THREE REASONS TO SAY *Yes*

JAIME CLEVENGER

BELLA
BOOKS
2018

Bella Books, Inc.
P.O. Box 10543
Tallahassee, FL 32302

Printed in the United States of America on acid-free paper

First Bella Books Edition 2018

Editor: Medora MacDougall
Cover Designer: Judith Fellows

ISBN: 978-1-59493-615-9

Other Books by Jaime Clevenger

Bella Books
Call Shotgun
A Fugitive's Kiss
Moonstone
Party Favors
Sign on the Line
Sweet, Sweet Wine
The Unknown Mile
Waiting for a Love Song
Whiskey and Oak Leaves

Spinsters Ink
All Bets Off

Acknowledgement

Thank you to my first-pass readers, Rachael and Carla, for your honest comments and encouragement. Thank you, Laina Villeneuve and Jane Chen, for your feedback and insight. Thank you to my editor, Medora, for making this presentable (since there was no chance you could clean me up). And most of all, thank you to Corina, for so many reasons.

About the Author

Jaime Clevenger lives in Colorado with her family. She spends most days working as a veterinarian, but also enjoys swimming, teaching karate, playing with her kids, and snuggling the foster kittens and puppies that often fill her home. She loves to hear a good story and hopes that if you ever meet her, you'll tell her your favorite. Feel free to embellish the details.

CHAPTER ONE

Calm, cool, collected. Julia Maguire repeated the mantra as she gripped the armrests of her window seat. The giggling kid in the row behind her had started up on another round of kicks. If she was trying out for a team, she was well on her way to making captain, but a soccer star wasn't what Julia needed at the moment. The turbulence had her stomach in knots and her boss's voice was on a loop in her head—"*You're going to Hawaii now?*"

"You okay?" Mo asked.

"Of course. I'm on my way to Hawaii." *Calm and cool.*

Mo peeked between the seats at the row behind them and then looked back at Julia. "Kate and I have a bet going. She's giving you five minutes before you lose it and make that preschooler cry. I told her you love kids."

"Why'd you tell her that?"

"Everyone loves kids."

Another kick thrust her seat forward and Julia shook her head. It wasn't that she didn't like kids. In fact, well-behaved children were cute in small doses. This kid, however, was not one of those.

"Why do people take kids to Hawaii anyway? Aren't they supposed to go to Disneyland?"

"My parents took me and my brother to Maui when we were little...I loved it." Mo paused, craning her head to sneak another look at the row behind them. "I know you've already made your mind up on this, but you should really take a look behind you. The kid's adorable. You'd have a hard time being mad at her if you saw her. And as for her mom—"

"I'm about to lose my breakfast. If I turn around, it will only be to glue those soccer cleats to the floor," Julia said.

"Suit yourself. But don't say I didn't warn you about this one."

Julia rubbed her stomach, wishing she had a Tums to pop in her mouth. The last thing she was interested in was checking out a mom with an annoying kid. She tried to focus again on the mantra.

Calm, cool, collected...

The conversation with Val interrupted. Conversations with her boss were one of the reasons she'd started seeing a shrink. Between the looming meetings with the Okinadi group and their rollout of the software upgrades for Pacific Powerlink, she had no business going to Hawaii for two weeks. Val was right. But this was the first real vacation she'd taken in five years. And she'd promised Kate and Mo that she wouldn't renege on the plans they'd made in college—one vacation with all three of them together before anyone got married.

Kate leaned forward in her aisle seat. "Jules, have you tried meditating? It can really help with nausea. Close your eyes and imagine a sunny beach lined with palm trees."

"I'll start us off," Mo volunteered. She took one deep breath, exhaling with a hum, then turned to Julia and whispered, "It's possible we'll need Kate's Xanax to get this right."

"I'm wearing earplugs, but I can still hear you," Kate said. "And I left the Xanax at home so watch out."

Julia decided meditation was worth a shot. As Kate and Mo argued, she closed her eyes and inhaled. Her seat jerked forward again and the palm trees were instantly replaced with an image of a grinning kid and a soccer ball. She cursed under her breath.

Mo eyed her. "I don't think you're supposed to swear when you meditate."

"I'm so done with this punk."

"Should I get the glue ready?" Mo chuckled.

"One more kick…"

When the next kick landed, Julia slammed her tray table closed and unbuckled her seat belt. Before Mo could stop her, she'd stood up, nearly smashing into the overhead compartment, and spun around to lean over her seat and stare down a tiny gremlin in an abundance of pink frills. The kid was frozen, mid-kick. Her rainbow-striped sneakers flashed like mini disco lights.

Julia opened her mouth, one millisecond away from a scathing lecture about personal space and respect, when she spotted the woman in the seat next to the kid. Short dark brown hair, sharp jawline, lanky athletic build…and unmistakably butch. The trendy designer glasses made her look more smart than sexy, but it was a close call. Dusk-blue eyes caught Julia's gaze. *Well, damn.*

Julia realized her mouth was hanging open. She closed it quickly and turned to the kid. As long as she didn't look back at the mom, she could pretend that her cheeks weren't burning up.

"Sweetie, my stomach's upset with this bumpy plane ride. Do you think you can stop kicking my chair? It would really help."

"Mom told me, but I forgot. Sorry." The little girl glanced at the butch woman and then back at Julia. She kicked the side of the plane and pointed at the flashing lights along the front of her sneaker. "My shoes light up."

"I can see that." Clearly having light-up shoes exonerated her. "I bet those are fun to watch when you run around in the dark."

"That's why Mom got them for me. I'm scared of the dark."

Julia couldn't help but look over at the mom then. She was convinced the universe was playing a cruel joke. The most attractive butch she'd seen in ages had not one but two kids. A matching burst of pink was sound asleep in her lap. The two girls looked to be about the same age, but the kicker had curly dark brown hair while the napping one had blond braids.

"I fell asleep for a bit. I hope she hasn't been kicking for long." The mom turned to her daughter and started in on how she'd have to take away the shoes if she couldn't be responsible for her feet.

Julia doubted a stern talk about foot responsibility would slow this kid down. She would have ripped the shoes off. Problem solved. She quickly scanned the nearby seats. No one else was obviously with this group and the mom wasn't wearing a ring.

"But I can't see in the dark without my shoes," the kid was saying. Her eyes had started to water. Crocodile tears.

"It's not dark in here, Bryn." The mom sighed. "Look, you can keep the shoes on as long as you don't kick her seat."

The plane lurched through a patch of clouds and Julia grabbed her chair's headrest. She swallowed, tasting bile.

"Are you going to throw up?" Bryn's eyes widened.

"I don't think so." Although she wasn't one for dramatic ploys, she finally had the kid's attention and knew she should play it up. "But this turbulence on top of all that seat kicking..."

Turning to her mom, Bryn said, "I know what she needs." She whispered something and the butch woman shook her head, but Bryn leaned forward to search her seatback pocket anyway. When she popped up again, she was holding a white paper vomit bag. "You can take mine in case you can't find yours in time."

Before Julia could stop her, Bryn had pressed the vomit bag into her hands. Julia stared at the bag, feeling the butch woman's eyes on her. She was officially sunk. No one could pull off looking sexy with a vomit bag. The most she could do now was make sure the kicking stopped.

"There's one problem." Julia tugged open the vomit bag. She already regretted her next sentence. "I ate a big breakfast and this isn't going to hold it all."

Bryn glanced from Julia to her mom, her panic obvious. "What should we do?"

"Well, we don't want her to overfill that bag. I think you better stop kicking." The mom looked up at Julia and winked.

Julia dared a smile and the look she got in return made her heart leap to attention. Maybe she wasn't sunk…Before she had time to process the buzz of feelings in her chest, Bryn covered her face with her hands and started making loud "ew" sounds. The mom tried to quiet Bryn as the sleeping kid in her lap stirred and Julia felt a pang of guilt. Ten minutes ago she'd cursed this stranger for not controlling her kid's feet. It was obvious now that she had her hands full.

Suddenly Bryn said, "I know what you need—a candy cane!"

"Oh no, I don't need any candy," Julia said.

"But Mom says peppermint helps when your tummy hurts," Bryn insisted, already pulling out a plastic bag full of mini candy canes and jelly beans that had been hidden under a sweatshirt. "She knows all about stuff like that because she's a doctor. Basically she knows everything."

"Basically." The mom grinned. "I primed her on that line."

Julia fought back the thought that this was her karmic retribution for always complaining about lesbians with kids. This woman was perfect. For someone.

"Bryn, how many jelly beans have you eaten? That bag was a lot fuller when I packed it."

"I only ate the ones that rolled on the ground."

"The bag just opened up and fell on the ground? Or you pulled it out of that zipped pocket?"

"This one's not even broken!" Bryn said, ignoring her mom's questions. "And it's still wrapped. That's lucky." She held it up to Julia like a peace offering.

"As fair warning, those were in the kids' Christmas stockings," the woman said.

"But they still taste good." Bryn inched the candy cane higher in the air.

Julia knew she wasn't going to win if she tried fighting this. At least Christmas was only two months ago. She reached for the candy. "Thank you."

"You're welcome!" Bryn's dimpled smile was triumphant. She looked over at her mom and squeezed her shoulders up to her ears. Cute enough to get away with murder. And as for her mom...

Julia stopped her thoughts right there. She wasn't interested in a mom. Even a sexy, smart, butch mom with amazing eyes and a sense of humor. Without chancing another look at the woman, she settled back in her seat, candy cane and vomit bag in hand.

Mo snickered and Julia waved the vomit bag. "Don't even start."

"What?" Mo pressed her lips together. "I was only going to say that you sure straightened that one out. Bet that kid never kicks anyone's seat again."

"And I'm sure her mom is happy for the parenting help. I hear it's hard to keep those preschoolers in line," Kate added, her grin unmistakable despite the magazine she was hiding behind.

Julia unwrapped the candy cane and licked the tip. She knew she shouldn't care what the butch mom thought about her, but she did.

"So..." Mo drew out the word. "She's your type, right?"

"I'm not interested." If she said that aloud ten times maybe she'd believe it.

"I'm not buying it," Mo said. "You're still blushing."

Of course she was interested. But even if the woman wasn't a mom, it wouldn't work between them.

When Julia didn't answer, Mo pressed on. "Okay, fine. Let's pretend you're not interested. Is it because she's a mom? Do moms have a certain look that you don't like?"

"You and I both know most moms don't look like her."

"Meaning most moms aren't butch," Mo clarified. "Although that's a very limited perspective and more gender normative than I would have expected from you." She chuckled at Julia's eye-roll. "Just tell me she's your type so I can say I called it."

"At least you made an impression, Jules," Kate said unhelpfully. "I saw her when we were waiting to board and wondered if you were going to say anything. I thought maybe the kids turned you off."

"Trust me, I would have said something if I'd noticed her."

"She's wearing sandals with socks. How could you not notice that?" Kate continued, "Plus she's tall and nerdy. Mo's right—exactly your type."

"She's a lot nerdy," Mo agreed. "But she's got the shy handsome thing going that Julia always likes."

"Did you see her legs, Jules? Great calves." Kate raised her eyebrows as if this would be the selling point. "I bet she's a mountain biker."

"I couldn't see her calves. She's sitting down. And, Kate, take out your earplugs. Half the plane doesn't need to hear our conversation." Julia silently hoped that at least one person on the plane was too distracted with her kids to have overheard anything.

"Hear what?" Mo turned halfway around in her seat so her voice would certainly carry to the back of the plane as she loudly continued, "That you like a woman who wears socks with her sandals?"

"Mo!"

Mo continued, "Or is it that you'd like to rip them off? I bet she looks good naked. What do you think?"

"I think this is the last vacation I'm going on with you." Julia wanted to melt into her seat.

"But you like her, right?"

"She can't answer you, Mo. She's too busy fantasizing about pulling off those mom socks." Kate cracked a smile, pleased with herself. "Who knew sitting in economy could be so much fun. Going back to first class will be boring after this."

"Welcome to our world, Kate." Mo turned to Julia, "The thing is, I can totally imagine you dating a soccer mom."

"You'd go to the games and be on the sidelines with a wagon full of juice boxes, yelling for the kids to kick the ball harder," Kate added.

"I'm getting you guys back for this."

"But what if she's *the one*, Jules? Maybe this is fate." Kate continued, "I could pass her a little note with your number. Or you could go to the bathroom and then when you're coming back, I'll get up to get something from the overhead and you'll have to stop and chat."

"Great. The straight girl's giving me tips for picking up women."

"You're right—why trust the straight girl's advice? You should listen to me instead." Mo chuckled at Kate's glare. "First step, hand her your number yourself. You don't need a friend to do that. Second step, bend down and take off her socks."

"I'm not *that* straight," Kate argued.

"You're engaged to a six-foot-two engineer who watches ESPN all day and you've never dated a woman," Mo said. "The fact that you're not *that* straight isn't going to help our case here."

"All I'm saying is that it's been a long time since she's been on a date. Just because I'm marrying Ethan doesn't mean I can't help her get a date."

"And all I'm saying is that she should listen to someone who actually dates women."

"Enough, you two." Julia held up her hand. "I'm on vacation. I don't want to think about dating."

"Why not?" Kate and Mo asked simultaneously.

"You needed some time after Sheryl, but it's been, what, six months?" Mo glanced to Kate for confirmation.

"Over a year. They broke up last January," Kate said. "Unless there's someone we don't know about."

"You know I'd tell you." Julia sighed. Since her ex had dumped her, she hadn't wanted to think about dating anyone again. But it wasn't because of a broken heart. "I suck at dating."

"Practice makes perfect," Mo said.

Julia nearly argued that she needed more than practice. She needed a whole semester of classes. But then she'd have to admit to her friends that she was terrible in bed. That was the other reason she'd started seeing the shrink.

Mo continued, "I think you'd be happier if you started looking around a little—that's all."

"Can we go back to thinking about palm trees and sunny beaches?" She sucked on the candy cane, avoiding Kate's and Mo's gazes.

Kate sighed and closed her magazine. "Sounds good to me." She pulled a black silk eye mask on, adjusted her neck pillow and then settled back in her seat. "Wake me when we're in Hawaii."

Julia avoided looking over at Mo, certain that she still wanted to talk, and instead stared out the window. Streaks of white passed below the wings and the distant blue ocean seemed cold and lonely. Maybe her friends were right. She could try dating again…

Her chair bumped forward and she overheard the whispered scold that followed. It took all her restraint to not peek between the seats. Another look at that butch mom was not what she needed. Finally she popped in her earbuds, picked out her favorite Pink song, and turned up the volume.

CHAPTER TWO

"I'm sweating already," Mo complained, handing her suitcase over to the shuttle driver.

"Get used to it," Julia said. "The weather forecast is in the eighties all week. Good riddance, Winter."

Julia had pulled her thick black hair into a ponytail, stripped off her long-sleeve shirt and stowed her jacket in her carry-on bag. Now in a spaghetti strap tank top, sandals, and a loose skirt, she was decidedly comfortable. Her plan to wear next to nothing for the rest of the trip was looking good.

She climbed onto the shuttle and headed for the empty back row. After the long flight, the thought of stretching out on the bench was tempting. Mo took the seat in the front row next to Kate, who was already applying sunscreen.

"Don't you think it's a little early for sunscreen? We've got an hour drive to the resort," Mo said.

"I burn in a walk across a parking lot," Kate said. "Knowing me, I'll get scorched sitting by this window."

Mo chuckled and offered to switch seats, but Kate argued that she didn't want to put Mo at risk. Predictably, she then launched in on a skin cancer spiel. Kate's job was to raise money for cancer research, and she was a walking doomsday report on anything cancer-related. Mo, usually optimistic and ready to chance fate, didn't challenge Kate on this one topic. She'd lost her dad two years after college to what she still called the Big C, as if not wanting to name the thing that had too much power already.

Outwardly, Kate and Mo were opposites. Kate had a petite, slender build with long blond hair and skin so pale you could see her veins at her temples. Mo was several inches taller with an athlete's physique, dark brown skin, and black curls clipped short against her head. They were both gorgeous, people always said, but so different. And yet in some ways they couldn't be more alike.

Kate leaned over the edge of her seat to look back at Julia. "What about you? Need sunscreen back there? We could go on for days about the high risk Irish-Americans have for skin cancer."

"I'm only half Irish."

"Being half Chinese isn't going to save your skin," Mo argued.

Kate pitched the sunscreen over the empty rows between them. "And I know how you feel about freckles."

Julia stuck out her tongue. She'd always liked freckles—on other people. Whenever she spent time in the sun and the freckles popped across her cheeks, she heard her mom urging her to wear a sunhat. Her father was the redhead, although now entirely bald, and she blamed his genes for the freckles.

"Mom, look! It's the woman from the plane who needed my vomit bag!"

Julia started at the voice, nearly gouging her eye as she hurried to rub in the sunscreen. Bryn, light-up sneakers and all, was half dragging and half leading her mom directly toward her spot in the back row. Her sister, who still looked mostly asleep, brought up the rear.

"Remember me?" Bryn shouted.

"Light-up shoes. How could I forget?" Julia wasn't sure if her stomach was buzzing with butterflies at the sight of the butch mom swinging suitcases onto the top luggage rack and now clearly fitting into the category of single with kids, or if her motion sickness was returning.

"Did you throw up?"

"Not yet."

"The candy cane worked." Bryn smiled. "I knew it would." She plopped down in the open seat next to Julia while her quiet twin took the seat by the window. Julia met the gaze of their mom for only long enough to feel a rush at the realization that she'd been checking her out. Then she reminded her body that she wasn't interested in dating anyone—not even an attractive butch who was giving her way too much eye contact. *But damn…*

"Hello again." The mom motioned to the remaining open seats. "Is it okay if we share this row with you?"

"Yeah—definitely." *Way too excited. Turn it down a notch.* Julia cleared her throat. "So, you're staying at the Sea Breeze Resort too?"

"Yep."

Of course that was where they were staying. The shuttle only went to the one resort. Julia knew she should quit talking before she managed to embarrass herself anymore. Still, what were the chances that they'd be staying at the same place? Kate's words repeated in her head: "*Maybe this is fate.*" Or maybe it was only dumb luck…Two rows in front of her she spotted Mo, who'd turned halfway around in her seat to make a kissy face. Later she'd be laughing out loud.

"I'm Reed."

"Julia." She stuck out her hand.

Reed had a strong grip, but her hand was decidedly feminine with smooth skin and shapely fingers. She met Julia's eyes and smiled. Realizing that she was still holding on to Reed's hand, Julia let go and tried to think of something to say to lessen the awkwardness. Who shook hands on an airport shuttle bus? What was wrong with her?

"Apparently I'm not in vacation mode yet. At work I'm always shaking hands with everyone." She mimed shaking hands with invisible people all around her and Bryn giggled. *Thanks, kid.*

"No problem. Takes a while to get out of work mode." Reed set her carry-on bag down and then took the empty seat next to Julia. "What do you do at work?"

"I'm in software." Julia hadn't meant to bring up work. In fact, the last thing she wanted to talk about was her job. But because Reed seemed to be waiting for her to say more, she added: "I'm a customer success manager—hence the hand shaking."

"Customer success? Is that like customer service?" Reed wondered.

Before Julia could answer, Bryn cut in with: "Mom, when are you going to introduce us?"

"You could introduce yourself, sweetie." At Bryn's crossed arms, Reed pointed to each girl: "Bryn—who you may have noticed never sits still—and Carly. Carly's my thinker. You won't hear much from her."

"I sit still sometimes," Bryn argued. "But it's hard because I'm four and a half. I'm the older twin. That's why I have more energy."

"Older by five minutes," Reed clarified.

Carly, the younger-by-five-minutes twin, was an inch or two shorter and frail looking. She was also clearly the introvert, glancing at Julia under long blond eyelashes and then quickly turning back to the window. Julia didn't blame her. The scene outside was beautiful—palm trees, flowers, and green everywhere—and they hadn't left the airport yet.

"Carly, what do you see out there?" Reed said.

"There's a little yellow bird in that tree with all the flowers." Carly's voice was a fraction above a whisper.

"Where?" Bryn said, climbing over her sister to squish her nose against the window. "I don't see it."

"You're looking too hard. He's right over there." Carly pointed at the branch where a small yellow songbird was perched. "Even the trees look happy here."

"I think so too," Reed said. "Bryn, sit down. The shuttle driver is ready to leave."

When Bryn didn't move and Carly started to whine about not having enough space, Reed reached across Julia's lap to pull Bryn back into her seat. "Bottom in your seat and hands to yourself." She met Julia's eyes. "Sorry about the reach."

Julia didn't have time to say that it wasn't a problem. She was still tingling from the contact of Reed's arm against her shoulder when Bryn slid into her lap. She tried to hide her surprise.

"Bryn, what are you doing?" Reed asked.

"Why do you think the trees are happy here?" Bryn asked Julia.

"Maybe because they haven't met winter," Carly guessed quietly.

"Bryn, get off Julia's lap and into your own seat. Now."

Grudgingly, Bryn finally looked over at Reed. She mumbled, "I was going to," as she slid off Julia's lap into her seat. A moment later, she'd popped off the seat. She turned to Julia and said, "Do you know that it's always warm in Hawaii? And if you live here, you don't need mittens—or a scarf. Or even a jacket!"

"Crazy, huh?" She smiled at Bryn's enthusiasm. Kid energy wasn't something she was used to and Bryn had it in spades. "I think you're supposed to be sitting down."

"Oh, right." Bryn smiled and the dimples were back. She dropped into the seat. "I'll try to stay in one spot, but I've got lots of energy."

Reed sighed.

Julia glanced over at her, wondering how she managed two kids alone. At least one of them seemed sane. "How long are you all staying?"

Before Reed could answer, Bryn said: "One week. That's this many days." She held up seven fingers, working hard to not let another finger slip loose.

Reed only smiled when Julia looked between her and Bryn. Maybe this was how it always went. Having kids interrupt every conversation was cute at first but would get old quick—not that she was entertaining the idea of dating Reed.

"Are all three of you here together?" Reed motioned to the row where Kate and Mo were sitting.

"Yeah. We were roommates in college and we always talked about going on a vacation together…Kate's getting married this summer so we decided it was now or never."

"Life ends when you get married?"

"That's what I've heard," Julia said.

Reed laughed and Julia was all too aware of the responding heat in her body. It seemed like an eternity since she'd flirted with someone and by some miracle, she wasn't blowing it.

"A vacation with friends sounds amazing," Reed was saying. "I wish I'd kept in touch with my college friends."

"I'm lucky to have Mo and Kate. Mo's our social committee. She drags us out to have fun against our will. But it's always worth it." Mo and Kate shared a two-bedroom flat in San Francisco while she'd moved across the bay to be closer to work. Julia still met up with them nearly every weekend however.

"Mom, when are we going to be at the ocean?" Bryn whined. "I want to swim."

"Soon. Look out the window and tell me if you can find a pink flower."

"Over there," Bryn said, jabbing her finger in the direction of a bush covered in bright pink blossoms.

"How about a yellow sign?"

The shuttle driver settled into the driver's seat and soon they were bustling down the highway and past fields of lava rock. Reed kept up with the color game, distracting Bryn and Carly, while Julia snuck sideways glances at her.

She guessed that Reed was in her mid-thirties—maybe a few years older than her. Her warm laugh matched her easy smile but the rest of her was easy to appreciate as well. Kate was right—even her calves were worth noticing.

Being in close quarters made it difficult to ignore her body's response to Reed, but worse than that, Julia found herself wishing they could have a long conversation. Maybe Reed's dark blue eyes and those glasses were to blame or maybe there was some deeper connection. *Or maybe I'm just horny.* As soon as she had that thought, she nearly laughed out loud. Since when had she been so attracted to anyone that she'd even used the word horny?

When Bryn popped out of her seat again and Reed had to lean past Julia once more to pull her back into her seat, their knees bumped together. It was an innocent touch, but the feel of Reed's skin against hers sent a flare up to her brain. Finally fate had sent her someone nearly perfect. She wasn't sure if she was glad that Reed's kids threw a wrench in the possibility of dating or if she was disappointed.

* * *

A wide stretch of grass and a handful of palm trees separated the condo's lanai from a set of black-bottomed pools with fountains and cascading waterfalls. Beyond this was a winding path down to the beach.

At least a hundred condos all shared the same pool area, but it hadn't taken Julia long to figure out which one belonged to Reed. Within minutes of arriving, Reed's kids had decorated their lanai with beach towels and blow-up pool toys. Towels were strategically hung to create a sort of cave that the girls took turns hiding in and then calling for Reed, only to shriek and laugh when she came out to find them. Reed played the game a half-dozen times before setting to cutting up a pineapple on the patio table. The girls clamored for her attention even more then and every few slices she'd pause to chase one back into the cave.

When she'd finished cutting up the pineapple, Reed handed out slices and then sat down on one of the patio chairs. She kicked up her feet, gazing out at the view, and then suddenly she was looking right at Julia.

Cheeks burning, Julia dropped her eyes to the pages of her paperback and reread the opening paragraph with her pulse thumping in her ears. She hated being caught staring. Hopefully, Reed was too far away to notice her embarrassment, but she'd seemed to sense that Julia had been watching her.

"How's the book?"

Julia jumped at Kate's voice. "Uh, good. Great, I think."

Kate craned her head to see the page number and then raised an eyebrow. "You know you've been reading for an hour. That must be an amazing first page."

"It's possible I've been distracted." Julia nodded in the direction of Reed's lanai, feeling a measure of relief at admitting her past hour's obsession.

Kate laughed. "Now that makes sense. Well, Mo and I are going to the pool. You should join us. You'll be able to spy on her better there."

Mo pushed open the screen door behind Kate. She was wearing a pair of flowery board shorts and a black sports bra-style swimsuit top. A wide-brimmed sunhat with a bright Hawaiian print band around the base completed her outfit. The hat was perfect for her, even if it challenged her usual butch image.

"Where'd you get that?"

"The resort store. Like it?" Mo pulled a matching hat from behind her back. "I bought three, but Kate won't wear hers. She thinks it makes her look gay."

"I didn't say that," Kate argued, swatting Mo's shoulder. In a serious tone, she met Julia's eyes and said: "You know I'd never say something like that."

"Because she can't say the word 'gay.'" Mo grinned and continued, "This place has everything. We can walk to the ocean, play tennis, golf…"

"Since when do you golf? And I can say the word 'gay.' Gay. Gay. Gay." Kate had her hands on her hips in open challenge.

"I love it when you talk dirty," Mo said. She winked and stuck out her tongue. "Too bad I know you're a tease."

"Mo!" Kate swatted her again.

Julia couldn't help laughing. This argument between Kate and Mo was old, but still funny. Mo was convinced Kate was a closet case and Kate was convinced Mo wanted everyone to be gay.

"I could golf if I wanted to," Mo argued. "But I probably won't make it past the pool bar. Speaking of, it's time for piña coladas." She walked over to the chaise lounge and balanced the second hat on Julia's head. "You can bring the book that we both know you aren't reading. But if you keep staring at that mom from the plane I'm gonna have to run a background check on her."

"Don't you dare." Julia didn't need to know more about Reed. She was having a hard enough time ignoring her as it was. Fortunately she knew Mo wasn't serious about the background check, but she worked in Internet security and had a knack for tracking down dirt.

"My best friend—who hasn't had a girlfriend in over a year and almost never pays attention to women who are interested in her—has a crush. I think it's my job to sniff around a little."

"I don't have a crush. I'm enjoying a good view." Julia's dating history paled in comparison to Mo's. High school had passed without any offers and she'd been too unsure of herself back then to ask anyone out. College came without much more success although she did manage to have her first kiss before she turned twenty-one. Still, in her entire dating life, she'd only slept with a total of two women and one guy. Mo had someone new every six months. "It doesn't matter if she has a police record. I'm only looking—not dating."

"I think I'd be more interested in her if Mo dug up a few misdemeanors in her past," Kate mused. "Who doesn't like a bad girl with great legs?"

"You have to stop talking about her legs," Mo said. "No one's going to believe you about the whole straight thing."

"I've already told you—I'm not that straight." Kate continued, "Did you notice that she took off the ankle socks by the time we got on the shuttle?"

Mo shook her head. "Let's go. My piña colada is waiting."

Kate often mentioned her attraction to women, but she rarely pointed out anyone she liked and not once had her interests matched Julia's. For the first time Julia felt a spark of jealousy at the thought that Kate was paying attention to Reed. Not that it mattered—Kate was about to get married and Julia wasn't going for someone with kids. She wondered how many times she'd have to remind herself of that fact over the next week.

Adjusting her sunhat, Julia followed Kate and Mo. She was planning on keeping her eyes on the path to avoid the temptation of looking at Reed's lanai, but the path went right past it and when she dared a quick peek, Reed raised her hand and smiled. Julia's pulse shot up, her cheeks likely matching the pink flowers on her hatband. She waved in return and then hurried to catch up with Mo and Kate. Reed seemed to have been waiting for her to walk by. She tried not to think about what that might mean.

Reed and the twins appeared at the pool not long after Julia had made it through the mystery book's first chapter. For the first ten minutes she pretended that she didn't notice them, but Bryn's squeals were hard to ignore and soon even the quiet twin was making noise. Finally Julia set down the paperback and leaned back in the chaise lounge to watch them. Since she had sunglasses on, she figured Reed wouldn't know that she was staring.

Reed's swimming suit gave Julia plenty to appreciate and the kids were a noisy but hilarious distraction. They alternated between splashing Reed, screaming for her attention and then careening down the waterslide to bump into her. Julia had to stop herself from laughing more than once at their antics.

"No way did twins come out of that belly," Mo said, jutting her chin in Reed's direction.

"She could have used a surrogate," Kate proposed, sipping her margarita. "Or maybe her ex had the kids?"

Mo's brow furrowed. "Maybe. Then why'd they break up?" If there was anything that bothered Mo, it was a woman whose history she didn't know. Being nosy was good for her job, but she couldn't take a vacation from the habit.

"Could have been an affair," Kate offered. "I bet she doesn't have trouble finding women to sleep with her. Or maybe she's a widow."

"Maybe her ex was terrible in bed," Mo said. "I've known lots of couples who stopped having sex after a few months. Imagine adding kids to the mix..."

Julia cringed. Mo had no clue about her failings in bed, of course, but this hit too close to home. "I don't want to marry her, remember? Let me enjoy watching her in peace."

Still, she was curious about a backstory. Reed's belly certainly didn't look like it had carried twins. In fact nothing about her body was motherly. She was all lean muscle. But how she'd ended up with kids didn't really matter.

Reed pulled herself out of the deep end without using the ladder, and Kate made a little moan. Mo rolled her eyes in response.

"She does have nice shoulders. You have to admit that at least," Kate said.

"I thought you were into her calves," Mo said.

"I'd take the whole package," Julia said, ignoring Kate and Mo's shared "I told you so's." They were right from the beginning. Reed was her type.

Reed dove off the edge of the pool, startling Bryn and Carly into a fit of giggles. When she popped up for air between their inflated dolphins, her mop of brown hair was sleeked back. She playfully lunged at the kids and then as they scattered, she looked over her shoulder and met Julia's gaze. Without the glasses, those blue eyes were even more amazing.

As soon as Reed looked away, Julia murmured, "Nice dive."

"I'd give it an eight point five," Kate said. "A little too much splash."

"I agree. She should hop out of the water and try again."

Kate pushed up her sunglasses. "That's what I was thinking."

"I can't take you two crushing on the same woman," Mo grumbled.

"I'm not crushing. I'm enjoying a good view—just like Julia." Kate winked at Julia. "It's like being at the gym. Eye candy is one of the reasons I stay in shape."

"Who's your eye candy at the gym?" Mo asked.

"Oh, I've got a few," Kate said evasively. "Anyone attractive is worth checking out."

"And you regularly check out men *and* women?"

Kate shrugged. "If they're good looking, sure. Why not?"

"Have you told Ethan that you're attracted to women?"

"I don't need to tell him every time I appreciate a nice body," Kate argued. "It doesn't matter."

"I think it might matter to him. One of these days he's gonna catch you staring," Mo said. "You're not that discreet."

"He's oblivious. Anyway, what exactly would you want me to say? 'Honey, I know we're about to get married, but I keep checking out women—and other men—at the gym. Do you think that's a problem?'"

"I don't think it's a problem," Julia said. "It's natural to notice attractive people. And it's not like you're fixated on one in particular, right?"

Kate hesitated before answering and Mo looked over at Julia with an arched eyebrow. Finally Kate said, "Well, there is one...She has really nice forearms and always saves me a spot in the spin class. But it's nothing." She reached for her sports bottle and took a sip. "Don't look at me like that, you guys. I'm not telling Ethan. And with the woman in my spin class I'm convinced it's only a forearm thing."

"I'm with you on nice forearms," Julia said. "Sometimes that's all you need. Did you notice the guy at the towel counter with those tats?"

"Mmm-hmm," Kate murmured. "I'd pay good money for him to take off his shirt and show me the other end of that dragon that went up his arm." She looked over at Mo. "Probably dumb as a box of rocks, but anyone can appreciate a good body. Although Mo would probably argue with that…"

Mo mumbled something under her breath and then said, "I want to hear more about the woman from the gym. I know a lot of people who work out there. I might know her. What's her name?"

"Careful, Kate. When Mo says 'know' she means it in the biblical sense." Julia dodged Mo's hand as she tried to swat her arm.

"This isn't about me," Mo said. She eyed Kate. "I'm only asking 'cause I could probably help you out. Introduce you."

"I'm marrying Ethan. I don't need any help getting a date."

"Kate, some guys are interesting. Ethan isn't one of them. I fall asleep when he talks about the Forty-Niners and you know how much I love football." Mo paused. "Look, I don't blame you one bit for marrying him. He's stable and I know you feel like you can trust him. But maybe you should look around a little more before you settle—"

"I'm not settling," Kate argued.

"Ethan's a little boring, maybe, but he's not a bad guy," Julia said. "I don't think you're settling either."

"This has nothing to do with Ethan anyway," Kate continued, her voice rising. "My point is, I'm not trying to notice women. It's like I can't help it." She shook her head. "Lately everywhere I go, I'm running into lesbians. The dog park is worse than the gym. That place is lesbian central. And it's not my fault that they're all hot."

"I'm not saying it's anyone's fault," Mo argued. "I'm only saying that I think you should consider your attraction before you marry a dude."

"Julia thinks the towel guy is cute," Kate shot back. "If she wants to marry a woman are you going to ask her if she's considered a dude just because she might be attracted to some men?"

"That's not what I'm saying at all," Mo said. "Julia help me out here."

"Honestly, I think Kate has a point. Although I've tried guys and it wasn't all that." Admittedly, the women she'd been with weren't any better. But she was convinced that she was either meant to be with a woman or meant to be single forever. "And I do think two women can have a deeper emotional connection."

"A deeper emotional connection? That's all you've got?" Mo's expression made Julia feel like she'd let down the entire gay rights movement.

"Well, I'm still stuck on the image of Kate in a crowd of lesbians at the dog park trying to get Peeves to hurry up and do his business." Julia said, hoping the change in subject would diffuse the tension between Kate and Mo. "I wish I could see that in person…"

Kate finally cracked a smile. "It's ridiculous. Peeves has to mark everything. Literally everything. You wouldn't believe how many women have given me their phone number."

"Jules, maybe you and I should get dogs," Mo mused.

"Or move next to a dog park. A string of lesbians walking dogs outside my apartment would be enough…Kate, what is it about the woman from the gym—beyond the forearms?"

"When you mentioned her you were blushing as bad as Julia does when she looks at that one," Mo added, jabbing her thumb in Reed's direction.

Kate didn't answer immediately. She looked over at Julia and seemed to be debating something. Finally she sighed and said, "Her name's Chris. I think it's short for Christine…And she looks a little bit like her." She nodded in Reed's direction. "Maybe even a little more masculine. Her head's shaved and when I first saw her I actually thought she was a guy. She has a rainbow flag on her water bottle so I know she's…well, you know."

"A big old homo?" Mo said.

"Maybe she just likes rainbows." Julia tried to hide her smile.

Mo added, "And sexy straight women in her spin class."

"She's not into me. We aren't even friends really." Kate shook her head. "Can we forget I brought this up?" She stood up suddenly, tossing her towel aside. "I wish you two wouldn't make it a huge deal when I notice an attractive woman. I'm straight, but I'm not blind."

Julia waited until Kate slipped into the water to look over at Mo. "I guess there's a chance she really is straight."

"Yeah right." Mo lowered her voice as she continued, "She drives me crazy. One minute she's arguing that she isn't that straight and then the next minute…Why can't she admit that she's bi? Her two best friends are queer. After all these years she still thinks it's a problem?"

"She didn't say that, Mo."

"She might as well have," Mo argued.

"You know how hard it is for her to open up. I think she was really trying that time." Julia changed her position in the lounge chair so she was facing Mo. "She's got baggage. You can't expect her to be as open as you are."

"Lots of us have baggage. We unpack it. Has she ever told you what happened to her?" Mo waited for Julia to answer and then when she didn't speak up, she continued, "I'm not saying she doesn't have issues. But we've been friends for this long—you'd think she'd have told us by now whatever the hell her issue is instead of just always saying that something happened…"

Mo followed Kate across the pool with her eyes. She was doing a graceful sidestroke with her face away from them. "And I'm not saying she needs to be with a woman. But I don't think Ethan's the right guy. She's gonna marry him and then realize it was a mistake."

"You know her better than anyone," Julia said. "But I think you might be biased against Ethan."

A brunette in light blue shorts and a dark blue polo shirt that had the resort's name embroidered above her left breast stopped in front of Mo's lounge chair. She held a notebook in her hand and her eyes went up and down the length of Mo's body before she casually asked, "Can I get you ladies anything? Something cool from the bar?"

Mo never seemed to mind a woman admiring her body but this time she hardly looked up as she handed the woman her room key. "I'll take another piña colada."

"Perfect." The server jotted down the room number and then handed Mo back the card. "Be right back." Her eyes lingered on Mo before she turned to head to the bar.

"I don't get it," Julia said. "You practically ignored her." She wasn't surprised when the server reached the bar and then glanced back at Mo.

"We said hello earlier, but I didn't want to give her the wrong idea."

"Why not?"

Mo shrugged. "I'm not interested."

"Too easy?" Julia laughed. "God, if I had half your mojo…"

"Tanya asked me to marry her on New Year's."

"What?" Julia nearly choked on the sip she'd taken. She leveled her gaze on Mo. Mo, the one who'd sworn she'd go to her grave single and free, only nodded. "What'd you say to her?"

"I said I wanted to think about it. We've only been dating for six months, but you know that's a long time in my world. Still, I kept thinking that we shouldn't rush things…Then I went and bought her a ring."

"Seriously?"

"I know it's crazy, but things have been going really well. It feels like the right decision."

Julia wasn't sure what to say next. She thought maybe she should say congratulations, but Mo marrying Tanya was among the worst ideas she'd heard in a long time.

She straightened up in the lounge chair. Regardless of how she felt about Tanya, she wanted Mo to be happy. The fact was, Mo wasn't smiling. Was it because she wasn't sold on the idea of marrying Tanya or was it because Mo had proclaimed more than once that she'd never marry?

"Have you told Kate?"

"No. I'm waiting for the right time." Mo exhaled. "It still feels a little surreal, but I love Tanya. So I figure, why not?"

Why not? Julia felt her stomach twist. She could give Mo about ten reasons why Tanya was not someone she should marry. Now both of her best friends were marrying people she didn't even like. What was worse, she was supposed to feel happy for them. "Well, Mo, I never thought I'd be going to your wedding, but if you're happy—that's what matters. Congratulations."

CHAPTER THREE

Julia slipped off her sandals and picked her way over the hot slate rocks to the water. She didn't go for the stairs. Instead, she went to the deep end and hopped straight in. The water skimmed over her skin, chilling her on contact. A squeal of delight slipped out. This, she realized, was exactly what she needed.

After a few laps across the central, bean-shaped pool, she made her way to the other pools. There were a total of four attached pools, but in order to get to the others, she had to either hop out or dip under the narrow bridges connecting the footpaths between them. Each pool had its own waterfall and an assortment of chaise lounge chairs and umbrellas surrounding it.

She swam until she found a quiet lagoon that she had all to herself. Lava rocks edged three sides of this small black-bottomed pool, helping to buffer the sound from the bar and making it feel like a hidden gem. Adding to the appeal was an underwater bench that made a perfect resting spot with a peek view of the sparkling blue ocean down the hill from the resort.

Julia settled in on the bench. If she planned it right, she could be in the same spot enjoying a sunset over the ocean that evening. She closed her eyes, leaning her head back against the cool tiles. Already work meetings were a distant memory.

Twenty-four hours in paradise had passed in a blink of an eye. But aside from spying on Reed, a long walk on the beach, and overindulging in the resort's dinner buffet, she hadn't accomplished much yesterday. Still when her head had hit the pillow last night, she'd dropped into what felt like a drugged sleep. She rarely slept longer than six or seven hours but she'd awakened ten hours later to the sound of a rooster crowing his head off. Beauty sleep, Mo had insisted, was why everyone looked better after a vacation. And maybe there was some truth in that. She'd spotted Reed at breakfast that morning, herding her kids to a table while balancing three plates stacked with fruit and pastries, and couldn't help but think she looked even better that morning than she had on the plane.

Reed would make a nice fantasy later. And there'd be plenty of time to squeeze in a nap back in the condo for exactly that reason. Once she'd accomplished a proper swim, her only other goal for the day was to eat a path through the resort's dinner buffet. She'd given up on her diet for the trip and only felt a pinch of guilt when she'd scanned the week's menu. Tonight's macadamia nut-encrusted fresh catch of the day was at the top of her list, followed shortly thereafter by pineapple shrimp kabobs and coconut sticky rice. Julia closed her eyes, letting the sun play on her skin.

"How much do you love me?"

"Hey, Mo." Julia smiled, rousing from the drowsy state the sunshine had drawn her into. "Where have you been?"

"Around."

Julia pulled herself out of the water and onto the smooth slate pavers edging the pool. "Why do I have the distinct feeling that you've been up to no good?" Mo's smug grin confirmed Julia's fears. "Do I want to ask?"

"Can you resist?"

"You've been spying on that mom from the plane, haven't you?"

Mo pulled a lounge chair over to the pool and sat down. "Better than spying. I've been researching."

"Coming from you that can only mean trouble."

"Did you know that they have a Kids Club here? Babysitter and everything. And get this. They'll watch the little boogers until ten each night."

"That's the research you've been doing?"

"Oh, I've got more," Mo said. "I got some good intel on your crush."

"She's not a crush." Julia swung her toes in the water, sending sparkling droplets into the air.

"Reed Baxter. Single. Thirty-eight. Prefers she pronouns, but I bet you could call her sir in bed." Mo winked. "Want more?"

Call her sir in bed? She was definitely not going there. "Mo, I'm on vacation…"

"That's funny. She said the same thing. Says she's not interested in dating, but I say that body of hers shouldn't be wasted."

"Wait a minute. Now you're into her too?"

"I'll admit, when she takes off those nerdy glasses and shows off her muscles in the gym—"

"Mo!"

"Relax, I'm not into her. Although Kate's right about her calves. Do you want to hear more or not?"

Julia stared at the ocean vista beyond the pool. She watched a wave crash on the sand sending up a white spray against the turquoise blue. Of course she wanted to know more. But what was the point?

"I'll take that as a yes."

"You can't resist telling me anyway."

"She's a doctor. Lives in Davis. That's only seventy miles from your apartment."

"And let me guess, you already googled the fastest route."

"Of course I did," Mo said. "I'm very thorough."

"Davis, huh?" Long distance wasn't something she minded, but it did present a whole different set of challenges. "Seventy miles is a long drive for a booty call."

"And here I thought you were going to complain about her being a doctor." Mo shook her head. "Just when I think I've finally figured you out, Jules, you surprise me."

"I already knew she was a doctor. Her kid told me that on the plane." Julia avoided Mo's gaze. She had sworn off doctors after Sheryl. But she'd had plenty of time to rationalize that not all doctors were self-centered pricks. Reed Baxter didn't strike her as self-centered. Nor did she remind her of Sheryl in any other way.

"Speak of the devil," Mo said.

Julia followed Mo's gaze to the entrance of the main swimming area. She felt a rush at the sight of Reed holding open the gate. The twins scampered past her toward the kiddie pool. Davis wasn't that far from Oakland if she timed the drive right, but in the evening commute, the freeway could be a nightmare...

What was she thinking? She'd hardly talked to the woman and she was already worrying about the ups and downs of a long-distance relationship. Besides that, according to Mo, Reed wasn't looking to date. And she had kids.

"By the way, she's staying all week here at the resort. Plenty of time to do more than ogle her."

"Mo..."

"And we were right—those kids didn't come out of her belly."

"Ex-wife?"

"I tried to dig out that story, but she wouldn't give. I said something about her having nice abs and then asked if she did a special post-kid workout." Mo grinned. "She said she wasn't her kids' biologic mom, and we left it at that. So what's your next move?"

"I appreciate you talking to her, but…I'm not interested."

"Why not?"

Julia watched as Bryn tackled Reed from behind. She buckled at the knees and tumbled forward into the kiddie pool, laughing. Soon both kids were crawling over her laughing and splashing. Julia smiled. Reed seemed to truly enjoy her kids, even if they hadn't come out of her belly. "Well, for starters, there's the kid thing. Hooking up with someone like her would be complicated."

"That's why they have Kids Club. Babysitting until ten every night. Think about it. A little afternoon nookie with a sexy stranger that you'll never see again…" Mo raised her eyebrows. "Come on, Jules. You need a vacation fling. Maybe she does too. And you're lying when you say you aren't interested."

Mo knew her well, but there was more than one thing holding her back. "I doubt I'm her type."

"Only one way to find out."

Julia shook her head. Even if Reed was interested in someone like her, Julia wasn't vacation-fling material. Although she couldn't help but wonder if she might be better at sex if feelings weren't involved.

"So you're saying she's fair game?"

"What happened to you being engaged?"

"Mo engaged? Yeah, right. And the Pope's in favor of birth control." Kate slipped off her flip-flops and dipped her toes in the water. She settled in next to Julia. "Ah, this is the life."

Julia hadn't noticed Kate walking toward them. She glanced at Mo, wondering if she was going to say something. Mo only mumbled something about birth control and straight women.

"The dinner buffet starts at six," Kate said. "I was going to make us reservations, but then I thought maybe you'd want to invite your gal and her kids to sit at our table, Jules. We could all get to know her."

"She's not my gal," Julia argued.

"I could ask her," Mo said. "She probably would enjoy some adult conversation."

"Mo, don't. Please. I've been looking forward to dinner all day. I want to enjoy the buffet and forget about my diet—not worry about making a good impression."

"I thought you weren't interested in dating her," Mo said. "You don't need to make a good impression."

"She sure looks good playing volleyball," Kate interrupted. "Now we know how she got those calves."

Julia followed Kate's gaze past the kids' area to the sand pit. The twins were carrying buckets of water from the pool to the sand and building castles while Reed had joined the volleyball game that was in session.

"Then it's settled," Mo said. "Kate can ask her to dinner."

Kate arched her eyebrow. "Maybe I will."

"Don't." Julia knew Kate was only playing along with Mo, but she didn't want their banter to go too far. She wouldn't put it past either of them to ask Reed. "I want to eat in peace. With my two best friends. Not with someone who has nice legs."

"What are you saying about Kate's legs?" Mo's straight face lasted only until Kate looked over at her. She busted up, clearly amused at her own joke.

"Watch it. Your legs were implicated too," Kate argued.

"Good thing you still check them out," Mo said, stretching out one leg and flexing her ankle to show off her muscles.

Kate's cheeks turned cherry red as she stammered out a response while Mo laughed it off. Mo always had the upper hand when they teased each other.

Julia interrupted with, "I appreciate you both looking out for my interests, but I swear I'm happily single."

"Well, you're certainly happier single than you ever were with Sheryl," Mo agreed. "Or with that woman you dated in college. She was a piece of work."

"But what if you could be even happier?" Kate asked.

"It's the what-ifs that get you into trouble." Mo stood up from her lounge chair and stretched. "All right, me and my sexy legs are going down to the beach. I'll meet up with you guys at dinner."

Julia wondered what Mo wasn't saying. She'd been quick to end the conversation. Was she thinking of Kate or Tanya in the moment that she'd covered with a smile and a joke?

Kate waited until Mo was out of earshot before asking, "Do you think something's wrong? She's been avoiding me all afternoon."

Julia shrugged. She didn't want to be the one to tell Kate about Mo's engagement.

Kate continued, "When I asked her to go to the beach after breakfast she got all moody."

"You know Mo. She'll tell you if something's really bothering her." Except this time she wasn't certain Mo would talk to Kate.

"That bartender with the big boobs keeps checking her out. I have half a mind to tell her that she's out of Mo's league."

"Mo's not interested," Julia said.

"Why not? She's attractive—if you're into that."

"I just know she's not." Julia wished she didn't have to keep a secret from Kate. She hated not telling her the truth.

Kate pursed her lips and glanced again at the bartender. She seemed to be turning some question over in her head. After a while she eyed the beach path Mo had taken.

"Maybe we should go after her…something's bothering her and I don't want to spend my whole trip waiting for her to tell me."

Julia considered talking Kate out of her plan. If Mo wasn't ready to talk, they'd only get in a fight if Kate tried to push her. But Kate had already stood up and was stepping into her flip-flops.

"You coming?"

"I think I'll go back to the condo to read for a while. If you find me passed out, wake me up for dinner."

Kate waved over her shoulder, clearly distracted now thinking about Mo. Julia moved from her seat at the water's edge to the lounge chair Mo had pulled over. A nap by the pool sounded nearly as good as another chapter of the mystery she was reading—and from here she could still spy on Reed.

She adjusted the umbrella's sunshade and picked Reed out near the volleyball net. The details Mo had gathered on Reed Baxter weren't enough to throw off her interest. In fact, she admitted, Reed had the potential to turn into an obsession. The safe plan was to simply imagine seducing her rather than to actually interact. In her fantasies, she couldn't disappoint anyone. She settled back on the lounge chair and closed her eyes.

Julia awoke with a start. She wiped her lips and sat up. She'd been drooling and the very real possibility that she'd also been snoring was enough to convince her to move her nap to the condo.

Unfortunately, the only way back to the condo was through the gate by the kids' pool. To get there, she either had to swim from the lagoon to the main pool and then cut through the bar, which was less appealing now that she was dry, or take the path that passed over a bridge between the pools and then cross in front of the volleyball net. To make matters worse, she'd left her towel and wraparound on a lounge chair by the gate.

Reed was still playing volleyball, and there was no easy way to avoid walking past her. But she had no reason to think that Reed would look in her direction anyway and she knew she shouldn't worry about covering up at a place like this. Still, she couldn't help wishing for something to tie around her waist.

Resolutely, she stood up. The sun and the short snooze had made her legs rubbery but waiting longer wouldn't improve that. She started down the path and only slowed when she reached the bridge.

From here, she had a perfect angle on the volleyball game. Reed had her back to her and the temptation to watch was hard to resist. The volleyball popped back and forth over the net a few times before Reed jumped to spike it. When the other team missed, a woman on Reed's team cheered and the guy on her left high-fived her.

Julia sighed. Sports had never been her thing. Dating sporty dykes wasn't her thing either. Not because she didn't appreciate athletic bodies, however. But if Reed was into sports, chances were she liked women who were in as good of shape as she was. Well, she didn't need someone like Reed anyway.

She turned from the game and headed down the bridge. On the last step, her left ankle rolled under as her right leg shot out in front of her. There was time to stretch for the railing, but she was several inches away and missed, striking a sharp slab of lava rock instead. By the time her slow-motion fall had ended, she was sitting in a puddle directly in front of the kiddie pool.

"Mom!" Bryn's voice was undeniable. "That woman from the plane fell!"

Julia saw a blur of pink life jackets and yellow sand buckets. Of all the places to land…She closed her eyes, willing her body to magically disappear. When she opened her eyes a second later, she was still in the middle of the pathway and the kids were getting closer.

She took a quick assessment of the damage. A good scrape on the palm of her left hand and another on her knee. Her hip was a dull throb, the pain in her left ankle was sharp, and her backside was soaked. Somehow she'd slipped on a wet spot. Too soon, Reed was standing over her with a look of concern on her face.

"I'm fine," she said, before Reed could ask.

"Okay." Reed squatted next to her. "But you look a little pale and you're bleeding."

"It's nothing. It looks worse than it is."

Julia didn't resist as Reed gently took her hand and examined the palm, but her heart immediately leapt to her throat. The fall was nothing. It was embarrassment that was going to finish her off. And did Reed's touch have to send shivers through her body on top of everything?

Reed glanced from Julia's hand to her scraped knee and then down the length of her outstretched leg and back up again. Just then Julia spotted the blush on Reed's cheeks.

Suddenly she didn't care that she'd left her towel on the lounge chair and happened to be sitting on her butt after a graceless fall. She also didn't care that she was twenty pounds over her weight-loss goal. Not when her curves could make a butch blush.

Reed smelled like coconut sunscreen and tangy sweat. The scent was perfect and Julia wanted to lean in closer. Good God, her hormones were throwing her for a loop.

"Mom, is she okay? Did she break her leg? Do you have to call an ambulance?" Bryn hollered. At Reed's bidding, the twins had gone back to the kiddie pool, but they were hovering at the edge and clearly hoping for permission to return.

"Pipe down, Bryn. She's going to be fine." Reed glanced back at Julia. "Sorry about that. They love ambulances."

"Maybe next time I'll try to break my neck." Julia bent her knee, ignoring the stinging sensation when she tried to stand. As soon as she placed weight on her left leg, pain shot up from the ankle.

Reed caught her, one hand slipping around her waist. "Easy does it." She helped Julia over to the nearest lounge chair. "You don't need to try for that ambulance ride."

"Well, paramedics are pretty sexy," Julia said, amazed that she could joke at the moment. Reed's grin made it worth the effort. Her ankle throbbed when she shifted her weight and tears sprang to her eyes. She wiped them away instantly and then gritted her teeth as she reached down to touch the sore spot. Definitely worse than she'd thought. "I think I twisted my ankle. I did this once before at band camp. Don't laugh."

"You went to band camp? That's cool."

"Band camp was not cool, but I loved it. I tripped when we were practicing our marching drills...only flute player to face plant." She sighed. "Look, I hate to ask but do you think you could wrap my ankle?"

"I could..." Reed hesitated, eyeing Julia's ankle. "But you might want to get an X-ray. You hit the ground hard and there might be a break. There's an urgent care in downtown Kona that we can get you to."

"I don't want to go to urgent care and end up in a cast. If I could just get some ibuprofen and an Ace Bandage..." Tomorrow Kate had signed all three of them up for parasailing and then surfing lessons the day after. This was not how she wanted to start the vacation. The tears threatened again and she bit the inside of her cheek to keep them at bay.

"Even if you did break a bone in your foot, they won't cast it. You'd get to wear one of those cool strappy boots that you can take off to swim."

"Cool?" This was getting worse by the minute. She glanced at her feet, picturing a big clunky boot paired with a flip-flop. "I'm not wearing a boot."

"As long as you don't wear it with socks, your friends will think it's a fashion statement," Reed said, her tone completely serious. "I mean, I'm not really a fashion person, but I heard somewhere that you should never wear sandals with socks and I think the same rule applies here."

Julia felt the blush come up her neck. Reed met her gaze, a smile at the edge of her lips. Clearly she'd overheard Kate's comment about sandals with socks. Kate did have a loud voice but...what if she'd also heard everything else they'd said on the plane? "Listen, I don't know how much you overheard in the plane—"

"Don't worry, I thought it was funny. I only brought it up because you looked like you were about to cry. I figured it'd be a good distraction."

"Gee, thanks."

Reed chuckled. "If you really want to talk about it, we can. Maybe over a drink..."

Julia wished the pain shooting up her leg wasn't distracting her. Had Reed seriously asked her to have a drink now? Before she came up with a response, Reed was hollering for her kids to get out of the water.

"They'll probably have a first aid kit in the gym. If you stay here with the kids, I can go run and ask."

"Uh, sure," Julia said, watching as Carly and Bryn sloshed out of the kiddie pool and scampered over. She had no time to rehash everything that had been said during the flight, but she already knew Reed had heard too much.

"Guys, I need you to stay with Julia. Keep her entertained while I find a first aid kit." She glanced at Julia. "I'll be quick."

Bryn stepped close to examine Julia's bloodied knee. "Too bad you didn't fall into the water. You're gonna need one of those big bandages like Mom put on my elbow when I fell off the porch swing."

Reed was gone before Julia could argue with the plan. As Bryn started firing off questions, Carly reached for Julia's hand, fortunately not the injured one, and clasped it gently. Julia wasn't sure if she was mad at her friends for deserting her—though they couldn't have predicted that she'd dive bomb the path—or glad that they'd missed this show. Mo would laugh her ass off if she saw Julia surrounded by kids and unable to get away.

Without a watch or her phone, it felt like ages before she spotted Reed at the gates to the pool. "You survived," Reed congratulated.

"Mom, it's only a scraped knee," Bryn said. "People don't die of that."

"Her hand hurts too," Carly added.

"And the ankle," Reed said. "But I meant that she survived you two."

Bryn and Carly looked at each other and shrugged. "Do you know what she means?" Bryn asked. When Carly shook her head, they both started to giggle.

"They're actually very sweet," Julia said.

"At least she didn't say 'cute,'" Bryn said, sticking her tongue out at her sister.

"Who would call you two cute?" Reed asked.

"You do!" the girls shouted at Reed, laughing as she scooped them out of the way. She deposited Bryn on the chaise lounge next to Julia and Carly by the first aid kit.

"Ibuprofen, as requested."

"Thanks. I'll take three," Julia said, extending her hand. Reed handed her a glass of water and three red pills, then knelt on the ground much too close for Julia to relax and started in on cleaning the scrape on her knee.

Julia chatted with Carly and Bryn, trying to joke with them about all the reasons you shouldn't run near a pool, and avoided the impulse to look down at Reed as she worked. The sensation of Reed's hand on her leg was sending a signal to an entirely too distracting place. When Reed dabbed an ointment on the scrape, Julia cringed, and Carly gripped her hand in response.

"Don't move," Carly said softly. "Mom's really good with Band-Aids, but if you wiggle it'll go on crooked."

Julia forced a smiled. "Is she also good at fixing egos?"

"What's an ego?"

"Something that hurts when people laugh at you," Reed said. "Or sometimes it hurts when you're embarrassed about something you did."

"Like when you farted at that movie theater?"

"Exactly." Reed pushed down the flap of Bryn's sunhat. "Thanks, kid. I can't even pretend to be cool with you two around."

Julia smiled. Reed was trying to impress her. That changed a few things. Before long, her hand and knee were decorated with Band-Aids. When Reed set in on the ankle, she had Carly and Bryn weighing in on how to wrap it. She'd found an Ace Bandage but was gingerly feeling the spot that had started to swell.

"You sure you don't want me to get you a ride to urgent care? If something's broken…"

Julia winced when Reed touched the inside of her arch eliciting something between a tickle response and screaming pain.

"Be gentle, Mom," Carly said. "That hurts."

Reed's eyes darted up to hers. How could she possibly be attracted to someone two little girls called Mom? "It's fine, really."

"She'll tell me if it hurts," Reed said. "But we should really get some ice on this…"

When Reed started to manipulate the ankle again, Julia pulled her leg back. "Okay, that hurts."

Bryn reached for her hand. "You have to try to be tough. She hasn't even put the bandage on yet."

"No, Mom has to be gentle," Carly said. She squeezed Julia's hand. "It's okay if you cry."

"Thanks," Julia said. But she definitely didn't want to cry.

By the time the ankle was wrapped, both kids had decided that Julia deserved an ice cream. She argued for a nap and they finally relented. It took longer than it should have to make it to the condo with Julia limping along on Reed's arm and the twins bouncing between them. Bryn spotted a gecko on one of the lanais and soon she'd taken off over the lava rocks after the scared lizard. Carly followed, hollering for Bryn to leave the lizard alone.

"You don't get a lot of down time with those two," Julia said, watching as the kids turned their attention to a butterfly that had made a sudden appearance.

"You have no idea." Reed eyed the girls. They had chased the butterfly to the end of the lawn where a tall wall of lava rock stopped their pursuit. "Sometimes I miss the down time…But life's more interesting with them." Just then, Bryn shoved Carly, hollering about her scaring away the butterfly. Carly argued back that it was Bryn's fault instead and then pushed past her to dash across the lawn. Reed sighed. "Then again, I wouldn't mind a quiet evening once in a while."

Julia leaned against the screen door. She wanted to ask Reed about her dinner plans, but the longer she hesitated the more awkward she felt. "Thanks for everything. I'm not used to needing anyone's help, but I appreciated being rescued."

Reed laughed. "I have no doubt that you would have managed on your own. But picking out your Band-Aids will probably be the highlight of the twins' day—right after looking for seashells. So, thank you for that."

"At least I made someone's day."

"You did." Reed met her eyes and then looked away quickly. She shifted on her feet and then squinted to see the twins, now chasing each other around a fountain in the center of the neighboring clump of condos. "I should probably go catch them before someone complains…"

"Probably." Julia smiled when Reed glanced at her again. She'd felt a sudden swell of confidence as she realized that Reed was the nervous one now. "Do they ever give you a break?"

"Not for long. But they do go to sleep." Reed paused. "Bedtimes are the hardest part of my day. But then I get a few hours of peace…Carly will be up late tonight worrying if your ankle still hurts and then Bryn will want me to call you to find out if your bandage is still on."

"You could call," Julia said. "But I'd rather you call because you wanted to talk."

Reed scratched her head. "It's been a while since I asked a woman for her phone number."

"I can tell," Julia said. "That's why I'm helping you out."

Reed chuckled. "Once upon a time I was better at this."

"Somehow that doesn't surprise me." But the fact that Reed wasn't smooth now was exactly why she was considering this. "Wait here."

Julia opened the screen door and hobbled inside, quietly cursing her ankle and hoping the meds would kick in soon. She found a pen and a pad of paper from the resort and quickly wrote her name and number. Maybe Reed hadn't asked a woman for a number in a while, but she couldn't remember the last time she'd given anyone her number either. With a new flush of excitement, she limped back outside. Reed was waiting for her, a warm smile on her face. She took the paper, folded it in half, and tucked it in the pocket of her shorts.

"I'm going to call room service and have them bring you some ice. You should lie down and put that foot up."

"Doctor's orders?" Julia said, trying to be funny but then worrying that she sounded suggestive instead. Quickly she added, "I promise I'll keep my leg up for the rest of the night."

"Then I'll have to catch you tomorrow for that drink," Reed said. "You'll hear from Carly and Bryn tonight. I know they won't go to sleep without checking in on you."

Julia wanted to ask Reed to come inside. But she knew she wasn't thinking clearly and if she suggested they have room service deliver those drinks now, she'd probably try and give her a thank-you kiss as well.

Reed held up her hand, gave a slightly awkward wave, and then turned to jog down the path toward Bryn and Carly. Julia watched her for a minute and then went back inside the condo. She sank down on the sofa, carefully situating her leg on the pillows before reaching for her phone.

After texting Mo and Kate, sparing them most of the embarrassing details, she called her mom. If anyone would understand the agony of missing the dinner buffet, it was her mom. And she wouldn't laugh about the fall.

CHAPTER FOUR

The condo was a bottom-floor unit, which meant no stairs, and although there was no view of the ocean, it certainly wasn't the worst place to be laid up. From the living room sofa, Julia could see out the sliding glass door, past the lanai to the lawn and the swimming pools. She'd been distractedly watching water cascade down a lava rock fountain for the past ten minutes and was convinced that the view alone would drain more stress than a year of therapy.

Aside from the living room decorated in bright Hawaiian-themed floral prints, the condo had a small kitchen, two bathrooms, and two bedrooms. Kate, whose parents owned the timeshare, had claimed the master bedroom, which left the smaller room with two twin beds to Julia and Mo. Kate's parents had offered their two weeks to the three of them for free. At that price, the place couldn't be beat. Despite that and the fountain, Julia hoped she wouldn't be stuck inside long. She adjusted the pillows under her ankle and cursed when a sharp pain made her muscle spasm.

"I bet this place has video cameras everywhere. We could probably find some footage of your fall," Mo said. She pushed open the screen door and came inside carrying a tin foil-wrapped plate. "Bon appétit." With a flourish, she set the plate on the coffee table and peeled back the tin foil. Plump prawns and chunks of pineapple filled half the plate along with a pad of coconut rice and several broccoli florets.

"This smells amazing. I've been lying here dreaming about prawns." Julia reached for the plate. "Have I told you how much I love you?"

"Tell me again. It never gets old." Mo beamed. She handed over the napkin-wrapped utensils and then pointed at the broccoli. "I know you're not a big fan, but there's a teriyaki glaze on that and even you are going to be a convert."

"I promise I'll eat my veggies," Julia said, choosing her first prawn. "After this." A burst of pineapple hit her tongue and she moaned her approval. The broccoli couldn't possibly taste as good. "Where's Kate?"

"She stayed to watch the hula dancers. The resort has them dance after dinner on Mondays and Thursdays—so don't even think about hobbling over there tonight. We're here for two weeks and you can catch them next time."

"Did you plan that speech out on your way over here?"

"Yes. Because I know you too damn well. Someone says hula and you're strapping on a grass skirt." Mo shimmied her hips and stuck out her tongue. "Am I right?"

"If you hadn't brought me dinner, I'd throw this remote control at you." She chose another prawn. "And, yes, you're right."

"Speaking of being right, I want news on Dr. Baxter." Mo held up her hand and added, "Not the part about you faking a fall so she could play doctor."

"Mo!"

"You blush so easy. I can't help myself." Mo patted Julia's cheek and then snagged a broccoli floret. She popped the broccoli in her mouth. "Now spill the juicy details."

"Her kids were there—no juicy details. But I may have given her my phone number so she can call and check on me later." Julia scooped a spoonful of rice and savored the sweet coconut. Between swallows, she added, "For the record, twisting my ankle on the second day of vacation isn't worth getting a date with any woman."

"You sure about that?"

Mo's serious tone stalled Julia's fork mid-dive. "Of course I'm serious. You don't think I did this on purpose, do you?"

"Of course not. Although I did wonder if you were playing it up a bit until you asked me to bring you dinner. Then I realized you'd be at that buffet table unless that ankle was damn near broke. But maybe it's your subconscious working…Maybe on some level you know this woman is the one."

"So my subconscious decides to lay me on my ass in front of her? And this is from the person who dates people based on their astrological signs and a palm reading…"

Mo chuckled. "There are worse ways to pick out a date."

"I've known Reed for one day—most of which I've spent looking like either an idiot or a klutz. I don't think my brain could have already decided she's the one."

"Things happen for a reason. That's all I'm saying." Mo sniffed. "You gonna try that broccoli or not?"

Julia stabbed a floret. Sesame, citrus, soy sauce, and a hint of honey beautifully disguised the broccoli. "I think even I would go back for seconds on this."

"Mm-hmm."

"Your turn, Mo. What's up with you avoiding Kate? You've got to tell her you gave Tanya a ring."

Mo sank into the empty loveseat opposite the sofa. "You know how Kate feels about Tanya."

"She thinks you can do better. And that's what you say about her marrying Ethan."

Mo met Julia's eyes. "But I'm right."

"You're a pain in the ass. We both know you two have feelings for each other. That's why you don't like Ethan and she doesn't like Tanya." When Mo didn't argue, Julia pressed on. "Why didn't you ask Kate out in college?"

"She was straight back then, remember?"

"But she would have said yes if you asked her out."

"You don't know that." Mo picked at the hem of her board shorts, avoiding Julia's gaze.

"Come on, Mo. She's had a thing for you ever since the first time you walked into our dorm room. Remember how she stumbled all over herself to give you the bed by the window? She'd already claimed it for herself, but she couldn't wait to give you the prime spot. You were dating Vivian then. After V it was Naomi. I don't remember who came next, but you were never single. And Kate was jealous of every one of them. She's jealous of Tanya and we both know why."

"Maybe she had a straight girl crush back in college, but that's not how she feels now."

"How do you know? Have you two talked?"

"I think you're reading more into this, Jules. She was with Travis all through college. It's not like she was pining away for me. And she's had plenty of chances to say something since then…"

"But we both know that she wouldn't volunteer anything unless you asked."

"I'm not going to ask," Mo said. "Look, you two are my best friends. I love both of you. But that doesn't mean I want to sleep with either of you."

"Secretly I'm glad you two never hooked up. I always worried that if you did, we wouldn't all stay friends after."

Mo picked up the remote control and turned on the stereo. Hawaiian music filled the room. She leaned back in the loveseat and stared at the ceiling. "Why is it that I love this music here, but as soon as I get back to California I can't listen to it?"

Julia finished off the last of the prawns and then started in on the rice. She eyed Mo. "I don't believe you about not wanting to sleep with Kate."

Mo looked over at her.

"And I think you two should talk about how you really feel before you get married."

"It's a two-way street. She could say something if she wanted to," Mo argued.

"She won't. You intimidate her."

"That's ridiculous."

"Why is it ridiculous? You're smart. You're confident. You've dated how many gorgeous women? You're funny. You're sexy."

Mo motioned with her hand. "Keep it coming. What else?"

"And you're cocky. Who wouldn't fall for you?"

Mo laughed. "You."

"If you keep bringing me platefuls of food I might yet." Julia paused. "Tell me why you've never asked Kate out. I promise I won't tell her."

Mo hesitated. Finally she said, "I'm only interested in women who know what they want. I don't need Kate's head trip."

Julia's cell phone rang and she glanced at the screen. Davis, California. "Shit, I think this is Reed." Her heart thumped in her chest.

"Girl, hurry up and answer it." Mo scooted to the edge of her seat.

"Don't listen, okay?"

Mo made a loud smooch and Julia rolled her eyes. She had to answer soon, but her hands were shaking now.

"Julia?"

Julia cupped her hand over the end of the phone and said, "Reed's kid is calling me." She couldn't help grinning.

"Ten bucks says you fall for her kids."

Julia shook her head and pulled her palm off the phone. "This is Julia. Is this Bryn?"

"Does your ankle still hurt?"

"Yeah. But I've got a pack of ice on it and I'm not walking anywhere—just like your mom told me."

Mo chuckled and said, "She wants you lying on your back with your feet up already?"

Julia waved off Mo's comment, but it distracted her enough to miss whatever Bryn had said on the other end of the line. "Can you repeat that, sweetie?"

There was a loud crash and then the sound of high-pitched voices all talking at once. Julia held the phone away from her ear and Mo raised her eyebrows.

"This is what you are getting yourself into," Mo said. "Consider yourself warned."

"I'm not getting myself into anything." Yet. She tentatively placed the phone against her ear when the noise died down.

"Um, Julia, um..."

"Is this Carly?"

"Yeah. Um..."

Carly's voice was hardly loud enough to hear and she couldn't seem to get any other words out. After a long pause, screaming erupted again. Julia guessed that Bryn had snatched the phone back. She held the phone away from her ear again and Mo murmured: "Sucker."

When she recognized Reed's voice, Julia felt her heart jump to her throat. "Hey." *Hey?* She wanted to do better than that, but her airway had tightened to the diameter of a coffee straw.

"You're probably going to regret giving me your number. The kids love calling people."

Julia swallowed. *Relax. She hasn't asked you out yet.* "Well, they're in luck. I love talking on the phone."

"That was before you met my kids." Reed chuckled. "Carly wants to know if you need more pain medicine."

Reed's voice was perfect. In fact, she wouldn't mind hearing that voice in bed. "I'm good. The ice is helping and I've got some Advil for later."

In the background, Julia heard Bryn say, "Ask her if she wants us to come over. She might need more Band-Aids."

"Do you need anything?" Reed asked.

"No, I'm good. Your kids are sweet, by the way."

"Sometimes."

Mo raised her eyebrows and whispered, "Told you so."

More screaming erupted in the background, and then the line went silent for a moment. Finally Reed said, "I've gotta get these kids to bed. They both skipped their naps. Maybe we'll see you tomorrow by the pool?"

By the time Julia hung up the line, Mo had enough ammunition to tease her for the next two weeks. Both girls wanted to say goodnight and she was certain that she'd blushed when Reed finally ended the call with her own goodnight. Fortunately, the screen door opened as soon as she set down the phone.

"You two missed a good show," Kate said. She held up a split coconut and wiggled her hips.

"How were the grass skirts?"

"Revealing. But I was paying more attention to the sweaty muscles of the guy with the torch." Kate set the coconut on the coffee table and went to the kitchen. She pulled a bottle of white wine from the refrigerator. "Who's drinking with me? I bought a deck of cards at the resort shop so Julia can beat us all at poker."

Kate's timing was perfect. Mo wouldn't have a chance to tease her about the phone conversation and she'd have a minute to digest the fact that she was going to be spending tomorrow at the pool with Reed and her kids.

"You guys are the best." Julia shifted the ice pack on her ankle and wiggled her toes. She was hoping for a miracle cure, but her ankle still hurt. "Kate, I have to bail on parasailing tomorrow. You and Mo will have to go on your own."

"You could come hang out on the beach anyway and take some pictures," Kate suggested.

Mo took one of the wineglasses from Kate. "She'd rather be taking pictures of a certain mom in the kiddie pool than hanging out with her friends."

"That's not true. You know I'd rather be parasailing with you two. Or hanging out on the beach. But I don't think I should walk on the sand until the swelling comes down..."

As Mo started to grumble about the trip being about spending time with friends, Kate cut in with: "Jules, this is fate. You're always so busy with work and you never let yourself relax. I think this is exactly what you need."

CHAPTER FIVE

Work was the last thing she wanted to think about. Julia stared at the phone number flashing on her screen and then eyed the swimming pool inches from her toes. She knew it was her boss. She also knew that Val would expect her to answer unless she was dying.

"How's Hawaii?"

"Good. What's up?"

Cut to the chase, Julia thought, *and please don't tell me that there's some emergency that you need me to come back to resolve.* She considered how much she needed her paycheck and how long it would take to find a different position if she told Val to screw herself for even thinking of asking her to come back to work.

"Did you know that this is the first vacation you've taken since you started here? I had Eileen pull up your file. You were hired five years ago. Since then, you haven't requested a single day off. Not a sick day, not even a long weekend. Eileen told me that you take one week off between Christmas and New

Year's to go see your parents in New York. That's it. And since the whole place closes for that week...Well, your record's impressive."

Or depressing. Julia wasn't going to admit that the reason she never took time off was that she had no one to spend it with. Val would probably congratulate her.

Val cleared her throat. "Anyway, I'm sure you're wondering why I'm calling. We've got a situation with the Chicago team."

Julia bit her tongue. Why had she answered the phone? "Okay. You'll have to get me up to speed. I haven't checked my email in a few days."

"Jason Gelfry is moving on. I haven't sent anything out about this yet, but we'll need to start a search for his replacement. I'd like you to talk to his team and put out any fires. Let them know that we're on top of this. He's not going to be replaced overnight and you know how people start worrying...In the interim, we need someone who can swing the meeting with D and J."

Val continued talking, but Julia had stopped listening. She wanted to argue that she was on vacation and so therefore she was not at work and therefore she was not going to be talking to the Chicago team. But she'd brought her laptop and could send a few emails...

"I'll be in Tokyo next week but go ahead and send me updates. Oh, and I've been hearing that there's trouble in Atlanta as well. Maybe you can send some feelers out to people on that team."

After Val hung up the line, Julia stared at her phone screen for several minutes. The wallpaper image was a shot of the Golden Gate Bridge that she'd taken over Memorial Day last year. She hadn't even gone out of town when she'd been required to take a three-day weekend.

Someone dove into the water a few feet away from her lounge chair and the splash hit her toes. Two teenage boys were roughhousing at the far end of the pool, taking turns dunking each other, and a third had come to join in on the fun. Julia had tuned them out until now.

"Hey. How's the ankle?"

She'd been waiting for Reed to show up at the pool, hoping to see her any minute, but now she was thrown off by the warm smile and gorgeous eyes looking down at her. Her body's reaction to Reed was ridiculous. She quickly glanced at the wrap on her ankle and wiggled her toes. "Feels great as long as I don't walk on it."

Carly and Bryn appeared on either side of Reed, each wearing a life vest and wielding pool noodles. Bryn eyed Julia's cocktail.

"What's that?"

"Punch for grown-ups," Reed said. "And, no, you can't have the little paper umbrella." Bryn's face dropped. Before she could get out an argument, Reed was pointing both kids to the pool. She glanced back at Julia. "Everything okay?"

Julia nodded.

Reed walked the kids over to the kiddie pool. As soon as she turned her back to set out their towels, Bryn pushed Carly into the water. Reed turned around when Carly bobbed up screaming. Bryn hopped in behind her. The kids fought for a moment and then were racing, somewhat awkwardly in their vests, toward the slide. Reed watched them for a moment and then walked back to Julia's spot. She sat down on one of the empty lounge chairs, keeping her gaze on the kids.

"Do they fight a lot?"

"All the time. They're best friends and best enemies." Reed sighed. "I know I could do a better job parenting Bryn...well, both of them, honestly."

Julia wondered if it was appropriate to ask if Reed liked being a parent and then decided that it wasn't. "Parenting looks hard."

"It's a lot harder than my day job," Reed admitted. She scooted her lounge chair over a few inches so the shade from the umbrella covered her legs. This also meant her chair was now sandwiched against Julia's.

With little effort, Julia could have brushed against her when she reached for her drink—which is exactly what her body wanted. Heart racing, she tried instead to focus on an intelligent conversation. "Do you like your job?"

"I'm happy enough. Some days I wish I'd decided on something with a little less stress, but this one pays the bills... And I like that I can help people." Reed paused. "Do you like yours?"

"I love it—most of the time." Julia shifted her leg so she was a little further from temptation. "My boss just called..."

Reed cocked her head. "She called you while you were on vacation?"

"She doesn't understand personal time."

"No kidding." Reed kicked off her sandals and shifted back on the lounge chair, bringing her even closer to Julia. "Is it urgent?"

"To Val, everything's urgent." Julia swallowed. *Focus on something besides how good she smells.*

"Maybe you should explain the value of vacation time. Increased productivity and all that."

Julia eyed Reed. "That would not go over well."

"No? What if you tell her that it's against the law to ask you to work when you're off the clock? Maybe labor laws will be more convincing. By the way, I'm completely unqualified to give career advice."

Julia laughed. "I was thinking you were doing a pretty good job, actually. For a doctor."

"I'm a radiologist. I give a lot of advice. But most of the time I'm talking to other doctors. Career guidance isn't usually part of the conversation." She paused. "You're looking at me funny. Did I say something wrong?"

"I was wondering how it is that you're a doctor and good at what you do, but you don't drive me crazy."

Reed chuckled. "How do you know I'm good at what I do?"

"Just a hunch."

"Hmm. What do you have against doctors?"

"I have something against know-it-alls. And cocky assholes. The last person I dated was both. She happened to be a surgeon—which I know is nothing like a radiologist—but I swore off the whole profession. I can't figure out why you're different," Julia continued. "But it's a good different."

Reed grinned. "Maybe not all doctors are assholes. It's possible you got caught up with a bad egg."

"Doubtful. I think you're an exception to a rule." Julia paused. "It wasn't only my ex. All of her friends were doctors and there was definitely a theme."

"The cocky asshole theme?"

"Exactly. Don't get me wrong—they were all smart and probably had every reason to act like know-it-alls, but it got old."

Reed's brow furrowed, seeming to consider her rebuttal. "I know a lot of doctors who are socially awkward. Maybe the cocky attitude is a cover. Most of us were the classroom nerd for too many years."

"Maybe. So what's your story?"

"What do you mean?" Reed squinted at her.

"You aren't cocky," Julia said.

"Do I need to work on that?"

"Please don't."

Reed chuckled. She was wearing her sexy glasses again and her hair was disheveled like she hadn't bothered with a comb. She ran her hand through it, as if nervous under Julia's gaze, and only managed to mess it up more. Julia resisted the urge to reach over and push the stray hairs into place.

"I'm sorry I asked you to check out my ankle," Julia said. "That's probably not part of your job description."

"Not exactly." Reed glanced at Julia's outstretched leg. "But how does it feel? We could get you to urgent care if it's still bothering you."

"It's getting better. I think I just need to follow doctor's orders and stay off it for a few days."

"You're going to let a doctor tell you what to do?"

"In this case, yes." Julia held back from saying that she'd do whatever Reed told her to do.

Reed's gaze had turned to the kiddie pool. Bryn was attempting a climb up the waterslide while Carly was teetering at the top, one hand gripping the top rail. Carly shouted for Bryn to get off the slide, her tenuous hold on the rail slipping, while Bryn was halfway up and shouting for Carly to stay put. A fresh surge of water pushed Carly and her hand slipped. Reed was on her feet and starting toward them.

Before she got to the pool, the kids had tumbled down the water slide and splashed into the sandy-bottomed kid pool. Someone had been thinking when they'd designed the little pool. The water was only knee height and with the sand, it was hard to get hurt. Still, Carly and Bryn were both wailing.

Reed scooped up one kid in each arm and carried them to the nearest chairs. Julia always had the impulse to run from crying kids, but now she was debating if she should hobble over to see if she could help or order everyone ice cream. She hailed one of the servers from the poolside café that was passing by with an empty tray.

"Any chance you could ask those three what flavor ice cream they'd like?" Julia handed the young man her room key.

"No problem." He glanced at the room number and then handed the key back to Julia. "Would you like a cone too?"

"Chocolate, please."

* * *

"Looks like you two had a fun day."

Mo was stretched across the living room sofa with an ice pack on her shoulder and another on her hip. Kate was on her yoga mat in the middle of the room, groaning as she stretched.

A cherry-red sunburn marked her thighs up to her shorts and her nose was decidedly pinker than it had been that morning.

"Don't rub it in," Mo said. "Turns out parasailing isn't as easy as it looks. And the brochure did not mention that you could fall getting back *into* the boat."

"Into the boat?"

"We had a good time until that mishap," Kate said. "But I forgot to reapply sunscreen."

"I noticed. Want some aloe?"

"Yes, please. Mo needs some on her feet, but she won't admit they got burned."

When Julia returned from the bathroom with the aloe, Kate said, "You're walking better."

Julia glanced at her ankle. She'd almost forgotten about the sprain. After her last dip in the pool, she'd left the wrap off. "I'm not going to tempt fate, but I think this sprain is a lot better than the last one I got."

"At band camp?" Mo grinned. "Or could it be that you were so distracted by a soccer mom that you spent all day lying on your back watching her and the swelling went down because of that?"

Mo's guess wasn't far from the truth, but Julia didn't want to give her the satisfaction of telling her so. She argued that she'd spent the day with her nose in her paperback. For the most part, that was true as well. "It's possible I may have had a few conversations with Reed, but I didn't spend all day ogling her."

"Any kissing?"

"No. Her kids were with us the entire time and I'm not going to start kissing someone I hardly know in the middle of the afternoon."

"You have a schedule for that?"

"Ignore her, Jules," Kate said. "Some of us take a while to get to know someone before we're ready to exchange saliva and that's completely reasonable." She raised her eyebrows at Mo and continued, "Do you know how many infectious organisms are transferred in one open mouth kiss?"

Mo let go of the ice pack she'd been holding in order to clap her hands over her ears. "Don't let her ruin kissing, Jules. You've gotta stop her."

But Kate pressed on anyway, a sly glint in her eye. "Eighty million bacteria in one intimate kiss. And that's only bacteria. That study didn't take into account viruses or yeast that could also be transferred."

"Yeast? In a kiss? Why do you always have to bring science in and ruin the good stuff?" Mo shook her head. "Anyway, Jules is kissing a doctor—there's no germs involved there."

"Turns out she's a radiologist," Julia said, mostly to change the subject away from bacteria. "Maybe it's because I'm slightly smitten, but I'm thinking there's a good chance radiologists are less likely to be assholes than surgeons."

"Give her time. Remember—she's on vacation at the moment. She's just as likely to be an asshole once you get to know her better." Mo added, "But less likely to have kissing germs."

"Well, she probably works in a hospital. Those places are cesspools of bacteria," Kate argued.

"Only if you touch the door handles."

Kate shook her head. "The truth is, we're probably at a higher risk of getting sick when we eat the fish tacos at the buffet tonight. Have you guys noticed that they leave that salsa out for everyone to reach their hands into? Norovirus central. And who knows if they wash the cabbage. Salmonella, anyone? It's all relative risk."

"Now you've ruined buffets and kissing," Julia said. "Do you realize those are two of my favorite things?"

Mo chuckled. "You're probably better off having sex. Germ free as long as you don't kiss."

"Not germ free," Kate said, shaking her head at Mo. "But probably safer than eating her taco."

There was a half second of silence before Kate busted up laughing. She laughed so hard that she had to stop for air and then busted up again. Her cheeks turned as red as her sunburned legs. Mo couldn't resist laughing at Kate and then Julia joined in.

When they'd all stopped, Julia said, "I'm so glad you two are my friends. I don't even care that I have a crappy dating life with you two around."

* * *

Her cell phone had been silent since Val's call earlier that day and Julia jumped when she heard it ring late that evening. She glanced at the caller ID and was instantly glad that Mo and Kate weren't back from the resort bar. This call she wanted to take alone. When she answered on the third ring, trying not to seem as if she'd been waiting for the call, she had to hide her disappointment at hearing Bryn's voice. Was it ridiculous to want Reed to call her herself?

"Can you come to the waterfall with us? Mom rented a car. It's red and there's a real window on the roof."

"A sunroof?"

"Yeah—can you come?"

Before Julia could decide how to answer, Reed's voice came on the line.

"Hope you weren't trying to have a quiet evening at home. My kids couldn't go to sleep without saying good night. Hold on a second."

"Julia?" Carly's voice was more distinct than it had been in their last phone conversation but still quiet. "Mom says one of the waterfalls has rainbows in it."

"That sounds beautiful."

"Can you come?"

As if on repeat from the previous night's conversation, a loud crash followed and then screaming. When Reed came back on the line, Julia said, "You all okay?"

"Oh, this is normal for us." She sighed. "Carly, Bryn, quiet down for a minute. I can't hear Julia."

The screaming died down some and Julia asked, "What's this about a waterfall?"

"You know your dating life has gotten bad when your kids start asking women out for you." Reed quickly added, "Not that I wouldn't ask you out on my own. I would definitely ask you out, but I'm not really dating right now and this isn't a date kind of thing. This is more like a field trip—with two insane four-year-olds who might scream the entire time." She paused. "I totally screwed that up, didn't I?"

"Not completely." Julia couldn't help smiling. "Maybe you should tell me what your plan is."

"We're taking a drive over to the Hilo side of the island. I want to show the girls some waterfalls and I need a break from the resort. We won't be walking much—you can see most of the waterfalls from the car. But we'll probably be gone the whole day…"

A day-long field trip with two four-year-olds. Julia knew she might be crazy, but she wanted to say yes so much that her brain was screaming the word. Sounding coolly ambivalent was a stretch. "When are you thinking of going?"

"Tomorrow morning. If you haven't been over to the rainy side of the island, the waterfalls are amazing…But no pressure. I won't blame you at all if you say no—four-year-olds can be terrors on car rides."

"Actually it sounds fun. And the drive will keep me off my ankle." She'd already told Mo and Kate that she wouldn't be joining them at their surfing lesson tomorrow, but she didn't have a good excuse for not going down to the beach to watch. Now she did.

"Really?" The happy surprise in Reed's voice made Julia smile even more.

"Really. I can't wait."

"Me neither," Reed said. "That was easier than I thought it'd be. I should let my kids ask women out for me more often." She chuckled. "For field trips, that is."

"I'll see you tomorrow. For our non-date."

"Perfect."

Julia ended the call and went straight to her room. Picking out what to wear often calmed her nerves and she needed all the help she could get at the moment. With Reed's kids in tow, she didn't want anything sexy, but the right outfit might make Reed wish they were actually going on a date. Although the good thing about a field trip with kids meant she could relax. There was no danger of anything intimate happening. Even if part of her wanted it to.

CHAPTER SIX

"No one has to pee, right?" Reed finished fastening the last buckle on Carly's seat. "'Cause this is your last chance for the next hour and a half." When she looked up, she caught Julia's eye in the rearview mirror.

The drive across the island was only an hour and a half, but then the plan was to go up the coast with stops along the way to find waterfalls. They were going to be stuck in the car for the better part of the day. Julia wasn't worried about the four-year-olds so much as herself. Given how many hours she'd spent last night fantasizing about Reed, the driver's seat was a little too close to the passenger seat.

She'd enjoyed one particular fantasy over and over again last night and now as Reed looked at her, everything she'd imagined seemed exposed. She swallowed. Reed was still holding her gaze in the mirror and she couldn't look away…

"It's not too late to change your mind," Reed said.

"I'm not changing my mind." That much was certain. She'd had the funny sense all morning that she was meant to go on this car ride. Forcing a smile and a light tone, she said, "I want to see some waterfalls."

"Me too," Bryn said. "Julia, did you know that this car only plays Hawaiian music?"

Reed settled into the driver's seat. As she buckled her seat belt she said, "Bryn wanted to play kids' music off my phone. Her favorite song is the Hokey Pokey with a close second being the Chicken Dance. We usually play the same album over and over again."

"That sounds like a party."

"Exactly." Reed's sarcasm was subtle. "Unfortunately, I can't hook my phone up to this car's stereo."

"What a shame. I'm sorry I'll have to miss those songs."

"You can come over to our condo later and I can play them for you," Bryn said. "I know how to use Mom's phone. You could even spend the night. Mom has a really big bed."

Reed looked in the rearview mirror, avoiding Julia's eyes as she said: "So, who wants to go see waterfalls?" Her blush was obvious though she was trying to hide it by focusing on backing the car out of the parking place. Thank God she was the one blushing—Julia's thoughts had gone straight to the image of an oversized bed with Reed lying relaxed in the middle of it waiting...

The kids banded together in a shouting match of "me's" and then Reed switched on the radio. Hawaiian music calmed the kids for about a second before they were back to shouting. This time the shouting match was about who could climb waterfalls.

They pulled out of the resort parking lot and Reed glanced over at Julia. "You're stuck with us now."

"I love road trips." The uncertain feeling in Julia's stomach had given way to excitement. "But I have to admit, this one's noisier than what I'm used to."

"They'll quiet down in a bit." The kids made loud dolphin squawking noises in the backseat as they battered each other with two stuffed dolphins and Reed added, "Hopefully."

"Don't worry. I'll get used to it."

"Can the dolphins be a little quieter back there?" Reed asked. "I think there's a shark around here and we don't want to get caught."

The noise immediately turned to whispers and Reed held up crossed fingers. "I love road trips too. Long drives feel kind of freeing, you know? No work to get to, no one expecting you anywhere...The summer before Bryn and Carly were born I drove from California to Boston to deliver a desk. It was one of the best vacations I've ever taken."

"California to Boston? That's a long drive to deliver a desk. Must have been a nice desk."

"It was more about the woman who wanted the desk. Unfortunately, it turned out she was more interested in the desk than she was in me."

"Ouch."

"Yeah. It was a long way to drive to get dumped." Reed slowed to a stop to let a pedestrian cross. "But the road trip was exactly what I needed. And she wasn't into kids so it probably was a good thing we broke up when we did. We'd been together for three years and she wanted me to move to Boston." Reed pulled onto the main highway and then said, "We're still friends. I give her a bad time about that desk whenever I think of it. I call it the break-up desk."

Julia wanted to ask if there'd been a girlfriend after that or, more to the point, if there was another parent in the picture, but she didn't want to seem nosy. If there was an ex-wife, the relationship must have been hot and heavy for them to decide to have kids that fast after Reed had gotten out of a three-year relationship.

When Julia didn't ask anything more, Reed said, "What's one of your favorite vacations?"

Julia thought for a moment. She knew the answer, but she wasn't sure it was a good thing to bring up. "After college, I went to Paris for two weeks with a friend. Well, a girlfriend." She paused. She was breaking her own rules by mentioning an ex-girlfriend. But she wasn't technically on a date with Reed. "It was the best vacation—but it was also the worst."

"What made it the best?"

She shook her head. "I know we aren't on a date, but I feel funny talking about an ex. I mean, you did it first, but…"

"Would this be a weird date? Dolphins that talk and arguing four-year-olds aren't the typical atmosphere for dates you've been on?" Reed smiled, glancing at the backseat. The stuffed dolphins were still on the lookout for sharks. "For the record, I don't usually bring my kids on dates. Or talk about exes."

Julia tried to gather her thoughts before she said something she'd regret. She wished she could take back what she'd said about this not being a date. "Actually this would be a nice date. Way better than a lot of past dates, in fact."

"Probably because we aren't really on a date. Which is why we can talk about anything we want—including all of our crazy exes." Reed winked.

"I think I've been the crazy one in my past relationships," Julia admitted.

Reed shook her head. "I'm not buying that. And you do realize that I'm not letting you off the hook about Paris, right?"

"I should have lied and told you that my favorite trip was the time I went backpacking in Yosemite. Alone."

"Too late. What happened in Paris?"

Julia instantly pictured the café where she'd had the fight with Emily. Yet she'd been so happy before the café. "The first couple days we spent roaming the streets and just taking it all in. I felt like we were in a scene from a movie. We stayed up late drinking wine and ate croissants for breakfast every morning… We went to this little cinema and watched French movies. I don't speak any French and I had no idea what any of the movies were about. But it was fabulous. If I could, I'd stop the memory there."

"Croissants for breakfast every morning and roaming the City of Light?" Reed met her eyes. "Sounds perfect. Maybe the memory can stop there."

But it didn't. All the hours of fighting burst from Julia's memory. Those first few days they'd pretended that everything was fine. Then Emily had asked if they could try having sex again. It wasn't Emily's fault. All along Emily had tried to be patient...That's what made it worse. They'd gone to Paris to repair a fatally damaged relationship, but the change in scenery couldn't fix the problem. Julia wasn't even certain what was wrong with her—only that as much as she loved Emily, she didn't want more than a kiss or a casual embrace.

Reed had turned her attention back to the road, leaving Julia alone with her thoughts. She stared out the window at the passing field of lava rock. For years, she'd refused to think about Paris. She'd tossed the photos she'd taken of Emily, along with every other picture she'd taken on that trip. She even threw out the ticket stubs from the movies they'd watched in the old cinema. The bad memories had tainted the good ones. Now she wondered if she could ever separate them.

"Those first three days in Paris were perfect. Definitely my favorite vacation." A moment later she added, "I need to go on more vacations. This is the first vacation I've had in five years. Most of the time I even stay home when there's a long weekend so I can catch up on work..."

"What would be a perfect long weekend?" Reed asked.

Julia considered the question for a minute. "I like new adventures. Maybe a drive down the coast to check out a town I've never been to. Or snowshoeing in the mountains. Or a hot air balloon ride."

"Wait, what?" Reed shook her head. "I was with you up until the hot air balloon. Those things go way too high. Plus there's no engine. You're trusting your life to a gust of wind and someone who's probably taken a summer course on aviation safety. If something goes wrong, you can't even control how you crash."

"How do you really feel?" Julia laughed, surprised by Reed's strong response. "Is it a control thing or are you scared of heights?"

Reed hesitated. "Since this isn't a date…we can be honest, right? I'm a control freak—total top—and I have a ridiculous fear of heights."

Total top? Had Reed seriously just admitted that? Julia felt a stirring between her legs she tried to ignore. At least the part of last night's fantasy when Reed had ordered her onto her knees wasn't completely far-fetched. "I'm not surprised that you're a top."

Reed chuckled. "That obvious, huh? What about you?"

"Uh, I don't think I have a category. Definitely not a top." She needed to change the subject. "So, how bad is your fear of heights?"

"Pretty bad. Don't tell me you live in a tall building?"

"Fortunately, no." She quickly added, "I hate stairs. Would you end things if you started dating someone who lived in a skyscraper?"

"Dealbreaker." Reed laughed. "Usually this stuff comes up in later conversations. I'm glad we're getting it all out in the open now."

"Before anything happens?" Julia couldn't believe the words had slipped out, but it was too late to take them back. She felt the flush go up her neck and avoided Reed's gaze, pretending instead to be suddenly fascinated with the view of the passing lava field. What was she playing at? Their bantering reminded her of conversations with Mo, but she wasn't only joking like she did with Mo. She wanted Reed's reaction. But what would happen if Reed wanted more in return?

At the stop sign, Julia dared to look over at Reed. The rush that went through her was overpowering. How was she going to get through the rest of the day pretending she wasn't wet at the thought of Reed's touch?

Feeling reckless, Julia asked, "Remind me again why you're single?"

"Everything changed when they came along," Reed admitted, a serious note in her voice.

"When are we going to see a waterfall?" Bryn asked.

Reed switched on the radio. "In about an hour. Tell me if you see a goat."

"A goat?"

The search for goats proved more entertaining than Julia expected and certainly distracted her from worrying about how much she wanted to feel Reed. Carly turned out to be the best at spotting the scraggly nomads. They seemed to pop up out of the lava rocks without warning, but the more Julia focused on finding them, the more detail she began to see in an otherwise desolate black moonscape. Soon the lava fields gave way to rolling hills and grassland and then a lush landscape of palms and flowering trees.

Reed pulled off the highway before they descended into Hilo. She drove down a winding, narrow, side road while leading a game of Twenty Questions, and Julia had the distinct feeling that wherever she was taking them, she'd been there before.

When a small green sign depicting a waterfall came into view, Reed said, "Oh good. I was worried we were lost there for a minute."

"You know this car does have GPS," Julia said, pointing to the map button on the darkened video display.

"But then we wouldn't feel like explorers who stumbled across something amazing." She leaned over the console and pointed out Julia's window.

A narrow river coursed through a jungle of green foliage and then dropped abruptly in a shimmering waterfall with a backdrop of lava rock. Below, a dark pool reflected the cascading water.

"That's beautiful," Julia said, surprised that the sudden appearance of the waterfall was enough to momentarily take her breath away.

Reed was smiling when she looked back at her. "It's even better close up. Think your ankle is up for a little walking?"

"As long as we take it slow."

"Don't worry. We never go anywhere fast." Reed looked over her shoulder at the kids. "Do you guys want to see the cave where the moon goddess lives?"

Getting out of the car took much less time than getting in, but there was considerably more name calling. Reed ignored the bickering for the most part, and soon both kids tumbled out of the car wearing sunhats and toting backpacks with water and snacks.

Bryn latched onto Julia's hand as they crossed the parking lot. "Do you think there's really a moon goddess here?"

"I don't know. I hope so," Julia said. "But she might be sleeping."

Fortunately, her ankle was feeling considerably better than she'd feared it might. Between the ibuprofen and the brace, she hardly felt any pain as Bryn dragged her over to the lookout point. She took out her camera and snapped a few pictures, catching the rainbow that the sunlight made in the spray, and then angled her lens toward Bryn who was staring, mouth agape at the dark cave behind the falls.

"I think she's hiding down there, Julia. Do you think she'll come out of her cave?"

"She probably only comes out when the moon is shining," Reed said. "If she exists."

Bryn and Carly were quick to agree that the moon goddess was real but that she was hiding because of all the people.

"Can you take our picture?" a woman asked, motioning to the man standing next to her and then holding her phone out to Reed.

After Reed snapped the shot, the woman glanced at Julia, the girls, and then again at Reed. "Would you like me to take one for you? You have such a beautiful family."

Julia felt a tinge of guilt as Reed said, "Uh, sure."

The woman reached for Julia's camera as the girls gathered close. Reed stepped in on the other side. A few camera clicks later and the awkwardness had passed. Julia took her camera back, thanking the woman, as Bryn and Carly started in on an argument over who had stepped on whose foot.

"There's a little spot over by those trees where we can have a snack and let the kids blow off some steam," Reed said. "Think your ankle's up for it?"

"Sure."

A well-trodden dirt trail, laced with tree roots and overhung with moss from the constant misting of the falls, followed the cliff above the waterfall for fifty feet or so before seeming to end in thick jungle growth. Reed pointed the way and Carly and Bryn set off at a run. When they reached the overgrown part, the kids stopped. Reed pushed back the brush, revealing the hidden path, and the kids laughed and shoved to be first as they took off again. The way was thick with hanging vines and bushes as tall as houses.

"You know your way around here."

"I came here a few years back. They were in diapers then. In retrospect, I was crazy for trying to go on a vacation alone with two toddlers." Reed paused. "They're easier now. In some ways at least. I feel like as soon as I get used to whatever stage they're in, they change on me."

"What stage are they in now?"

"I'm not sure. It's a mix of boundless energy and constant curiosity fighting with a shitty attention span. Plus there's a little self-centered asshole thrown in." Reed grinned. "I kind of love the challenge."

She pointed at Bryn who'd been in the lead until she ran headfirst into a bush and got tangled up. She shrieked as Carly pushed past her. Tugging her shirt off a branch she'd snagged,

Bryn turned to tear after her sister. "They'll sprint for about twenty feet, then stop dead when they see a bug or a lizard. Then they spend two minutes poking and prodding the poor creature, another three arguing about who saw it first, and before you know it, they're off at a run again."

As if on cue, Carly stopped in her tracks and Bryn bumped against her. "Look! Tarzan vines!"

The tree ahead of them was enormous and Julia guessed by its size that it was ancient. "What type of tree is that?"

"I think they call it a banyan tree," Reed said. "And the things that look like vines are actually roots of little fig trees."

The dangling fig roots, although Julia agreed with Carly in that they looked more like Tarzan vines, added to the prehistoric feel of the tree. As they drew closer to the spot where Carly and Bryn had stopped, Julia realized the path didn't end at the vines but turned toward the center of the tree, dipping down a short slope to a clearing at the base of the tree. Several logs in varying states of decay made haphazard benches underneath the tree's canopy.

The girls dashed down the slope and then began wildly whooping as they circled the tree trunk. Julia took her time choosing her steps down the slope. Reed stayed close, likely so she could catch Julia if she slipped, though she pretended to be studying the roots that overhung the path.

When Julia stubbed her foot on a half-buried rock, Reed's hand was on hers immediately. She let go as soon as Julia had righted herself, almost as if she were embarrassed that she'd caught her so quickly. Julia felt a heat flare inside her at the innocent contact. She wanted to reach for Reed's hand again but this time she wanted to hold on.

They reached the bottom of the slope and Reed said, "Not too bad, right?"

Julia arched her eyebrows. "You came here with toddlers? How did they get down here without falling?"

"My memory of that entire year is a little fuzzy to tell you the truth. They'd just learned to walk and I wasn't sleeping much…I have a vague recollection of them scooting down the hill on their butts."

Reed went over to one of the nearest logs and slipped off her backpack. Julia followed, grateful to sit down and give her ankle a break. As Reed called the kids over, handing out triangle-cut peanut butter and jelly sandwiches along with juice boxes, Julia wondered again if there had been a wife in the picture at one time. Maybe Reed had decided to adopt kids alone, but she doubted that. She'd hinted that her life had changed course because of the kids. But had she gone into it alone and wanting this?

Julia pushed the questions from her mind. She didn't want to pry, and how kids had come into Reed's life didn't matter anyway. If anything happened between them, it would be a vacation fling—nothing more. They didn't need to exchange life histories.

The fact that she was even considering having sex with Reed was crazy. But she was certain Reed was drawn to her and there was no doubting her body wanted at least a kiss. Was she really up for more?

Thoughts of having Reed's hands on her had been nonstop since she'd bandaged her up after the fall. But the likelihood that she'd freeze up if they tried to be intimate made her want to stop at the fantasy alone. Still there was a chance she could relax this time—and actually enjoy sex—since there was no risk of a long-term commitment.

"Here, I made you one too," Reed said, handing her one of the triangular pieces. "I could only find pineapple jelly at the resort store. It tastes a little weird with peanut butter, but the combination kind of grows on you."

Julia took a bite, thankful to have food to focus on instead of sex. She'd skipped breakfast since Reed wanted to make an early start and her stomach had been grumbling for the past hour. "This is good."

"You must be hungry," Reed said. "People only like my cooking if they're starving."

"I don't know if peanut butter and jelly qualifies as cooking."

"It does in my house." Reed took a bite of one of the sandwiches and murmured her approval. When Julia shook her head, Reed said, "Let me guess: you're secretly a gourmet chef?"

"No. But I am a good cook. One of these nights, I'll make you all dinner as a thank-you for taking care of my ankle."

"That was nothing. And you probably shouldn't cook anything too good because I already like you more than I should."

Julia swallowed her bite, feeling a rush of delight at Reed's words. "More than you should? Do you have a rule on how much you can like someone?" She couldn't hold back her smile. Reed was charming, no two ways about it.

"When I meet someone while I'm on vacation, yes."

The reality check hit Julia like a punch to the stomach. What was wrong with her? This wasn't even a date and she was busy planning future family meals.

Reed continued, "The truth is, I haven't met someone I liked in a long time. I don't go on dates very often but when I do...I never seem to click with anyone. And then the kids come up." She met Julia's eyes. "I'm probably breaking more of those dating rules, aren't I?"

"Good thing this isn't a date."

"Right." Reed glanced at Carly and Bryn, who had emptied their own backpacks and set up a picnic on one of the other logs. "Thanks for coming today. I almost forgot how nice it is to hang out with another grown-up."

After a stop at a playground in Hilo and then ice cream, they started the trek northward up the coast. Out one side of the car were distracting ocean vistas and out the other side was waterfall after waterfall coursing down brilliant green gorges. A light rain started after they pulled out of Hilo. Carly and Bryn fell asleep quickly and Julia thought of all the personal questions she wanted to ask Reed, starting with how she'd ended up with twins. Instead they talked about the landscape they passed and about places they'd lived. Safe topics.

When the rain came down in sheets, Julia let Reed concentrate on the drive. She distracted herself by taking note of the places she could steal glances without drawing attention: Reed's hands on the steering wheel, the curve from her shoulder to her neck and the shaved start of her hairline, the line of her jaw when she hummed along with the radio. If Reed glanced at her, Julia turned her interest to a passing car or a street sign. She needed to not let herself get any more attached than she'd already gotten.

Out of the blue, Reed asked, "You aren't used to being around kids, are you?"

"Why do you ask?"

"You seem a little nervous around them. Especially when Carly wanted you to help her get off that climbing structure at the playground. She likes you—which is saying a lot. Most people can't even get a hello out of her."

"Don't tell Carly, but that was the first time I've ever picked up a kid."

"Seriously?"

"I didn't realize they were so light."

"Try carrying two at a time for a while." Reed stopped the windshield wipers. They'd finally gotten to a patch of blue sky and the thick jungle vegetation on either side of the road was glistening in the sunlight. "I can't believe that was the first time you've picked up a kid. No younger brothers or sisters? No babysitting jobs?"

"My parents got married late in life. They didn't think they'd have kids at all and then I came along. And definitely no babysitting jobs."

"What was your first job?"

"I was a bagger at ShopRite. My dad used to say I was acquiring lifelong skills, but about all I learned was how to pack a week's worth of groceries in under a minute."

"You never know when that might come in handy." Reed grinned. "Are you close to your parents?"

"I talk to my mom a lot. I can tell her everything. And if I needed help, my dad would go to the moon for me. But I don't get to see them often. Overall, on the parent department, I got lucky." She paused. "They've always supported me—even with the gay thing. My first semester in college I dated a guy and then my second semester I dated a woman, and my mom's response was, 'It's good to test out your options. That's why everyone loves all-you-can-eat buffets.'"

Reed laughed. "Your mom sounds awesome."

"She is. It's important to her that people are with the person they love. She had a lot of pressure from her family to marry a Chinese man—ideally someone from their church. When she fell for a tall, skinny redhead from the Bronx, my grandparents thought she'd lost her mind. They wouldn't talk to her for months. It's marginally better now."

"Your grandparents are still alive?"

"Everyone in my family lives forever. My Chinese grandma says it's the rice and my Irish grandpa says it's the whiskey." Julia smiled. "I think it's because they're all too stubborn to be the first one to go."

"Where do they all live?"

"New York." Julia paused, a sudden rush of homesickness catching her off guard. Although her parents had visited her, she hadn't been back to New York in years. She made a mental note to call everyone soon. "So, what about you? What was your first job?"

"Babysitting. Then lifeguarding." Reed glanced at the backseat. The kids were still sound asleep. "I was the oldest of five so there was a lot of babysitting."

"Five kids? Is your family Catholic or Mormon?" Julia added, "Don't take that the wrong way—both of my parents were raised Catholic. We never went to church when I was a kid, but I always wished I had a big family like my cousins.

You don't hear of people having that many kids unless they're religious."

"They weren't religious. My mom just always wanted a big family."

"Well, I'm officially jealous. How many brothers and sisters?"

"Three brothers, one sister." Reed seemed reluctant to add more. The respite in the rain had been brief, and she switched the wipers on again, concentrating on the wet pavement.

"Are you close to them?" Julia noticed Reed's jaw muscles clench as soon as she'd asked the question. It was too late to take it back. "I'm totally prying. You don't have to answer."

"It's fine. You're not prying." Reed stalled, concentrating again on the road. "My sister passed away a few years ago. She overdosed."

"Oh, jeez. I'm sorry for asking—"

"Don't be. You didn't know and I should be able to talk about it." After a long exhale, Reed said, "McKenna was the kid who was always the life of the party. Would talk to anyone— flirted nonstop with the boys—and had plenty of girlfriends too. Everything changed in her world when our mom died. She was a freshman in high school. The rest of us had already moved out...It was just her and my dad at home. I was in med school three thousand miles away and our brothers were in college. We should have been there for her, but none of us realized how much she needed us.

"My dad was a mess. All he could handle was getting to work. He didn't notice when McKenna stopped going to school. She dropped out, started hanging out with a different group of friends, and then it wasn't long before she was on the streets looking for ways to get high.

"And I was in my own world. I had no idea what was going on with her until my dad called one day asking for help. He'd reported her as missing. She'd been gone for three days and he'd been driving around the city all that time looking for her, asking all her old friends if they knew where she was...Then the police called. She'd gotten arrested for stealing a bottle of vodka. It was her fifteenth birthday." Reed paused. "That was when it went from bad to worse. She was fourteen when our mom died and she got into heavy drugs less than a year later.

"My dad tried so hard to turn her around. She was in and out of treatment programs for years. But she didn't want to stop using. Not really.

"Part of me always knew that one day she'd go too far. But in my head too far meant she'd hit bottom and we'd pull her up from there. Then she overdosed and that was it. She was gone."

"I'm so sorry, Reed."

"Me too." She met Julia's eyes briefly before turning back to the road. "I still have trouble talking about it. All I can think about is what I could have done...should have done..."

"Her overdose wasn't your fault. It wasn't your fault that she dropped out of school and got into drugs in the first place either. You were three thousand miles away—how could you know what was going on?"

"That year after my mom died I could have done something. I could have called her every day to check in. I could have taken some time off." Reed's voice faltered. She took a breath and continued, "Hell, I could have asked her to move in with me. She could have come to Boston and finished high school there...I was her big sister. I was supposed to take care of her."

Before Julia could think of anything to say, Reed pointed out the driver's side window at a brilliant green gorge and a thread of blue water that seemed to have no end to its drop. "Can you see that waterfall? That's one of my favorites. You can hike right up to the base of the falls. Once you get there, when you turn around, you have a perfect view of the ocean. But you can't hear your own voice even if you shout. The waterfall is so loud, you can hardly hear yourself think."

"It's gorgeous."

"Yeah. It is." She paused. "On some level, I know I can't blame myself. But I do. There's so many things she never got to see—like that waterfall. I can't help thinking that if she'd only known there was more out there…Maybe we should go back to talking about vacations we want to take. I probably broke another first date rule with depressing conversations."

"I'm pretty sure you broke more than one."

When Reed glanced over at Julia again, her eyes were wet, but she was smiling. "Good thing this isn't a date. That's what you're thinking again, right?" She chuckled.

On impulse, Julia reached across the car's console and set her hand on Reed's leg. Her heart was pounding in her chest and she could hear her pulse in her ears. Maybe she was making a mistake, but she had to reach out. Reed glanced down at Julia's hand and then back at the road. Tears slid slowly down her cheeks. She didn't make a sound, and she didn't wipe them away. Somehow she seemed the stronger for the tears and for not caring if Julia watched her cry.

Julia didn't shift her hand off Reed's leg for the next half hour. Carly and Bryn slept on and the sound of the windshield wipers and the rain took over where their conversation had ended. She'd never felt so close to anyone, not even Kate or Mo and certainly no girlfriend, and she'd never felt such a heavy grief for someone she'd never met. Reed had opened a window into her soul and then stood there shaking, not bothering to cover herself up, and Julia had no idea what to say or do next.

The twins woke when Reed pulled off the highway onto a bumpy side road. "Where are we going?" Bryn asked, rubbing at her eyes.

Julia was wondering the same thing.

"It's a secret," Reed said.

The dirt road passed a clump of houses and then made a few hairpin turns before ending abruptly at a small parking lot. Turquoise blue water lapped a short stretch of sandy beach flagged on either side with outcroppings of black lava rock. The parking lot had a few cars, a boarded-up ice cream stand, and plenty of scraggly trees that had dropped a mess of leaves everywhere. This clearly wasn't one of the beaches that catered to the resort crowd with manicured paths and palm trees. And it was stunning.

"I think I could sit in this parking lot all day."

"I promise the view is even better on the beach." Reed got out of the car and popped the trunk.

"Julia, unbuckle me first," Bryn said from the backseat.

"No, me first," Carly whined. "Bryn's always first."

Before Julia had opened the door to the backseat, the kids were screaming at each other. Since Carly was on her side of the car, she started with her first, but this made Bryn's screams worse.

Reed poked her head in on Bryn's side and quickly unlatched her. She scooped her out of the car and swung her onto her back, then poked her head back in to grin at Julia. "Welcome to my world. They'll be better after they eat."

"I'm not hungry. I want to get in the water," Bryn hollered.

The screaming didn't lessen until they reached the sand and Reed opened the cooler she'd brought. She handed string cheese sticks and baggies of apple slices to the twins and then held the same out to Julia. "Gourmet cheese stick?"

Julia smiled. "I love string cheese."

"You wouldn't prefer dinner at a fancy restaurant with a waiter telling us about the day's fresh catch?"

"This view is hard to beat," Julia said.

"Good answer." Reed reached into the cooler again and pulled out sliced salami, a box of crackers, and two bottles of water. "'Cause nothing here is gonna impress you."

"I'm already impressed."

Reed looked up at her and grinned. "Is that so?"

"You sound surprised."

"Well, my food doesn't usually have that effect…"

"You've got room for improvement." Julia laughed at Reed's mock look of indignation. "But the rest of this day has been pretty amazing."

Before Reed could say anything, Bryn called out, "Last one in is the rotten egg." She started a sprint toward the water, cheese stick held high.

"Bryn Mawr, hold it right there," Reed said. "You need sunscreen and a life jacket—unless you've learned to swim in the past twenty-four hours."

Bryn stuck out her tongue when Carly repeated Reed's words and soon the fighting started again. When Bryn jabbed her cheese stick at her menacingly, Carly swung her bag of apples as a block. The apples connected with Bryn's nose and soon both were shrieking as they pushed each other to the sand.

Reed stood up and started toward them. She looked over her shoulder at Julia. "What were you saying about the view being nice?"

"Maybe we should build sand castles while we finish our snack? I saw some sand buckets and shovels in the trunk..."

Surprisingly, Bryn and Carly stopped crying at this. "I want to build castles with Julia," Bryn said.

"Me too," Carly cried. "She always gets to do everything first."

"You can both do it. I'm sure Julia wants help from both of you." Reed scooped the kids up from the sand and then pointed them toward Julia. "She has no idea that with us, you get what you ask for."

Julia met Reed's eyes. "And all I have to do is ask?"

Reed stopped, mouth agape, and then stammered for a moment about what she meant. The kids looked up at her, foreheads wrinkled in confusion, and Reed said, "I'll go get the buckets and shovels. Julia's in charge of sunscreen."

Before they'd gone two steps, Bryn said, "I'm building sand castles with Julia. You can build them with Mom." When Carly started to argue, Bryn reached over and grabbed her sand-covered cheese stick. In one quick move, she managed to hurl it into the water.

Crying burst out again and Reed caught Bryn's shoulder to spin her around. She took Bryn's cheese stick, and said, "I know you want to spend special time with Julia. So do I. But we're all building sand castles together."

When Reed tossed the second cheese stick into the water, more crying ensued. It was several tearful minutes before everyone was chewing quietly on apples and salami slices, and fortunately, Reed didn't leave Julia alone with the kids after all. Once they'd settled down to eat, Reed dealt with the sunscreen too. She glanced over at Julia as she applied the lotion to Bryn's cheeks and said, "You should have seen them at three. This is way better."

"I thought two was the hard year."

"I'm waiting for the easy year," Reed said. "Bryn Mawr, stop wiggling or this is gonna end up in your eyes."

Bryn squeezed her eyes tight at that but kept wiggling.

"Bryn Mawr, like the college?"

"Yep. We're all named after colleges." Reed pointed to Carly and said, "I went to Carleton for undergrad. My parents met at Reed. And my grandmother used to teach at Bryn Mawr. Grandma was a spitfire like Bryn."

"I'm not a spitfire," Bryn argued. "What is that anyway?"

"Someone with a lot of attitude. And sometimes remembering how amazing Grandma was keeps me from pulling out my hair when you are acting, well, like you."

"Like a spitfire?"

"Like Bryn." Reed grinned at the stinky face Bryn made in response. "There's a story behind all of the other names in the family too. My sister was named after Claremont McKenna College—my mom's alma mater. My brothers got Wellesley, Macalester, and Davidson—Wells, Mac, and David, for short."

"Can we build sand castles now?" Bryn pleaded.

"Yes. If you promise to be good for the three minutes it takes me to run and grab the buckets."

"You better go fast," Bryn said, crossing her arms.

Reed sighed and kissed the top of Bryn's head. "I'll be fast."

They spent the next half hour digging trenches and making mounds of sand. Once the base was done, Julia and Carly worked on decorating the front of the castle with shells while Bryn and Reed fortified the rear to withstand the assault of a dragon that was due any minute. Nearly every time Julia looked up, she caught Reed's eyes on her and more than once Bryn complained that Reed needed to pay better attention.

The sun beat down, but a breeze kept the sweat off her neck and Julia felt a swell of happiness. She sat back on her heels and looked over the results of their work. It took some imagination to see a castle, even with the moat and the drawbridge.

"You okay?"

Julia met Reed's eyes. "I'm great." Nothing about the day was what she'd expected when she'd daydreamed about the trip to Hawaii. But it was perfect.

Ten seconds later, Bryn stood up and said, "I hate sand castles." She marched over to the section of moat Carly was digging and dumped the contents of her bucket. Reed sighed as Carly stood up, fists curled.

"I think it's time to get in the water. Who wants to get wet?"

"Me!" Carly and Bryn screamed. They pushed and shoved their way over to the life jackets and then fought to be first to get strapped in.

Reed peeled off her T-shirt, revealing a black bikini top, and Julia couldn't help but stare. Fortunately, Reed didn't notice. She'd jogged over to where Carly and Bryn were arguing, picked one kid up in each arm, and started toward the water.

Soon Bryn and Carly were laughing and splashing Reed. The sibling argument was forgotten over their desire to soak their mom. Julia stretched out on the sand to watch them play. She hadn't thought to bring her suit, but she wasn't sure her ankle was ready to hold her up against the waves anyway. Plus, she didn't mind taking a quiet break from the kids.

The warm breeze pushed puffy clouds overhead, and every so often one of the waves would crash hard enough to send up a cool spray of water. Julia got out her camera and snapped shots of the water and then a few of Carly and Bryn chasing after the foamy break. More than once, she angled her lens on

Reed. Between the bikini and the black-and-white board shorts that hugged her butt, Reed was breathtaking. Julia gave up the pretense of watching the surf and focused on Reed. Kate was right—Reed had nice calves. But that wasn't where the nice ended.

After a handful of shots, Julia eyed the images on her screen. She felt a wrench in her stomach. Reed's profile as she glanced back at Julia was perfect. So were the sinewy muscles of her back and the curve of her butt. But in less than a week, Reed would be gone from her life, and she didn't need a memory card full of pictures to remind her of something that couldn't be. Her finger hovered over the delete button.

Finally she decided she'd send the pictures to Reed. She'd ask for her email later. The truth was, she wanted an excuse to keep the image. If nothing more happened, she wanted to hold on to the memory of their afternoon and of everything that had been said and left unsaid.

CHAPTER SEVEN

"I was about to call search and rescue," Mo said, shifting on the couch. "Do you know what time it is?"

"Almost eight." Julia dropped her purse on the coffee table and went to pour herself a glass of water. Unbelievably, she'd survived ten hours with two kids. And what was more, she couldn't remember the last time she'd had a better day. But that was mostly Reed's fault. "You knew I was going to be gone all day."

"You've got a sprained ankle and we hardly know this person," Mo argued. "Aren't you supposed to be lying on your back with your foot up?"

"Mo, you're worse than my mom. Give Jules a break. She's allowed to go on a date." Kate held up the knife she was using to slice pineapple. "But you should let this woman know that I'm a skilled knife thrower and if she breaks your heart..."

"I wasn't on a date."

"Right." Kate raised her eyebrows. "Which is why you look like you're glowing…How were the waterfalls?"

"Beautiful." Julia did feel like she was glowing, but she wasn't ready to share all the details. She went to her room, snagged a towel and her bathing suit, and then came back to the living room. "How was surfing?"

"Wait, are you leaving again?"

"Relax, Mo. I'm going for a swim. I was in a car all day." She was not going to admit that she was hoping to catch Reed after the swim. Reed had mentioned that after she got the kids in bed in each night, she'd been spending her evenings alone out on the lanai. She hadn't made it sound lonely—more as if it was her own quiet time to refuel. Julia didn't want to intrude, but something in Reed's voice made her think that she might want company for a change. There was a risk to seeing Reed tonight however.

"Did you guys stand up on your boards?"

"You should have seen Mo ripping it on the waves," Kate said. "She's a natural."

"Unfortunately, now I can't move. Every muscle in my body is in lactic acid overload."

Kate scrunched her nose. "That's attractive." She filled a bowl with pineapple slices and set it in front of Mo. "You'll feel better after you eat."

"I'll feel better after I sleep," Mo argued.

"Pineapple first. The pizza should be here any minute. And I promised you a massage after you saved my butt in that big wave."

"You would have been fine even if I wasn't there."

"I thought it was the end." Kate shook her head. "When that big wave tossed me…I think I'm taking a break from the ocean for a few days."

"Thanks for saving her life, Mo. Maybe you two could do something safe tomorrow like sunbathe? I'd like to go home with the same two friends I came with." Julia snagged a slice of pineapple. "See you guys."

"Wait a minute. I want the real scoop on your day," Mo said. "I don't want to hear about waterfalls. I want to hear about the date part."

"I wasn't on a date," Julia argued, heading for the door.

"You can't leave without telling us the details."

Julia looked back over her shoulder and waved at Mo before she slipped outside. Mo's voice followed her for several yards down the path. Then it was the music from the distant pool bar she heard, laughing voices from folks gathered around one of the barbecues, and finally the sprinklers. She passed Reed's condo, slowing her steps long enough to steal a quick look. The lights were dimmed in the living room, but all the shades were up and she could see through the sliding glass door right into the kitchen.

The kids were sitting at the table, an open box of Cheerios and a gallon of milk between them. Bryn had a bowl balanced on her head and Carly was peeling a banana. Bedtime snack. Julia felt a surge of longing to join them. She'd said good night only twenty minutes earlier, getting hugs from both Carly and Bryn, and yet she missed them already. Reed crossed the living room to close the open sliding glass door and Julia ducked her head and hurried down the path.

It wasn't embarrassment at being seen—she could have called out to Reed and waved. But she'd felt suddenly exposed. And unsteady. The emotions that had come in unsettling waves all afternoon were hard enough to classify. She didn't want to try to explain herself to anyone else. Three days ago she would have laughed at the thought that she'd want to tuck two kids into bed and then wrap her arms around their mom.

She changed in the locker room and then went out to the pool. The first few laps were full of images of waterfalls. Then all she could think of was Reed. After a half hour in the pool, she got out and showered.

Julia took her time drying off. The locker room was nearly empty and quietly comfortable with potted palms everywhere, a wicker patio sofa, and several chairs set up in lieu of benches.

She sat down on one of the benches and set to combing out her tangles. Her ankle was starting to ache and she knew she ought to ice it, but she wasn't ready to go back to the condo. The thought of going to Reed's instead was both tempting and terrifying. She stared at her reflection in the mirror, wishing she had no fear of sex—if only for one night. God, the things she wanted to do with Reed. And the things she wanted Reed to do to her…

The locker room door swung open and a resort employee entered. She smiled at Julia and then said, "How was the pool?"

"Lovely."

"It's a perfect night for a swim. The moon's almost full."

Julia agreed. The woman went to one of the locker bays. She quickly changed out of her blue resort polo shirt and khaki shorts and into a slim-fitting dark pink tank top and flowered skirt. She was strikingly pretty with an olive complexion and long dark brown hair that framed her face.

"Basically the whole day has been perfect," Julia said, more to herself than the woman, who was focused on touching up her makeup.

"Welcome to paradise." The woman smiled at Julia in the mirror's reflection. "When I first saw you, I thought you were this girl I went to school with. You and Kalea could be sisters."

Julia had been mistaken for someone else many times. Mostly it was annoying, but this time it was strangely nice… What had always made her different seemed common here. For once she looked like a local.

"You and your partner have the cutest kids," the woman said, interrupting Julia's thoughts. "I was watching the four of you play in the kiddie pool yesterday. Adorable. All of you. How long have you been together?"

"Oh, we're not together. We met a few days ago—on the plane ride here."

"You're joking. A few days ago?" The woman turned around to squint at Julia. "Huh. Go figure. But you're into women, right? Do you like her?"

Julia nodded, thankful she didn't have to admit out loud how much she liked Reed.

"Well, in case she hasn't told you, the feeling's mutual." She spun back to the mirror and finished with her lipstick. "She was giving you some long looks yesterday."

"Maybe, but she's not interested in dating. She's got the two kids and she's busy…"

"So don't date." The woman raised her eyebrow. "My girlfriend would kill me if she heard me say that. She doesn't believe in having sex unless you're in love. We've agreed to disagree." She laughed and closed her locker. "If you're looking for something to get your mind off her, there's a band playing over at the bar. The crowd at that place is always straight, but the music's good."

"Thanks for the tip."

"Sure thing. See you around." She smiled and swung her purse over her shoulder along with the tote.

By the time Julia left the locker room, the sky had darkened to a deep indigo. The full moon, still low in the sky, competed with a sea of stars, and music from the bar carried down the path between the condo buildings. Her steps slowed when she reached the lawn outside Reed's condo, as if her body was in charge of where she went. The lights were off and she couldn't make any distinct shapes out of the shadows. She took out her cell phone, debating if Reed would think she was coming on too strong if she texted tonight and then she spotted several messages she'd missed. Three were from Mo, wanting Julia to spill the beans on her day. But the most recent text was from Reed.

I know I'm probably breaking some more dating rules, but I can't stop thinking about you. Am I crazy if I want to see you tonight?

Julia stared at the words. Thank God she wasn't alone in this. She swallowed back a rush of emotion. Maybe in Hawaii she could do this—maybe she could have sex without thinking so much that she ruined it all. Maybe she could be normal.

Since we haven't gone on a date yet, I don't think you're breaking any rules.

Reed took a moment to respond: *Good. Want to come over for a drink?*

Julia's finger hesitated over the letters. If she went over now, she had one thing on her mind. To say this was unlike her was the understatement of the year. But she could simply have a drink and leave if her old anxieties returned. Or maybe she should go home to Mo and Kate before disaster struck.

The urge to be close to Reed was making her feel insane. Worst-case scenario, the same issues that always came up would strike as soon as they got into the bedroom—she'd choke and they'd have to stop before things got started. She'd admit she was terrible in bed and then apologize for leading Reed on. Then in the next few days they'd probably run into each other over and over again at the resort and everything would be awkward.

Julia started to type that she'd promised to hang out with her friends that evening, but before she pressed the send button, she deleted the sentence. She hadn't promised anything. Kate and Mo were probably watching a show and planning on an early night. They had both looked exhausted. She didn't want an early night and her therapist's voice sounded in her mind. She'd say that Reed was an opportunity. Reed was much more than that, however, and if she screwed this up...

But if she went home, she'd never know what might have happened. Reed was asking and her body was begging her to say yes.

Maybe they could stop at kissing. With all of her past lovers, her cold feet didn't come up until after they got past that. Then her brain took over and the sex that followed was an abysmal failure. She had no clue what the cause might be, she only knew she wanted it to stop. Her therapist was convinced there must be some underlying reason, but if so she had no clue what the cause might be. Emily had guessed that the problem was they had been friends first and her body couldn't make the leap to more. But there was no explaining what happened over and over again with Sheryl. Julia would want the intimacy and she'd even start things most of the time, but then she pulled back. She didn't blame Sheryl for getting upset.

If it was a lack of desire for more than cuddling with her exes, that couldn't be the case with Reed. Desire for her was there in spades. She'd been fantasizing about kissing her, undressing her, feeling Reed's body on hers and actually being fucked, for the past two days. Whatever was different this time, one thing was clear—her body was responding in a way it never had before.

Before she could second-guess herself again, she hastily typed: *I'd love to. When?*

Reed's response was immediate: *Now?*

*You caught me on my way back from the pool. My hair's wet and I'm in a wraparound.*Julia stared at the text wondering if she'd said too much.

Not sure what a wraparound is but your hair looks great wet. There was a pause and then Reed added: *I probably shouldn't have admitted that last part.*

Julia smiled. If Reed was trying to win her over with charming honesty, it was working. A light switched on in Reed's living room and Julia's heart jumped to her throat. It was ridiculous to be nervous considering she'd already spent the day with Reed and yet she was. She willed her feet to move, telling herself she could stop at one kiss…

But she'd been coming on strong all afternoon and Reed might be expecting more. Hell, her own body was expecting more. If Reed was as much of a top as she'd said, maybe Julia could let her be in charge. She took a deep breath, exhaling slowly. This was part of what got her into trouble in bed. She overthought everything. Tonight she wanted a break from thinking.

Reed stepped out onto the lanai, her profile outlined by the living room light behind her. She had a pitcher in one hand and two glasses in the other and she struggled to close the screen door. As soon as she turned, she took one step and stubbed her toe on the cooler she'd left outside. Hopping on one foot and cussing, she bumped into a tower of pool noodles and splashed some of the contents of the pitcher. Julia couldn't help smiling. Thankfully Reed wasn't as smooth as she looked.

Weaving between the pool noodles that were now spilled across the lanai, the inflated dolphin and shark, and a pile of snorkel gear and bathing suits, Reed finally reached the table. When she'd set down the pitcher, she adjusted her glasses and looked up. "Oh, hey. You're here," She bit her lip, looking down at the mess around her feet. "How long have you been standing there?"

"Not long." Julia smiled. "How's your toe?"

"Fine, thanks." Reed chuckled. "Now you know why I'm scared of heights. I trip walking from my bedroom to my bathroom."

For Reed's own safety, she'd be happy to keep her in the bedroom. Julia wondered how she was going to hold up a conversation when she was being completely disrupted by thoughts of sex. Her hormones had amped up instantly and the stirring between her legs was more than a little distracting.

"Turns out I like wraparounds," Reed said. "I thought those were called sarongs."

"Same thing." Julia glanced down at her outfit. She'd quickly tied the wraparound above her breasts leaving her shoulders and neck exposed. "Not what I would usually wear on a date…"

"You should consider changing that dating rule. You look amazing." Reed hastily looked down at the pitcher. "Can I pour you a margarita?"

"Is this what you're out here drinking every night when you're enjoying your quiet time alone?"

"Not usually…This is for a special occasion."

"What's the occasion?"

"I had a good day." Reed poured. "My kids spent most of the day playing with each other instead of fighting and I got to spend an entire day with an adult that I wasn't working with.

Besides that, I can't drink more than one margarita or the tequila gives me a headache."

Julia took the glass from Reed, making a mental note to go slow. Her body didn't need alcohol on top of the hormones. She took a sip and pursed her lips as the burn hit the back of her throat. "How much tequila is in this?"

"Is it too strong?" Reed tasted hers and then made a sour face. "In case you were wondering, I wasn't planning on giving up my day job to bartend."

"Don't tell anyone, but I'd rather date a radiologist anyway." Julia quickly added, "Not that we're dating. Sorry—we've been joking about the dating rules all day and…" She broke off her sentence.

"You don't have to apologize."

The look on Reed's face made Julia's heart skip a beat. She had to stay focused or she'd say—or do—something she'd regret. The impulse to kiss Reed was getting stronger by the minute.

"Today did feel like a date," Reed continued. "If that's possible with kids in the backseat."

"Can I tell you something I probably shouldn't?" Reed waited for her to go on and Julia pushed back the uncertainty. "I feel like we're connecting in a way I haven't with anyone in a long time. And I keep wishing this was the start of something."

"I know what you mean."

Julia hoped that Reed would say more, but the silence stretched and then Reed glanced over her shoulder at the lit living room as if she'd heard a noise. The Cheerios box was still on the kitchen table, as were the kids' empty bowls. Towels were hung off every chair and toys were scattered about as if an entire daycare had blown through.

Reed looked back at Julia and her expression was difficult to read. "I don't want to give you the wrong idea. I'd love more." She took a deep breath. "But I can't. I'm not in a place where I can date. Today was perfect, but when this vacation ends, we go back to different worlds."

"You're right. And I'm not looking for more. But if I was…" Julia forced a smile. *Damn it.* She wished she could take back what she'd said. Reed was right. They were on vacation and this reality wouldn't last. Reed had kids and a job that was probably more than full-time while she lived nearly two hours away and had a boss who didn't believe in weekends. "If I was looking for more, you'd be perfect. Since I'm not—and you're not—we might as well live for the moment, right?"

"That's an option for you?" Reed squinted at her drink. "Don't let this terrible margarita influence your answer."

"Well, when you put it that way…" Julia laughed at Reed's scrunched-up face. "All I'm trying to say is I think we both want the same thing." When she heard the obvious suggestion in her words, she quickly added, "I mean, we're on the same page."

Reed took another sip of her margarita and then set the glass on the patio table. "That suddenly awkward page where you hope the other person is going to make the first move?"

"Totally my fault." She smiled. Somehow, despite what she'd said, maybe this evening still had a chance. Unless of course she froze up as soon as Reed touched her. As soon as the thought crossed her mind, she felt a rush of her old fears.

"Want to sit down?" Without waiting for her to answer, Reed began clearing pool toys from the lounge chairs.

Julia didn't move to sit down. What was she thinking coming here tonight? She needed to admit that she was a disaster at sex before something happened. But she didn't want to be a disaster tonight. She sipped the margarita, wishing for an instant cure. Then she ran through all the possible excuses she could give for leaving.

Reed straightened up and looked over at Julia. "Did I say the wrong thing?"

"No, it's…it's nothing."

"I can tell I've made you uncomfortable." Reed ran her hand through her hair. "We don't have to sit down. Or do anything…I don't want this to be weird."

Shit. Julia gritted her teeth. Why did Reed have to be perfect *and* perceptive?

Reed continued, "I had a really nice day with you. In fact, I think I might have a new favorite day of vacation."

Julia let out the breath she'd been holding. Relax. Nothing has to happen tonight. "Me too. I think waterfalls might win over croissants in Paris."

"Even with the sprained ankle?"

"Hard to believe, but yes. Paris didn't have a picnic lunch on a secluded beach. With pineapple for dessert. And you weren't in Paris." Julia swallowed, willing herself to go on. "I loved spending the day with you and your kids."

"What about the part with me breaking down about my sister? That wasn't enough to ruin it?" Reed continued, "I don't know what came over me...I guess it was the waterfalls. I swear I don't usually act like that. I'm not the type to spill my darkest secrets to someone I just met. And I'm not a big crier. Doesn't exactly help me pull off the tough butch look."

"As much as I like your butch side I loved seeing that other part of you. I wouldn't have changed anything about today."

A long moment passed where the only sounds were of the dance music far in the distance, the cicadas, and a sprinkler. Reed glanced at her drink, still half full, and then at Julia's. "When I was getting the kids into bed, Bryn asked me if you could read their bedtime stories tomorrow night. You were really sweet with them. I know they can be a pain in the ass—Bryn especially—but you roll with it."

"What'd you tell her about me reading the bedtime story?"

"I didn't make any promises. Anyway, I'm not sure I want to share you."

Julia smiled. "Who said you had me?"

Reed stepped forward, closing the distance between them. She rested one hand tentatively on Julia's hip. Through the thin cloth of the wraparound, Julia could feel the warmth of her palm. Her breath caught in her chest. She wanted Reed to kiss her more than she'd ever wanted a kiss.

"Can I ask you something?"

Talking was not high on her list at the moment, but she managed a nod.

"What does a customer success manager do?"

Seriously? Reed was asking her about work now? She couldn't think standing this close to Reed and with those blue eyes on her. "Well, a customer success manager…" Oh jeez. She looked up at the dark sky, trying not to focus on how good Reed smelled or how nice it felt to have that hand on her hip. How was she supposed to think about work? Stars blinked down at her. She needed to go for this, that much she was sure of. "The easiest way to describe it is that I make sure the customer is happy with our product."

"And your company sells software?"

"We build software programs—mostly for big companies. When they buy software from us, I make sure they get their money's worth and that they're happy with what they bought."

"So they'll come back and buy again."

"You got it."

"Why isn't your position called customer service manager?"

Julia met Reed's eyes briefly and then needed to look away again before she could go on. Reed either needed to take her hand off her hip or she needed to kiss her. Waiting for her to do one or the other was torture.

"Well, you call customer service when something isn't working, right?" At Reed's nod, Julia continued, "It's my job to get to you first and show you all the ways our product works. We show you the bells and whistles you didn't know the product had. When you buy something from us, you might not realize all the tools at your fingertips. I teach you how to use the tools you already have. And I help you like what you've bought even better than you thought you would."

"So hopefully I won't need to call customer service."

"Right."

"Okay. That makes sense."

"Any other questions?"

"Can I kiss you?"

"After making me wait this long, I don't know if I should let you." Julia laughed, but one look at Reed and she stopped short. Yes, she could kiss her. All night if she wanted.

Reed's lips touched hers and everything around her went quiet. The distant music from the bar, the sprinklers, and the chatter of the crickets. She closed her eyes, moving into the kiss. Reed felt perfect.

When the first kiss ended, Reed pulled her close for another. There was no doubt that Reed wanted this as much as she did. Her desire made Julia's knees weak.

Slowly Reed moved them over to the lounge chair, still kissing her as they shifted onto the seat. She loved that Reed had taken over. All she wanted was to relax and enjoy this without worrying about what she was supposed to do next.

If the next step was moving to the bedroom, she was not going to back out. Not this time. For once, she was ready to go for what she wanted without thinking about contingencies.

"Mom!"

Reed pulled back. Her hand was still on Julia, but she'd turned to look through the screen at the empty living room and kitchen. The voice called out again, this time with an urgency.

Reed exhaled and met Julia's eyes. "This is my life." She murmured an apology as she stood up.

Julia followed her with her eyes, watching her cross the length of the condo and disappear into the back bedroom. The interruption was forgivable, of course. She had to check on her kid. Still, Julia wished she'd hurry.

Reed's hands had felt too good. Their absence only made Julia want them more—all over her body. There was no place she didn't want Reed to touch. She'd managed to stop herself from slipping her hand under Reed's shirt, but that wouldn't last long.

Since the beach, she'd wanted to run her hand up and down the muscles she'd seen there. And she couldn't wait for Reed to undress her. Reed's scorching gaze had made it clear she wanted to do exactly that. If she was lucky, Julia thought, and if Reed wanted to go there, she wouldn't stop her from putting her fingers inside or even going down on her. That was something she'd stopped her other lovers from doing, but it was all she could think of now. She realized they'd be in full view of whomever walked by if they continued out on the lanai and decided to suggest they go inside as soon as Reed got back.

Julia reached for the margarita and drained the remainder of the glass. This was what Mo joked about—the blinding desire for sex that made her mind check out and left her mouth dry while other places got embarrassingly wet. She hadn't admitted to Mo that she'd never felt that sensation—her mind never checked out if sex was on the horizon. Now she understood.

Reed reappeared, her expression set. "Bryn's got a stomachache. She wants me to lie down with her for a while."

"Oh…"

"You have no idea how much I'd rather be doing something completely different at the moment."

"I have some idea," Julia said. Letdown landed like a brick.

"If I don't get her back to sleep, she'll wake up Carly and then—"

"No, I get it. You have to take care of her." Julia stood up, adjusting the wraparound and trying to hide her disappointment with a wide smile. "This was probably going somewhere that would have made tomorrow awkward anyway."

"I don't think it would have been awkward," Reed returned. "But tell me if I crossed a line. That's the last thing I wanted to do."

"You didn't. I was—"

"Mom," Bryn interrupted. She stuck her head through the opening in the screen and rubbed her eyes. Her expression was puzzled as she took Julia in, but then she turned to Reed and said, "Mom, I'm hungry. That's why my tummy hurts. Why's Julia here?"

Reed glanced between Bryn and Julia. She sighed and went to pick up Bryn. "Let's get you some toast." Bryn nestled against

Reed's chest and yawned. Her sleepy eyes closed. Reed looked back at Julia. "I'm sorry."

"Don't be."

Reed turned to go inside. Tomorrow was going to be awkward—Julia was sure of it. First, however, she had to get through tonight uncomfortably wet with a swollen clit and no vibrator. With luck, Mo and Kate had decided on an early bedtime. She wasn't ready to rehash tonight with them. The mixed-up emotions she was feeling needed to sort themselves out before she could talk about it—and hopefully that would happen before she saw Reed again.

CHAPTER EIGHT

"Are you going to eat that?"

Mo pushed the bowl of pineapple toward Kate. "All yours."

Kate licked her fingers after she'd finished the last slice. Her slim frame seemed an unlikely reservoir for two-thirds of a pineapple, but that was true for everything she ate. Meanwhile Julia looked at a slice of cake and gained an inch on her belly.

"You're quiet," Kate observed, picking up their empty breakfast plates. "What's wrong?"

"She's still thinking about kissing Reed." Mo studied a picture in her magazine as she leaned back in her chair. She'd picked up the surfing magazine that morning and had been poring over the pages.

"No, I'm not." Julia sighed. "Or at least I wasn't. Now I am—thanks."

"That's why I'm here," Mo said.

"That was sarcasm." Julia sighed. "Guys, what if everything about yesterday was a mistake?"

"You had a good time, Jules. Stop overthinking this." Mo held up the surfing magazine. "Look at this wave. Can you imagine surfing that? It's as tall as a house."

Julia shook her head and Kate gave her a sympathetic smile. Of course she was overthinking. That's what she did best. When she'd gotten home last night, Kate and Mo were in a heated battle of Go Fish. They'd all stayed up late playing cards and analyzing Julia's date—that wasn't a date. Mo had come down squarely on the side of Julia needing to have sex with Reed to get it out of her system and then recommended moving on—quickly. Kate thought she should quit while she was ahead, convinced Julia was setting herself up for heartbreak, or ask Reed point-blank if she'd consider a friends-with-benefits scenario long term. By the time they'd gone to bed, Julia's drive for sex had died down enough to let her sleep. But her mind was still spinning.

Kate cleared the rest of the dishes and started filling the sink with water. She eyed Julia, her finger checking the temperature. "You need to ask her about the kids if you're really going for this."

"Why would she do that? Only a straight person would ask a lesbian how she got kids." Mo didn't look up from her magazine. "I'm thinking of renting a car. There's this beach about a half hour north of here that sounds amazing. This article says the place almost always has good waves for beginners...unless there's a red flag warning. Sounds like people drown there only occasionally."

"Don't drown today, Mo. Who's going to watch the telenovelas with me? Jules won't sit through an episode."

"I don't speak Spanish."

"You could learn," Kate argued. "But seriously, why can't she ask her where the kids came from?"

"Because a straight woman would never get asked that," Mo said. "Think about it—you meet a straight woman in your spin class. You hit it off. You find out she isn't married and has two kids. Are you going to ask where her kids came from?"

"How do I know she's straight? You're the one who's always telling me that you can't always tell if someone's really straight."

Mo rolled her eyes. "Let's say she tells you she's straight to stop you from hitting on her."

"I wouldn't hit on a woman I'd just met." Kate arched her eyebrows in retaliation. "And, yeah, maybe I'd ask her about the kids. If there's an ex I need to know about…In this case, Jules needs to know if there's someone who's got dibs on part of Reed's heart—even if she's an ex. If she's the mother of her kids, there's a bond between them. What is Jules getting herself into if she starts dating Reed?"

"She's not dating Reed—she's only having sex. Well, with any luck she will be. We've got to figure out a babysitter for the kids."

"You could babysit," Kate said. "Kids love your robot dance."

Mo cocked her head to the side and then made a robot motion with her hand as she set the magazine on the table. She jerked her other hand up and in her robot voice said, "Jules—this robot has your back, dude."

Julia laughed. "Well, now I'm not worrying about if it was a mistake to kiss Reed. I'm worrying about what happens when you start doing a robot dance at the pool."

"What if I asked Reed?" Kate continued. "About the kids, I mean. I won't ask her why she made moves on my best friend last night and then totally bailed."

"Her kid woke up," Julia said. "You can't blame her for that."

"I love that you're coming to her defense. Last night you weren't as understanding." Mo grinned. "Got over your blue balls?"

"That's disgusting," Kate said. "When are you going to grow up?"

Mo shrugged. "I don't have any set plans. When are you going to act less straight?" Before Kate could answer, Mo turned to Julia and said, "Whatever you do, don't ask her how she got the kids. The only time it's okay to ask a dyke that question is if you're hoping she'll give you the leftover sperm."

"What?" Kate shot a look from Mo to Julia. "Are you serious? That's a thing?"

"Why not? And don't start with all the germs you can get from sperm." Mo wagged her finger in the air. "We're talking about the washed kind that comes in a little glass tube. Not the gross stuff you get all over your hands."

Kate opened her mouth, as if about to argue with Mo, and then unexpectedly burst out laughing. Mo looked over at her with a goofy smile on her face and Julia said, "I will never understand half of what passes between you two."

"I don't know why she's laughing either," Mo said. "I figured she was about to yell at me."

Julia shook her head. "Well, I get what you're saying, Mo, but what if I can ask Reed in a way that won't sound like I'm judging? I do want to know how she decided on being a parent. And if there's an ex in the wings, I need to know."

"What do you want out of this, Jules?" Mo turned to face her, suddenly serious. "Last night you told us you only wanted to get laid. I'm hearing other things now. Do you really think this is someone you're going to try dating when you get back to California?"

"How can she answer that question until she knows Reed's story? She needs to know if there's an ex in the picture," Kate said, finally sobered. "Or she needs to walk away before her heart gets involved."

Julia glanced from Kate to Mo. What *did* she want out of this? She didn't have an answer, but she'd spent hours of last night sleeplessly wondering if she should ignore Reed for the rest of the trip precisely because her heart already wanted more.

"Mo, you're always the one who wants a background check on everyone Kate or I date. I want to know more about her."

Mo shook her head and turned back to her surfing magazine, Kate stared down at the sink full of dishes, and Julia exhaled. She couldn't wait to see Reed again, but she was all nerves now. She needed to get out and stretch her legs—and think of something besides what hadn't happened last night.

"I'm going for a walk on the beach. Anyone want to come?"

Kate and Mo both shook their heads. Mo mumbled, "Surfing," and Kate said, "I'm spending today in a lounge chair."

Julia slipped on her sandals and plunked the sunhat on her head. "I'll see you two later then." She'd skipped the brace and her ankle didn't wobble at all. In fact, it felt as good as new.

The ocean shimmered in the morning sun as a hot breeze whipped up triangles of white along the blue surface. Julia took off her sandals when she got to the sand. She walked the length of the beach, keeping to the dark, hard-packed sand along the shore break. The bottom third of her wraparound was dripping after she miscalculated the first few waves. After that she gave up trying to get out of the way and let the water splash up to her knees. She was on her way to a shady spot between a clump of trees at the edge of the beach when she spotted Carly and then Bryn making their way down the path from the resort.

Carly had a sand bucket and a shovel. Bryn had one of their pool toys, an inflatable shark that was nearly as big as her, perched on her head. The shark fell off every few feet and she had to stop to pick it up and then work on repositioning it. Reed followed several feet behind with a large beach bag, towels, and another shark.

Julia watched their progression, not moving from her spot. She wasn't in their path toward the beach, but she found herself hoping Reed would look in her direction anyway. They passed the clump of trees and Julia fought back a wave of disappointment. It wasn't only that Reed wasn't looking for her. It hit her now that Reed wasn't looking for anyone. Her life was full.

Mo was right. It didn't matter if an ex-girlfriend was involved or if Reed had used a surrogate to conceive two kids. It didn't matter what she did for a living or how many girlfriends she'd had in the past. If it was a fling, life details didn't matter.

Julia glanced again at Reed, watching her awkwardly attempt to apply sunscreen to her shoulders. Oh, those shoulders would be nice to rub…

As Reed spread out a beach blanket, Bryn chased after Carly with the shark and Julia turned away from the scene. She made her way over to a bank of rocks facing the ocean and settled on one, staring out at the never-ending blue. Maybe a fling would be good for her, but what she didn't need was to fall for someone who wasn't looking for her.

* * *

"What do you think about taking one of these boat tours tomorrow?" Kate held up a brochure with a picture of dolphins playing in the wave break alongside a catamaran. "They have snorkeling trips that promise manta rays and a coral reef."

"Sounds perfect. Where's Mo?" Julia dropped her sunhat on the coffee table and sank down on the sofa.

"Surfing. Or making out with one of the resort employees. When they left together I figured either option was fifty-fifty."

"Who was it?"

"Long dark hair. Curvy. Looks Hawaiian. And gorgeous." Kate sniffed, her gaze on the snorkeling brochure. "Whatever. Mo can make her own choices."

"You're jealous."

Kate didn't look up from the brochure. "I'm not going to say yes because if I do, you're going to get all on my case about it. But you're spending all of your time with Reed—which I totally understand, don't get me wrong—and I was hoping to at least have Mo's company. Now she's taken off with the Hawaiian goddess…"

"'Hawaiian goddess'?"

"Seriously, Jules, the woman is stunning. As soon as she offered to take Mo to the surf spot she goes to after work, I knew we'd lost Mo for the rest of the trip."

"I have a feeling I know exactly who you're talking about. Outgoing, great smile, and a diamond nose piercing?"

"Bingo."

"I ran into her in the locker room last night after my swim. She mentioned that she could give us advice on where to go dancing...definitely a lesbian." Julia took the brochure out of Kate's hand and scanned it. "Let's call and see if we can reserve a spot for tomorrow. I need a break from thinking about Reed Baxter. If you'll have me as a substitute for Mo, this is exactly what I need."

Julia dialed the number on the brochure and waited for the ring. She tapped Kate's leg. "We need to talk about you and Mo. And why you're jealous of every woman she checks out."

"I never said I was jealous. You did." Kate dropped her head back on the sofa cushions. "I'm engaged to Ethan."

"Do you love him?" When Kate didn't answer, Julia turned to stare at her. "You're marrying him. You really need to be sure he's the one."

"I think I'm sure."

"You *think*?" Before Julia could ask her more, a voice on the other end answered the line. Tomorrow's morning cruise was full, but there was still space in the afternoon one. As the details of the trip were reiterated, Julia eyed Kate. She'd covered her face with a throw pillow. When the snorkel guy finished with his spiel, Julia hung up the phone and reached over to tug the pillow off Kate's face.

Kate's eyes were moist. "Mo drives me crazy."

"You drive her crazy too."

"So why do I love living with her so much?" Kate sniffed.

Julia set her hand on Kate's. "Do you love her?"

Kate closed her eyes. "I don't know. I keep telling myself it's like a sister thing. Or a really close friendship. But lately...I'm worried there might be more to it. Ever since I started having that weird crush on that woman from my spin class I started comparing the two of them. Don't tell Mo, but she always wins.

And I've started wondering what it would be like to kiss her. Do you think that's normal?"

"Totally," Julia returned. "For a lesbian."

"Don't joke, Jules." Kate pulled her hand back. "I'm serious. Come on, you know I'm a wreck with this emotional stuff. Is it weird that I think about kissing one of my best friends?"

Julia reached for Kate's hand again. She laced her fingers through Kate's and then gave a squeeze. "You're scared you'll lose Mo when you move in with Ethan." At Kate's tentative nod, Julia continued, "I think she's scared too. You guys have been fighting a lot lately. Maybe you need to talk about what you want after you move out. Set up a plan—you know how much Mo loves to schedule everything. You could still see each other."

"It won't be the same. And what if I don't like living with Ethan as much as I like living with Mo?"

"Maybe you need to figure that part out before you get married. You could move in with him now." Julia paused. "You're not an emotional wreck, but you're terrible at deciding what you want. This time, you have to pick."

What Kate and Mo had was definitely more than a friend thing. Yet Kate's indecision was exactly why nothing had happened. Mo wouldn't risk it and Julia didn't blame her. If Kate hadn't figured out how she felt about Mo by now, Mo was right to have moved on.

Kate shifted on the sofa. "I've never had to choose any guy over Mo. Not really, anyway. I could always come home and know she'd be there. It's probably not Ethan's fault, but I blame him for it. If only we could keep dating and never get married…"

"What happens when Mo gets married? Eventually one of you will move out."

"Mo married?" Kate laughed. "Could you imagine?"

Julia knew she could be making a mistake with what she was about to say. Mo hadn't told her not to say anything, however. "Mo's engaged to Tanya. She's been waiting to tell you."

"Engaged? Are you serious?"

Julia nodded.

Kate was quiet for a moment as she processed the news. "Why didn't she tell me?"

"I think she was waiting for the right time—"

"The right time? We've spent every waking minute together for the past two days—she could have told me anytime." Kate's anger was building. "Of all the women she's dated, why'd she have to pick Tanya?"

"That's part of why she hasn't told you. She knows you don't like Tanya."

Kate cussed. "She used to tell me everything."

Julia took a deep breath. Kate rarely let a swear word slip. "This engagement with Tanya is a new thing. Mo told me Tanya popped the question when they were up in Napa. How much time have you two had for a heart-to-heart? You were paragliding and surfing together, yeah, but you know Mo gets distracted."

"Distracted? That's the stupidest excuse I've ever heard."

"You're right. Want to hear what I really think?" When Kate didn't answer, Julia plunged ahead. "You two have been more than friends for years. You should have slept together back in college and gotten it out of your systems."

"That's ridiculous."

"But it's true." Julia stood up and went to the kitchen to pour a glass of water. "Want something to drink?"

Kate didn't answer.

"You and Mo have been a thing since forever. It's not like this is earth-shattering news."

Kate pulled her knees up to her chest, sinking back against the sofa. Julia eyed her, knowing when she took that position, the conversation was over. Whatever issues Kate had faced in the past, she was a pro at shutting down.

Julia took a sip of water and then found the chocolate-covered macadamia nuts. "Whoever decided to cover macadamia nuts in chocolate was brilliant. I love everything about Hawaii. Even their damn nuts." She sat back down on the sofa and reached for the brochure. "Do you think we'll get to see dolphins?"

* * *

Mo didn't turn up for dinner that evening and it was after ten when she finally slipped into the bedroom she shared with Julia. Julia was still awake. At first she blamed the buzz of the overhead fan, then the fact that she was worried about Mo, but thoughts of Reed, who she hadn't seen since the beach that morning, were more likely the culprit. She'd held out hope for a phone call from the girls or at least a text from Reed, but there'd been nothing all evening. Of course, she hadn't tried to contact her either.

Mo slumped into bed, clothes still on.

"You okay?"

Mo rolled onto her side and looked over at Julia. "Why are you awake?"

"Couldn't sleep. What happened to you?"

"I was surfing…"

"I heard. Kate said a Hawaiian goddess invited you to some secret locals'-only spot."

"Kate called her a Hawaiian goddess?" Mo chuckled. "Her name's Alana."

"How was it?"

"Amazing."

"Maybe don't tell Kate that. She's already jealous another woman is stealing you away. By the way, Mo, I told her about you and Tanya. I know I should have let you tell her about the engagement, but…"

"It's fine. You saved me from having a conversation I didn't want to have."

Julia shook her head. "You're not getting off that easy. You two still need to talk. What happened after the surfing? Even I know no one surfs this late."

Mo shifted onto her back and stared up at the fan. "I didn't sleep with her if that's what you're wondering. After the waves died down we stayed at the beach talking…Then she took me to this little barbeque place that's open late. She dropped me off after that, but I wasn't ready to go to bed so I went for a walk."

"You're engaged to Tanya—I know you're not going to screw around. You don't need to convince me that you were loyal to your gal. Kate was worried, but I'm not."

Mo looked over at Julia again. "I think Kate and I have been spending too much time together. I mean, it's been good, you know, but…"

"But?"

"I don't know."

"You live in the same apartment. You're always spending time together."

"Not like this. We're both busy with work and we're gone nearly every night. She's over at Ethan's and I'm with Tanya. We haven't hung out this much since college." Mo sighed. "I think she's getting feelings for me that are going to make things complicated."

Julia felt a pang in her chest for Kate. Her guess was right— Mo *had* moved on. Or she was trying to at least.

Mo sat up in bed, pulled her shirt over her head and then took off her sports bra. She shifted back in the bed, rubbing the underside of her breasts and mumbling about sand getting everywhere. Mo had perfect plump breasts with prominent dark nipples. When she took off her bra, Julia had a hard time not staring. But Mo never seemed to be showing off her breasts when she went around topless. It was clear that she wasn't ashamed of her body and she didn't seem to mind if anyone else appreciated what she'd been gifted with.

After a while, Mo said, "I still think Kate's making a mistake marrying Ethan."

"Well, I think you're making a mistake marrying Tanya," Julia returned.

Mo leveled her gaze on Julia. "Why?"

"I think you love Kate."

"Does it matter?"

At least Mo wasn't trying to deny it. Julia considered her response. "It matters if you marry the wrong person, yes. If Kate wasn't marrying Ethan, would you have bought Tanya a ring?"

"I don't know." Mo closed her eyes. "But I do know that I love surfing. When I lay still like this, I can still feel the waves."

"I love you, Mo," Julia said. "And I want you to be happy—with whoever you end up with."

Mo smiled, eyes still closed. "That's what I want for you too. Did you see Reed tonight?"

"I'm trying to avoid her. I think something's wrong with me. The more I try not to think about her, the more obsessed I get."

"It's called hormones. Send her a text. Tell her you can't sleep because you can't stop thinking about her."

"Not on your life."

Mo laughed. In a more serious tone she added, "She's only here for a few more days, Jules. Clock's ticking…"

Two more days and Reed would be flying back to California. Julia hadn't forgotten. "I was hoping she'd text me first…I think maybe I came on too strong last night. She's focused on her kids and not really looking for anyone. I think I need to back off and wait for her. Right?"

"You're doing what you always do." Mo kicked off her sandals and then wiggled her toes. "You make excuses so you don't have to do something that scares you. Why wait for her to text you? If you want this, go get it. Gather ye rosebuds while ye may and all that crap. Do you want to have sex with her or not?"

"I've never gone after someone only for sex." She was not going to admit that sex with Reed had been on her mind all day, however. "That isn't me."

"But this time that's your only option. Do you want it or not?"

Julia eyed Mo. "Do you want to be with Tanya or not?"

Mo sighed. "Yes. And I don't want to lose Kate as a friend, but it feels like I have to choose."

Julia's phone interrupted, buzzing with a text. The phone was plugged into the charger on the nightstand between the two beds. She glanced over at it but didn't reach for it.

"Ten bucks says it's Reed," Mo said, reaching for the phone. She smiled smugly. "Listen to this: 'Can't sleep. Thinking of you.' Blah, blah, blah…'Hope you're having good dreams.'"

Mo looked up from the phone screen. "No, she doesn't hope you're having good dreams. She hopes you're awake to read this and you want to come over to talk."

"Talk?"

Mo grinned. She tossed the phone to Julia. "What type of woman do you think she is? Someone who makes a booty call at ten o'clock at night?"

"If only…"

Mo laughed. "Read the text. She's horny and wants you now."

Julia felt her heart lift as she read the rest of Reed's text: *Saw you at the beach today. Wanted to say hi but…looked like you were enjoying some time alone. Hope you're having good dreams.*

"What text did you read, Mo?"

"The one she wrote between the lines." Mo got off the bed and picked a nightshirt out of the dresser. "Text her back before I do."

Julia stared at the phone for a moment and then texted: *Still awake.*

Reed's reply was instant: *Missed you today.*

Julia missed her too. Too much for her own good. She tapped out a quick reply: *Want company?*

Julia stared at the text she'd sent. It was too late to take back the words, but she worried Reed would think she was being too forward. "Dammit, Mo. I think I just invited myself over."

"Nice going."

"No—not nice going. What the hell am I doing? She's gonna think I've been sitting here waiting for her call all night. She'll think I'm desperate. And horny."

"You're saying one of those things isn't true?"

Julia rolled her eyes at Mo.

Mo laughed. "Relax, sweetie. She's not gonna think you're desperate. But she is hoping like hell you're horny. She couldn't ask straight up if you wanted to come over because at this time of night we all know there's only one thing she wants. She opened the door and you chose to walk through. This is how you play the game."

"I can't play this game." Julia dropped the phone facedown on the nightstand, her heart thumping in her chest. "Who invites themselves over to someone's place at ten o'clock at night?"

"Someone who wants the same thing you want. She texted you first. That was your invitation." The phone buzzed again and before Julia could stop her, Mo picked it up. "Get dressed, honey. Your booty call's waiting."

Julia pulled the phone out of Mo's hands and stared at Reed's brief answer. Before she could gather her thoughts or figure out what to put on, another text appeared on the screen.

You wearing a wraparound? Kidding. Sort of.

There was a short pause and then:

Reread that last bit.

Going to stop texting before I ruin my chances.

By chances I mean

Chances at a convo that isn't awkward

Not chances of anything more

Unless that is what you were thinking.

Mo snagged the phone back. By the time she'd read all of Reed's texts, she was laughing out loud. "Can I screenshot this and send it to Kate?"

"Don't you dare. What should I wear?"

"Clearly a wraparound. Are you sure I can't screenshot it?"

Julia wrested the phone from Mo and went over to the dresser. She sorted through her clothes. Unfortunately, she hadn't brought any sexy underwear. Only cotton bikini style. The thought of skipping the underwear sent a tremor to a distracting spot. This was crazy—she'd never gone to someone's place simply for sex. But she wanted Reed so much she could hardly think. Then the nauseating fear rose up inside her. She dropped the underwear back in the drawer. "Mo, I'm terrible in bed. Maybe the worst ever."

Mo looked over at her. "What are you talking about?"

Aside from her exes and her therapist, she hadn't talked about her sex issues with anyone else. Now she wanted to tell Mo everything in the ridiculous hope Mo could fix what no one else had.

"I haven't had sex with anyone since Sheryl and sex with her was a disaster. It wasn't any better with Emily either. And you should have seen me in bed with Cal—not that you would have wanted to. He was so nice about it, but—"

"Stop. You're going to be fine." Mo paused. "You need to forget about Sheryl and her drama. Forget about the others too. You're right—I don't want to know the details. But it doesn't matter anyway. This time's gonna be different. Don't worry about what you're supposed to do—or what you aren't supposed to do. Get dressed and go stand in front of Reed looking like your sexy self. Let her take it from there. Trust me—she will."

"But you don't understand. I literally suck in bed. And not in a good way."

"Oh, sweetie." Mo seemed to realize Julia was painfully serious and changed her tone. "Okay, look. I'm gonna tell you a secret. You know what would make any butch's day? Tell her you're gonna need some help. Tell her you want her bad but you aren't good at sex. She'll make it her personal mission to change that. Then stick to what you know. You're good at kissing, right? Stick to kissing."

CHAPTER NINE

Mo was softly snoring by the time Julia came back from the bathroom. She'd decided on the wraparound after all—a new one she'd bought that afternoon. It was too late to ask Mo if she was crazy for skipping the underwear. She grabbed the house key and switched off the bedroom light. Mo's advice ran round her head. "Tell her you're gonna need some help." Hopefully Mo was right and Reed would take over after that.

Outside, stars lit the clear sky but the night air was still warm. Only the back porch light shone at Reed's. Julia crossed the lawn between their condos, avoiding the spray of the sprinklers and wondering with every step if she should turn back. Fantasies and a vibrator were always better for her than the reality of sex, but this time her desire for the real thing was overwhelming. She wanted to see Reed naked, wanted to feel her body, wanted to be wrapped in those arms, and yes, she wanted to be fucked. That feeling hadn't lessened since she'd recognized the urge for what it was last night.

Reed was leaning in the doorway and Julia's heart skipped a beat when she spotted her. Tall, lean, tousled hair, and comfortably relaxed. Glasses and all. God, she was handsome.

Reed raised her hand, a soft smile curving her lips. Julia gathered her courage and picked her way between the pile of pool toys and the lounge chairs crowding the lanai, grateful she had to focus on where she was walking instead of gaping at Reed. She stopped when she was standing only a few feet from her, then worried she'd stepped too close.

"I swear I'm not drunk," Reed said. "But I realize those texts I sent made it sound as if I were. I had a beer with dinner—that was it."

Julia smiled. "I finished a bottle of wine with Kate tonight so you might be the sober one."

"Does that mean you're up for making bad decisions?" Reed quickly added, "That was totally inappropriate. You don't have to answer that. I should apologize in advance for the next dumb thing I say. I didn't get much sleep last night."

"You don't seem like a bad decision." Julia crossed her arms to stop herself from reaching for Reed. She wanted to kiss her, but she had to think of something to change the subject. Her body was too keyed up. "Up all night with the kids?"

"No—Bryn went right to sleep after the toast. But then I couldn't stop thinking about you. And the mistake I'd made sending you home."

"Is that an apology?"

Reed grinned. "Should it be?"

"Yes." Julia felt a rush at the look Reed gave her then. It was easy to flirt. But what would happen when she wasn't as forward later?

"How's this: I'm sorry I didn't sleep with you last night. I really, really wanted to."

"Not bad for starters."

Reed's eyes traveled up and down Julia's body. Her desire was obvious, and Julia couldn't wait for her to reach for her. She knew it was coming, knew by the muscle flex in Reed's forearm how much those hands wanted to be on her. The space between them was filled with a heat that made it hard to breathe, hard to swallow, and impossibly hard to hold Reed's eyes. Her body was practically begging her to step forward.

"I spent all day thinking about how much I wanted to kiss you again. When I saw you on the beach…" Reed's voice trailed. "I wondered if you regretted the direction things went last night."

"I don't regret kissing you." She did, however, regret going back to the condo especially now that she knew Bryn had gone right to bed. But she didn't want to admit she was the type to regret *not* sleeping with someone. She'd never been that person.

Reed touched Julia's elbow, sending shockwaves to points that shouldn't be connected to an arm at all. Her warm fingertips slid gently up to Julia's shoulder.

"This time don't leave if the kids wake up. I'll get them back to sleep."

Julia nodded. She'd agree to anything with Reed's hand on her bare arm. She waited, hoping. When Reed's hand slid behind her neck, she closed her eyes. Lips met hers and she moved with Reed's lead. The feel of Reed's hand, holding her in place, wasn't something she wanted to fight. Instead she wanted to give in. She'd been wanting this all day.

When they parted, Reed's expression was almost bashful— as if she'd taken liberties that weren't hers to take. She rubbed her lips. "Uh, do you want to come inside and talk?"

"We could do that," Julia said.

Reed glanced over her shoulder at the mess that was the living room. A puzzle had been overturned and magazines with pictures of beaches were spread out like a carpet.

"I probably should have cleaned up…"

"It's okay. I don't really want to talk," Julia said.

Reed met her eyes, a half-smile on her lips. "Oh, really? Why not?"

"It's not that I don't like talking to you," Julia added. "But I have other things on my mind." She wasn't sure where this person had come from—this version of her that could stand in front of a handsome butch and basically admit she wanted sex— but it was a thrill all the same. She didn't have time to temper her request. Reed had caught her hand and pulled her through the doorway. As Reed brought her closer, Julia felt her knees go weak.

She kissed her hard. Julia parted her lips, wanting to give Reed the opportunity for a deeper kiss, and as her breasts brushed against Reed's chest, she savored the feel of Reed's body against hers. Another kiss and then another. She was already wet and if Reed kept this up, she'd have trouble standing. But she didn't want her to stop kissing her anytime soon.

Reed let up only to close the screen door and then the blinds. She pushed aside a few magazines to clear a path through the living room, keeping hold of Julia's hand as she did this.

When they passed the kitchen table, Reed seemed to remember her manners and said, "I should get you a drink, shouldn't I? Do you want something?"

Julia shook her head. Reed was as ready for this as she was. She wondered when she should tell her the one problem in their plan. Before she could speak up, Reed's mouth was on her lips with another kiss. This was exactly how she wanted it to go—all reflex on her part as Reed took charge. Every part of her was telling her to keep giving in to whatever Reed wanted. Reed's hand moved down her back, over the thin material of the sarong, and then settled on her hip.

"You feel so good," Reed murmured. "Tell me if you want me to slow down." She kissed her again, pushing the sarong up Julia's thighs. "'Cause if you don't say anything…"

She didn't want to slow down. The worry of one of the twins waking briefly crossed her mind, but then Reed was pulling her into the master bedroom and she forgot about the kids. Reed closed the door and then held her gaze for a moment.

Julia gasped as Reed moved against her, pushing her back against the wall as she moved the bottom of the sarong up to her hips. When Reed pressed against her, murmuring her appreciation of the fact she'd left off the underwear, Julia felt a thrill that was nearly as good as an orgasm. Nearly.

Reed's hands moved up and down her thighs, pushing the sarong whichever way she pleased. She kissed her again, more demanding now of Julia's lips. Her tongue pressed inside just enough to nudge at Julia's. Mo's advice to stick to kissing echoed in Julia's mind. "I'm not that great at this," she managed. "Actually I'm terrible."

Reed kissed the curve of her neck. "At what exactly?"

Shit. She needed to be upfront, but she hated admitting it. "At sex. I really want it but…I need you to do everything."

"Everything?" Reed's voice let on her pleasure at the request. "That's an option?" She chuckled. When Julia didn't respond to her attempt at banter, she murmured, "I got you."

Julia felt her body relax. It was as if something bound up in her chest unlaced on its own accord. She closed her eyes, kissing Reed back when her lips lingered near hers.

Instead of her hands going to the places Julia wanted to feel them, Reed held onto the wraparound. She had a section of it taut and the material moved over Julia's butt and up her backside, sending a delicious shiver through her body. She didn't want the material on her skin—she wanted Reed's hands. But Reed seemed to know exactly what she was doing and didn't appear to care if she was making the wait agonizing. Finally she ran one hand up the inside of Julia's thigh, stopping only when she got to her center.

For a moment, Julia felt a pulse of uncertainty. This was always when she froze—when it was clear the encounter was going beyond a make-out session. Reed was much stronger than she was, could do what she wanted, but Julia knew if she said anything, the hand that was pinning her would drop off instantly. Her breath quickened as Reed undid the knot of her sarong. This was happening. The material dropped to the ground and then Reed's tongue swiped over each nipple, making them harden with desire. There was no questioning what her body wanted.

"That feels good...really good...but..." Damn it. Why was she talking at all? She was going to mess everything up.

"But?"

Julia squeezed her eyes closed. She didn't want to stop. She definitely didn't want to talk. She wanted to be normal and enjoy it.

Reed had straightened up and now gently cupped Julia's chin. She tilted it up so their gaze met. "Can you tell me?"

Julia shook her head. She closed her eyes again. This is where she'd stopped Cal. She could hear him tenderly asking if it was because she wanted to be with a woman instead. This was where Emily had wondered if she didn't love her enough. God, that wasn't it, but it still hurt knowing the pain she'd caused. And this was where Sheryl had called her cold. "You need professional help," she'd said. "You need to deal with your issues." Issues. She'd tried that but counseling hadn't fixed her.

Reed's hand traced the curve of her neck to her shoulder. Soft fingers played down the length of her arm. Then Reed clasped her hand. Julia looked down at their entwined fingers. She could sense the desire moving like a current through Reed, barely contained. Reed wanted this. Wanted her.

"I want you to fuck me," she breathed out. The words were hardly more than a whisper, but she knew by the change of Reed's grip that she'd heard her. "But I might stop you again. Before we get all the way."

"Okay."

That was it? "Okay"? Julia wanted to insist that she was going to screw this up. That Reed was going to be disappointed. Clearly she didn't understand.

But Reed kissed her before she had time to plan out her next sentence. "*Stick to kissing*," she heard Mo say again.

Kiss after kiss distracted her as they moved closer to the bed. Reed's clothing, a button-down, short-sleeved cotton shirt and a pair of canvas shorts, were rough against her skin. She wanted Reed naked, but every time she fumbled with the buttons, Reed found her lips again. She knew she wouldn't be able to please

Reed anyway. Tonight she needed a stone butch who wanted to fuck her until she couldn't move and she desperately hoped Reed understood that. Hopefully Mo would be right and the only satisfaction Reed would need would be getting Julia off.

Reed pulled down the bedsheets when they bumped against the bed. One hand stayed on Julia's hip while she pushed the extra pillows off and then a moment later, she was moving them both to the mattress.

Julia sucked in a breath and Reed whispered, "Remember I got you," as her hands moved up from her hips to her neck and then down to massage her breasts. Reed tugged a nipple until it was swollen and tender, then she let go of it and shifted between Julia's legs. She was still dressed.

"I want you naked," Julia said. She heard the whine in her voice, noticed Reed's reaction, a guilty smile, and realized she wasn't going to get that unless she worked for what she wanted.

Intent on accomplishing that, Julia started in earnest at undoing Reed's buttons, realizing as she did so that she appreciated it all the more because this distracted her from what was coming next. She managed to get the first few undone before Reed shifted away from her. Reed had moved lower, kissing her way down Julia's chest and then past her belly. Her face dropped out of sight, and soon Julia was staring at only tousled brown hair. She shuddered as Reed's tongue slid along the inside of her thigh.

Reed found her swollen, wet clit and pressed hard with her tongue. Julia couldn't contain the sound that slipped out of her, part moan, part hungry cry. Then she remembered the kids in the room next to theirs. She bit her lip. Staying quiet was going to be a whole separate challenge.

Reed pinned her hips and slipped a finger inside. She gasped and had to stop herself from reaching for Reed's hand. *Relax. You want this*. She did want it. Desperately.

What was more, she knew Reed was enjoying her body. Reed didn't hide her soft low sounds of desire. Closing her eyes, she willed her mind to focus on how good Reed felt and how good her own body felt. She was dripping wet and Reed knew just how to touch her.

Julia whimpered softly when Reed's finger slid out. She waited, hoping Reed would push in again and then looked down to see Reed staring up at her. Reed drew a wet line down the inside of her thigh and then up again, making a wide circle around the place Julia wanted her to touch.

"You feel so good," Reed said, drawing out the words. Her hand moved down Julia's other thigh. "I need you to stop me if I do anything you don't want."

Julia pushed her hips up, hoping that was enough answer. She didn't want to stop Reed from doing anything.

"Good. That was what I was hoping for." Reed bent her head and stroked her tongue over Julia's clit.

Julia moaned. The certainty in Reed's desire, her confidence in what she was doing, made Julia finally let go. She dropped her head back against the pillows and spread her legs further. Reed murmured her approval and then slipped her finger inside again.

Maybe it was only sex without feeling attached, but for the first time it felt good. Julia closed her eyes, enjoying the sensation of Reed's tongue and her expert hands. Those hands… Julia could feel that as long as she didn't fight it, Reed was going to get her all the way. She was close. So close. A little more pressure from Reed's tongue and she wouldn't be able to hold back.

Reed thrust faster with her finger, somehow also keeping up with her tongue. As good as that all felt, Julia suddenly wondered if Reed had a strap-on. She wouldn't have packed a dildo for a family vacation, would she?

As much as she would enjoy letting Reed fuck her with a cock, something she'd never let anyone else do, she realized it was unlikely that she'd have brought sex toys on this trip. But now that the thought of a strap-on had entered her mind, she had to ask. *After*. She was too close. She tried to slow down her body, wanting to enjoy Reed's tongue more. *After*—Julia thought again, enjoying a warmth that was already pushing through her and almost laughing at the thought of wanting more. Where had this version of her come from? How could she possibly be thinking about a second round?

But for the first time she knew she was going to want more after she'd come. She was nearly there. She reached down to comb her fingers through Reed's hair, then arched her hips off the mattress. The fact that she'd never had an orgasm with a partner, but she knew she was going to with Reed, was less of a surprise than the realization that one wouldn't be enough.

She wanted to be on her knees in front of Reed. Then she wanted Reed standing, looking down at her, while she licked… Or she'd let Reed pin her exactly like this all over again. Oh, God, she couldn't hold off for much longer.

Julia cried out when she came, gripping a fistful of Reed's hair, and arching off the mattress to push into Reed's mouth. She fell back on the bed a moment later, tingling with a delicious warmth that rushed through her body. Her teeth were clenched. She could feel the orgasm clear down to her toes.

Yes, she wanted more, but it would be a long minute before she could move. Reed settled her weight on top of her, heavy in all the right places, and an aftershock gripped Julia's body.

It was minutes later before Julia dared to open her eyes. Reed was watching her. She smiled and then kissed her lips softly.

"That was amazing," Reed said.

"And you still have your clothes on," Julia replied, aware her words were slurred.

"Yeah…I thought you were taking them off."

Julia gave in to another kiss. She couldn't fight off Reed's advances even if she wanted to—but she didn't want to. She wanted to lie there with Reed on her, not fighting anything, taking whatever was given. In a while, when she'd recovered, she could beg for a little present—a little taste of Reed.

"I want you naked."

"Mmhmm," Reed murmured, kissing her again. She combed her fingers through Julia's hair. "I like you naked. And on your back."

Julia smiled, her eyes still closed. "I think you would like me in other positions too."

"You're right. But then I wouldn't be able to see your expression when you climaxed. Or see your breasts." Reed's hand moved to Julia's breast, cupping it gently and then tracing lightly around the areola before pinching the nipple.

A spasm shot to her clit. She gasped when Reed's teeth grazed her nipple. "Gentle."

"That wasn't gentle?" Reed's voice held a certain playful tone that made Julia open her eyes. Reed smiled. "Hey, gorgeous."

"Hey, yourself. And, no, your teeth aren't gentle."

"I didn't want you to fall asleep."

"I'm not sleepy," Julia murmured. "I just can't move at the moment." She closed her eyes again. She had no intention of sleeping, but she needed a minute to regroup. Had she ever felt this good? No vibrator had ever made her feel this way—that much was certain. And no other lover had gotten her there...Maybe all along she'd needed someone who wanted to overpower her, someone whose desire for her made resisting seem pointless.

Reed shifted off her and reached for something on her nightstand. The overhead fan chilled her skin, wicking off the sweat, and she thought of reaching for the sheet, but her muscles were still too lax. Julia longed to have Reed back on top of her, satisfyingly strong as she pinned her and deliciously warm.

"Want a sip?" Reed held out a glass of water. "You were doing a lot of heavy breathing. Not that I'm complaining."

"You better not. All of it was entirely your fault. Do you think I was too loud?"

"For the kids? No. They're exhausted tonight and once they're out for the night they won't wake up. Last night Bryn just couldn't fall asleep."

Julia sat up and took a sip. Her parched throat was eager to drain the glass, but she handed it back to Reed, not wanting to have to pee later. "Then why aren't you naked?"

Reed shrugged. "I had better things to do than take off my clothes."

"I want you naked."

"You keep saying that." Reed took another sip and then leaned past Julia to set the glass down on the nightstand. "Maybe you should do something about it. And, by the way, you are definitely not terrible at sex."

Julia grabbed the tail of Reed's shirt. She tugged on the fabric until Reed was moving to straddle her. Once Reed had settled on top of her, the rough canvas of her shorts rubbing Julia's still sensitive center, she crossed her arms. Her eyes dared Julia to go further.

"Maybe the therapy sessions are actually helping," Julia said.

"You're seeing a therapist to talk about sex stuff?"

Julia nodded. Her throat felt tight. She wondered if Reed would think that was ridiculous.

"Definitely money well spent," Reed said. "Do they have group sessions?"

"Why? Do you want to go?"

"Do I want to go sit in a room full of women talking about sex?" Reed grinned. "Um, yeah."

Julia laughed. "Why are you so sexy?"

"Years of practice. What about you?" When Julia didn't answer, Reed continued: "Too sexy to even answer that?" She traced the curve of Julia's breast. "It's kind of a problem for me...how attractive you are...Do you know how many times I've had to stop myself from staring these past few days?"

Julia shook her head. All the years of not liking her reflection in the mirror, of not liking how tightly her clothes fit, couldn't be erased by words alone. And yet...The look in Reed's eyes was hard to argue with. Tonight she felt sexy. She worked another one of Reed's buttons loose to avoid answering.

"What are you thinking about? You just got this look on your face like maybe I should get off you."

"No. Don't move." Julia's fingers stalled on Reed's next button. She bit her lip and then looked up to meet Reed's gaze. "I'd like to return a favor."

"I like the sound of that."

"Unfortunately, I don't have a lot of practice topping a butch so you might have to help me out a little."

"What exactly did you do in those therapy sessions?"

"Talk about feelings."

"Hmm. How would you feel if I told you I'm not going to let you top me?"

"Frustrated." Julia let her hand drop off Reed's shirt. "But the truth is, I don't think I'd be able to satisfy you anyway."

"That I can help you with." Reed leaned down and kissed Julia's lips. She pulled a few inches away and said, "Why don't you start by finishing what you started? I think you wanted me naked."

Julia felt a new spasm at her clit as Reed straightened up, a definite challenge in her gaze. She watched Julia's fingers work. After another two buttons, the shirt fell open. Reed wasn't wearing a bra, but her small breasts hardly needed to be held in.

Julia reached up to touch one of the hardened nipples—small but responsive. Reed leaned down and kissed her again. "You're on the right track. What do you want to do next?"

Julia shifted and kissed Reed's neck, then ran her tongue over the edge of her earlobe. She loved the salty taste of sweat and the approving murmur wherever she kissed Reed. Mo's words repeated in her mind again—"Stick to what you know." Kissing. She could do that all night.

"You better hurry up. I might get ideas about fucking you again if you take too long getting these clothes off." Reed's voice was husky now. Clearly she was turned on by what was happening.

Julia hoped that would last. If Reed was going to talk her through this, maybe she wouldn't be a total failure. She reached down to Reed's shorts. Not only did she want to feel how wet she'd made Reed, she wanted her scent all over her, and then she wanted to find her clit. She managed to get the snap undone and then pulled the zipper. Reed hitched the shorts down herself before kicking them off. She was stripped down to a pair of black boxers with a red waistband and one red button.

Julia eyed the red button that fastened the opening in the front, hoping she could save the image of Reed straddled over her, shirt gaping open and nothing but boxers below this.

"More buttons?"

Reed grinned. "I think you can handle that one. It's little."

Julia could hardly swallow, let alone undo another button. She loved a woman in boxers. That had only been the stuff of fantasies before now. Emily preferred underwear that capitalized on feminine curves and Sheryl even liked wearing lacy lingerie. But none of their expensive panties were as sexy as Reed's boxers.

Somehow, she focused enough to work on the button and once it was undone, she slipped her fingers between the folds in the fabric. Reed's short curls brushed against her hand. She pushed forward, finding the wet warmth underneath. Reed's sudden intake of breath and then a soft moan came when Julia found her clit. When she stroked her index finger over it, Reed pushed into her hand and murmured her approval.

Julia wanted to give Reed the same overwhelming orgasm she'd just experienced, but her fingers felt suddenly all thumbs. She knew it was likely she wouldn't get Reed off, despite how turned on she clearly was. Sheryl had laughed at how clumsy she was the first time, but by the time it became a running joke so many other things were wrong that it was useless to try. Emily hadn't laughed, but she'd hardly given her a chance. A wave of the old panic started in her chest. She felt the flush hit her cheeks, knowing she was about to mess up this perfect night.

When she pulled her hand back, thinking of an apology, Reed caught her wrist and brought her back to her wet warmth. "Don't go anywhere. You're perfect right there."

Julia looked up, but Reed's eyes were closed, her lips parted. She'd started grinding on Julia's hand, soaking her fingers as she did. Reed pushed herself back and forth over Julia's hips, dragging her clit over Julia's index finger as she did. The lines of concentration on her face mingled with the shadows from the open window and the whirling overhead fan behind her. Reed was stunning.

Julia's wrist ached, but she didn't dare move. If she held still, Reed would take care of everything. She felt a pang of regret. Yes, clearly, Reed could take care of everything. But she hated being incompetent, hated she couldn't be doing more. Without stopping to analyze if it was a good idea or not, she thrust her middle finger inside Reed. Reed's body clenched as she pushed inside the vault.

"Oh, right there," Reed breathed.

Reed ground down on Julia's hand once more before her climax. She squeezed Julia's legs, still between both of hers, so tight Julia nearly cried out. But it wasn't from pain. It was pure pleasure feeling Reed come on her hand. She could almost feel the orgasm course through Reed, noticing how her muscles tightened and then relaxed. But she hardly had time to enjoy it. Reed pulled on Julia's wrist a moment later, letting the middle finger slip out of the warmth that had held it so fiercely a second earlier.

"Is it my turn again?" Reed asked.

"Again?" Julia laughed. The truth was she wanted more if Reed was offering. But how was that even possible? She'd always been thankful when an attempt at sex was finished and she could simply cuddle with a lover. Not this time...

Reed pinned Julia's hand on the pillow behind her head waiting for permission. The scent of their sex was thick in the air. Delicious and intoxicating. Julia licked her lips. The hunger in Reed's eyes made her nod.

Reed let go of Julia's hand and slipped off her partially undone clothes. She stood naked, at the side of the bed, surveying Julia. "I wish I'd brought some toys."

Well, that answers that question, Julia thought. "Me too."

"You like a cock inside?"

Julia hesitated. She hadn't expected such an upfront question. Reed was standing there, naked, asking her if she liked cocks and her brain was stumbling for an answer. How many fantasies had she enjoyed with a butch woman in the centerfold of her mind, cock brandished? She decided on the truth. Most of the truth. "I'd like yours."

"I think you would…" Reed got back into bed, kissing Julia as she settled in alongside her. Her fingers traced Julia's curves, from her exposed armpit, down the side of her chest to her hip. Julia shivered and started to reach for the sheet, but Reed stopped her hand. "I want to enjoy you like this for a minute longer. I can turn off the fan if you want."

"I'm fine as long as you're on me." It was a warm evening and she was still hot from what had happened only minutes ago. But Reed's gaze was so intense. She would notice Julia's flaws now, the extra weight around her middle, the dimples of fat at her thighs. Reed's body seemed perfect in comparison—nothing but taut, smooth, tanned skin over sinewy muscle. "I'm not used to someone looking at me like that," she admitted.

"Like they can't get enough of you?"

Julia felt a blush on her cheeks. She crossed her arms over her breasts. "That was not what I meant."

"You'll have to explain what you meant later. I'm a bit distracted at the moment." Reed moved on top of her then. "I'm sorry to let you down about not having a strap-on…Think I could make it up to you other ways?"

Before Julia could say she wasn't let down—none of this evening had been a letdown—Reed's lips were on hers again. She felt Reed's hand shift between her legs, heard Reed murmur about how wet she was, and then felt a rush as Reed entered her again.

For a moment there was pain but then only satisfaction. A deep need being filled. She relished Reed's desire, her strength, relished even the brief sting that came when Reed pushed in another finger.

Reed was rougher this time than during the first go, but Julia heard herself begging breathlessly for more. *More.* Reed shifted then, riding on the ridge of her own thumb as she stroked.

It wasn't long before Julia heard the change in Reed's breathing. Reed was getting close, rubbing her own clit as she worked over Julia, and the sounds she made were pushing Julia further. She felt her own orgasm coming even as she tried to hold it at bay. When Reed gasped, she gave in finally.

The climax was hard and quick. Julia squeezed her eyes closed, feeling her body contract on Reed's hand. She relaxed a second later, letting the release wash over her.

Reed pulled her fingers out too soon and when Julia complained she only got a kiss on her cheek in response. It wasn't as if she could keep Reed inside her all night, though the thought of asking for exactly that crossed her mind. She was empty now, her pussy tender and dripping, and somehow still wanting more.

Reed was quiet and Julia wondered if she would fall asleep. No way could she sleep anytime soon. She felt Reed shift against her, turning on her side.

"You okay?" Reed asked.

"I'm good." But she wanted more. Minutes ticked by and still her body begged for Reed. She knew by her breathing that Reed wasn't asleep yet. Finally, she reached for Reed's hand, and placed it back on her center.

"Right here," Julia murmured.

Reed chuckled, kissing her neck, then her earlobe, and again her lips. Reed's hand settled on her mound, and a warmth spread over Julia as if she'd pulled up the blankets. Slowly Reed parted her folds, fingering her gently where she was swollen and tender.

Julia wasn't prepared to be entered again, but she didn't want Reed to stop touching her either. She relaxed under Reed's tending and closed her eyes, body spent. Could she take a little more? There was no chance she was going to come again, but if Reed wanted it...

"I should let you rest," Reed said.

"Do you have to?" Her tongue felt thick. She didn't want to sleep tonight and she didn't want this to end. But she didn't want to ask Reed to keep going if that made her sound crazy or desperate or both.

"I think you'll be sore tomorrow. I went a little hard there at the end..."

"What if I want more?" Julia admitted.

Reed pushed inside then and Julia rode out the twitch of pain as more waves of pleasure followed. All of her senses seemed heightened this time. She drank in the scent of Reed's sweat, tried to memorize the look on Reed's face, lips parted and eyes closed, and savored the feel of hot skin against hers. Slowly she let her knees slack open and Reed shifted so she was penetrating deeper. The sensation of being filled, of being thoroughly satisfied, and thoroughly fucked, was exactly what she needed.

CHAPTER TEN

Julia awoke from a deep sleep. She took a moment to get her bearings in the unfamiliar room. The overhead fan still whirred and light was stealing into the room through the crack between the curtains—bright light that could only mean late morning. She reached across the bed to find only emptiness and then lay on her back for another moment. Her pussy ached. She reached down to touch the tender places, gently exploring. The edge around her hole stung and the bony places felt almost bruised, but her clit pulsed when she swiped over it. Still eager. She nearly laughed. Her body had never reacted to a lover the way it did with Reed.

She wiped the wetness off on her thigh and sat up in bed. The sense of floating hit her then. Last night had been perfect. For once she'd satisfied a lover and the orgasms Reed had given her were like nothing she'd experienced before.

Slowly the sounds outside the door made their way to her. Utensils clattered against dishes. Small high-pitched voices spoke all at once, then Reed's voice filtered through the door, asking for a little quiet. By the bedside clock it was ten on the dot. She couldn't remember exactly when she'd fallen asleep. She was certain, however, that Reed's hand had still been between her legs.

She eased out of bed and went to the bathroom, grateful Reed had a master suite and she wouldn't have to face anyone before she'd rinsed off. She turned on the shower and stepped in while the water was still cool.

Reed came into the bathroom with a stack of towels. "Sorry about the kid noise. They can only stay quiet for so long." She set the towels on the bathroom counter. "Morning delivery from room service. We used up all the others at the pool." She paused, eyeing Julia through the glass door now splattered with water and smiled. "Last night was nice."

Before Julia could agree, one of the kids called for Reed. A loud clatter followed.

'That's probably Bryn throwing the remote control," Reed said. "She's in a mood. I've already had to talk to her about not punching her sister."

Julia fought back a wave of disappointment as Reed slipped out, carefully closing the bathroom door behind her. She wanted a shower and then she wanted Reed to pull her back to bed so they could make love again. *Sex, not love*, she quickly corrected. What had happened last night was only sex. No matter how good it felt, Reed wasn't making love to her. They both got a release and that was probably going to be the end of it. Maybe they'd have one more night together, but then Reed was going back to California. And this was only a vacation fling. Part of her knew that's why she'd relaxed last night. She hadn't worried about what would happen next.

She lathered the coconut hibiscus shampoo in her hair. Hawaii was perfect and so was Reed. But neither were long term. The wild sex they'd had was worth remembering, especially considering how sore she was while still longing for more, but feelings weren't involved. She'd have heaps to talk about with her therapist later.

Reed poked her head back into the bathroom. "I wanted to say you have no idea how much I would love a babysitter at the moment."

Julia smiled. Reed was gone again a moment later. She turned into the stream of water and closed her eyes, letting the shampoo rinse out. At least Reed wanted more…That helped some.

* * *

Mo and Kate were still asleep when Julia got home. As quietly as she could, she rummaged through the few items in the fridge to come up with a breakfast of a hard boiled egg, sliced cheese, and more pineapple. Once outside on the lanai, the view certainly better than the meal, she settled in to eat. She couldn't remember the last time she'd been this hungry. "Famished" was more appropriate. The food disappeared before she was full, and she leaned back in her seat, trying to decide if a donut was worth the trip to the resort café.

She'd turned down the offer of a bowl of Cheerios at Reed's, feeling somewhat torn as she did. Bryn had asked—not Reed. If there was only a playbook for how it was supposed to go when you were having a fling with someone who had kids…Morning-after cuddles, which had always been higher on her list than the sex itself, was of course out of the question. Though given how last night had gone, she'd prefer sex over cuddles this one time.

But was she supposed to leave immediately or linger and chat? Chatting seemed impossible—that was one of the reasons why she'd gone with her instinct on leaving before breakfast. How could she have a conversation about anything other than the mind-blowing sex she'd had the night before? She wasn't even certain how to say good-bye when she'd left. Reed had decided that by walking her to the back door and planting a kiss on her lips when the twins' backs were turned.

Julia touched her lips now, remembering the warm reassurance Reed had given her with that kiss. Without a word, she'd seemed to promise that they weren't finished.

Her cell phone buzzed and Julia looked through the screen at the kitchen counter where she'd left her phone. The master bedroom door opened at the same moment and Kate emerged wearing a white terry cloth robe. A towel was wrapped around her hair and she looked as if she'd stepped out of a magazine ad on resort living. Yawning, she went over to start coffee and then paused when she noticed there was already a full pot waiting. Julia waved when Kate glanced out at the lanai.

"You're up early."

"It's almost eleven," Julia returned. Her cell phone buzzed again and Kate walked over to it.

"You got a text," Kate said, holding up the phone. "It's from Reed. One word—'Tonight?' Well, that's cryptic."

"Is there a question mark?"

Kate nodded. "Do you two have dinner plans?"

"No...no plans." Julia smiled at the delicious thought of Reed planning their evening in bed. She wondered what would be on the menu.

"Still cryptic. I need coffee," Kate said. "Did Mo come home last night?"

"Right before I left." Julia noted Kate's furrowed brow. Recognition crossed her face a moment later.

"You went to Reed's place last night. Did you spend all night there?" Kate set the coffeepot down. Julia couldn't stop smiling. "And?"

"Sounds like she wants me back tonight. I guess it couldn't have been awful on her end, right?" Julia knew it wasn't. Maybe she hadn't blown Reed's mind, but she'd clearly enjoyed herself. For once she hadn't been a disappointment.

Kate laughed. "Good for you. I don't think I've ever seen you smile like that," She cocked her head, still studying Julia. "That good, huh?"

Julia smiled again. She didn't want to share any of the details, but if Kate asked, she'd admit it was the best sex she'd ever had—not that her past history had set much of a precedent. Reed had made it easy for her and Mo had given her the guts to go for it. Later she'd have to thank Mo for the pep talk.

Julia replied to Reed's text with one word: *Yes.*

She couldn't wait to be alone with her again. Getting through the rest of the day was going to be tough, especially with her body reminding her exactly what they'd done.

* * *

"You've got to blow out. Don't worry about the water getting into the snorkel."

"I feel like I'm drowning," Julia argued. But Kate's look made her dip her head back under the water. A bright yellow fish darted past her and she inhaled, choked on salt water, and pulled the snorkel out of her mouth. When she came up for air, Kate was waiting. She shook her head when she spotted the snorkel hanging loose.

"I think there's something wrong with my snorkel."

"You give up too easy."

Julia wanted to blame the equipment, but she knew Kate was probably right. Kate slipped under the water then, leaving her alone on the surface. The boat had dropped them off in a sheltered cove along with a half dozen other passengers and the cove was wide enough for them to be spaced about without feeling crowded. No one else seemed to be having any difficulty. Partly it was the snorkel for her, but the other issue was the strange sensation of not knowing how deep the water was and the sloshing waves. She'd never been a strong swimmer, but she could manage treading water and a halfway decent breaststroke. Being in the open water was entirely different than being in a swimming pool, however, and she was glad to have a life vest.

The few glimpses she had below the surface were mesmerizing—a kaleidoscope of colors and fish in every direction she'd looked. But every time a wave crested overhead, the snorkel filled with water. Finally she gave up fighting the snorkel and floated on her back instead, eyeing the cloudless blue sky and the lush green above the rocky shore. Maybe she was missing out on the underwater show, but the one above was nearly as gorgeous.

The sun warmed her and the waves lulled her into a half-sleep state. Thoughts of Reed filled her mind. She'd been fighting the urge to rehash everything that had happened, trying to stay in the moment and enjoy her time with Kate, but she gave in to the temptation of Reed now.

Last night hadn't been an abysmal failure, that much was clear. But the insecurities she'd carried for so long couldn't be wiped away with one good roll in the sack. Yet...She felt different now, buoyed with a confidence she hoped she could hold on to. And she was exhausted. She smiled at this thought. Later she'd wrap her arms around Reed and tell her how tired she'd been all day because of her. Then, just maybe, she'd act on her new confidence and do something truly crazy like play out one of her fantasies.

Rolling onto her belly, she fit the mask on again, determined to give the fish show another try. Before she had the snorkel set, a turtle surfaced only an arm's stretch away. Julia felt her breath catch. She wanted to motion for Kate, but she was frozen in awe.

Exposed as she was, she didn't feel any danger. The wrinkled face examined her own, ancient eyes peering into her soul, and time seemed to pause as they considered each other. Snapping its mouth a few times, the turtle indelicately crunched on something before slowly turning to reveal its huge shell.

Julia expected the turtle to drop under the water then, but it floated for a while longer, apparently in no rush to leave. The waves sloshed between them, pushing the turtle closer and then farther from Julia, and still one eye stayed trained on her. Some message seemed to pass in that steady, cool gaze, but Julia had no idea how to decipher it.

Before she lost interest, the turtle did, disappearing as unceremoniously as it had appeared. The sun sparkled on the water, making it difficult to see where it had gone, and Julia worked the snorkel into her mouth, resolved to catch one last glimpse.

The hour and a half of snorkeling promised in the brochure passed entirely too fast, but Julia realized she was too spent to do any more as soon as she tried to pull herself out of the water. The boat captain, a tawny older woman with a hint of a Texas accent, helped her manage the rope ladder and then took her snorkel gear to store along with the rest.

After they'd eaten a bag lunch of a deli sandwich and chips, the captain, who'd been watching some gathering clouds in the distance, gave the order to pull up the anchor. A light breeze had picked up and the waves that had seemed gentle earlier were now tipped with white.

"Weather changes quick around here. We might get some rain," the captain warned. "We'll pick up some speed and head back to Kona a little faster than planned to see if we can stay ahead of the clouds."

Along with the captain there were two teens working the boat, one boy and one girl, and another woman who seemed to hold the position of first mate. All three jumped into motion with the captain's warning and the boat was soon cruising away from the cove.

"Let's go up to the front of the boat," Kate suggested. "The captain told me they sometimes see dolphins on the ride back."

Julia's legs were shaky and the ankle that hadn't given her any trouble in days was complaining, but she followed Kate anyway. A promise of dolphins was too good to miss. She spent the first ten minutes of the ride staring at the blue water. The turtle had definitely been the highlight, but she was amazed by the sheer number of fish she'd seen at the cove and now the world under the waves seemed entirely changed.

"Look," Kate said, pointing at a blur in the distance.

Julia squinted and then spotted something lurching out of the water. "Is that a flying fish?" Another blur appeared over the waves followed with a splash.

The captain answered: "Dolphins. They're coming our way."

Julia looked over her shoulder at the helm. The captain had leaned out from the enclosed glass cockpit to point at the blurred objects that were decidedly coming toward the boat now. As they neared the boat, their dolphin shape became clearer, and Julia counted over a dozen in the pod.

For the next several minutes the only sounds aboard were oohs and ahhs as everyone watched the dolphins play in the boat's breaker waves. Some of the dolphins managed spins as they leapt from the surface, their sides gleaming; others surfed alongside the boat, seemingly racing the captain.

A light rain started, and the dolphins took this as their cue, turning as one to head back the direction they'd come from. Kate reached over and caught Julia's hand. Her face was shining with the biggest smile Julia had ever seen on her.

"That was the best thing ever."

Julia smiled back. "I forgot you had a thing for dolphins."

"Remember that poster I used to have up in our dorm room?"

Julia nodded, instantly picturing the ocean poster that had hung on the ceiling above Kate's bed. "Mo used to joke that you had to be a lesbian because no straight girl would ever like dolphins enough to have a poster of them."

"I had posters of Orlando Bloom and Will Smith too."

"But you kept those in your closet."

Kate laughed. "Think that meant anything?"

"You love dolphins more."

Kate leaned back, holding the rail and letting the rain splatter on her face. She closed her eyes. "When I was a kid, I used to want to be a dolphin. Part of me still does."

Kate rarely mentioned anything from her childhood and when she did, her face usually would change immediately. The gloom that appeared was painful to see. Julia knew that Kate's parents were well off and she'd mentioned that she'd been spoiled. But there was something that had happened that she never wanted to talk about. And despite having everything she could have ever wanted in material things, it was clear that she hadn't been a happy kid.

Today was the first time Julia could remember when Kate had shared a memory that hadn't changed her expression. She was relaxed and still smiling. Julia set her hand on Kate's knee. She closed her eyes too, letting the cool spray from the water mix with the warm rain on her skin.

CHAPTER ELEVEN

Julia tried not to check her phone compulsively. She knew she wouldn't miss the buzz of Reed's text and the number of times she checked the blank screen wouldn't speed up the evening. But by nine o'clock she was fighting back a wave of annoyance. Why did Reed have to have kids? If she'd been single, they could have spent the entire day in each other's arms. As it was, Julia only got a few hours of her. It wasn't enough—especially considering Reed was leaving tomorrow.

When her phone finally buzzed at nine thirty, Julia was too annoyed to rush to pick it up. They were watching a documentary that had been filmed in Hawaii, mostly because Kate and Mo were carefully avoiding each other but also because the landscape from the helicopter shots was stunning. Mo got to the phone first, tossing it across the sofa into Julia's lap without reading the text. That was serious restraint on Mo's part.

Kids are asleep.

Julia stared at the words for a minute, then she turned back to the television. She considered texting that she was busy watching a movie. Tomorrow Reed would be gone anyway. Why had she thought a fling would be a good idea? She'd never get Reed out of her mind, and yet she hadn't had nearly enough of her. And what was worse, she'd compare her to everyone who came after.

"Everything okay?" Kate asked.

"She's trying to decide if she wants to answer Reed's booty call," Mo said, her gaze not leaving the television screen. "What do you guys think about going on a helicopter ride?"

The helicopter was soaring above one of Kauai's waterfalls. Julia felt her stomach clench. Now every time she'd see a waterfall she'd think of Reed. She sighed, and Kate reached over to pat her hand.

"Don't overthink this, sweetie. This is her last night here."

"Wait," Mo said. "You're giving advice on not overthinking something?"

Kate held up her middle finger to Mo but kept her eyes trained on Julia. "You want another night with her, right? Don't beat yourself up worrying that this is only sex. She's asking you and you want it. You can regret it later. Tonight you might as well go enjoy her."

"Do I know you?" Mo asked. "Seriously, who stole the Kate who worries about getting STDs from dance clubs?"

Kate ignored Mo. "Jules, we both know what's going to happen if you don't go. And, quite honestly, I don't want to listen to you whine about how you let this slip out of your hands. I actually like Reed—unlike the other women you've dated."

"This is just about sex—you do realize that, right?" Mo was staring incredulously at Kate. "She's not signing up to date Reed."

"Well, maybe she should," Kate returned, finally looking at Mo. "Maybe they need one more night together to realize they're meant to be. Why not?"

"Meant to be? Are you kidding?" Mo shook her head. "They've known each other for less than a week and the only thing Reed's wanting out of this is—"

"I need to pee." Julia stood up. "You two finish this discussion and let me know how it turns out."

Julia headed to the bathroom while Mo and Kate argued over the likelihood that a relationship initially based on sex could turn into something more. She didn't need to pee, but she needed a break from Kate and Mo. The reflection in the mirror above the sink didn't hide her disappointment. She knew Mo was right. For Reed, this was only about sex. The irony was, that's what she'd needed last night, even if part of her wanted more. And now she didn't want to miss out on another night with Reed simply because she wanted the promise of a relationship. If only she could convince her brain that a fling was a good idea.

She stuck her tongue out at her reflection. One thing was certain—she needed to get out of her head and go enjoy sex with possibly the only person she'd ever enjoy sex with. After a long minute spent convincing herself that she wouldn't get any more attached than she already was with one more night in the sack, she hopped in the shower for a rinse and then decided on eyeliner and lipstick. If she was hoping for hot sex, she might as well show up looking good. And it wouldn't hurt if Reed ended up wishing this weren't good-bye.

Kate and Mo both noticed the makeup and the fact that she'd changed into the one nice outfit she'd brought—Mo reacting with whistles and Kate with oohs and ahs. She headed for the door, pretending to ignore them but couldn't help smiling. The fact they knew exactly what she was about to do was more than a little embarrassing. But their catcalls also felt strangely like another pep talk.

When she stepped outside she felt a rush from the warm night air. Something had broken loose inside her—something that was fully charged and rattling around with excitement.

Two steps in front of Reed's lanai she paused to take a deep breath, worrying her courage was already wearing thin. She had a plan in her head for what she wanted to do tonight, but maybe this was all a bad idea. Maybe last night had been a fluke and she'd be back to her usual level of incompetence.

Reed was in the living room, feet kicked up on the coffee table and a book open in her lap. As Julia watched, she reached for a glass tumbler of something amber colored, took a sip, and then glanced at her phone.

Julia hadn't returned her text and she felt a pang of guilt now. A couple walked by on the path, chatting and laughing. She returned their waves and then, once they'd gone, glanced back at Reed's living room. *Now or never.* She crossed the wet grass and slipped between the lounge chairs.

She tapped on the edge of the screen and Reed looked up from the book. A smile spread across her face and Julia's heart thumped faster in response. It was useless pretending her feelings weren't already involved, but she'd deal with that tomorrow. After Reed had gone.

"Wow," Reed said, opening the screen door. Her gaze swept down the front of Julia and then returned to her eyes. "You look amazing. Are you going out with your friends?"

"No. I'm coming over to hang out with you."

"You got dressed up for me?" Reed scratched her head and then glanced down at her own clothes. "And I'm in my pajamas."

"I didn't give you much warning," Julia admitted. "But I like your outfit anyway."

Reed was barefoot and wearing a white tank top and a pair of thin, light blue cotton pants with a drawstring. The pants hung loose on her hips while the tank top was tight enough to show all her muscles. Julia had to fight the urge to reach out to snag the drawstring. Reed was too tempting. "A little bit comfortable, a little bit sexy…"

"These are my lucky scrubs," Reed said, smoothing the thin cloth. "I've had them since senior rotations. They're too comfortable to throw out. But as far as being sexy—this is not what I would have picked out if I knew you were on your way over." She grinned. "I'd try a little harder to impress you."

"Lucky scrubs, huh?" It helped that Reed wanted to impress *her*, but the fact she had lucky scrubs was more intimidating. "I don't think I want details."

"Not lucky like you're thinking." Reed held up her hand. "It's a long story…but the pants are innocent, I swear."

"Hmm. Not sure I believe you."

Reed laughed. "It's good to see you."

"You too." Julia smiled. A little too good.

"When you didn't text back, I started to worry that you were upset."

"I'm not upset with you."

Reed cocked her head. "But you are upset?"

The only person she was upset with was herself. As much as she wanted to, she couldn't pretend she wasn't going to miss Reed tomorrow. The ache was already starting.

Reed leaned against the doorframe. "Did we go too far last night?"

"Last night was perfect," Julia said. "And since then, I haven't been able to stop thinking about sex. I feel like a horny teenager."

"Is that a good thing or a bad thing?"

"That depends on what you're doing tonight. And if I lose my nerve." Not able to resist any longer, Julia reached out and tugged on Reed's drawstring. She bit her lip.

"I thought about you all day," Reed said. "And I can't stop wishing tomorrow wasn't when we say good-bye."

Before Julia had a chance to respond, Reed closed the distance between them. The desire in her lips sent a rush through Julia. Did it matter that Reed was going to miss this too? Julia knew the answer was yes. She wanted Reed to long for her. But it wouldn't make tomorrow any easier.

With Reed's lips still on hers, she untied the drawstring and slipped her hand under the material. Reed's soft gasp was what she needed. She pulled back and said, "I think we should go inside before the neighbors get a show."

Reed chuckled, rubbing her lips. She stepped back inside, catching her pants only after they'd slipped down to reveal her boxers, and then deftly retying the strings. The brief peek Julia had of Reed's boxers was enough to make her mouth dry.

"The kids are asleep, right?"

"Out cold," Reed said. "We spent all afternoon playing in the waves. They've been asleep for an hour."

"So you're sure they won't wake up?" Julia asked, catching Reed's hand.

"We could probably have a rave and they'd sleep through it," Reed promised. She cocked her head as if about to ask why, but Julia pressed one finger across her lips. She turned then and pulled the blinds closed.

The fantasy she'd had in mind all afternoon came racing to the forefront of her thoughts. When she turned back to see Reed watching her, she felt brave enough to go for it. She kissed Reed, pushing her backward toward the sofa. She had the drawstring undone in a moment and then the scrub pants slipped down before Reed sank onto the cushions.

"And here I was worried that maybe I'd moved too fast yesterday." Reed grinned.

"I've been thinking all day about what I wanted to do to you," Julia said, dropping to her knees. She was emboldened by her own words as much as Reed's response when she pushed her legs apart and shifted between them. Before she could lose her confidence, she slipped her hand through the flap in Reed's boxers. The warm wetness she found under the short curls made her body tremble with a longing she could hardly hold back.

Reed's chin dropped and a gasp slipped out of her lips. When Julia started to pull her hand back, Reed moved her hips forward so her butt was at the edge of the sofa. The way she pushed herself onto Julia's hand made it clear she wasn't wanting her to slow down.

Julia pulled the boxers down past Reed's knees and then off her ankles. The familiar musk she'd had all over her skin last night turned her body on again. Reed spread her legs further when Julia slid her hand up the inside of her thigh. She'd never been good at this, at going down on someone, but she'd never wanted to do it as much as she did now. In her fantasy, her lover was giving her the orders to be on her hands and knees and then talking dirty. She wasn't about to ask Reed to do that, but she could imagine it.

She slipped her arms under Reed's thighs and pulled her center closer. She inhaled, taking in the scent that was making her feel reckless. Reed's hands moved through her hair.

Finally she dipped her chin and pressed in with her tongue. She found Reed's clit and circled it. The sounds of Reed's pleasure, soft moans mixed with words encouraging her—"yeah, that's it, oh yeah, keep going"—she was aware of, but the rest of the room blurred as she worked her tongue on Reed. She felt hands move from her shoulders, to her hair, and then up and down her arms, but she had trouble keeping track of what was happening when. At some point, Reed pushed into Julia's mouth, one hand holding Julia's head in place. She wasn't talking dirty, but the feeling of her controlling Julia was a huge turn-on.

Julia sucked on the swollen clit, knowing as Reed's rhythmic hip thrusting increased that she was getting close. She'd stopped worrying about doing it wrong. Whether Reed came or not she wanted to be exactly where she was and she had no intention of stopping until Reed pushed her away.

Too soon she felt Reed's thighs tense. She seemed to be trying to keep quiet, but the orgasm hit and her moan slipped out. Her head dropped back on the sofa cushion as the rest of her muscles clenched. Julia watched her, holding her in place when a second tremor came a moment later.

Before she could enjoy more of the scene, Reed's hand slipped behind Julia's neck and pressed her head back between her legs. She thrust her tongue hard this time and heard Reed's low groan. She sucked again, swallowing the salty cum and wanting more of it. Reed's body tensed, her hand holding Julia in place as the climax moved through her.

The fact that they were in the living room with the lights on hit Julia as Reed's grip on her relaxed. *Those kids better stay asleep.* She kept her lips on Reed's center still, kissing the inside of her thighs and lapping up what dripped.

Now that she'd felt what she could do to Reed, how she could turn her on and bring her to the edge, she wanted to do it all over again. But Reed had collapsed back against the pillows, all of the tense lines gone from her face and her legs spread. When Julia started to lick her clit again, Reed slid her hand between her legs blocking her. "Uh-uh. No more."

"But you taste so good."

Reed opened her eyes then, a slack smile on her lips. "There's only so much lovin' my clit can handle." She reached for Julia. "Come here."

After only a few kisses, Reed eased back on the sofa, eyes closing again. "What were you saying yesterday about not being good at sex?"

"You make me want to try things."

Reed smiled, eyes still closed. "And you turn me into a puddle. A satisfied, happy puddle."

"That's how I felt last night. I'm glad I could return the favor." That was putting it mildly. She was still heady from the rush of Reed's climax, but she didn't need to admit how well Reed was patching up her insecurities. She picked up the half-full glass Reed had been drinking from earlier. "Can I have a sip?"

Reed nodded.

Julia took a sip, surprised at the sweet pineapple mint flavor. "What is this? It's delicious."

"Pineapple mojito. Did you know the resort bar delivers to your room?"

"No...Too bad you didn't discover that a few nights ago. Could have saved us from your margaritas."

"Ouch." Reed laughed and took the glass from Julia. "For that comment, I shouldn't let you have any more."

Julia pulled the drink back before Reed had a sip. She finished it in one gulp, Reed laughing all the while. When Julia set the empty glass on the coffee table, Reed shook her head, a grin still playing on her lips.

"You've changed this past week. Or maybe I'm just getting to know you better."

Julia knew both were partly true, but she didn't want a deep conversation about it now. She only had Reed for a few more hours. Fortunately, Reed seemed to sense that she didn't want to talk. She wrapped her arms around Julia and brought her into another kiss.

As she pulled back, she said, "I think it's my turn now. And don't think I'm going to let you fall asleep tonight."

Julia felt a surge as Reed stood up, pulling her toward the bedroom. Yes, she was ready to let Reed have her. But as much as she wanted it, an equal part was holding her back. She didn't want this to be the last time Reed led her to a bed. If only they could keep this up when they got back to California...

"Second thoughts?" Reed was watching her, one hand on the open door to the master bedroom. Before Julia could explain, Reed continued, "We can stop whenever you want. I'm not going to lie—I want more—but if you want to leave..."

"No, I don't want to leave." She paused, knowing she shouldn't say more but unable to stop herself. "I was thinking about how far I'd drive to sleep with you. We wouldn't have to say good-bye tomorrow...I know you're not in a place to date but what if it was just sex?"

"How far would you drive for that?" Reed asked. Her tone was playful, but there was a seriousness in the gaze Julia felt boring into her.

"At least two hours. Probably three or four depending on my mood. But it's only eighty miles from Oakland to Davis."

"Hmm. I think maybe we need to talk logistics then." Reed smiled, pulling Julia toward her. She closed the bedroom door and immediately started inching up Julia's tank top. "But that conversation is going to have to wait til morning because I need something else from you now."

All the other questions disappeared as Reed leaned in to kiss Julia's neck. Her kisses traveled down to Julia's collarbone. She slipped the spaghetti straps of Julia's tank top off her shoulders and then finished tugging it all the way off. Reed's hands were deliciously warm against Julia's chilled skin as she cupped first one and then the other breast.

"This might be inappropriate, but I love your breasts. They're a really nice size. I mean, obviously they're nice, but they're—I don't know how to put this—satisfying?" Reed stopped. "That was probably saying too much, wasn't it?"

"When you're holding my breasts I think we've gone past the stage where you have to worry about what's appropriate." Julia smiled. "But at the moment I'm hoping you're about to put that in your mouth instead of just talking about it."

Reed rolled Julia's nipple between her fingers and then licked the tip. She straightened up. "I mean, that's not all I like about you. It's just that I've never really been with someone who had nice boobs. I mean, like these."

"Boobs?" Julia laughed again. "You're blushing at the word boobs? After what you did last night?"

"Well, yeah. And I remembered we're not supposed to talk about exes."

"As long as you like me better than your exes, I'm okay with it."

"I like you way better than my exes. All of them put together. But it's not just your body. I like being close to you… Standing next to you makes me feel like I'm buzzing on the inside."

"I didn't think you only liked me for my body. In fact, if you did, you'd be the first." Julia hadn't felt self-conscious until that moment. She dropped her gaze down her chest and saw the swell of her belly over the tight band of her skirt.

Reed tipped Julia's chin up to her. "If I'm being honest, it was your smile that caught me first. On that flight...I could tell you were about to chew out Bryn and then you looked over at me and smiled." Reed paused. "I noticed your boobs right after I noticed your smile, but in my defense, you were leaning over that seat and, well, they were at eye level. But just so we're clear, everything about your body is exactly what I like. I wouldn't change a thing."

For once, Julia didn't doubt a compliment about her body. Reed's hands had moved down to her hips and then her fingertips slipped under the waistband. She could feel how much Reed wanted her in the firmness of her touch, in the way she stroked over every inch as if it was her right. And every part of her that Reed touched seemed to be lit like a slow-burning fuse. She wanted more of Reed's hands caressing her body, more of her eyes taking all of her in and clearly liking what she saw. It didn't seem possible...but she knew it was.

"By the way, I like your eyes too. Can we say that was where I was looking?"

"Too late." Julia laughed and started to pull away, shaking her head at Reed's honesty. She let Reed pull her close again without a fight and then leaned into another long kiss. The truth was, she liked Reed for her body too. She liked how tall Reed was, how strong her arms felt as they held her, how close her body pressed against hers, how her eyes seemed to always be waiting for Julia's.

Reed was slow to take off Julia's skirt. Her hands traveled up and down, but she seemed in no hurry to get her naked. Julia tried to quell her anticipation. Even after the skirt was off, Reed made no move to touch her below her waist. Unlike last night when she had taken them from first base to home plate in the blink of an eye, the slow massage she was doing on Julia's arms and back only made Julia want to feel those hands other places.

Reed knew exactly what game she was playing, grinning between kisses and trying to chat when Julia had no interest in talking. Finally Julia gave up pretending she wanted to talk, antsy for Reed's fingertips and wanting to move to the bed. Reed kept up a steady stream of a one-sided conversation, noting more parts of Julia that she liked as her hands moved over her body: "And don't get me started on your legs," she was saying. "These curves are perfect...And I love how your hips move when you walk. And this trim pussy..."

"Trim pussy?" Julia laughed.

Undaunted, Reed continued, "Yeah. I like how neat the lines are where the hair starts."

"I got a bikini wax before the trip."

"It's a good look." Reed grinned. "What?"

"When are you going to fuck me?"

"When I'm ready." Reed kissed her, tracing down her chest to her belly button and then back up again.

Julia wanted her to move lower, but she kept up a slow tease, never going to the warm, wet place where her body was waiting to be touched. By the time they'd moved to the bed, she was positively dripping and Reed still hadn't reached between her legs. She'd gotten chilled in the air-conditioned room and welcomed the cover Reed pulled over her.

"Do you want anything?" Reed asked, not climbing into bed yet. "Are you thirsty? Hungry?"

"You're doing this on purpose."

"Doing what?" Reed was clearly trying not to smile.

"Making me wait. And if you think I'll want you more, it's possible you're right." Julia pushed the cover off her body and spread her legs. Reed's expression changed immediately. Yes, she had her attention now. Julia reached for her hand. "But I think you should know what you're doing to me."

Reed's sharp intake of breath was almost as satisfying as the rush Julia felt. She loved how she could turn Reed on—and turn the tables. Reed's finger dipped inside and then a moment later she was on the bed, pressing her weight on Julia.

If only this night didn't have to end. If only Reed could stay exactly where she was, her hands doing exactly what they were doing, her lips covering Julia with kisses…

CHAPTER TWELVE

"Mom, wake up!"

Julia pulled the sheet up to cover her chest and quickly rolled on her side, away from the open doorway where Bryn stood. There was a slim chance Bryn hadn't seen her.

"Julia?"

Julia opened her eyes, rubbing away sleep. Carly was inches away from her face, smiling as she teetered on tiptoe on her side of the bed. "Uh, hi, sweetie."

"Can you stay and have breakfast with us?" Carly asked.

"Um, well…"

On the other side of the bed, Bryn interrupted with, "Mom, you had a sleepover with Julia again?" She climbed onto the bed, pushing her way over Reed to see for herself. "Julia, can you sleep in our room the next time you sleep over? It's not fair that Mom gets you two nights in a row."

"Yes, it's fair," Reed said, laughing as she playfully wrestled Bryn back to her side. "My bed is bigger. She'd fall out of your bed."

Carly climbed into the bed then as well, wiggling over Julia to get in on the wrestling. Reed had Bryn at arm's length only long enough to have Carly sneak in from the side. At some point in the night, Reed must have gotten up and put her clothes on. She was wearing the tank top and scrub pants again, both decidedly more wrinkled now, and her hair was a disheveled mess. In short, Julia decided, she was sexy as hell.

When they lost the wrestling match, the girls turned to tickling Reed. Julia watched the scene, carefully keeping hold of her sheet and laughing along with the twins when Reed nearly fell out of bed. Out of breath, Reed finally stood up and caught hold of Carly and Bryn. She kissed each kid on the head and planted them on the floor.

"Okay, time out. Julia might stay and have breakfast with us if you two give us a minute to get dressed. Go on." Reed pointed to the door. "Bryn, can you get the Cheerios out? And Carly, you know where the bowls are…Close our door for a minute. Julia's shy."

Grumbling, Bryn and Carly filed out of the room. When the door closed, Reed sank back in the bed. She ran her hand through her hair and then looked over her shoulder at Julia. "I promised you a conversation about logistics, but if that changed your mind…"

"It didn't," Julia said. "As long as I know morning tickle competitions are part of the deal, I won't go to sleep naked."

"I should have warned you. Most of the time they call for me around dawn. I don't often get to sleep in." Reed stretched and then tried unsuccessfully to pat her hair into place, strands of which were sticking out in every direction.

"I love how you are with them. By the way, you should stop messing with your hair. It looks good." When Reed gave her a skeptical look, Julia said, "I'm being honest. The just-fucked look suits you."

Reed chuckled and then moved to straddle Julia. "I won't mess with my hair if you stop covering up your sexy body. The just-fucked look suits you too."

"I need clothes. You have kids."

Before Julia could worry about having morning breath, Reed was leaning over her. "But they're not here now." Julia wiggled, laughing as Reed tugged down the sheet, exposing a nipple. Reed kissed the tip and her body's response was immediate. She realized then she was still wet between her legs despite the fact it had been hours since Reed had touched her there. She fended off a second nipple kiss by messing up the section of hair Reed had flattened into place. When Reed tried to kiss her lips instead, Julia playfully pushed her back.

"You should know I'm pretty good at wrestling," Reed said, climbing on top again with a devious smile. She pinned Julia's shoulders and then leaned over her. "What's your plan now, sexy?"

Julia reached up to tickle Reed's armpit. As she fell back laughing, Julia sat up in bed. "You should know I'm very good at tickling."

Before Reed could plan a counterattack, Julia hopped out of bed. "So I hear you're making me breakfast?"

Reed swung a pillow at Julia's backside as she skirted around the bed toward the bathroom. "Sure. How do you like your Cheerios?"

* * *

"We've got an hour to finish cleaning. That means finding all of the toys you two hid and getting our suitcases out the door. Checkout is eleven," Reed said, handing out the last of the pineapple speared on toothpicks. The pineapple temporarily halted the argument between Bryn and Carly over a wheelie suitcase. They were taking turns pulling the suitcase around the condo until Carly discovered she could ride the suitcase. Then Bryn insisted the suitcase belonged solely to her.

"You could leave your things at my place and stay a few hours longer. What time's your flight?" Julia almost hated to ask. She didn't want Reed to leave.

"Not until six."

"Can we stay at Julia's?" Bryn asked, hopping off the suitcase.

"Well…" Reed glanced from Bryn's face to Carly's. Both kids were nodding in unison and then laughing as they faced off, trying to get their nods perfectly in sync. This was how the past two hours had gone—giggling and then fighting and then giggling again. It was exhausting, but Julia hadn't once wanted to leave. Reed looked over at her, "What about your friends?"

"Mo's probably surfing already and Kate will be in a lounge chair by the pool. Besides, these two will want to play in the water one last time."

Carly and Bryn started their nodding in unison, laughing again. "Please, Mom," they begged.

"Okay. But no more fighting, you two, or Julia might change her mind."

"I won't," Julia said. She caught Reed's hand and squeezed.

Reed met her eyes. She leaned close and kissed her—it was only a peck on the lips—but as she pulled away, she said, "I don't think I told you how much I enjoyed last night."

"You didn't."

"I wish I could pull you back into bed now to explain…"

Julia laughed when Reed pulled her into a tight hold. The twins had wheeled their suitcase off to the back bedroom and they finally had a moment alone. It wouldn't last, Julia knew, but with Reed's body pressed against hers she longed for one last session naked. Reed, she'd discovered, came quick whenever she sucked on her clit and the thought of getting one more time with her was almost worth asking about childcare options.

"But this is my last day on vacation with them," Reed said, letting go. She glanced down the hall to the twins' bedroom. "Tomorrow they'll go back to full-time day care and I go back to work."

"Then let's get this place cleaned up so you guys can go play at the pool," Julia said, forcing a smile.

"You don't have to help. You could go relax…"

"This way I get more time with you."

Reed seemed to stop herself from arguing more at Julia's determined look. She smiled and let go of her hand, heading to the kitchen table to clear away the remaining dishes from breakfast.

The next hour passed quickly. Every time Reed looked over her shoulder at her or bumped into her—clearly not on accident—Julia longed to pull her back to the bedroom. Instead, she busied herself by tossing the remaining leftovers in the fridge and then gathering the crop of pool toys spread throughout the condo. Whenever she thought of sneaking a kiss, the twins wheeled through the kitchen holding up a new item they'd found. Everything from missing goggles to Legos turned up in their search. Their excitement almost made up for Julia's frustrations. Almost.

Eleven o'clock came too soon. The morning was slipping away, and Julia knew she wouldn't be ready to wave Reed off that afternoon. As soon as they were back in California the fantasy life she'd been dreaming of, where she spent weekends in Davis and commuted back and forth to Oakland, would come face-to-face with reality. It wasn't only the kids that had her worried. Reed had a career and a busy life—once she went back to that world, would she really want Julia to take time away from those things? She hadn't mentioned any shared parenting or ex-wife, but that lingering question kept nudging at Julia's mind as well. Every minute that passed without that conversation about logistics made Julia wonder if Reed was purposefully postponing it for some reason.

"I think that about does it," Reed said, tossing a hand towel onto the counter. "You ready for two little gremlins to drop in at your place?"

"Can't wait."

Reed came over to help squish the suitcase Julia was trying to zip. The girls had tried to add a T-shirt and a book on Hawaiian birds to the already jam-packed case and she couldn't close it now. Reed sat down on the suitcase and managed to pull the zipper closed. She met Julia's eyes, now sitting only inches away from her.

"Since I've had them, I've never tried to be with someone," Reed said.

"I thought you said you'd dated…"

"Well…by dates I meant…" She hesitated.

"Hookups."

"Yeah." Reed sighed. "It's complicated with kids. Mostly I meet people at their place and…"

"I get it." Julia didn't want details on Reed's usual arrangement. She imagined the women Reed might have hooked up with and tried to ignore the swell of insecurity. Reed was confident, attractive, and smart—which meant she probably had women coming on to her if she was paying any attention. And the women she hooked up with weren't going to be disappointed in bed.

Reed continued, "I feel like I should have a disclaimer or a warning label whenever I meet someone—some flashing neon sign that says, 'By the way, I'm a mom of four-year-old twins. I'll probably disappoint you in more ways than one. Even if this is just about sex…'" She glanced toward the back bedroom where Bryn and Carly were bouncing between the two beds and calling each other poo-poo heads.

"Between work and them, I don't have extra hours in the day. I can't tell you how many times I've had to cancel on going out because one of them is sick. It takes two weeks of planning to schedule in dinner and a movie. And I can't do romantic weekend getaways. I can't show up unexpectedly with a bottle of wine and flowers."

"I'm not asking for that."

"I know you aren't but…" Reed shook her head.

Maybe Reed had spent the morning thinking of logistics and decided that even hooking up wasn't worth the trouble. Or maybe she only liked the thrill of someone new and had decided the past few days were enough. A week ago, Julia would have agreed she had no business letting herself get attached to someone with kids. "Part of me wishes I didn't like you so much. Or that there was something really annoying about you."

"I could give you a list," Reed said. "For starters, I can be a terrible communicator. Or so I've been told."

"I hadn't noticed." Julia smiled when Reed looked sideways at her, but her heart was beating hard in her chest. "Tell me what you want."

"If there's a chance we could make this work—without pretending we're actually dating—I'm all in. I don't want to say good-bye to you today."

"Then we're on the same page. Your kids come first. I get that. And I know I only get part of you. But I don't want to end things before we've even started." Julia felt shaky, knowing she was only admitting part of the truth. "Although I do have another week in Hawaii to find some attractive single butch to have mind-blowing sex with so if you need to pull out of the deal…"

Reed didn't laugh or say anything in response, and Julia felt the room start to close in on her. "I was kidding about finding someone else," she added. "I want you."

"But are you really okay if this is only about sex?"

"I think it's what I need," Julia said.

Reed held her gaze with those gorgeous blue eyes. She had to be able to see right through her, had to know how bad she already had it for her. Julia held her breath, waiting for Reed to say something in response. She felt like a fool, still wishing that Reed would admit the past few nights had been about more than sex for her. The longer she didn't say that, the more doubts and the more her crazy insecurities came back in full force.

"Honestly now I just want the option for more time with you. These past few nights have been amazing and I don't want to say good-bye." They'd known each other for a week; she shouldn't be ready to commit to more anyway. "You don't have time for a relationship and the truth is, I don't either. But maybe we could pull off a weekend every once in a while…or even a night here or there. Yeah, we'll run the risk that it'd be about more than sex for me, but I don't need a full-time relationship."

"A weekend with you sounds amazing." Reed paused. She reached for Julia's hand. "And I don't want to say good-bye either. I'm just worried I'll be a disappointment."

"It's possible. And it's possible the mind-blowing sex will get old."

"Anything's possible." Reed grinned. "Okay. This is gonna sound nerdy, but I'm going to send you my calendar so we can pick some dates. In my normal life, everything gets scheduled. I have categories for everything from dropping off kids at day care to eating meals."

"I want to know what category you're going to put me under in your schedule."

"Oh, you're going in under the heading of mind-blowing sex."

Julia laughed and Reed pulled her close. The kiss she got in return sent a rush through her. Why did she have to love kissing Reed so much? She nearly whimpered when Reed pulled away from her lips. She didn't want to think about logistics or the fact she'd only get Reed for a weekend every once in a while. At the moment she wanted to take Reed back to bed and not think at all.

CHAPTER THIRTEEN

"I can't believe you haven't figured out the kid thing yet." Kate handed Mo her carry-on bag and then dropped into the window seat. "With as much time as you two were together, she must have dropped some clues."

"We didn't spend a lot of time talking," Julia said.

Mo chuckled until Kate gave her a side eye.

"Well, you could text her and ask. You've had that phone in your hands an awful lot this past week."

That much was true. She'd felt like a teenager with as many times as she'd been caught checking her phone. Kate and Mo had taken turns teasing her. If only they knew how often she was thinking of Reed and longing to see her…Unfortunately the texts from her had been few and far between.

Mo hefted Kate's bag into the open space in the overhead compartment and then jammed her own bag alongside it. "We've already been through this. You can't ask a queer mom how she ended up with kids."

"She can if she needs to know," Kate shot back. "And now that they're going to keep up seeing each other—"

"Turns out I still don't need to know." Julia sank into the middle seat. They'd agreed on rock-paper-scissors to determine their seating for the return flight and she'd lost both rounds. She settled in, squishing her purse under the seat in front of her, and then decided to pull her phone out, knowing she'd want to send Reed one last text before takeoff.

"Can I ask her for you?"

"What does it matter? It's not like the kids are going anywhere." Mo settled into the aisle seat. "Besides Julia says she actually likes them. And although that's hard to believe given how that one kid with the curls whined nonstop—" Mo waved off Julia's defense of Bryn. "I understand."

"Understand what exactly?" Kate asked.

"You can like something you've never liked—kids, in Julia's case—if it's part of the person you're really into. You accept it as part of the package. Maybe you even start to love that about them."

"Mo, you're completely missing my point," Kate said. "I'm not saying she doesn't like Reed's kids. All I'm saying is that she deserves to know if there's another woman involved. If she's divorced and—"

"And what? Julia likes Reed. She's going to accept that part of Reed as well. Anyway, who cares if she's divorced?"

"All right. That's enough you two. Reed doesn't want to date—we've been through this. We're meeting up for sex. I don't need to know everything about her." Julia motioned to one of the flight attendants passing their aisle. "We'll be needing three rum and Cokes as soon as you start the drinks."

"No problem," the woman said, glancing briefly at Julia and then settling her gaze on Mo. "Anything else I can get for you?"

Mo smiled up at her. They began to chat about Hawaii and Julia heard Kate murmur, "Here we go again," under her breath. Julia had always found it endearing that Mo could flirt with any woman she met and Kate's jealousy wasn't always so obvious.

Now she felt decidedly uncomfortable sandwiched between the two of them.

The mood between Kate and Mo had turned cool over the last few days. Something had happened the last night Julia had gone to Reed's condo, but neither wanted to talk about it. Mo insisted nothing was wrong, and Kate simply waved off Julia's questions. They'd been spending more time apart; Mo had the excuse of surfing and Kate had signed herself up for more snorkeling day trips. Both of them were happy as long as they weren't talking about each other. When they did try to interact over dinner or at breakfast, the tension between them had been impossible to ignore.

Aside from the spats between Mo and Kate, the second week in Hawaii had passed for Julia in a slow blur of unimportant moments. As much as she'd enjoyed relaxing by the pool and snorkeling in the ocean, she'd caught herself thinking of Reed nearly every free moment. She wanted to see her again so much that she had trouble concentrating on anything else. She was ready to be home. Or, more close to the truth, she was ready to see Reed again.

Reed had invited her over for dinner on Friday night—six long days away. Julia knew the invitation was for Friday so she could spend the weekend like they'd talked about. But if Reed had asked, she would have driven to Davis as soon as their plane landed.

Kate already had her headphones on and was staring out the narrow window at the gathering darkness. The red-eye would drop them in San Francisco early Sunday morning and then Julia would have the rest of the day to face the mountain of work emails she'd ignored. Reed would be a much nicer prospect. The flight attendant returned with her credit card, promising the drinks shortly, and then the pilot's voice buzzed in the speakers overhead.

Mo leaned back in her seat, sighing. "I don't want to go home."

"You aren't missing Tanya?"

Mo reached for her phone. She pulled up the text message screen and then clicked on Tanya's name and passed the phone to Julia. "We're in a fight at the moment. Remember that first time I went surfing with Alana? I forgot to call Tanya to say goodnight. I always call her before I fall asleep, but I was so tired that night…She decided I must have been sleeping with someone else if I didn't call her."

Julia scrolled through the texts. At first the idea of Mo cheating was only hinted at—the tone of the message was almost playful—but then when Mo had directly denied this, Tanya's texts took a different turn. She went on a rant, essentially blaming Kate for every failing in their relationship. The last text ended with Mo promising to drive straight from the airport to her place to talk.

"Oh jeez, Mo. She's pissed. What are you going to say?"

"I'm going to tell her the truth—for the fiftieth time. I don't cheat."

"I think that's only part of it. Tanya never actually accused you of cheating. She's worried that you aren't really in love with her."

"That's ridiculous. I've told her—"

Julia interrupted, "This isn't about how many times you've told her you love her." She glanced quickly over at Kate to make sure she was still wearing her headphones. In a lower voice she said, "She thinks you're in love with Kate. And clearly this trip to Hawaii has stirred up some of her insecurities. Honestly, if I was in a relationship with you, I'd be jealous of Kate too. You're a total flirt—don't try and argue that one—but it's different with Kate. It's not a game with Kate. You don't flirt the same way."

"Wait, now you're siding with Tanya because I don't flirt with Kate?" Mo shook her head. "Look, I know she's right about some of that stuff, but nothing's going on with me and Kate." Mo took her phone back without meeting Julia's eyes. She turned it off and dropped it in the seatback pocket. "I'll fix things with Tanya as soon as we get home. Work was so busy last month and then with this trip coming up…I didn't make time for us."

Julia wanted to tell Mo that it was too late. It was everything Tanya hadn't said. There'd been no "I love you" and toward the end of the texts, it was clear that she'd already pulled away.

Mo continued, "I told Alana I was going to come back to see her compete in her next surfing competition. And don't worry—I've already asked Tanya to get a week off in July so she can come too."

"July? That soon? After this trip I doubt my boss will ever give me another day off." Julia had successfully avoided thinking about work for days, but she'd have to face reality soon. "On the other hand, even if she did, I'm too broke to pay for another plane ticket."

"Which is why we should just stay here," Mo said.

* * *

By noon, Julia was halfway through her emails and on her third cup of coffee. Some of it was good news—quarter sales were up—but Val's firestorm of emails overwhelmed the few positive points. Her meetings in Tokyo hadn't gone well and with the changeover looming on the VP post in Chicago, Val had doubled down on butt kicking. Everyone from the PR secretary to the engineer assigned to head of product design had been advised they'd be working overtime. Unfortunately, Julia was no exception.

Julia was ready to put in the hours through the week, but no matter what Val said, she wasn't giving up next weekend with Reed. She'd sent Reed one text when the plane had landed, and it had taken all of her restraint not to ask if she could squeeze an extra hour between working out and sleep. As promised, Reed had sent Julia her schedule. Unfortunately, one look at the tightly organized chart made Julia's heart sink. All the colored rectangles arranged in thirty-minute increments made her realize that Reed's real life didn't have room for her. And as much as she wanted to see her now, she worried that any impromptu visit would only add stress.

Julia went to her kitchen to search for food. Canned minestrone wasn't her favorite, but the shelves were nearly empty and she'd cleaned out the fridge before the trip. She'd planned on hitting the grocery store on her return, but now that she was home and changed into her most comfortable sweats, she had no intentions of leaving—unless she could drive up to see Reed.

She turned on the stove and emptied the can into a pot. Twenty-four hours ago, soup would have been the last thing she wanted, but the balmy tropics had been replaced with the damp cold of her insulation-free apartment. The view through the window was a palette of grays and the San Francisco Bay seemed to be seeping in through the walls. When she was in the mood for fog, she loved the heavy stillness that came with it. But today the fact the sun refused to show itself seemed to make a point that vacation was over.

The doorbell rang as soon as she'd finished dishing the soup into a bowl. Guessing it was the neighbor returning her mail key, Julia left the soup on the counter and went to open the door.

"Tanya broke up with me." Mo's eyelids were puffy and she was wearing the same shorts and Hawaii surfing T-shirt she'd been in when Julia had waved good-bye to her at the airport.

"Oh, sweetie. I'm sorry." Julia pulled Mo through the doorway and into a hug. "When can I say that I've never liked her?"

"Right about now."

Mo let herself be led down the hall to the living room. She plopped down on the sofa and then grabbed Julia's quilt, wrapping it around her shoulders. "Why is your place always freezing?"

"The landlord controls the heat. Anyway cold air is supposed to strengthen your immune system." When Mo shot her an incredulous look, Julia added: "I read it somewhere, but it seemed bogus to me too. Kate would probably know."

Mo's smile was lukewarm at best. She rubbed her eyes and then rolled onto her side. "Not only did Tanya break up with me, I can't go home because Kate has Ethan over at our place."

"You could still go home."

"I don't want to see them together." She waved her finger in the air. "It's not what you think. I just don't want to see two people who love each other hanging on each other's arms and kissing—that's all."

"Well, in that case, you're safe here." She sighed. "Although, now that I think about it, I've never actually seen Kate kiss Ethan. Have you? I've seen her hold his hand one time, but that was when she was getting out of a cab."

"They'll look at each other and act all lovey. That'll be enough."

"Well, I promise not to act lovey with anyone." She sat down next to Mo. "I know you feel horrible right now, but I'm proud of you for skirting disaster."

"Proud? She broke up with me, remember?" Mo leaned back into the pillows. "I don't even care that she wants to keep the ring. But she better give me back my lucky Niners sweatshirt."

"I'm proud of you," Julia said again. "Because you could have changed to be the person Tanya wanted. But you didn't. You kept your values, you didn't sink to where she was to make her happy. And you feel like shit right now, but the truth is you were too good for her from the beginning."

Mo looked over at Julia, her dark eyes wet. "Thanks. I wish that were true but…"

"It is true. Do you want me to start listing all of the reasons you are the hottest, most eligible butch in San Francisco?"

"Maybe." Mo grinned, wiping away the tears in the corner of her eyes. "But after that, you're gonna have to tell me why you're sitting here instead of driving up to Davis to see Reed."

Julia wished she had a better answer than the truth. Unfortunately, Reed had made it clear she wasn't up for a real relationship and didn't have time for hookups that weren't scheduled.

Julia's cell phone rang and she glanced at the kitchen counter where she'd left it, not wanting to leave Mo. "That's probably Val wanting me to come into work. She's sent me about a dozen emails in the past hour."

"It's Sunday."

"Val doesn't believe in weekends." The ringing stopped when the call went to voice mail and Julia tried to ignore the guilt. She didn't need to be available for her boss on Sundays.

"Want a roommate? I don't think I can stay with Kate anymore."

"You can have the couch anytime you need it."

Mo leaned against Julia's shoulder and exhaled. "I don't want to hear Kate say 'I told you so' about Tanya."

"So don't tell her. At least not right away."

Mo squinted at the coffee table, clearly lost in her own thoughts. "I feel like I can't talk to her about stuff anymore. Things are different between us…"

"Something happened with you and Kate that last night I was with Reed, didn't it?" When Mo didn't volunteer an explanation, Julia pressed on, "I'll get it out of you eventually—you might as well tell me now."

"I screwed up."

"What's new?"

Mo rolled her eyes. "Thanks, Jules. Hit me when I'm down." She hesitated for a long minute before she said, "Kate tried…" She paused again. "You know, I don't think I'm up for talking about it now. Someday I'll tell you. Promise."

What had Kate tried to do? Julia had trouble not running through the possible options aloud. But that wouldn't help Mo. She set her hand on Mo's knee. "Okay. But you keep too much stuff inside. Sometimes you have to talk with someone."

"You're my someone," Mo said.

Julia's cell phone buzzed with a text and she looked over at the counter.

"Val again?"

"Possibly Reed." But Julia didn't budge. "She can wait."

Mo cocked her head. "Tell me that every fiber in your body doesn't want to jump up and go check that phone."

Julia sighed. "You know I can't say that."

"Go check your phone before I do. What if that was her calling you?" Mo continued, "And ask her about the kids."

"What about all that stuff you told Kate—how you can't ask a lesbian how they ended up with kids?"

"I changed my mind and started a little betting pool. My money is on her being a widow."

"Please don't tell me that you're serious. We are not betting on how Reed ended up with kids."

Mo scrunched up her face. "That ship already sailed."

"What do you mean?" Julia guessed the answer a second later. "You and Kate placed bets on how Reed ended up with kids?"

"Alana and her girlfriend are in on it too. Alana thinks Reed adopted the kids. Her girlfriend is betting on a surrogate—which I told her was ridiculous at first although the more that I think about it, she might be right. Kate is convinced Reed's got an ex-girlfriend with part custody. And she's sure the woman's crazy."

Julia shook her head. "And you're betting on her being a widow. Did you guys actually place money on this?"

"What bugs me about the widow story is that the one with the braids looks a little bit like Reed when she smiles." Mo pointedly ignored the question about money.

"Well, you may never know because I'm not asking." Julia was more determined than ever that it didn't matter how Reed had come to be a mom. "If Reed wants to tell me, she will."

"I'm running the background check then."

Julia pushed Mo's shoulder. "Don't you dare. After next weekend, who knows if I'll see her again." When Mo squinted at her, Julia continued, "From the beginning she told me she didn't have time for a relationship. We agreed to try it out, but I already know I'm going to want more than she wants. And I may have lied a little bit when I said I was okay with it only being about sex." Julia shifted closer to Mo. "Vacation's over and reality isn't looking so good."

"Tell me about it." Mo clasped her hand. "But what if she texted you asking you to drive up to Davis tonight? Would you go?"

"Tonight she doesn't get me," Julia said, snuggling closer. "My best friend needs me." Besides, it would only be about sex. Julia was torn between desperately wanting whatever part of Reed she could get and knowing she owed it to herself to ask for the whole package or not date at all.

Mo wrapped her arm around Julia. "Can we order a Hawaiian pizza? Tanya hated pineapple."

"Are you serious? Pineapple?" Julia shook her head. "Good thing you got out when you did."

CHAPTER FOURTEEN

At four o'clock on the dot, Julia closed her laptop. Five days had never dragged on so long, but she'd finally hit Friday afternoon. She skirted an attempt at chitchat over weekend plans with two colleagues in HR and then beat a path straight to the elevator. Instead of riding the train as she usually did, she'd taken her car, and for the first time all week, she was leaving the office before dark.

Unfortunately it was pouring and the street was already clogged with traffic. Holding her briefcase over her head, she stepped onto the sidewalk and hurried toward the parking garage. Maybe rain was a sign. If she was late for dinner because of a terrible commute…

The past week had been filled with mounting anxiety. Trouble was brewing in the Atlanta office and Val's tantrums about how the Chicago team was falling apart had only amped up, but work wasn't the issue. The real problem was Reed. On one hand, Julia wanted to have amazing sex and not think about anything else. On the other, she wanted to sign up for a real relationship and not settle for less. But then there was a sneaky third hand that kept bringing up the fact that Hawaii might have been a fluke. What if her old sex issues manifested now that they were back in the real world? The cartwheels her brain was doing over it all were making her dizzy.

What made it all worse was that she'd hardly heard from Reed that week. Since Reed had invited her to spend the weekend, there'd only been two phone calls. Julia had limited her own calls and texts in response, not wanting to seem needy, but then the silence between them made her all the more uncertain.

Though part of her desperately wanted to spend the weekend, Julia had avoided a direct commitment to anything beyond dinner. Mo argued that spending the night might actually help her figure things out, but Julia wasn't convinced. Until she was certain of what she wanted, she needed to keep some distance.

Her cell phone buzzed as soon as she reached her car. She climbed in, damp from the knees down after unsuccessfully dodging puddles on the crowded sidewalk, and read another text from Mo. Mo had been hitting up her phone all afternoon with everything from traffic reports to advice on picking up something fun for the bedroom.

Julia texted back: *No to lingerie and no to swinging by Good Vibes. Only staying for dinner. Remember?*

Mo: *Tomorrow you can tell me how you wish you'd brought lingerie.*

Cars sloshed through the city streets and when she hit the highway the traffic was no better. Julia turned on the radio, hoping to tune out her thoughts. The realization she'd be standing in front of Reed in a few hours had butterflies terrorizing her stomach. Should she hug her when she walked in the door? A kiss implied too much but a handshake would be awkward...

Reed's house was on a tree-lined street in the middle of town. The front yard was covered in leaves, two bicycles, and an assortment of other kid toys. The scene wasn't entirely unfamiliar. Reed's lanai had had the same feel: welcoming and messy at the same time.

Julia went up to the front door and raised the brass knocker, but before she rapped it, the red door swung open. Bryn hesitated for only a second and then lunged forward, wrapping her arms around Julia's legs. The ache she felt when Bryn hugged her was an unexpected curve ball. Since when had she even liked kids? *I can't already be attached to her kids.*

Bryn let go and beamed up at Julia. "I was watching you from the window because I wanted to scare you. Did I?"

"No." Julia smiled.

"I'll get you next time."

"You can try, but I'm really hard to scare."

Bryn pointed at Julia's car. "Is that your car? It looks really fancy."

"Fancy? Well, I guess so." Her shiny red Lexus with the dealer plates still on definitely stood out. Even soaked in rain, the car was gorgeous. She'd splurged with her end-of-year bonus and loved everything about the car. But suddenly it looked a bit ostentatious parallel parked between a scratched-up minivan and an old Honda. Julia bit her lip, wondering what Reed would think.

"Can I ride in it sometime?"

"Sure, but we'd have to put your car seat in there..."

"Mom's really good at that," Bryn said. "My car seat's pink and Carly's is blue. We got to pick our favorite colors."

Before Julia could say anything more, Reed's voice came from down the hallway: "Hey, guys, I thought we were going to try and pick up these toys before Julia came. Who took out the Hungry Hippos game? There are little marbles all over the place."

Julia's heart leapt up to her throat. Hearing Reed's voice was enough to make the blood rush to her cheeks and send the rest of her body to cloud nine. She was going to have to stay focused. *No matter how good she looks, you are not spending the night.*

"That was me," Bryn whispered to Julia. "I wanted to play Hungry Hippos with you."

"I bet you're good at Hungry Hippos," Julia said. Playing with the kids would be a good diversion. Maybe she could avoid being alone with Reed until she regained her sanity.

"Really good." Bryn's dimples appeared. "Julia's here," she hollered. "And she wants to play Hungry Hippos!"

Reed came into view suddenly at the end of the hall. She was wearing a button-down collared shirt with a tie. Her slacks were tailored perfectly. The tie alone convinced Julia that her logical mind was going to have a tough fight over her body's desire tonight.

"Hey," Reed said, smiling warmly as she came up behind Bryn. She opened the door all the way and Julia stepped inside.

Before she could decide on a hug or handshake, Bryn bounced between her and Reed, chattering about all the rules of the hippo game. All Julia could do was smile briefly at Reed as she tried to pay attention to Bryn.

"Sweetie, why don't you go set it up?" Reed said. "We'll only have about ten minutes to play."

"I get to be the red hippo," Bryn said, darting down the hall. "It's my turn this time."

"Talk to Carly about that."

When she'd gone, Reed closed the door and turned to Julia. "Thanks for driving up in the rain. I wondered if you'd cancel…"

"It wasn't a bad drive," Julia said. But she wondered if Reed sensed that she'd nearly backed out for other reasons.

"Can I take your coat?"

Julia unbuttoned the navy pea coat and felt Reed's eyes on her. When she looked up, Reed quickly glanced at the floor. But it was too late. Julia had seen Reed's desire and she couldn't ignore the heat that rushed through her body in response.

"I like your dress," Reed said, awkward now.

"Thank you."

Reed took her coat, brushing against Julia's arm as she did and then apologizing a moment later. The touch might have been accidental, but she didn't move to hang up the coat and instead held Julia's eyes.

"Hawaii feels like a long time ago," Reed said. "It's really good to see you again."

Julia's heart was thumping hard, and she didn't dare take her eyes off the pea coat still hanging in Reed's hand. Reed stepped forward and met her lips. What the hell had she been thinking? No way was she leaving tonight. She moved into the kiss, and Reed's arms wrapped around her.

Maybe this was only Reed's release from a long week. But did her reasons matter? After all, Julia was getting something out of the deal too. Simply feeling Reed's body close to hers, she was nearly certain her old sex issues were truly a thing of the past. Reed's kiss was a reminder of everything they'd done— and everything she still wanted to do. To think that earlier she'd debated canceling altogether…Thank God she'd packed an in-case-you're-too-horny-to-leave bag. She only opened her eyes when Reed pulled back.

"It's good to see you. I already said that, didn't I?"

Julia smiled. "You did."

Reed eyed the coat in her arms and said, "So…the babysitter's not here yet. We have a little time before our dinner reservations for that game of Hungry Hippos."

"Oh good," Julia said. "I didn't want to miss out on the chance to be a marble-eating hippo."

"Bryn's been obsessed with that game. We've played it every night since we got back from Hawaii. She rediscovered it under the bed in her room when we were unpacking." Reed paused.

"I probably shouldn't admit this, but I've been nervous about tonight. I kept wondering if it was going to be different now that we're both back in our real worlds…"

"I've been prepping myself on not overthinking this," Julia said.

"Is that working?"

Julia laughed. "Not well."

"Maybe we can help each other out." Reed grinned. "How's this? 'Thanks for coming over. You look even more amazing than I remembered.'"

"Nope—that didn't help." Julia smiled. "Try again."

But Reed looked more embarrassed with that admission. When she turned to hang up the coat in a hall closet, Julia reached out to caress the low of her back, surprising even herself. Five minutes with Reed and she'd lost her mind. But she didn't move her hand. Reed glanced over her shoulder, catching Julia's eye. She fumbled for a hanger as Julia's hand strayed up her back to her shoulders. The muscles of Reed's back were firm, tensed by the touch, and Julia could feel the warmth of her skin through the shirt.

Emboldened, Julia stepped forward as soon as Reed turned back around to face her. She ran her finger down Reed's tie. "We could skip dinner."

"Something else you'd rather do?" Reed asked.

Julia nodded and Reed swallowed hard. Although Reed kept her hands at her side, Julia could feel the heat building between them. It was easy to reach for Reed's belt. Reed kept her gaze on Julia's eyes, however.

"This is one of those times when you'd pay a babysitter double if they showed up early."

Julia smiled. She ran a finger over the buckle and then undid it. Reed was motionless, watching her. Any lingering uncertainty about what she wanted from tonight was gone now. But when she found herself wanting to unzip Reed's pants, she knew she needed to stop. The entryway had gotten way too warm.

Bryn called Julia's name and Reed looked down at Julia's hand, still on her belt. She didn't step back, but she made a soft whimper.

"I think we're wanted for that game of Hungry Hippos," Julia said.

"Some days it's hard being a parent."

"I bet." Julia left Reed to fix her belt and followed the sound of Bryn's voice. From the entryway, a hall led past a messy front room with toys scattered all about and a staircase to a second floor. Despite the mess, the house itself was as inviting on the inside as it had been from the curb. It was an older Craftsman but clearly renovated with a loving hand.

The hallway opened up to the kitchen, where Julia had to pause for a moment. From the expansive counters, custom cabinets, and vaulted ceilings with overhead fans and skylights to the windows above the sink and the breakfast nook, a six-burner gas range and high-end appliances that looked unused, she could have spent the evening admiring every nook and cranny.

"Julia—do you want to be the green hippo or the blue hippo?"

The kitchen was open to the living room where Bryn and Carly were waiting. Two big couches faced each other and a rug covered with puzzle pieces and more toys filled the space between. A fireplace with a crackling log took up the far corner.

Bryn stood up and came to lead Julia over to the game. A shy Carly only briefly made eye contact as Julia greeted her. At Bryn's request, Julia sat next to her. When Reed claimed the hippo on Julia's left, she knew it was going to be difficult to concentrate on the game.

The babysitter arrived after the third round and Julia smiled at how fast Reed jumped up to get the door. She gave the excuse of dinner reservations, but Julia guessed at her thoughts as they headed out and Reed caught her hand, pulling her into another kiss.

"You're terrible at Hungry Hippos," Julia said.

They cut through the soggy backyard to a detached garage and Reed held the door open for her. "I was letting you win."

"You're terrible at lying too."

Reed laughed. She hit the unlock button and then went to open the passenger door. Julia glanced at the car. Unfortunately, Reed noticed. "What?"

"Nothing." She went to the passenger side and tried to slip past Reed. Reed had her hand on the door still, partly blocking her way.

"Who's the terrible liar now?"

Julia laughed. "No, really, it's nothing. I just didn't picture you as a Volvo driver."

"Why not?"

"I don't know. It's just…it's such a mom car."

Reed grinned. "Guess what? I'm a mom."

"Yeah, I know but…" Julia shook her head. "Okay, don't take this the wrong way, but you seem cooler than a Volvo wagon."

"Cooler?" Reed raised her eyebrows. "Don't take this the wrong way, but you seem less shallow than a Lexus."

"Take that back. I love my car," Julia said, laughing as she tried to swat Reed's chest. Reed dodged her hand and then caught her arm and pulled her close. She kissed her with all the desire that she'd had in the entryway earlier, and Julia found herself wishing the garage was a little warmer. She wouldn't mind if Reed decided to take her right there.

But Reed pulled back and said, "Volvos have amazing safety ratings. And this one gets great mileage. Plus it came in silver so you can barely tell when it's dirty." She leaned close and pecked Julia's cheek. "Now get in my cool mom car so we can go eat."

Julia hardly noticed the drive. Reed's hand was on her thigh as soon as they pulled onto the freeway and stayed there until they parked. It was a short walk to the restaurant, a hole-in-the-wall place that only had a handful of tables but amazing smells coming from the kitchen. Julia's stomach stirred to life as they waited to be seated. She wanted Reed, but dinner first wasn't a bad idea. Then she could have energy for a late night.

When a server came to seat them, Reed joked with him and Julia wondered if she'd been to the place before. She didn't want to ask. It was definitely the type of restaurant for a date, not a family meal, and if this was part of Reed's routine with the women she met up with for sex, she didn't want to know.

It wasn't until after they'd ordered that Reed said, "Is everything okay?"

Julia hesitated answering. "I wanted to see you way too much tonight."

"And that's a problem?"

She hesitated. "Bordering on a problem, yes."

"Do you want to talk about it?"

"No. You're supposed to be helping me not overthink this, remember?" Julia clinked her glass against Reed's and then took a long sip. Red wine wasn't usually her drink of choice, but Reed had ordered it and this one slid down easily. She looked everywhere but at Reed.

Reed reached across the table and touched the back of Julia's hand. "It's the Volvo, right?"

Julia laughed as she shook her head.

"Phew. I thought that might be one of your deal breakers." Reed pulled her hand back, grinning. "Do you want to play a game?"

"What kind of game?"

"You ask me whatever you want to know—no restrictions or judgments on the questions—but you don't get to respond to my answer and I can't give any explanations. No follow-up questions either. Then it's my turn to ask you something."

"Sounds dangerous," Julia said. "Any question?"

Reed nodded. She took another sip of her wine. "You start."

Julia took a deep breath. She knew she might regret asking this but…"How many women have you brought here?"

"You're the first," Reed answered immediately. "Are you sure you want to date someone with kids?"

Julia opened and closed her mouth. She hadn't expected Reed to ask that, and she was still trying to digest Reed's answer to her question. "No. I'm not sure. But I thought we were only keeping this to sex anyway."

Reed slid her finger down the stem of her wineglass. She looked over at a couple seated a few tables away from them. Julia's stomach had clenched into a tight fist.

"I want to say more. No explanations makes this hard," Julia said.

Reed nodded. "Your turn to ask a question."

"Do you still want me to spend the night?"

"Is that a follow-up question? Technically follow-up questions are off-limits."

Julia sighed. "I'm starting to realize what you meant when you said all doctors were big nerds."

Reed grinned and then said, "I want you to spend the weekend."

"Okay, I want to go back to your question about kids. I already lost this game anyway."

The waiter came to take their order, and Julia felt as if she were sitting on pins and needles despite the fact her chair was incredibly comfortable. The whole place was perfect. Reed was perfect. Unfortunately.

As soon as the waiter left, Julia said, "I want to explain my answer."

"Your answer was honest."

"Yeah. It was honest. But the thing is, your kids are the first ones I've ever gotten to know. And I like your kids," Julia said. "I don't want to get attached if we're keeping this casual. It's not fair to them or me. If this is only about sex—"

"What if I'm not sure about that part?" Reed paused. "Can we have something that's more than friends but isn't a commitment?"

Julia wanted to say yes. That would give her an excuse for staying the whole weekend. "I don't know."

Reed picked up her glass and took a slow sip. "Me neither. I thought maybe you were upset after our last conversation—you know, about keeping this casual. No commitments can make it sound like I don't want more from you. That isn't it. But I know I can't offer much more than a fun weekend every once in a while. Or a fun night if we keep the kids out of it."

"Some things you aren't sure about until you sign up." Julia reached for her water glass. She'd drunk too much of the wine already. "I think it's your turn to ask a question."

"Ever wear handcuffs?"

Julia nearly choked on the water. She shook her head and then caught Reed's smile. "I'll get you back for that one." Thinking quickly, she asked, "Favorite toy?"

"Oh, that's a good one." Reed didn't act the least bit fazed by the question and only seemed to want to give it serious thought. "I've got a vibrator I love, but when I have a reason to wear the strap-on...I guess if I have to pick a favorite, I'd go with the strap-on."

Julia could feel her own blush. She'd intended to make Reed squirm, but the question had backfired. Reed was entirely confident with sex. Julia wasn't certain if that made her own feelings of inadequacy better or worse. "Have you worn handcuffs?"

"It's not your turn to ask," Reed said. She winked and added, "But I'll give you a freebie. Yes. I like bondage, but only when I'm comfortable with someone. It's been a while."

"Now that's an image I want to think about," Julia said.

Reed smiled. "Maybe sometime you could do more than think about it."

Reed tied up and entirely at Julia's disposal was a fantasy she'd used more than once in the past week to get to sleep. Of course she'd also turned the fantasy around—the idea of Reed tying her up was as terrifying as it was arousing.

"I've got a whole box full of things you could go through sometime," Reed tempted.

"Tonight?"

"Not tonight. I already have plans for you." Reed finished her wine and leaned back in her seat. "Unless you decide to go home after dinner."

"I want to stay for the weekend." The doubt had gone. Reed was exactly what she wanted. All she needed to do was keep her head out of this.

As soon as they stepped out of the restaurant, Reed clasped her hand and she kept hold of it while they walked. Julia felt disoriented, not remembering where they'd parked or even knowing exactly where they were. She'd been distracted on the drive here, but now she was hyperaware of every detail—of how warm Reed's hand was, of how close she stood when they stopped at a traffic light, of how the cool air felt against her cheeks...The rain had let up and the clouds were clearing overhead, but the city lights made it impossible to see any stars.

"Where are we?"

"The Capitol Building's over there." Reed pointed down a long city block. "And the rose garden's over there. I used to live a few blocks from here over by the hospital."

Sacramento. Of course. Julia let Reed open her car door again. She wasn't going to stop her from doing anything she wanted to do tonight. The realization that she wanted Reed in control wasn't new, but it was strange how easy it was to relax and let it happen. She'd never let any of her past dates open a car door for her. Then again, she'd never dated anyone who took charge quite so well.

Reed pulled out of the parking spot and zipped into traffic. When her hand settled on the gear shaft, Julia felt a stirring between her legs that was both ridiculous and impossible to ignore. She loved Reed's hands. That was the root of the problem. Another complicating factor was that Reed handled the car exactly the way she'd handled Julia's body. Her movements were smooth, no mistakes, and there was no doubting she was focused on the road even as she kept up a conversation about music. She'd asked Julia to pick the radio station and then asked about her favorite musicians. Julia tried to keep up with the questions, tried to maintain her side of the conversation, but all she wanted was for Reed to reach across the console and slide a hand up her thigh.

Twenty minutes later, they pulled into Reed's garage. Reed led the way through the backyard, passing a swing set, a sand box, and an assortment of tricycles and scooters the twins had probably outgrown, before they reached the back door. Through the French doors, Julia could see the living room where the babysitter was settled on the couch watching TV. The kids seemed to be already in bed.

Julia waited in the living room while Reed paid the babysitter and then walked her to the front door. She looked like a college student—a much too attractive college student— and was annoyingly sweet to Reed. *Oh jeez, I'm jealous of the babysitter.* To stop herself from eavesdropping, Julia occupied herself with picking up the pieces from the Hungry Hippo game. The little red marbles had rolled under the coffee table and across the room. Knowing Bryn, there was a good chance she'd been throwing them on purpose.

When Reed returned, she switched off the TV and then came over to help finish picking up the game. Julia closed the lid and held the box out for Reed. Instead of taking the box, Reed leaned in for a kiss. Soft lips met hers and then Reed pressed in with an intention that left Julia breathless. Reed pulled away too soon. Again. She only seemed to give enough of herself to remind Julia of her thirst—not enough to quench it.

"I have to go check on the girls. Sometimes they're only pretending to be asleep when they have a babysitter."

Julia followed Reed down the hallway and then up to the second floor. The twins shared a room and she waited in the doorway as Reed went to check on them. Both were sleeping soundly in the two side-by-side beds. Reed switched off a light someone had left on and then kissed each forehead before pulling both blankets up to their chins. She closed the door carefully and then turned to Julia.

"Do you want to go back downstairs?"

Julia shook her head. She glanced down the hall at a closed door and guessed it was the master bedroom. "Your room?"

"If we go in there I won't be able to concentrate on a conversation—if that's what you were hoping for."

"I like conversations," Julia said. "But I think we did that already."

Reed smiled, stepping closer. "It's been hard waiting these two weeks…"

"Tell me about it. That's why I want to see your room."

Julia closed the distance to Reed's lips. She wanted to strip Reed—tie first. They kissed the length of the hallway with Julia only managing to loosen Reed's tie before they reached the bedroom door. Reed had her distracted. She'd unzipped Julia's dress and her warm hands had slipped under the fabric to move up and down her back. By the time they'd crossed the threshold, Julia was ready for Reed's hands to move lower on her body.

Reed closed the bedroom door, kicked off her shoes, and started undoing her belt. She caught Julia watching her and stopped. "Am I going too fast?"

"Not fast enough."

For a split second, Julia was embarrassed by her answer, but then she saw Reed's face—a hint of a smile and then the longing in her eyes. She pulled Julia into another kiss, her chest pressed close against hers.

When they got to the bed, Reed let go of Julia's hand long enough to push the comforter down. She'd dropped her pants along with the belt but was still wearing the tie and her pressed white shirt was still perfectly buttoned.

Julia smiled. "I like your outfit."

"I like yours better." Reed slid her hand up Julia's leg, pushing the dress up to reveal the red silk underwear. One fingertip traced the edge of the silk. When her fingertip came to the middle seam, Julia held her breath. If Reed wanted to push the fabric aside and dip inside she wouldn't resist. She was having trouble waiting as it was. But instead, Reed traced the curve of Julia's underwear up the other leg hole.

Tonight she didn't want foreplay. She wanted Reed to take her hard and fast. She started to take off her own dress and Reed caught her hand. Julia moaned softly. "Please?"

The word slipped out but before she could be embarrassed, Reed responded with a half smile that made Julia realize it was exactly what she wanted to hear. Reed had the dress off a moment later and then ran her hands up and down Julia's arms, kissing from her bra strap to her lips. Julia was too turned on to wait much longer. She kicked off her heels and sank down on the bed but Reed only looked down at her.

Julia shifted to sit on the edge, wondering if that was what Reed wanted. Reed watched her, licking her lips. When Julia parted her legs, Reed swallowed and stepped toward her. She pushed Julia's knees further apart and then moved between her legs. Kissing her again, she slipped her hand around to unhook Julia's bra.

Reed murmured her satisfaction as she cupped Julia's breasts. She plied her nipples, rolling the tips between her fingers only hard enough for Julia to want a little more pressure as she found Julia's lips. Their kiss deepened and Julia longed for Reed to reach between her legs.

But then a moment later Reed was guiding her up to the pillows as she moved on top of her. With every kiss, Julia wondered if she'd come before Reed even touched her clit.

When Reed finally reached between Julia's legs, her satisfied moan turned Julia on even more. As Reed's fingertip brushed over her swollen clit, Julia silently begged her to push inside. She circled and stroked, bringing Julia close but not giving her the satisfaction of what she wanted. "I want something inside," Julia finally asked.

"I know you do," Reed returned, still holding back.

"Please," Julia murmured again. When Reed only stroked her clit, Julia met her gaze. She'd beg if that was what Reed wanted. "Please...I need you to fuck me...Please."

Reed's eyes darkened. "That's better."

Julia couldn't hold back a moan when Reed entered her. Pressing against Reed's hand, she clutched the sheets, enjoying the pulse of pleasure mixed with the pain. Reed was clearly turned on by the power play, while Julia realized in that same moment that playing submissive was her natural inclination. Giving in to Reed's dominance only added to her own bliss. She'd say please to anything that made her feel this good.

Reed moved so Julia's leg was between hers and started grinding on her thigh. With every thrust, her thumb raked across Julia's clit. The roughness of it and the intensity of Reed's desire was exactly what she wanted. A climax was starting and she didn't try to slow it down. She didn't need to. Reed wanted her like this.

When the orgasm caught her, she clutched Reed's arm, desperate to keep her hand in place. Reed's thumb pressed into her swollen clit and she couldn't hold back. As she cried out, her nails sank into Reed's wrist.

Reed held her, one arm wrapped around her back and the other still between her legs, until she finally relaxed. Julia dropped back onto the pillows, her whole body tingling and her mouth slack. Reed kissed her cheek and then her neck. Julia couldn't move her lips to kiss her in return.

Slowly she became aware of the fact she was lying diagonally across the bed. Reed had stretched across the length of her body and her weight was so satisfying Julia didn't want to move. She ran her hand up Reed's leg to her boxers.

"You're still dressed," Julia said. "How'd that happen again?"

Reed shifted onto her side and met Julia's gaze. "Do you want me to take off my clothes?"

"Can you keep the tie on?" If Julia wasn't still under the effects of the orgasm, she was certain she would have stopped at that. But now she was ready to voice her fantasy aloud: "I know you said you had your own plan, but..." Okay. Maybe she wasn't quite ready. She couldn't bring herself to ask out loud for the strap-on as much as her body was begging her to.

"But?"

"I've been thinking about what you said at dinner. Well, I was thinking about it before then too..."

"Thinking about what?" Reed had already started unbuttoning her shirt. She slipped the tie off her collar and then pulled off the shirt. The tie hung loose around her neck and down her naked chest.

Julia's words caught in her throat. Reed leaned close and kissed her. She wanted her to guess what she wanted without having to ask. One kiss and then another. How was Reed so good at this? Must be practice. Lots of practice. Julia wished that thought hadn't crossed her mind. Yes, of course, it was obvious Reed was better at sex than she was—but who wasn't? And what difference did it make if she'd had more partners or more sex?

Reed pulled away from her lips. She stared at Julia for a moment and then drew a line across her brow. "You okay?"

Julia nodded. What had happened? A minute ago she'd nearly asked for a strap-on and now she was thinking she had no business being in Reed's bed at all. Reed could have anyone she wanted. It wouldn't have been hard at all for her to catch someone more attractive, someone more adventurous, or at least someone who was competent in bed.

"Should we talk?"

Julia shook her head.

"Still trying to leave the thinking for later?" When Julia didn't respond, Reed continued, "The thing is, I am really wet. Almost embarrassingly wet. And my clit needs a little something."

"Embarrassingly wet?" That was enough to rally Julia's resolve. If part of why she was here was to get better at sex, she couldn't let her mind get in the way.

"It's a problem," Reed said, reaching between her legs.

"I want you to wear your strap-on," Julia blurted out.

Reed grinned. "That's what you were thinking about earlier?"

"All through dinner."

"And now you tell me." Reed leaned over Julia and kissed her again.

"Please?"

Reed shook her head. "Tomorrow."

Julia almost argued, but Reed caught her hand and brought it up to her lips. She kissed her fingertips and then guided Julia down to her groin.

Reed moaned when Julia pressed between her legs. She was wet, exactly as promised, and her clit was as hard as one of the marbles downstairs. As Julia compared it, she knew she'd never be able to pick up a marble again without thinking about Reed.

Reed moved against Julia's hand, murmuring as she did, "Tomorrow I can show you the box I keep in the closet." Her eyes closed and her lips parted. "Keep doing that to my clit...I have handcuffs, silk ties...Cocks in about every size you could want. Lots of vibrators. And rope if you're into that."

"Maybe." Julia didn't want to admit she'd never tried any of it. She wanted to start with the strap-on, but the idea of being tied up was appealing too. She circled the edges of Reed's center and then back to her clit, dragging a finger over it.

Julia stroked back and forth, wondering if this was what she'd meant when she'd told her to keep doing what she'd been doing and then wondering how long she should keep it up. A familiar twinge of uncertainty made her fingers unsteady. She'd never gotten Sheryl off this way, but Reed had moved so her center was squarely on Julia's hand and she was grinding faster. Still, her fingers were uncoordinated, and she wanted to tell Reed she wasn't good at finger sex despite that one night in Hawaii and also she had no clue on how to use toys with someone else. But then she noticed the expression on Reed's face. Julia held her hand in place and Reed stroked over it a few more times before she climaxed.

It was almost too easy. *But damn did it feel good. There's no way she's faking either*, Julia thought, unable to hide her smile of satisfaction. She loved how Reed didn't hold back the sounds of her pleasure.

Reed lay on her for a minute, recovering, and then when her breathing slowed, she rolled off. Julia tried to relax too, but she knew sleep wasn't coming for her.

"It's not that I don't want to play with toys," Reed said, several minutes later, her voice relaxed with the afterglow. "I used to be really into all of that. But tonight I wanted your hand."

"I noticed." Julia turned on her side and moved her hand over Reed's chest. "Can I tell you a secret?"

Reed nodded. Her eyes were closed, which made it easier to go on. Julia exhaled. "You're the only person I've ever gotten off."

"I don't believe you."

"I'm serious. You should talk to my ex-girlfriends."

Reed opened her eyes and shifted onto her elbow. "I think we already established that you are not terrible at sex. Did you notice how fast I came?"

"I love that about you. It's a big confidence boost for me."

"Confidence boost?" Reed laughed again. "Happy to oblige."

"This is going to sound weird, but I want to see your toys before we use them. So I'm not nervous." And then of course she was nervous. But she pressed on anyway. "I've never been with someone who I felt comfortable with trying things like that. Don't judge."

"No judging," Reed said. "But…you know it's possible your exes were the issue, not you."

Julia shook her head. "It's all me. Fortunately, you're good enough at this for both of us."

"This isn't all me," Reed argued.

Before Julia could explain exactly why it *was* all her, Reed had gotten out of bed. She opened the closet door and then stepped inside, half closing the door to get something from a shelf on the other side that Julia couldn't see. A line of shirts filled one rack and pants half-filled the other. The closet was one of the most ordered she'd seen. No mess in sight. Even the shoes were all on a rack.

Julia closed her eyes. Reed had her life together, that was clear. Which was why this worked. Reed took care of details and didn't expect her to do anything on her own. They weren't making love; they had an arrangement for sex. At least one benefit was that she could be honest.

The room was warm and she felt perfectly comfortable lying on the bed nearly naked without any blankets. She reached between her legs and felt the wetness there. Although the orgasm had been exactly what she needed, she wanted more. She'd have to wait until tomorrow. Tomorrow. No way was she leaving tonight. That plan had gone out the window. Julia eyed the trail of her clothing from where her dress had landed to her heels. She liked seeing her mess in Reed's space. Spreading her legs, she fingered her folds, thinking of what she'd let Reed do to her. She stopped as soon as the closet door opened again.

Reed came back to the bed. Julia heard her footsteps, then felt the mattress give as she climbed into bed, but she only opened her eyes when she set a wooden box alongside her.

"Looks like a pirate treasure box."

Reed chuckled. "Close."

Julia sat up and eyed the contents. She picked up a dildo, dark burgundy and ribbed with fake veins that she found herself tracing. The shaft was longer and wider than some she'd seen. She found another smaller version under this one and then a leather harness. "This harness is nice."

"I like it too," Reed said. She picked up a bullet vibe. "This goes at the base of the little cock. The bigger one doesn't have a spot for a vibrator. I have a midsized one somewhere in here that has a life of its own...the more you stroke it, the more it changes up the speed." Reed sorted until she found what she was looking for and held up a different dildo. "If you're new to this, we'll probably start with something like this. You can turn it off so it doesn't start vibrating until you need it. And it goes in easier than the bigger size, but it's not going to slip out like that little one. Judging from how much you like my fingers inside you, I think you can take this."

Reed was so matter-of-fact that Julia decided to search through the rest of the box. She picked up something that looked like a cheerleader's pom-pom crossed with a whip.

"Flogger. Gotta be in the right mood for that." Reed picked up a pair of velvet handcuffs. "Maybe you'd like these? My suggestion with all of this is to start tame and only try what you're ready for. It's more fun that way." She held up two metal pieces that Julia recognized as nipple clamps and then a handful of scarves in different colors next. "Or we jump right in and go straight for the tie downs…"

"What's in here?" Julia had pulled out a small, unmarked box that was still taped as if no one had opened it yet.

"Um, yeah. That…" Reed grinned. "That's a butt plug. I was going to take that out of the box, but I couldn't find it when I was in the closet looking for it."

"I was wondering why you were in there for so long." This time, Julia laughed. "It looks new. Have you tried it?"

"No." Reed scratched her head, further messing up her already messed-up hair. Julia loved the look. The sheepish expression on her face was endearing. "It's been on my to-do list."

"I want a peek at that list." Julia smiled. "What about everything else in here?"

"I've tried everything else," Reed admitted. "And don't worry, I'm ridiculously clean with all of that. Everything gets sanitized or I use a condom."

"Why am I not surprised?"

Reed leaned back on the pillows, eyeing the mess on the bed and then reaching for Julia's hand. "The thing is, I like vanilla too. We don't have to do anything crazy."

Julia gathered up the toys and placed everything back in the box. If this was only about sex, she was going to learn all she could. "I think I need to try crazy."

Reed pulled her close and kissed her lips gently. The fire was gone, but the desire was still there. "Then we'll start tomorrow. Tonight I just want to hold you."

CHAPTER FIFTEEN

Mornings are supposed to feel exactly like this, Julia thought. The house was still quiet and Reed's arm was draped over her. Reed was still naked and pressed up against her back—a perfect combination of warmth and strength.

A thin light slanted in around the edges of the shutters. She had to pee, but she stayed put for another minute. The room smelled of sex. Reed had made her orgasm more than once. But the feeling of Reed climaxing on her hand was better than all of that. If only what they'd done last night could be every night...

When a knock sounded on the door, Reed shifted away from Julia and sat up. She rubbed her eyes and carefully climbed out of bed, probably hoping to let Julia sleep. By the time she'd reached the door, she'd pulled on a shirt and boxers. Bryn was standing on the other side, bouncing on her toes. Reed held her finger up to her lips to stop Bryn from asking whatever question she was dying to ask and then slipped out of the room. The door closed softly behind her, and Julia felt the first swell of regret.

Even if last night had been perfect, this wasn't the start of a real relationship. She had to be okay with that.

* * *

"When are we going to the park?"

Bryn had asked the same question five times in a row, and still Reed only smiled and said, "Soon, kid. Are your shoes on yet?"

Carly was standing by the door with her shoes and her jacket on. She was fussing with a bicycle helmet but refused any help. Reed checked her phone—she'd done so more than once, apologizing when she did and murmuring that it was something to do with work—and then glanced at Julia. "You ready?"

"Ready."

Getting out the door had taken a little under an hour, but Reed had warned her the kids would be difficult the morning after a babysitter. Disrupted routines...They'd been a disaster all through breakfast, culminating with Bryn throwing her bowl of fruit at Carly and then a piece of buttered toast was hurled in retaliation. Ear-piercing screams had erupted a moment later. At one point, Julia was certain Reed was going to lose it and yell, but she managed to keep her cool and eventually she had both kids cleaning up the mess of fruit and toast. It was only then that Julia wondered if there was ever another parent involved. She didn't ask, of course, but more questions came to mind. Did Reed ever get a break? Did she have help in the beginning and then that other mom bailed?

"The park's not far from here," Reed said. The two girls were pulling their bikes onto the sidewalk and jabbering about who was faster at putting on a helmet. Carly had hers fastened before they'd left the house, though in Bryn's defense she'd taken a fraction of the time getting hers on when they stepped outside.

The girls biked ahead of them and Julia fell into step next to Reed. She was surprised when Reed reached out and caught her hand but guarded her face from showing any reaction. "I love your neighborhood. All these old houses and the big trees…"

Reed glanced up at one of the trees. "It'll be even nicer in a week or two when the new leaves come out. Spring is gorgeous here. Unfortunately summer lasts forever."

"You don't like summer?"

"I love fall," Reed answered. "Bryn and Carly—stop at the corner, you two. We have to cross the street together." She looked over at Julia. "You're a little quiet this morning. Everything okay?"

"Everything's good." Partly that was true. She had nothing to complain about. "I like that you check in with me. You know, make sure I'm not freaking out."

Reed eyed her again. "Turns out I want you to be having a good time." She looked like she was going to say more, but before she could, the kids reached the end of the sidewalk and they had to jog to catch up. Both of the bikes had training wheels so they couldn't get too far ahead, but Bryn didn't seem inclined to wait long before crossing the street.

Four blocks from Reed's house was Central Park. It was a block wide and two or three blocks long and half of the space was taken up by an open grass area and a playground. The other half was a farmers market. When they reached the playground, the bikes were shoved against the fence and both kids tore off in different directions—Carly toward the swings and Bryn toward the slide. The playground was fenced off, but with dozens of other kids darting about it was nearly impossible to keep track of both kids.

"Don't worry," Reed said. "I haven't lost them yet. I know that look of panic when you think you've got eyes on them and then they take off on you."

Reed sat down on the bench facing the slides and Julia settled in as well, leaving a space between them in case Reed wasn't comfortable being close in public. She tried to ignore the swell of happiness when Reed reached over to clasp her hand

and then shifted closer so there was no space. *Dammit. Why does this have to feel so perfect?*

Julia kept her gaze trained on the playground until she finally picked out Carly's blond braids on the kid climbing the monkey bars and then Bryn's yellow raincoat on the kid towering at the top of the slides. They'd switched places so quickly there was no way she'd keep track of them for long. Reed, however, was relaxed and staring up at a puffy white cloud passing overhead in an otherwise blue sky. Bryn had insisted on wearing the raincoat despite the clear forecast and Reed had only shrugged.

"You're good at parenting. I think I'd yell more if I was doing it alone," Julia said. "Not because I wanted to yell, but because I'd be trying to control them—watching Bryn ride her bike through those intersections while she was pretending she was a cowgirl with a bucking bronco was a little unnerving."

"Sometimes I yell. Not that it helps." Reed sighed. "Do you want kids?"

Julia hesitated. "I don't know. For the first time I'm thinking about it." That was the honest answer, she realized, but if anyone had asked her a month ago, "absolutely not" would have been the truth.

"When we first met I thought you weren't a kid person. But you're getting more and more comfortable around them." Reed paused. "At the restaurant last night I asked you a question that wasn't fair."

"What do you mean?"

"The one about the kids…"

"I do like your kids."

"I can tell." Reed paused. "Usually by now I've gotten the question of why I decided to have kids. It doesn't take people long to start wondering. I figured you'd ask last night."

"I feel like that question is off limits."

"But asking about my favorite toy was fair game?" Reed grinned.

"Julia, look!"

Julia followed the direction of the voice hollering for her and spotted Bryn balanced on the top of a climbing structure. She lifted one foot up in the air, as if trying to tempt gravity. Julia started then, surprised Reed hadn't already jumped to her feet. "Shouldn't we go catch her?"

"She'll be fine," Reed said. In fact, a moment later, Bryn had slipped off, caught herself and was climbing again. "That one I don't worry about…Carly's a different story."

Carly appeared, as if on cue, at the edge of the fence. She waved to get their attention, then slipped out between the rails of the gate and raced over to them. Before Julia had time to register what was happening, Carly was climbing into her lap.

Once she got herself settled, she looked over her shoulder at Julia and asked, "Why aren't you guys playing?"

"Grown-ups like to sit on benches," Reed said.

Carly squinted at Reed. "That's boring."

"Not if you like the person you're sitting with," Julia said.

"You like my mom." Carly giggled. "When we were in Hawaii I saw you kiss her."

"I do like your mom." Julia didn't dare look over at Reed. She wasn't ready to tell her how much directly. "But you can like someone and be happy sitting on a bench with them even if they aren't someone you kiss." She wrapped her arms around Carly and hugged her. "I like you too."

Carly tucked her feet under her knees, pulling all of her small frame into the lap she'd claimed before relaxing back against Julia's chest. "Did you see me on the monkey bars? When I was three I couldn't reach the bars at all. Now I can go all the way across."

"I saw you. It was impressive. I don't think I'd make it across."

Carly looked over her shoulder at Julia. "Really? Mom can. She's really good. Maybe she'd teach you."

"Carly! Come push me on the merry-go-round!" Bryn hollered, hopping up and down on the red metal rungs.

"I get to ride too," Carly hollered back. "We have to take turns pushing." She hopped off Julia's lap and dashed off to join her sister.

"She's not like that with most people," Reed said. "Bryn will strike up a friendship with anyone. But Carly's different. I haven't ever seen her climb into someone's lap—except mine."

"I was shy like that when I was little," Julia admitted. She watched as Carly pushed the merry-go-round and Bryn spun round. "I've been wanting to ask about them—about why you decided to have kids—but I didn't want to pry. It's not that I'm not interested in that part of you. I know how important they are to you."

Reed shifted on the bench. "My sister called me up one night. I hadn't heard from her in months...I figured she wanted money. McKenna was always asking for money. This time it wasn't about that.

"She told me she was pregnant. Eight months. She'd been kicked out of the hotel room she was living in and was staying in some friend's car. I told her she could move in with me—gave her my address and wired her bus money. She never showed up. I called her, sent her texts, tried everyone who'd ever known her...Then a few weeks later I got a call from a hospital in Fresno. She'd delivered the twins and walked out of the place a day later. The only contact information she'd given them was my name. She'd used my address and phone number when she registered."

Reed stopped. She smiled and waved to Bryn, now a fuzzy yellow blur spinning round, who was hollering to get their attention. Her smile dropped off her face when she continued: "The kids were three when she overdosed. They'd never met their biological mom—and suddenly they'd never have a chance to. I'd been trying to send her pictures, trying to track her down at least for a phone call, ever since that day in the hospital. I kept thinking of myself as their aunt until she died. That was the day it all hit me. This was my life. I was a mom to twins.

I know it should have occurred to me before then, but it all seemed temporary."

Julia reached over and clasped Reed's hand.

"One of the nurses at the hospital had told me to have them call me Mom from the get-go. I didn't think about it much then, but I realized later she was trying to tell me McKenna wasn't ever coming back for them. And all they know is that I adopted them—that they didn't grow in my belly. I haven't told them my sister was their biological mom. I know I need to, but every time I try to start explaining things I end up crying. It's not fair how things turned out for them."

Reed's jaw clenched. A long minute later, she said, "I'm lucky they're both healthy. Well, healthy enough. Carly's got some issues with her kidneys."

With Julia's look of concern, Reed continued, "They're working, but not at full capacity, and she has to get regular blood work done. They don't think she'll have problems until she's older and maybe not even then...Anyway, I can't fault McKenna for that. It's a genetic thing. As far as I know, she stopped using when she found out she was pregnant." Reed glanced at Carly. "Both kids were tested at the hospital and they weren't positive for anything...At least she did that much for them."

Julia felt the sting of her words. It was the first time she'd heard any negative tone from Reed. Not that she blamed her. "It might not be fair how it turned out, but they're lucky to have you. Incredibly lucky."

"Most of the time I feel like it's the other way around," Reed said. "Although there are days I want to go back to that time when I wasn't a parent and could spend a weekend in bed with someone."

"Well, then you should know that part of the reason you had this particular someone in your bed last night is because you're a mom. If Bryn hadn't kicked my seat..."

Reed chuckled. "Oh, man—that flight!"

"Worst flight ever?"

"It was in the top three. But then you dropped in." Reed squeezed Julia's hand. "Don't get me wrong, I love my kids more than anything. McKenna made her choices. Mostly I just wish they could have known her—before she was an addict—and that she could see the amazing little people they are."

"Mom, can we have kettle corn?" Bryn shouted. Carly seconded this, clapping her hands and starting for the playground gate. The merry-go-round was quickly forgotten.

Reed stood up. "They both inherited my sweet tooth."

Julia smiled. "They also have your good looks."

"You might be biased." Reed met Julia's eyes. "Thanks for spending the night."

Before Julia could answer, Bryn and Carly crashed into Reed's legs, both laughing and out of breath.

"Can we have kettle corn? Please?"

"Who brought money?"

"You have money, Mom!" Bryn said, laughing. She bumped into Carly. "Let's go pick out flavors."

They both took off at a run toward the kettle corn stand with Reed and Julia following several yards behind.

"I thought farmers markets were for fresh fruits and vegetables."

"Corn's a vegetable, right?" Reed smiled. "Does it help if it's locally grown and possibly organic? Most of the time I do buy fruit and vegetables along with the kettle corn. Well, some of the time. I'm not the best cook, but I can peel a carrot."

"We might need to teach you a few new skills," Julia said, eyeing the overflowing tables of gorgeous produce.

"Are you volunteering?"

Julia smiled at the innuendo. "Maybe I am." They'd reached the kettle corn—the first stand of the farmers market and conveniently located next to the playground—but the way Reed was looking at her, Julia suddenly had no interest in popcorn.

"I'd take lessons from you," Reed said.

Julia had to focus not to give in to the urge to say something inappropriate with the kids now standing next to them. They were jabbering on about the popcorn flavors but still…"How about I cook tonight and you watch?"

"Are you gonna be naked?"

Julia shook her head. Reed had said the words quietly enough that only she heard, but her cheeks were blazing anyway.

"You don't have to cook," Reed continued. "I was thinking we could get takeout from the Thai restaurant we passed on our way here."

"How often do you get takeout?" Julia wasn't completely happy the conversation had changed direction, but she knew it was for the best. As much as she wanted to spend the day having sex or at the very least making suggestive comments about it, she had the next eight hours to get through before the kids went to bed.

Reed's brow wrinkled. "On average? Three nights a week. But it's frozen meals on the other nights. Or something out of a box. Don't judge. At least it's not fast food. If the kids had their way, it'd be chicken nuggets or pizza every night."

"I'm not judging. But let me cook tonight. It's my pleasure, really. Especially with that kitchen of yours." Julia scanned the booths beyond the kettle corn, surveying rows of greens and winter squash and already planning what she'd make. "And we can find all the ingredients we need here."

"As long as you realize that about the only thing I can do in a kitchen is chop."

"I thought you could only peel a carrot. Keeping things from me?" It was impossibly hard not to reach for Reed then. She wanted to slide her hand under Reed's shirt and feel the warm skin she'd kissed last night.

Reed grinned. "Well…"

"Tonight you're not doing anything but sitting back and watching me."

The kids were arguing over popcorn flavors, and Reed stepped up to the counter, ostensibly to keep the twins in check although her hand slyly caressed the low of Julia's back. Julia thought of all the ways she'd enjoy having Reed in the kitchen. But first she had to focus on what she'd make for dinner.

Maybe a creamy sweet potato coconut curry with chicken skewers on the side? Or sautéed green beans and bell peppers with popcorn shrimp?

Reed's kitchen was something out of her fantasies. The non-erotic ones, that is. Between the double oven and the six-burner gas stove, wide counters open to the living room with bar seats, the chopping block, and the huge sink, the place had clearly been designed for a chef.

As they stepped away from the popcorn stand and made their way down the aisle of produce, Reed slipped her arm around Julia. "So you cook. Any other secrets I should know about you?"

"I plan on parceling them out slowly." Julia stopped at a table chock-full of baskets of dark red strawberries. The next table over had broccoli and bok choy that were at their peak. "How do you feel about a vegetable stir-fry with some strawberries for dessert? I could make some whipped cream, although these look like they wouldn't need it."

Reed reached for a basket of strawberries. "Sold."

After another hour in the park, they started back toward Reed's house. Now that they were tired, the kids rode their bikes alongside them and didn't argue about stopping at the intersections. Reed led them on a different route home, passing through two blocks of the downtown section. It wasn't until Reed stopped and glanced at her watch, something she'd done more than once over the past hour, that Julia wondered if something was wrong.

"Hold up, guys," Reed called to Bryn and Carly, who'd biked ahead of them twenty feet or so. She turned to Julia and said, "The kids don't nap anymore, but they need some downtime in the afternoon so I usually let them watch a show...I figured you'd probably be more interested in a massage than kids' cartoons."

The door opened in the shop they were standing in front of and a woman stepped out. She smiled at Reed and then turned to Julia. "You must be Julia."

"Perfect timing," Reed said. She turned to Julia. "I hope you like massages."

"I love them," Julia said. But she didn't want a break from Reed. Was this her way of making sure they each had space while they spent the day together?

"Good. Kara gives amazing massages." Reed reached for the bags of produce Julia had filled at the market. "I'll carry these home and see you in a few hours."

Julia glanced from Reed to the woman standing at the open door. She noticed the sign on the door a moment later. A massage sounded nice, but not as perfect as staying with Reed…

"Don't worry. Kara will take good care of you." Reed turned to call for the kids to wait for her and before Julia could say anything, Reed had squeezed her hand and then jogged off to catch up with Carly and Bryn.

"Come on in. I'll give you a little tour first." Kara held open the door.

Julia started to follow her but hesitated on the threshold. She stole a glance back at the intersection. Reed and the girls had already crossed with Bryn in the lead and started up the adjacent street. Just then Reed looked over her shoulder and held up her hand. Her heart was tugging to follow them.

"She's one of my favorite customers," Kara said, noticing Julia's gaze. "But she doesn't come often enough…Always a wreck of balled-up muscles when she does. But sweet as pie."

"*Sweet as pie.*" Julia smiled. Those weren't the first words she'd use to describe Reed. She wished again that she wasn't already in too deep. The lingering concern that Reed wanted space made her turn to follow Kara into the front waiting room. Nature music playing from a hidden stereo—raindrops mixed with a chatter of birds and crickets—and the warm earth tone decor soon put her at ease. There was no counter or cash register. Instead the room had one long leather couch, two love seats, a coffee table, and a hutch with a teakettle and an assortment of Japanese-style teacups next to a wide array of teas. If she had to take a break from Reed, this wasn't a bad consolation prize.

"Reed made me promise to pamper you," Kara said. "But she'd only let me have you for three hours so we'll have to get right to it."

Three hours? That was longer than she'd ever spent at a spa. Time was money and she didn't want to ask how much three hours typically cost. Kara had already set off through the waiting room to a back hall and Julia hurried to catch up. She was older—likely in her late fifties and stout enough to promise a thorough massage. Her faint accent made Julia guess she wasn't originally from the states. Maybe German? They passed a hallway of closed doors and then an atrium before stepping outside again to a back patio.

"This is our salt water spa," Kara said, lifting the cover on the tub. A rush of steam greeted the cool air. "But I promised Reed I'd show you the tub in our tearoom. She thought you'd like that."

Kara headed toward a small cabana-type building. The floor was a cool flagstone and the walls were natural cedar planks. In one corner was a shower. A bench was against the sidewall and a stretching area with a yoga mat took up the opposite wall. A large ceramic tub claimed center stage and a huge skylight took up most of the ceiling above this. The back wall was a bamboo thicket so dense there was no light through to whatever was on the other side. Julia took a deep breath, enjoying the faint scents of eucalyptus and mint. This would do.

"We ask everyone to shower first. Then you're free to soak as long as you want. When you're done, come back inside and I'll get you set up for that massage. There's a sauna on the other side of the patio if you'd prefer that and of course the salt water spa outside…"

"I think I'll stay right here. This feels like a mini-vacation. In fact, I might not want to leave once I get in that tub."

"Well, my job is done." Kara laughed. She went over to a cupboard and pulled out a towel and a robe. "I'll go get your hot water and our tea selection. Oh, I almost forgot. We have a nail salon two doors over and one of my girls does facials and waxing. Before you say no, remember Reed made me promise to pamper you." Kara smiled again. "I'll be back with the tea and then I'll let you soak."

* * *

"The house is so quiet. Are the girls napping?"

Reed shook her head. "They have Grandpa time every Saturday afternoon. My dad takes them for a few hours to give me a break. Today they're going to the train museum. You just missed them."

"Trains? That sounds like a quintessential grandpa fieldtrip."

"He takes his role seriously," Reed said. "And he's great with them. Even Bryn listens to him. But she's also got him wrapped around her little pinky." Reed walked over to Julia and kissed her cheek. "How was the massage?"

"Perfect. And I found my way back without getting lost," Julia said. She leaned toward Reed and met her lips. "But I have to admit, I missed you."

Reed kissed her back, but Julia wanted her to press close and she could feel her holding back, as if she wanted some distance between them. Why did she have to be more into Reed than she was into her? Before she could worry about this, Reed went around the center island to the kitchen sink and filled two glasses of water. She took a sip of hers and handed the other to Julia.

"I worried about what you might think with me dropping you off there. It wasn't that I wanted a break from you. But I thought...well, I wanted to make sure you weren't feeling done with the kids. I know how they can be."

"I wasn't."

"You're mad at me?"

Julia sighed. She hadn't meant to let her tone give her away. "Frustrated. And feeling slightly ridiculous for how much I want to be around you."

"I'm glad you liked the spa anyway," Reed said, skirting Julia's comment. "Kara's great, but I mainly go for that tearoom tub."

"That was the best part." Julia paused. She didn't want to argue. "I couldn't have asked for a better surprise. Thank you. And now I'm feeling very relaxed."

Reed glanced at her watch. "And we've got three hours to kill…Any ideas on what we should do?"

"Well, I do want to get started on dinner, but it's a little early." Julia walked around the island and met Reed in front of the sink. She ran her hand up Reed's sleeve until she reached her shoulder. Then she followed the line of her collarbone over to the start of the buttons on her shirt. "Before I get to that, maybe we could get out that box you have in your closet."

"Something in there you want?"

Julia nodded. This time, she wanted it enough to ask. "I was thinking about that strap-on…"

"You were?"

"Practically the whole time that I was in that tearoom soaking, I kept thinking how nice it would be to have you there. And then I started to think about what I wanted you to be doing."

Reed smiled. She caught Julia's hand, already undoing the third button of her black shirt, and guided it down the front of her chest to her jeans. Julia felt the bulge there and sucked in a breath. *Oh fuck. This is happening.* She'd pulled her hand back instinctively. She trusted Reed wouldn't do anything without her being ready. But here was Reed's open invitation, and she needed to decide what she wanted.

When she reached forward to feel the outline of Reed's cock, her clit responded with a twitch. This was only about sex, her body reminded her. And there was no doubt about what her body wanted.

"Is that what you were thinking about?"

Julia didn't trust her voice to answer. Instead she unbuckled Reed's belt and, when Reed didn't stop her, undid the front of her jeans. Reed watched her, hands moving to the edge of the counter she was now leaning against. Black boxers. Julia undid the button closing the fly and then hesitated. Reed stepped forward and kissed her, turning her around so she was the one pressed up against the counter. When Reed moved against her, she could feel the cock. She imagined Reed pushing it inside and knew she was ready. She was already wet and wanting it.

"We could go upstairs…" Reed's voice trailed as her hands slid down Julia's sides. She pushed the skirt Julia was wearing up a few inches and then moved up her thighs. As she moved closer to her middle, her lips distracted Julia with kisses. Warm fingers traced along the edge of Julia's underwear.

Reed made it easy to not worry about what was coming next. She knew what she was doing. Julia stepped out of her underwear and then felt the cock press against her skin. Reed murmured something about lube, but Julia knew she was so wet she wouldn't need it. A moment later, Reed discovered as much. Her fingers slipped inside Julia's folds and a little moan escaped her lips.

"Never mind. You're wet enough." Reed leaned close and kissed her neck. "You smell so good."

Reed didn't let up with the kisses. The desire in her body was so hot it filled Julia. When she pressed her against the counter, Julia wondered if she'd push inside, but she pulled back a moment later.

Julia realized then that Reed was waiting for her. What was she supposed to do? She thought of reaching down to feel the cock, but she wasn't certain she even knew what to do with it. Rub the tip? Stroke the shaft? Reed seemed to sense her hesitation.

"Don't think too much. We'll do whatever you feel comfortable doing."

Julia reached down then and traced over the leather straps. When she reached the center, she circled the shaft. Reed pushed her hips forward a half inch. If Julia hadn't had her finger pressed at the base of the shaft, she might not have noticed the subtle thrust. Her center pulsed and she knew that even if it hurt, she wanted it inside. That was how she wanted to play with it.

She drew a line down the shaft, following one of the ridges until she reached the tip again. Reed's hands had stilled. She was watching her.

"I want it inside."

Reed tilted Julia's face up to hers, kissing her lips.

The tip pressed at her rim, but still Reed waited to push inside. Julia ran her hand through Reed's short hair, disheveling it. *Please push inside*, she thought silently. Her fingers had a nervous energy she couldn't decide what to do with. Part of her wanted to grip the dildo and push it inside herself, but then part of her was nervous she wouldn't like it. And that Reed would notice. Julia breathed out, trying to relax. Reed was still waiting.

Finally she arched her hips up, matching Reed's rhythm and shifting so that the tip of the dildo barely penetrated. Reed met her eyes. When she moved her legs apart, Reed pushed forward.

First the tip, then the shaft, slid inside, and all the while, Reed's hands and lips were on her, massaging, caressing, and kissing. Julia's eyes watered at Reed's first thrust. It wasn't the little dildo with the bullet vibe. Reed was wearing the medium-sized one and her body tightened around it, causing more pain but then more satisfaction with every inch. When she thought Reed had filled her and that she couldn't take more length, she looked down and realized only half of the cock was inside. She gripped Reed's elbow when she felt her thrust.

Reed's eyes met hers. "That's hurting you?"

"But I like it," Julia said. She loved it, actually. Loved feeling the connection between Reed's groin and her center, loved the way Reed had thrust inside her. It was almost too much.

"Let's go to the couch," Reed said, inching back slowly. "I don't want this to hurt."

Although she was clearly trying to pull out gently, Julia gasped when the bulb at the end of the shaft caught her rim as Reed stepped back. Still, the moment Reed was out of her, she wanted her back inside. "I want you back."

"And I want you to enjoy this," Reed returned. She caught Julia's hand and tugged her toward the couch, shaking her head at the argument on Julia's lips. Reed tossed the throw pillows off and then turned back to Julia. "Lie down."

Julia hesitated, feeling a twinge of her old nerves. But her body wanted to feel that cock inside again. Finally she sat down on the edge of the cushions and then when Reed only waited, she stretched across the length of the couch.

"Comfortable?"

"I could be better..." Julia parted her legs and Reed licked her lips in response.

Reed had snagged a bottle of lube off the counter and was squeezing some onto the tip of the cock, making the dark purple glisten. "You're wet but this will make it slide in even easier."

The anticipation of letting Reed fuck her had her palms sweaty and the look of desire on Reed's face was intoxicating. Reed's hand stroked up the shaft, coating the lube over the length of it.

Julia let her legs slack further open and Reed groaned. This was her own power play and she loved the effect it had on Reed. But still Reed took her time settling on top of Julia, first stroking a hand slowly up from Julia's hip to her breast and then dragging a finger over her clit. Reed seemed to want to torture herself a little, drawing this out.

When she finally settled between Julia's legs, and angled the tip of her cock, Julia was practically panting with need. Reed pressed inside in one smooth stroke and Julia pulled up her knees and let out a moan. Reed pulled back and repositioned before dropping her hips against Julia's and sinking all the way in.

"Oh, God…"

"Is that okay?"

Julia managed a nod. She reached down to feel Reed, her short hair rough against Julia's waxed skin and then touched the cock tying them together. When Reed began to pump, Julia closed her eyes, matching the rhythm.

Reed's breath was coming faster, hot against her neck, and Julia realized she wasn't going to take long coming. She wanted Reed to come like this, wanted it so much that she lost track of her own body as she matched Reed's thrusts. She wasn't paying attention to Reed's hands until she felt one finger stroke up the inside of her thigh. Reed's thumb found Julia's swollen clit. She was going to come too. How'd she get this close and not realize it?

Another few thrusts, and she couldn't hold it back. She came in a shudder, her body gripping the dildo as her thighs tightened around Reed. She'd wanted to wait for Reed, hadn't even thought she was going to come at all with the thrusting, but then when Reed found her clit, she couldn't help it.

Before she could murmur an apology, Reed's arms wrapped around her back, lifting Julia's butt up off the sofa and changing the angle of the dildo. When Reed thrust again, Julia felt the deeper penetration. With a few more fast thrusts, Reed climaxed hard, collapsing down on Julia's body and moaning with clear satisfaction.

Julia held Reed then. Her eyes had closed and her lips were parted. Julia didn't think she'd seen anything quite as beautiful as Reed in that moment. Reed didn't pull the dildo out. She stayed inside Julia, her arms slack but still holding them together. Julia reached down to touch the cock again, most of the length inside her and what she could feel slick with cum. She wanted to keep Reed inside her longer, but she could feel her already stirring.

"Please…stay…" She wrapped her arms around Reed and then felt Reed's lips brush her neck. She knew Reed would pull out soon and she wouldn't stop her, but she wanted to savor the connection they had in that moment.

When Reed slid out finally, Julia shuddered again. She was going to be sore later, but she wouldn't regret it. Reed kissed her lips, softly this time, and then got off the sofa. She turned the shaft of the cock in the O-ring, pointing it downward, and stuffed it back in her boxers as Julia pulled her skirt back into place. When Reed did up her jeans, it was as if nothing at all had happened.

"You look almost presentable," Julia said, sitting up gingerly and buttoning one of Reed's shirt buttons that she'd undone earlier. Would she sound crazy asking for more?

"So do you," Reed said. "That went a little faster than I'd planned. Sorry. I got distracted and kind of skipped the foreplay."

"You weren't the only one who got distracted." Julia touched the bulge in Reed's jeans. Her mouth was dry with want. "I liked that. A lot."

Reed met her eyes. "Want to go upstairs?"

Julia nodded, thankful that Reed didn't seem to think she was crazy for wanting her again. She already knew what she wanted next: Reed on her back. But she wasn't going to let her take off that strap-on.

CHAPTER SIXTEEN

How could it be morning? Julia rubbed the sleep out of her eyes and glanced at the clock. Late morning. She blinked, trying to get her bearings. She was alone in the bed and the sheets were a tangled mess around her legs. The strap-on was gone — Reed must have put it away before she'd gone to sleep—as was the vanilla lube that tasted more like mint.

She heard the shower shut off and then a minute later Reed stepped out of the bathroom. A towel was wrapped around her waist, but she was naked above the white terry cloth.

Julia smiled but didn't say anything. Reed was as handsome as ever in the morning light. Her dark hair was slicked back and still wet. She was wearing her glasses again. Sometimes she wore contacts, but Julia loved it when she wore the glasses instead.

Her last memory had been fighting sleep with Reed still on top of her. The dreams that followed had gone past what they'd done to a strange land of kink. She wanted to ask Reed to repeat everything, but she wanted to be tied up when they did it again.

When they did it again…she wondered how long she'd have to wait.

"You missed breakfast. Can I bring you something?"

"The kids are quiet."

"I'm letting them watch cartoons," Reed said. "Sometimes I don't have the energy to parent."

"That's possibly my fault," Julia said. "Did you see what time it was when we finally went to sleep?"

"Four o'clock. And it's completely your fault, but I'm not complaining." Reed came over to the bed. She sat down on the edge nearest Julia. "You okay with everything we did last night?"

"Better than okay." Julia shifted off the pillow to rest her cheek on Reed's thigh. "If the kids weren't awake, I'd convince you to go get that pirate chest out again. I think I'm up for that cock that vibrates on its own."

Reed ran her fingers through Julia's hair. "I love how much you like me inside."

"Is it weird that I feel guilty about that?"

Reed shrugged. "We're not supposed to like sex." She moved to massage Julia's scalp, her fingers pressing and releasing points of tension that Julia didn't even realize were there.

"I also love a good head massage," Julia murmured.

"You're in luck. I'm a pro."

In fact Reed was making it hard for Julia not to moan. "What aren't you good at?"

"Cooking."

"Oh, right. That's too bad. I'd love an omelet."

"I have eggs and some fancy cheese someone at the co-op convinced me to try. And I bought a bell pepper and a tomato even though I knew I probably wouldn't eat them…I might even have an onion."

Julia sighed. "Sounds perfect. Unfortunately I can't move at the moment because someone's giving me the world's best head massage."

Reed's fingers stopped. "I'll chop if you'll cook."

Reed had made a perfect sous chef last night. They'd managed to get out of bed and chop most of the veggies before Reed's dad dropped off the kids.

Reed's dad reminded Julia of a quintessential absent minded professor. He had a cane, although he didn't seem to use it, a trim gray beard that added to his distinguished look, and he'd even worn a button-up sweater with leather elbow patches. On first impression, Julia thought he seemed sweet, if not a little clueless. He didn't bat an eye when Reed wrapped her arm around Julia as he was leaving, but then he did ramble on way too long about the train museum. Of course Julia had been more than a little distracted by how close Reed was to her. She couldn't wait for him to stop talking. Somehow they'd gotten through dinner and the kids' bedtime before their clothes were off again.

"Now that I know that you give head massages, I think we might need to have a little competition," Julia said.

"You give head massages too?"

"I was once a resident champion." Julia laughed at Reed's feigned shock. "You weren't expecting that?"

"I feel like you've been holding out on me."

"I'm parceling out secrets slowly, remember? There's still a lot you don't know about me." Julia shifted off Reed's leg and stretched. Reed was watching her with a bemused expression. "What?"

"Nothing." Reed smiled. "Just that you're beautiful and I love that you're making me an omelet."

"We're making an omelet together," Julia corrected. "I hate chopping onions."

"Another tidbit I'll have to file away. And now I'm wondering how to get you to tell me more. Maybe I'll grill you about your past while you're distracted cooking for me."

"Not a chance. I won't be distracted cooking unless you're still naked," Julia said. She picked up a pillow and swung it at Reed.

Reed held up her arm to block but still got a face full of feathers. Laughing, she reached for a different pillow but before she could throw it, Julia pushed her back on the mattress and kissed her. When she sat up, Reed was still on her back laughing. She stopped when Julia stood up and reached for a robe.

"Is the secret thing one of your dating rules? Too many secrets told and the date's a bust?"

"We're not dating," Julia returned. "Casual sex, remember? That means you don't get all of my secrets. Can I borrow this?" She held up the robe.

"I left it out for you." Reed's expression had sobered.

Before she could say more, Julia swung the robe over her shoulder and headed to the bathroom. Tears had welled up in her eyes from out of nowhere and she didn't want Reed to see, much less ask any questions. She needed a shower and a few minutes to sort out the mess of emotions that had caught her off guard. Reed was only joking around—and she had been too. But then her mind had gone on the defensive. She knew she'd surprised Reed with her sharp tone and she hadn't meant to lash out. She'd been upset, but she should have explained why. Now an apology would only make it into a bigger deal. She wiped the tears off her cheeks and scowled at the reflection in the mirror.

Exactly when she'd decided she could swing a sex-only relationship and not get caught up thinking Reed was the one, her emotions were trying to sabotage her. She had to be okay with the ground rules Reed had set out. Or she could leave. She couldn't get mad at her now because she wanted more.

* * *

The drive home on Sunday morning took less than an hour, thanks to the lack of traffic. As she parked her car, Julia tried not to think about how easy it would be to turn back around. She sat listening to the pop song playing on the radio as her mind wandered.

Ever since getting out of the shower she'd been antsy to leave. Breakfast had taken too long and then when Reed asked if there was something wrong, she knew she had to go. She couldn't pretend she was fine for a minute longer than necessary. Still, the moment she'd walked out of Reed's house, the heaviness in her chest had only gotten worse. The weekend had been surreal. Reed was perfect and sex with her was amazing. Every hour she spent with the kids, she got more attached. She even loved Reed's house. But she only had a temporary visitation pass to all of it.

When the song she was listening to ended, she turned off the radio and stared out the windshield. A wet fog cloaked her street, and the sun didn't seem to be making much of an effort to dispel the gloom.

Hearing her phone buzz, she immediately hoped it was Reed. She chastised herself a moment later for the mutinous thought. "Hey, Mo."

"Why are you sitting in your car?"

"Where are you?" Julia craned her neck to see the cars behind her and across the street. She didn't see Mo anywhere—nor her car.

"I'm in your apartment. Before you ask, it's a long story. And not a very good one. I lost my keys last night."

"You lost your keys? Then how'd you get in my place?"

"She only took my car keys. I got a ride to your place and let myself in."

"Wait, someone taking your keys is different than losing them."

"I know. Like I said, it's a long story." Mo sighed. "Kate has them. She told me I wasn't allowed to drive home, so I came to your place instead."

"Where were you guys? And why did Kate take your keys?"

"Ethan's place. And I was drunk…Are you coming up here or do I have to go down to your car? I don't want you to call me an idiot over the phone. I'd rather you do it in person."

"You know I won't call you an idiot. Ever. You're the smartest person I know."

"Aside from Kate."

"That's debatable. What happened?"

Mo sighed again, heavier this time, like she was doing it for dramatic effect. "I told her she was making a mistake marrying Ethan."

"And then you got drunk together?"

"No. I showed up at his place drunk."

"You showed up drunk at Ethan's house? Why'd you do that?" Julia straightened up in her seat. "Hold on a minute, Mo. I'm coming up."

Mo grumbled about how she was a total idiot and Julia didn't need to tell her because she already knew. Before Julia could argue, the line went silent. Mo had a habit of hanging up to avoid conversations she didn't want to have. And giving up without a fight. But had she tried to fight for Kate finally?

Julia jogged up to her apartment and punched in the code. "Was Ethan there when you told Kate not to marry him?"

"He was already asleep." Mo was in one of Julia's T-shirts and her sweatpants from San Francisco State. Mo had a pair too, but hers actually fit her long legs. Julia's only reached the top of her calves. "She tried to get me to spend the night on his couch 'cause she didn't want me driving. Can you imagine Ethan waking up and finding me sound asleep drooling on his priceless leather couch?"

Julia sank down next to Mo. She clasped her hand and brought it up to her lips, kissing the knuckles. "Sweetie, why'd you go to his place?"

"Kate called me. They'd had a fight and then he went to sleep. She was upset...And I was drunk. She didn't want me to come over, but I had to make sure she was okay." Mo shook her head. "She can't marry him."

"What was their fight about?"

"Wedding stuff. How much money it was going to cost and how many people they wanted to invite—stupid stuff. She wants to keep it small, but he wants to impress everyone he knows… Kate said it was no big deal, but he'd yelled at her and you know how she gets when someone yells. She sounded shaky on the phone and I knew she'd been crying." Mo paused. "I really don't get what she sees in him. He's too boring to be an asshole."

"I don't think the two are mutually exclusive. And he can be really sweet."

Mo met Julia's eyes. "Why are you home early?"

"It's already noon. This isn't early."

"Yes, but you were spending the weekend having wild passionate sex. I figured I wouldn't see you until dinnertime."

"She's got kids, Mo. We aren't going to be having sex in the breakfast nook. Although yesterday while the kids were out with their grandpa, it did get a little hot in her kitchen. She's got these long counters…"

Mo scrunched up her nose. "I don't need that image. As much as I love you, Jules, I like to imagine you only get to second base with your beaus."

Julia smiled. "You're the one who asked."

"So it was good?"

"Better. There were toys involved."

Mo held up her hand. "We're going to pretend you kept it to passionate kissing, remember? No sex talk, but tell me the rest of it. Maybe that will take my mind off rehashing everything I did wrong last night."

"Where do I start?" Julia sighed. The weekend had been perfect until she'd ruined it by thinking. "Friday night we went out for dinner and talked. I was so nervous about seeing her again but then…it was really nice. And after was even nicer— but I'll spare you the details. Then on Saturday she surprised me with a massage and facial at a teahouse where you soak in a private tub for as long as you want. And that night was even better than the first. But then this morning came…

"I'm not sure if it's her or me. There's this weird hot and cold vibe I get from her. First she doesn't want a relationship, but then she says she's not sure…She doesn't want to get close, but then she lets me in. And then there's the kid thing which I haven't decided how I feel about completely…She drives a Volvo."

"A Volvo?" Mo grinned. "Any mention of a crazy ex?"

"No. But I did finally solve that mystery."

Mo sat up straighter. "Who won the bet?"

"No one did. Unless someone was betting that the kids were technically her nieces. Reed's been their legal parent since the beginning. Her sister was a drug addict and overdosed a year ago. Apparently she never even met the kids."

"I've got to text everyone who was in on the bet." Mo reached for her cell. "If I were you, I wouldn't worry about the hot and cold thing. You had a great weekend. Remember, the trick is not thinking about this too hard."

"You know how I get, Mo. I overthink everything."

"Well, this time you're going to have to let go and enjoy the ride."

Julia wondered if that was possible. It certainly was tempting…"It's not like I have time for a long-distance relationship anyway. I work late every night and now Val wants me to do more of the face-to-face meetings, which means I'll be traveling more. Maybe a sex-only thing would work. Every roll in the hay doesn't have to be about making love. Sometimes it's only sex, right?"

"Are you trying to convince yourself or me?"

"Me." Julia gave Mo a wan smile. "I love sleeping with her. She makes me want to try things that I've never done before. She has this whole toy box with bondage stuff. Blindfolds, handcuffs, a half dozen dildos…even a whip."

"La la la…" Mo stuck her fingers in her ears.

"Sorry. I forgot. No details." Julia pried Mo's hands down. "Relax. We didn't use anything more than a strap-on. But it was my first time, so there's that."

"Really?"

Mo's surprise made Julia blush. "Yes, and please don't tease me. I told you I'm not good at sex. Or I wasn't before I met

Reed." She grinned. "I've never been this horny before. Do you think I'm thinking about sex too much?"

"I don't think that's possible." Mo chuckled. "This is a new relationship and you're in the honeymoon phase—even if it isn't a real relationship. As long as you're enjoying it and you manage not getting attached, I don't think you have anything to worry about. Besides that, she's got kids. If you were really dating, you'd have to deal with all of that."

"Unfortunately I think they're part of the reason why I'm already attached."

Mo shook her head. "What happened to the Julia who said she'd never understand why anyone would willingly get pregnant? And that if a condom ever broke—"

"I know, I know," Julia held up her hand to stop her. "It doesn't make sense. I know kids make everything more complicated. And at least half of the time, they're a total pain in the neck. But the other half…" She thought of Carly climbing into her lap at the park and of Bryn whispering silly words to her that morning at breakfast to make her laugh. "Turns out I want kids. I've never dreamed I'd say that sentence aloud, but it's true."

"So you need someone exactly like Reed. But not Reed."

"Tell me the next time you run into a sexy butch who's an amazing kisser and happens to be single with kids."

"And if she's a rich doctor, you wouldn't mind that either?"

"I don't care how much money she has. It's everything else…It's the way she stands there looking at me, the way I feel in her arms…" Julia leaned against Mo's shoulder. "I know I'm being ridiculous. How can I be this into someone that I met three weeks ago, right?"

"Maybe it's only the sex clouding your thoughts. I think we should go back to the idea that this one's your learning curve."

"And pretend I'm not already wanting to say 'I love you'?"

"Jules, tell me you haven't said that."

"She didn't hear me. She'd already fallen asleep."

Mo gave an exasperated sigh. Julia knew it was a problem.

"Learning curve," Mo repeated. "Let her show you the ropes in bed—not literally, or if she does, don't tell me about it. So you're not good at sex and need some practice. Reed's perfect. You'll practice with her and then when Ms. Right shows up—"

"You're saying I should use her for sex and then dump her when I meet someone who wants a relationship?"

"I hate to break it to you, but she's using you for sex. As long as you move on before your heart gets hooked, this could work. But absolutely no more 'I love yous.' Even if she's snoring."

Julia wanted to argue that Reed wasn't simply using her for sex or that if she was, the benefits were not one-sided. As far as heartbreak, she wouldn't let it get that far. The first "I love you" she'd said was only a reflex to a good orgasm. But then she'd whispered the words to Reed's shoulder later…

"What do you think we should do with Kate?"

"You're changing the subject," Mo said.

"Yes."

Mo shrugged. "Kate's marrying Ethan. There's nothing we can do except throw her a big bachelorette party and then get drunk at their wedding. C'est la vie."

"What about your heart?"

"My heart's fine. I think she's making a mistake, but I'm not in love with her." Mo looked sideways at her and then held up her hands. "Don't look at me like that. I'm not."

"Why'd you get drunk last night?"

"Remember how I got dumped last weekend?"

"Oh. Right. I'd already moved on for your sake."

"Yeah, well, I'm trying to. Unfortunately Tanya's texted me about a hundred times this past week. She had one of her friends drop off some stuff I'd left at her place and she said she didn't want to see me…but my voice mail is full of messages from her."

"You could block her number." Julia wrapped her arms around Mo when she shook her head. Mo always managed to be friends with her exes. This time Julia hoped she wouldn't try. "Can I be glad you aren't marrying her?"

"Yes." Mo smiled sadly. "I think I'm mostly upset about how close I came to that disaster. Never again."

"Maybe we're both meant to be single."

"I've started a list and so far the pros to staying single are winning." Mo reached into her pocket and pulled out her phone. She opened the notes screen and handed it over to Julia.

"Unlimited sex? Is that a pro on the single side or the married side?"

Mo rolled her eyes. "Single, obviously."

Julia read through the rest of Mo's list and then handed back the phone. The truth was, she thought most of the positives listed for being single only applied to someone like Mo. In her case, women weren't standing in line to have sex with her. And Mo didn't even have cuddling on the list of positives for being in a relationship. For Julia it was at the top—or had been until she'd discovered that sex with some people was better than cuddling. Sex with Reed anyway…

"Should I call her tonight to apologize for leaving in a bad mood?" Julia wondered. "Reed knew I was mad this morning… She kept being extra nice to try and make me feel better. But I wouldn't tell her why I was upset."

"Absolutely not. You're not dating—that means you don't have to worry about drama. So you left upset. Next time you see her, it won't even come up because all you'll be doing is—"

"What if I text instead of call?"

Mo smacked her forehead and groaned. "Jules, Reed isn't looking for an endgame. For your own good, don't text her again until you want sex."

CHAPTER SEVENTEEN

Mo's advice kept popping up in Julia's head over the next several days. She didn't want it to matter that she wasn't Reed's endgame, but she couldn't pretend that it didn't. Despite the fact Reed hadn't done anything wrong, Julia was too ticked at her to answer the phone when she called to check in. She sent her straight to voice mail. That particular power play didn't feel as good as she'd hoped, however, and she nearly broke down and called her back when she heard Reed's voice on the message.

The problem with Mo's theory was that Reed treated her as if she genuinely cared about her. That's where her thinking got stuck every time she decided not to see her again. But for how long could she have sex with her knowing this wasn't going anywhere?

"It's Friday night and you're going out with me," Mo said, walking through Julia's front door. "Don't try and come up with an excuse because I know you don't have any plans."

"How do you know that?"

"You're wearing sweatpants."

"It's been a long week," Julia complained. "Val's been on my ass about every little thing and I've got two presentations to make Monday morning. Can't we stay home and watch something on Netflix?"

Mo shook her head. "Go change. We're going dancing. You and I are getting ourselves out to meet people."

Julia crossed her arms. "What's the point?"

"Well, for starters, I need someone to check me out—at least a good long stare and maybe a little chin lift. Preferably someone attractive, but I'm not going to be picky. Second, you need to be reminded of the fact that single people have more fun."

"Do they?"

"Yes. There's no drama." Mo straightened up and tugged down the bottom edge of her leather vest. "What do you think about the vest? Too much?"

"Actually you look hot. I especially like the hat."

"Good." Mo tipped the brim on her bowler hat and winked. "Now go change into something sexy."

Julia stared at the ice cream she'd scooped for herself. "One bite of ice cream first. And I'm only doing this for you."

After Julia took one bite, the cold chocolate chunk melting on her tongue, Mo snagged the bowl. "We shouldn't waste the ice cream."

"You owe me. I'm sacrificing my movie and ice cream night just so someone will flutter her eyelashes at you."

Mo nodded, spooning a big bite into her mouth and following Julia to her room. "By the way, we're meeting up with a few friends of mine." She shook her head at the first shirt Julia pulled out of the closet and then went to sort through the clothes herself. Mo picked the tightest pair of jeans Julia owned and a red V-neck that showed off too much cleavage.

"I'm not squeezing myself into that tonight. I had Noodle Express for lunch."

"Work with me here, Jules. You've got a great butt in these jeans."

Julia sighed and picked up the clothes. "Who are these friends anyway? Anyone I know?"

Mo pulled up a picture on her phone and held it out for Julia. "Meet Andi. She's going to be at the club tonight along with two of her friends. Cute, right? And she's single. I know her from work."

"Cute, yes. I'm not interested." Andi had a great smile and was butch enough that Julia was certain she would have given her a second look if she'd run into her on the street a month ago.

Mo switched off the phone and then said, "Have you talked to Reed?"

"No." Julia held the jeans up to her waist. "But I almost caved tonight. It's probably a good thing you showed up."

Mo sat down on the bed, playing on her phone while Julia took off her sweatpants. "I'm surprised you've held out this long. It's been, what, five days?"

"It helps I got my period on Monday. I think that's why I was such a mess on Sunday." Julia pulled on the jeans. "She's called twice to ask me if I was okay."

"And?"

"I didn't call her back."

"Good," Mo said. "But you should call her this weekend."

"Why? I thought I wasn't supposed to call her until I was horny?"

"You don't want her to think you're done. She's butch, but she's got feelings. If she thinks you're done with her, she'll go get drunk and find someone new to screw around with."

Julia was instantly upset at the thought that Reed might do exactly what Mo said. "If she's that type of person then maybe she should find someone new now."

"But she's not. She'd do it because you hurt her feelings." Mo held out another picture of Andi. She was wearing a cheese hat and was otherwise dressed entirely in green. "You're going to like Andi. She's a programmer. Total nerd. But great sense of humor. Laughs all the time. At first it kind of annoyed me but…"

Julia zipped the jeans but held off on the button, wishing she hadn't finished the huge plate of noodles. She took the phone from Mo's hand and eyed the picture. "I don't know, Mo. On one hand, you're telling me to go meet Andi, and on the other hand, you're telling me to call Reed. This is why being single is easier."

"Of course it's easier," Mo said.

"So let me stay home and binge watch Netflix."

"Do you want to know why I'm making you go out tonight? Because you want someone on the couch with you when you're watching Netflix. You want someone to eat ice cream with. And then when you go to bed, you want someone to spoon you." Mo arched her eyebrows, knowing she was right.

When Julia didn't argue, she continued: "Text Reed tonight. Tell her you're thinking of her. If she texts you back, which she'll do, tell her you're out at the club and none of the women are as good-looking as she is. Not only will it make her feel good that she's the one you want, she'll be jealous you're out there on the market looking for someone else to have sex with."

"But I'm not."

Mo held up her hand. "Let me finish. Next thing you know, she's gonna start thinking about how she wants to have rights to your pussy."

"Mo, she's not going to be thinking that."

"Trust me—that's exactly what she's gonna be thinking. And she's not gonna like the idea of someone else kissing you, let alone putting their hands all over you. I know it sounds crude, but all that is gonna go through her mind as soon as you tell her you're at a club thinking about her."

"But if I'm at the club thinking about her—"

"If you're thinking about her, you're thinking about having sex." Mo paused as if her point couldn't be more obvious. "Now if she doesn't text you back because she's a boring parent who forgot what a club scene was like, flirt your ass off with Andi. It's a win-win for you."

"Do you offer classes in this?"

Mo grinned. "Hurry up and get your dancing shoes on."

Andi laughed too much. Not only did she laugh at inappropriate times, her laughter was high-pitched and way too loud. Julia guessed it was like a twitch that would ease up once she got to know her better, but it was hard to ignore. An annoying laugh shouldn't be a fatal flaw when it came to dating potential and yet...

"Everything okay?" Andi asked, laughing again. She took a sip of beer as if to calm her nerves.

"Yeah. Everything's fine."

"Do you want another drink?"

"No thanks." Julia lifted up her glass, still half full. "I'm savoring this. I drove tonight."

"Oh, right." Another laugh.

The problem wasn't only the weird laugh. Andi also stood too close and her cologne-to-body size ratio was seriously off. Julia knew these were minor offenses and that probably none of it would bother her if she were actually in the mood to meet someone new. Unfortunately, she was in the mood for Reed.

Irritated again at her predicament, she glanced around to see where Mo had gone. Not surprisingly, Mo was on the dance floor with one arm around Camille. Camille was Andi's friend— now Mo's friend, Julia clarified—as Camille saddled up to grind against Mo. The two had instantly connected. Julia sighed. This was Mo's scene, not hers. She didn't fault Mo. On the contrary, she was happy for her. But seeing her hit it off so easily with Camille only made her realize how she never connected that quickly with anyone. Except Reed.

Julia set down her drink. "I need to pee."

"Oh, sure. Want me to keep you company?"

"No thanks," Julia said. "I'm good peeing alone."

Andi laughed again. "Some people like to pee with a friend."

"Yeah, not me." Julia knew her tone was unnecessarily sharp. It wasn't Andi's fault that she wasn't Reed. She forced a smile. "I'll be right back."

"There's a long line for the women's, but if you sneak around behind the DJ, there's a stall in the back that no one ever uses. I think technically it's only for employees." Another laugh.

"I'm fine waiting in a line," Julia said.

"Okay, well, I'll be here."

At Andi's sweet smile, Julia almost explained everything— that although she technically wasn't in a relationship, she wasn't single either. She felt awful that Mo had let Andi think she'd be interested and worse that she hadn't given her a chance all night. But instead of admitting all that, she nodded and said, "Don't hold my spot. If some hottie asks you to dance, go for it."

Andi's look of confusion only spurred Julia toward the bathroom. She didn't have any experience on letting someone down gently. It was always someone else letting her down.

The line was long, but she didn't have to pee that badly anyway. She pulled out her phone and started the text to Reed that she'd been working on in her head all evening.

Wish you were here.

Reed's response was immediate: *Me too.*

You didn't ask where here is. Could be a gas station.

Reed sent a smiley face emoji and then: *I love gas stations. That's where all the cool people hang out.*

Julia smiled even as her heart clenched in her chest. Why did she want Reed so much? Was Mo right—that she wanted her more because she couldn't have her? And what was so wrong with Andi? Single, attractive, interested in a relationship, and available now Andi…

All these women—why do I have to be stuck on the one person who isn't here?

There was a long pause with no response from Reed, and Julia felt sick, thinking once again she'd said the truth too plainly. She jammed her phone in the back pocket of her jeans. A second later it buzzed against her butt.

Reed: *Close your eyes and pretend?*

Won't help. They won't sound like you either. Julia reread the line she'd just sent. It was probably too honest, but she didn't care at this point. She added: *I want someone who looks sounds and feels exactly like you.*

Hmm. Tricky. There was a pause and then Reed texted: *Have you tried kissing someone with your eyes closed and your fingers in your ears?*

Julia burst out laughing at that image. The woman next to her in line turned and smiled.

Reed continued: *Been thinking about you so much that I'm having trouble sleeping. When can I see you again?*

I could be in Davis in an hour. Julia realized it was a crazy idea. It was already after ten. She wouldn't get there until close to midnight. And yet she hoped Reed would say yes.

I want to say yes…

But? Julia waited for Reed's response and then added: *For the record, I'm not drunk. This isn't a drunk text sort of thing.*

And, Julia thought, tonight she'd proven to herself it wasn't that she was desperate either. Other people were interested. If she wanted a relationship, she knew possibilities were out there.

Reed finally texted back: *I'll leave the lights on.*

CHAPTER EIGHTEEN

"The question is, are you happy?"

"Happy enough," Kate answered quickly. She'd clearly considered this question. Her answer sounded practiced. "What about you?"

Julia set her latte on the table and shifted back on the cushy chair. This was Kate's favorite café, two blocks from the apartment she still shared with Mo and boasting the best scones in town. Geared toward San Francisco's work-from-home crowd, the place was filled with all the comfy features needed to make you want to stay for hours. Buttery scones and overpriced coffee was their reward for having spent the past two hours dress shopping. Unfortunately Kate still hadn't found the one.

"I thought we were talking about you and Ethan here. You're the one about to get married."

Kate shrugged. "I've made up my mind. Besides, I'd rather talk about you and Reed. I'm sick of thinking of the wedding."

Julia thought that was a bad sign but didn't say as much. At least Kate wasn't annoyingly obsessing about the details. Still, she wanted her happy, really happy. Not simply happy enough. And what could she say about her and Reed?

"Every time I drive up to Davis, I think I'm crazy for going. I know this isn't going anywhere—she doesn't want more. But the thing is, on the drive home, I'm always convinced that long term doesn't matter. She makes me feel amazing and she doesn't hide how much she enjoys me. What we have works. Why mess it up?"

Kate narrowed her eyes. "You're sure this is still only about sex for her?"

Julia nodded. Reed made no secret of the fact that it worked precisely because of that. She seemed to think, although she hadn't said this part aloud, that they wouldn't work as a couple. And as much as Julia wanted to ask why she felt that way, she couldn't bring it up, sensing she'd ruin what they had if she questioned it.

"In some ways, I wish I didn't want her and that I wasn't so happy when we were together...I tell myself I'm going to quit seeing her and then four or five days go by and she's the only thing I'm thinking of. I call her up and we're back on again. Of course I haven't told her I'm trying to break this habit." Julia paused. "I know I want a real relationship someday. Reed's made me realize that much. But I don't want to let go of what I have with her simply because it isn't enough."

"You're attached."

"Completely." Julia sighed. "I'm even attached to her kids. They're so sweet. I love mornings when we're all together."

Over a month had passed since she'd starting driving up to Davis on a regular basis. Following Mo's strict guidelines for a sex-only relationship, she only went when she wanted to sleep with her and only for one night at a time. No long weekends of bliss were allowed—that was her own rule to keep her sane.

In some ways, it was a perfect set-up. She got the closeness she wanted and never felt pushed. Every time they met up it was her call on what they did—although she often asked Reed to be in charge as soon as she showed up. Reed's dominance was a turn-on in ways she'd always longed to feel. And their attraction didn't seem to be in any danger of lessening. In fact, Reed had joked that she was enjoying keeping up with her appetite. Since when was she the one with the insatiable appetite for sex?

But she knew it wasn't only sex. She loved being with Reed. The kids were a whole separate problem. Although not at all in the way she would have guessed before things with Reed had started. Mornings were definitely her favorite time. They had breakfast together before she drove home and either Carly or Bryn was in her lap snuggling after the cereal was finished. Both "helped" her with her hair and makeup and then, before she left, she had to hug each one. In those few morning hours they all spent together, she was happier than she thought she'd ever be.

"I know it sounds crazy, but I'm thinking of moving to Davis. I could commute down for work and make fewer trips than I'm doing now."

"Absolutely not. No."

Kate's quick veto of the idea made her laugh. "Why not?"

"You're not serious, are you?" Kate was incredulous.

"Not really…but it's so good when we're together. The problems come up when we're apart. I go up there for one night and then we have too many nights apart."

Kate shook her head but then was quiet for a long moment. "Who knows—maybe you have the right idea. Maybe Ethan and I would be better off seeing each other only for sex."

"Tell me the truth. Does Ethan make you happy?"

"Lately? No. But we've both been busy…We'll be better after the wedding." Kate nodded into her coffee mug and didn't make eye contact, a sure sign she was holding something back.

"What's wrong?"

"Nothing."

"When you say nothing there's always something." Julia picked up the lemon biscotti and bit off the corner.

"Well, nothing major. A few fights here and there…" Kate set down her mug and exhaled. "Things aren't always great, but I can't tell how much of that is normal with wedding stress… And there's that other thing I'm trying to ignore."

"What other thing?"

"That woman from my spin class. And that woman from the snorkeling boat tour."

"What woman from the boat?"

"You know…the boat captain."

"Wait, you were attracted to her too?"

Kate covered her face with her hands. "The problem's getting worse. I swear I'm starting to obsess over lesbians. And suddenly they're everywhere."

"Invasion of the lesbians? If only…" Julia laughed. "You had a thing for the boat captain? How'd I miss that?"

"Are you kidding? That woman was gorgeous and you stared too. She was older but…hot. I hope I look that good when I'm her age." Kate paused. "But shouldn't those feelings be going away?"

"Well, you're going to be attracted to other people even if you're in love with Ethan. You've always been attracted to men and women, so this isn't that different, is it?" Julia knew that in Kate's case, however, there was a significant chance that she was more attracted to women than she'd ever been to men. "Do you want to talk about what happened with you and Mo that night you guys got in a fight in Hawaii?"

"No. I don't want to talk about Mo at all."

Julia sighed. "Okay, then let's stick to Ethan. Do you want to marry him or not?"

"Should I be debating if I want to marry him on the same day I'm shopping for a wedding dress?"

Julia smiled. "I love that you're as terrible at relationships as I am."

"Possibly worse. The truth is, I don't know. He isn't a bad guy…And not agreeing on the small stuff is normal, right?"

"Probably."

"But what if we can't decide on the big picture? We argue about the wedding almost every time we talk. We made a down payment for that fancy resort in St. John, but the cost is ridiculous considering how many people he wants to invite. And we need to send out invitations yesterday..."

"Why did he nix your parents' yacht?"

"He didn't think getting married on a boat would be a good plan." Kate shook her head. "At first he said the weather would be an issue...then it was the size of the boat. Honestly, I think he wants to impress his friends and he didn't think a boat was fancy enough. With the stress and everything else, I haven't been in the mood for sex for months now. I know he's starting to wonder why." Kate shook her head. "Do you think getting married is supposed to be this hard?"

"You're asking the wrong person. I've fallen for someone who doesn't even want to date me."

Kate reached across the table to squeeze Julia's hand. "We make a good pair. How would you feel if we gave up the wedding dress hunt for the day and went to a movie instead?"

"Is popcorn part of the deal?"

"Have you met me?" Kate smiled. She let go of Julia's hand. "If you really like Reed and her kids enough to be thinking of moving in with them, I think you need to have a trial run. Call her up and tell her you want to take some time off work and spend a week at her place. See what she says."

"I can't take a week off."

"You could," Kate countered. "Just ask her."

* * *

"Atlanta?"

"We need someone to rescue this deal. Kasper's one meeting away from losing the KleenPac contract and I can't call on Joe or anyone from his team...You're the best I've got at the moment," Val said.

That was Val's compliment of the year. Not that Julia was the best customer success manager she had but that she was the best "at the moment." Julia exhaled. She had to say yes. "I'll call Kasper and get the details. I can schedule a flight out Monday morning."

"They're making a decision tomorrow. You need to fly out tonight."

"Of course." Julia forced a smile. She stood up when Val's attention turned back to her computer screen. Clearly their meeting was over.

"And, Julia, remember—this isn't one deal. This is our foot in the door for food packaging. If they're not happy with our software, you need to make them happy." Val didn't look up from her screen.

Julia walked back to her desk, wishing she'd left an hour ago. Although, knowing Val, she would have called her at home. She sank down in her chair already formulating her email to Kasper. Andrew Kasper didn't know yet that he was being relieved of his duties, and she'd have to sugarcoat the details to get the information she needed from him. She decided on a call rather than an email, thinking Kasper would appreciate that and reached for her phone. No new texts. Not that this was a surprise.

Two weeks had passed since she'd asked Reed about spending a week in Davis. She'd left the message on a voice mail and then days slipped by with no response. Finally a text came from Reed saying she wanted to talk about it in person. As reasonable as that request was, Julia found herself fighting back a wave of rejection. That wave only worsened when she tried to set up a time to drive up and Reed ignored her next several texts.

In a weak moment, she'd finally sent Reed an email saying she was thinking of her but work was keeping her busy and the idea of spending a week in Davis probably wouldn't work. Reed sent a brief note in response saying she was busy too and it was no problem. Julia had read that email while she was still at work—fortunately after nearly everyone in the office had left—and she hadn't been able to hold back the tears. Reed couldn't have made it clearer that she didn't want more. Thank God she hadn't delivered the blow in person.

A few days after that exchange, Julia's temper started to work. She left a voice mail saying the current arrangement wasn't working for her. She missed her more than she should and it wasn't that she was too busy—she was trying to put some space between them. Probably she'd admitted too much, but there was no way to erase the message once she'd left it.

The next morning she got a text in response. Carly had been sick. Something to do with her kidneys and multiple doctor visits involved. When Julia deciphered that she was in the hospital, she had to hold herself back from driving straight up to see her. Why hadn't Reed told her sooner?

Julia sent dozens of texts and left more voice mails—some with questions but the rest with offers to help. Everything went unanswered. The only reason she'd stopped trying to reach her was because she'd finally gotten the message. Reed didn't want help and didn't need to tell her what was going on. Obviously Reed didn't think she would have gotten attached to Carly.

Now with Atlanta on the horizon, all she wanted to do was drop everything and drive up to see Carly. She knew a better plan would be sending flowers or balloons to the hospital, but she had no clue which hospital they were in and only a faint idea of what was wrong with Carly. Although she knew she shouldn't fault Reed, she did. How hard would it be to shoot back a text? Or pick up the phone and call?

Julia tried to refocus on work—the mess in Atlanta was at least a distraction. Kasper's number came up after a quick search through the company's phone list, but she hesitated making the call. Before she had time to think about what she was doing, she dialed Reed instead. She listened to the ring, surprised she hadn't been directed straight to voice mail like the other times.

"Hello?" Reed's voice was strained.

"Hi. It's Julia."

"Yeah, I know. Caller ID." Reed paused. "Can you give me a second?"

Julia started to say she could call back later, but the line had gone quiet and she guessed Reed was holding her hand over the speaker. Seconds ticked by and Julia pulled up flights to Atlanta on her computer screen. She could take an early morning flight and be there in time for a lunch meeting. As exhausting as it sounded, she clicked on the four a.m. option.

"Sorry about that," Reed said. "A nurse just came in…Hey, I know this is probably weird, but Carly wants to talk to you."

Except it wasn't weird. Julia felt her eyes water when Carly's small voice said a timid hello.

"Hi, sweetie. I hear you're not feeling well. Wish I could give you a hug." There was a long silence, and Julia finally added, "I'm at work and you won't believe what's on my desk."

"What?"

"Trolls. I've got twenty-seven of them."

"Twenty-seven?"

Julia would never have admitted this to Reed. In fact, the troll collection had not been intentional and she was a bit embarrassed by it, but the awe in Carly's voice convinced her to launch into a description of a few of her favorites. The whole thing had started as a joke when she'd bought ballpoint troll pens for everyone in her work group on a last-minute Valentine's Day splurge. Then the larger five-inch trolls with their crazy hair began to appear mysteriously on her desk.

"Do you have one with purple hair?"

Julia scanned the collection, counting quickly. "I have four with purple hair. One has a cowgirl outfit and one is a ballerina. Most of the trolls are naked, but a few are in costumes. I like the one that's supposed to be a doctor. She's got big pink glasses, crazy blue hair, and a doctor's coat. She even has a miniature stethoscope."

"I wish I could see…"

"How about I text your mom a picture of my desk? I'll have to squish some of them closer together so you can see them all."

Julia didn't care what Reed would think. If the trolls that were balanced on her computer monitor and crowding the ledge behind would make Carly happy, it was worth it.

"Most grown-ups don't have toys," Carly said.

"I know. Isn't that weird?"

"Mom says I have to say good-bye. The nurse came back… Can you call me later?"

"Maybe I should let you rest. How about I call you tomorrow?"

"Okay."

Reed's voice came back on the line. "I don't know what you said, but you made her face light up. She hasn't smiled since we've been here."

"Do you need anything? I could drive up tonight and bring some dinner. Or I could watch Bryn…"

"Bryn's staying with my dad. I've got everything covered, but thanks for asking."

Julia hadn't expected Reed to accept an offer for help so the quick dismissal wasn't a surprise. Maybe she did have everything covered, but Julia could hear how exhausted she was. Instead of asking what was going on with Carly, she asked for the name of the hospital and their room number. She knew Reed wouldn't want to answer a bunch of questions.

Reed got off the line after that, and Julia tried not to worry about the terseness in her voice. Her kid was in the hospital and she wasn't going to be thinking about anything else. And as understandable as that all was, part of her worried that Reed didn't even want to talk to her.

"I need a favor, Mo."

"For you—anything. By the way, Andi just texted me asking me for your number."

Julia sighed. She'd gone to the club again this past Sunday only for Mo's sake. Andi was nice. And cute. But she definitely didn't want to go out on a date with her. "Can you tell her I'm not interested in dating anyone at the moment?"

"Except that would be a lie."

"Then tell her I don't have a phone."

"She'll buy that," Mo grumbled. "What's the favor?"

Julia held up the troll doll. "Any chance you can meet Kate at the bakery on Macarthur Street? She's cake tasting. I promised I'd help her out, but Val wants me in Atlanta for a meeting tomorrow morning and I'm running up to Sacramento tonight to drop something off..."

"Cake tasting?" Mo hesitated. "Why isn't Ethan going with her?"

"He hates cake."

After Mo complained about Ethan, she said, "If Kate asked you, she might not want me to show up instead."

"She didn't ask me," Julia admitted. "I told her I was going because I didn't want her doing it alone. And you know how I feel about cake."

"Are we talking chocolate or vanilla?"

"No clue."

"I love those fancy fruit fillings they do in layered cakes. Do you think she'd go for that? Raspberry is always good with chocolate, but strawberry is better with a vanilla cake. Or maybe she'd want to go with a chocolate ganache over a layer of whipped chocolate cream..."

"You're making me regret skipping this cake-tasting thing." Julia longed for a bite of everything Mo had listed. Skip dinner and she'd go straight for cake. But tonight's plan was more important. "Knowing Kate, she won't be able to decide on any of the options. That's where you come in."

"Okay. I've got this. By the way, you can ask me for this kind of favor anytime."

"Thanks, Mo."

Julia got off the line before Mo asked why she was driving up to Sacramento. What Mo would have to say about all of this she didn't want to know—although she had a good guess. She'd been pressuring her all week to give Andi a chance and forget about Reed.

Grinding her way toward Davis through heavy traffic, in a downpour, and in a car whose backseat was filled with an oversized helium balloon, she had to admit it would have been easier to call a florist in Sacramento and have balloons delivered. She questioned her judgment for not going with that original plan, but the problem was how to get the troll to Carly as well.

At the last minute, she'd also swung by her apartment and snagged the photos she'd finally gotten printed from the Hawaii trip. She had a few great shots of Reed and the kids at the beach, although her favorite was the one of all four of them at the waterfall. She kept the waterfall shot for herself, taped to her fridge between the menu for the Indian restaurant with delivery and Kate's wedding invitation. The other pictures she stuffed into an envelope to drop off at the hospital, hoping Carly would be cheered by the silly fish faces she and Bryn had made as they'd posed in front of their sand castle.

She wasn't planning on going up to Carly's room. If Carly was asleep she didn't want to chance waking her, but she also wasn't ready to see Reed.

The hospital was a huge maze; it took several minutes to locate the front entrance and then another few wrong turns before she found an information desk. She waited in line, doubt nudging at her thoughts. Hopefully Reed wouldn't analyze why she'd driven all this way to deliver a troll. The fact was, this was about Carly, not Reed.

"Can I help you?"

"I was wondering if someone could make a delivery for me. I think visiting hours are probably over, but I wanted to drop this off," Julia motioned to the balloon with the troll tied on the end of the string and then held up the envelope with the photos. "Room 210."

"We have visiting hours until eight. You can go up to the nurses station on the second floor and ask if you can see the patient."

"Well, I don't want to disturb her. Is there any way I can pay someone to drop this off in her room?"

"No. That's not a latex balloon, is it? Because we don't allow that. And no flowers."

The woman was the least cheerful greeter ever. "No flowers," Julia agreed. "And I don't think it's latex." She glanced at the balloon with the dangling troll, thinking again she was crazy for being at the hospital at all.

"Looks like a Mylar balloon so I think we're safe."

Julia turned at the sound of Reed's voice, her heart pounding in her chest. So much for the plan to avoid her. She stepped away from the information desk, managing a thank you to the woman who was already helping the next visitor. Apparently Reed's voice of authority had convinced her the balloon wasn't worth fighting.

"Cute troll." Reed's smile seemed forced.

"She's supposed to be a doctor troll."

"Yeah, the stethoscope gives it away. Although she looks a bit like a mad scientist with that hair."

Julia glanced at the troll, more to avoid Reed's gaze than anything else. She tapped the troll and sent it into a spin. "I was hoping to do a drop-off and not bother you guys."

Reed had her hands shoved in the pockets of her jacket. She glanced at the door, which swung open as someone hurried in, and then over at the elevators. "She told me you were going to text us a picture of your desk. Twenty-seven trolls, huh?"

"You probably think I'm ridiculous for coming all the way up here...I was going to have a florist deliver flowers—now I'm glad I didn't."

"Who knew flowers were dangerous, right?" Reed's tone was flat. It wasn't clear if she was trying to joke and just tired or if she was annoyed that she was having this conversation at all.

Reed took something out of her pocket and it took Julia a moment to realize it was a cigarette. She was caught off guard and spoke up before she thought, "You smoke?"

"I used to…A friend of mine from med school is one of Carly's doctors. She got one of the nurses to read her a book and then gave me this. Told me I needed to take a walk. I know they're all doing everything they can for her, but…" Reed paused, eyeing the cigarette.

"How bad is it?"

"The infection's bad. The first antibiotic didn't do a thing, but we got the culture results back and we're hoping the new antibiotic works." She paused. "Her fever came down this afternoon so there's that. But we don't know how much damage was already done and since her kidneys didn't start out perfect…

"I can't remember if I told you this or not but my mom died of kidney disease. She was older, obviously, but Carly has the same genetic issue my mom had and the infection's compromised everything. I don't know. I can't even think straight. I've been awake for days."

"I'm so sorry, Reed. You must be so worried." Julia couldn't think of what else to say. When she reached for Reed's hand, it was quickly pulled away. Julia tried to hide her disappointment.

"I'm gonna go outside and decide if I want to smoke this. You don't have to go in to see her. Just drop that off with the nurses on the second floor. They'll take it to her room for you."

Julia stared at Reed's back until the automatic doors swung closed behind her. Reed had turned and walked away before she could try to stop her—not that anything she'd have to say would make a difference to her at this point.

The air seemed to have gone out of the lobby and Julia couldn't decide if she should leave or drop off the balloon, after all. She glanced again at the dangling troll. Why had she thought that a balloon and a dumb troll would help? If Reed had only told her how sick she was…But maybe the antibiotics would fix everything. Maybe there wouldn't be any long-term damage.

Not at all sure she was making the right decision, she headed for the elevator. The second floor was quieter than the lobby, and she had no trouble finding the nurses station. A nurse looked up and smiled as she approached.

"Can I help you?"

Julia felt her spirits inch up a notch. "I'd like to drop this off for Carly Baxter. Room 210."

Another nurse glanced up from her file and noticed the balloon. "Carly was telling me about trolls when I took her last TPR. If you want, you can wait until her mom gets back—she just stepped out for a minute—and then you can take that in yourself. I'm sure Carly would love to see you."

Julia hesitated. As much as she wanted to hug Carly, she didn't want to make things harder for Reed. The fact she'd come to the hospital at all was clearly not what she wanted. She stepped back from the desk as a doctor approached. Instead of addressing the nurses, she turned and held her hand out to Julia.

"You must be Reed's girlfriend. I'm Terri."

Julia shook the offered hand, wondering if now was a bad time to state she wasn't the girlfriend. "I'm Julia. I don't want to get in the way…I was hoping to drop this off for Carly."

"I'm sure Carly will want to see you. We all heard about the trolls." Terri grinned. "We were expecting a picture. Twenty-seven, huh?"

"I know it's ridiculous…It's this joke at work."

"Well, you made Carly smile, which is the important part." She paused. Her own smile slipped off her face when she continued. "Reed and I went to med school together and we've been friends ever since. This has been really tough on her. I told her she needs to stop blaming herself for missing signs that weren't there. She seems to think it's her fault Carly got this sick. Sometimes these things come on quick and there's nothing we can do.

"Reed's helped me more times than I can count," she continued. "I can't tell you how many times I've called her about a case. If you ask her, she'd say she's just a radiologist, but she's brilliant and knows way more than she lets on…This is the first time she's ever asked me for anything in return. And I know how hard it is for her to ask at all. Anyway, it's good that you're here—for Carly and for Reed."

Julia wasn't convinced about the last part, but she nodded anyway. Terri was clearly a good friend and would probably do anything for Reed. What could she do for her? "I don't want to disturb Carly if she's resting. It's late…Could you maybe just take this in and tell her I said hi?"

"How about I take you to the door and you can wave," Terri said. "She won't fall asleep until Reed comes back anyway. A nurse is in there reading to her now."

Before Julia could bring up her concerns about overstepping, Terri was leading the way down the hall. If she was crossing a line coming here, she wondered if Reed would be even more upset to find out she'd gone to Carly's room instead of dropping the balloon off with the nurses. But it was too late to worry now. Terri had pushed open a door that was ajar and stepped inside.

"Someone came to drop off a present for you," Terri said.

Carly looked up from the mass of pillows where her small frame was propped up. "Julia?" A smile spread across her face. "That's a really big balloon."

She'd told herself she would stay in the doorway, but seeing Carly with machines all around her and a tube taped to her arm, she couldn't. She went up to her bedside and handed her the balloon string. "I got the biggest one I could find. And I brought my favorite troll to keep you company."

Carly's eyes lit up. She tugged on the balloon a few times making the troll flop in the air and then looked up at Julia again. As she spread her arms for a hug, Julia was certain her heart was not going to be the same after this visit. She leaned close and wrapped her arms around Carly, barely holding back the tears.

"So what do you think? Does the troll look like me?" Terri had snagged the troll and held it up alongside her face.

Carly shook her head. "Maybe if you had pink glasses."

"And blue hair," Julia added.

"But I've got the doctor coat," Terri argued, playfully puffing up her chest. "And a real stethoscope."

Reed appeared in the doorway. "Good thing. Otherwise no one would believe you were a doc with all those tattoos and piercings."

"I usually keep my artwork covered up," Terri whispered, feigning a contrite look as she tugged the edge of her sleeve down to cover the tattoo that had peeked out on her forearm. In her defense, the tattoos had been hidden until she'd reached for the troll. She winked at Carly and added, "But maybe I secretly am a pirate."

Carly shook her head, grinning. "No, you're Doctor Terri."

Terri put her hands on her hips in mock frustration. "What if I want to be a pirate?"

Julia couldn't help but smile as Terri pretended to be a swashbuckling pirate. Reed was the only one in the room with the somber expression. She was exhausted, Julia realized, and sick with worry. It wasn't fair to be mad at her for not smiling at Terri's game.

Julia eyed Terri again, wondering how close a friendship Reed had with her. She certainly wasn't the image of a doctor—particularly with the tattoos and multiple ear piercings. But the bright red hair in a messy shag cut also gave off a queer femme vibe. Julia felt a kinship with her for that and more importantly because she'd made her feel as if she ought to be in this room with Carly tonight. She only wished Reed felt the same.

"Can I talk to you for a minute?" Terri asked Reed, motioning to the hallway. Before she stepped out, she passed the troll to Carly and added, "I think I would look good with blue hair, don't you?"

Carly shook her head, sighing in mock exasperation at the grown-ups she had to put up with. The nurse who'd been reading to her stood up to leave then as well, saying they'd finish their book later.

When they'd all gone, Carly turned to Julia. "Do you have to leave too?"

"Not quite yet." She sat down on the edge of the bed. "Do they let you watch TV here?"

"I've been too sleepy. It's really boring being sick. But I watched a movie on Mom's iPad tonight."

"What'd you watch?"

"*The Tigger Movie*. I wanted to watch *Trolls*, but she didn't have it on her iPad."

"They have a movie about trolls? How did I not know about this?"

"In the preview, the trolls sing." Carly stifled a yawn and then settled back on her pillows. "Maybe Mom will let us watch it sometime."

"Maybe…"

"I get to go home soon." Another yawn.

Reed came back into the room then, her focus drawn to Carly's yawn. She went to the far side of the bed and leaned down to kiss Carly's forehead. "You've had a long day, sweetie. I think we need to say good-bye to Julia."

"I want her to stay a little longer. I'm not even tired yet." But she rubbed her eyes.

"Can my troll stay and keep you company?"

"She might get sick," Carly warned.

"She's a doctor. I think she can handle a few germs." Julia fished through her purse for the manila envelope with the pictures. She set it on Carly's bedside table and then straightened up.

"What's that?"

"When you wake up tomorrow, you can open it. There are some very silly pictures inside," Julia promised.

"You could stay until I fall asleep."

"You're in good hands here with your mom." Julia glanced at Reed, but her gaze was on Carly. "Good night."

Carly looked up and gave a slack smile. It was obvious how spent she was. She didn't try waving in return, and her heavy eyelids were already starting to close. Reed raised her hand but didn't meet Julia's eyes.

A weight pressed down on her chest as she turned to leave. *If Carly didn't get through this*…She knew that thought had to be tormenting Reed and there was nothing that would comfort her until Carly was in the clear.

As she let herself out of the room, the start of a lullaby made her pause in the hallway. With the door still ajar, she could hear Reed's melodic alto. She listened, ignoring a pang of guilt for intruding on the moment. Even exhausted, Reed's voice was soothing and perfect.

Julia thought of waiting for the song to end. She wanted to give Reed a hug so much her whole body ached. But after a long moment, she resolutely turned toward the elevator. She'd never thought much about antibiotics or how they worked exactly. But now the only thing she wished for was they'd miraculously do their job. Reed could handle everything else.

CHAPTER NINETEEN

Atlanta was a whirlwind of a flight fueled entirely on caffeine. Julia had trouble falling asleep after the trip to the hospital and then couldn't rest on the plane ride either. Worrying about Carly kept her from focusing on preparing for her day's meetings too. She could only imagine how the strain was wearing on Reed.

With three hours of sleep, she'd arrived in Atlanta and gone straight to meet with Andrew Kasper to convince him to divulge everything that had happened with KleenPac. Then she had to woo her way through an afternoon of meetings with the same folks he'd disappointed. Against Val's wishes, she'd decided to bring Kasper's assistant to the meetings. The assistant, Danielle, was two years out of college but surprisingly adept at soothing tempers, and she seemed to know everyone at KleenPac from the CEO down to the guy who operated the forklift. When Julia asked, she'd explained she'd been managing the client for the past six months and had met a lot of people in the process.

Things had soured with KleenPac only when Kasper had stepped in.

At the end of the day and five cups of coffee later, Julia had called Val to explain all the reasons they needed Danielle to take Kasper's job. Besides Val, she'd need to convince two others to sign off on the promotion, but she had no doubt it was the right decision. Without Danielle, Julia doubted she would have convinced KleenPac to renew the software contract. What was more, they'd requested a review of their outdated software system at a sister fruit distribution plant as well. By the time she got into bed Friday night, her exhaustion sent her right to sleep without worrying about how Carly, or Reed, was doing.

Saturday was spent getting Danielle up to speed in the new role she'd doubtlessly be promoted to and then wrapping up the Atlanta visit with more meetings. When Julia fell into bed that night, she turned off her phone determined to get a solid night's sleep before her flight home.

As she sat in Bay Bridge traffic on the airport shuttle bus the following morning, she forced herself to check her phone messages. Not surprisingly, Val had texted her before she'd gone to bed Saturday night and then a dozen times between five and six a.m. She'd clearly been working on the elliptical. Julia grumbled about her boss's workout schedule and then noticed Reed's text sandwiched between several of Val's. Julia couldn't stomach Val's diatribe until she knew if Carly was okay.

When she clicked on Reed's text, the first two words: "Hi Julia" were followed by a paragraph of emojis. Seeing an entire line of smiling poop emojis interspersed with happy faces, sad faces, meh faces, random food, and green aliens, she was certain Carly had been in charge of the phone, at least briefly.

Julia shot back a thumbs-up, a puppy face, and another green alien to Reed's phone. She added the probably unnecessary salutation: "Hi Carly." A prompt reply came with more alien emojis. If Carly was feeling well enough to be playing on Reed's phone, the antibiotics had to be doing their job. Julia couldn't stop smiling.

The phone rang and she answered immediately. Expecting Carly's voice, she was surprised instead to hear Reed's. Thank goodness she wasn't driving. Her brain stopped working as soon as Reed said hello.

"Carly's feeling better—in case you couldn't tell."

"Are you guys out of the hospital?"

Reed hesitated. "For the moment. She wanted me to ask you if you could come up for another visit. I told her we couldn't make it a long visit. She needs to rest."

"Tell her I'd love to. When would work for you guys?"

"Tomorrow?" In a quieter voice, Reed added, "Let me step outside for a minute." A door opened and closed and then Reed cleared her throat. "She goes in for more blood work next week. We may need to start dialysis."

Dialysis? Wasn't that only for kidney failure? Julia's heart sank. "Shit."

"The infection seems to be gone, but there was a lot of damage done…" There was a pause and then when Reed came back on the line, Julia wondered if she'd been trying not to cry. "So maybe around two or three?"

"Yeah, sure. I'll send you a text tomorrow morning to make sure she's still up for it. And Reed—" Julia wasn't sure how to explain the mess of feelings tugging at her heart. She understood that this wasn't about them at all. This was about Carly. Reed was letting her in for Carly's sake. "Thanks."

* * *

A quick Internet search on kids and dialysis did nothing to diminish Julia's fears. Reed hadn't explained what sort of genetic kidney issue Carly had been born with, but none of the possibilities sounded good.

Julia pushed all of this out of her mind as she pressed the doorbell and listened to a scurry of feet. Bryn appeared in the narrow window alongside the door. She pressed tight against the glass, squashing her nose so that she resembled a pale piglet grinning ear to ear. Her brown curls were more tangled than usual and she was wearing pajamas at three in the afternoon. Bryn disappeared from the window and the door swung open a moment later.

"I'm a flying hippo!" She took one step back, wiggled her butt, and then launched herself into the air.

Julia caught her, taking a step back so she wouldn't lose her balance, and then spun her around in a circle, laughing. She set Bryn down on the threshold. "You're getting too big to jump into people's arms, little hippo."

"Mom can carry two hippos at once. She's really strong."

"I'm pretty strong," Julia said, flexing her arm muscles. She looked at where the bump should be and pushed up the material of her jacket. "See those muscles?"

"Not really," Bryn said, squinting.

Reed poked her head through the doorway, and Julia immediately dropped her arms to her sides. "Oh, hi."

Reed smiled. It was the same forced smile she'd had at the hospital. "Come on in." She glanced at the bag at Julia's feet.

"I brought you guys lasagna. Homemade. You can freeze it and heat it up whenever…"

"Can we have it tonight?" Bryn asked, hopping up and down in front of Reed. "Julia can stay and eat with us!"

"Sorry, sweetie, I can't stay that late." Julia reached into the bag and brought out a big bottle of bubbles. "But maybe we can go into the backyard and blow bubbles after I say hello to your sister?"

"She's sleeping at the moment," Reed said. "She's been sleeping a lot. I almost called to tell you not to come up, but I thought maybe she'd wake up by the time you got here…"

Bryn snagged the bubbles. "Let's go outside!"

"Why don't you go outside and get set up. We'll be there in a minute," Reed said.

Bryn looked as if she were about to complain about that plan, but then she eyed the bubbles and said, "Don't take forever."

Julia watched as she dashed down the hallway, feeling sorry for Bryn, who probably hadn't gotten as much attention over the past few weeks. She handed the casserole dish of lasagna to Reed as she stepped inside. Reed took it, glancing around for somewhere to set it and then looking somewhat awkward as she decided to hold it instead. She met Julia's gaze, and in that moment, unfortunately, she was as attractive as ever.

"If you want, you can go check to see if Carly's still sleeping. It's been a while now."

"I'll go blow bubbles with Bryn first. I want Carly to get her rest. I'm sure she needs it." From the look of it, Reed needed a nap as well. Julia almost suggested it but stopped herself with the worry that she'd take it the wrong way.

Reed was eyeing the stairwell. "She's been through a lot these past few weeks."

"So have you." Julia wanted to wrap her arms around Reed. Fortunately, the lasagna stopped her. If she hugged her now, there was no telling what she'd say. Or if she'd let go.

Reed seemed to remember the casserole dish then. "I should go put this in the fridge."

"And I should go blow some bubbles."

"You know you don't have to. You don't have to bring us food or bring them anything—"

"Stop," Julia interrupted. She wasn't going to argue. Not now. But it stung that Reed would think she was here out of some feeling of obligation. "I know I don't have to. I want to."

After a half hour of bubbles and tag out in the sun-drenched backyard, Julia convinced Bryn to take a break. Reed had left them to play alone, which was just as well since Julia wasn't ready to face her again, but she wasn't in the living room or the kitchen when they came back inside. Bryn settled in with a video game and Julia headed upstairs with the plush purple troll she'd brought for Carly. She'd also found a copy of the movie she'd mentioned, *Trolls*.

At the top of the stairs, Julia paused, noticing the mess around her. Clothes were half-folded in laundry baskets along one side of the hallway, Barbie dolls and Legos battled for floor space down the middle, and someone had given up on an art project involving glitter glue, duct tape, and construction paper. The remnants of the artwork, some of which was partially attached to the walls, made it hard to even get to the kids' bedroom. When she'd last been over, the house wasn't spotless, but it wasn't at this level of disaster. She'd assumed Reed had a house cleaner, but now it was apparent she'd been doing everything on her own.

Julia pushed open the door, expecting to hear Carly's shy soft voice call out. The room was quiet and it took a minute to spot her asleep in the bed. The drapes were drawn and the one light in the room on the bedside table was dimmed. Julia tiptoed around a figure eight train track set up in the middle of the room and gently set the stuffed troll at the foot of the bed. She placed the DVD on the bedside table and then switched off the light.

The dark room was a strange disconnect to the brilliant sunshine-filled backyard, and Carly couldn't be more different from Bryn in that moment. She'd always seemed frail compared to Bryn. One the quiet bookish kid and the other the outgoing athlete. But now she looked younger as well. Curled on her side and with her thumb in her mouth as she slept, she looked more like a toddler than an almost kindergartner.

Julia thought of the pictures of the kids undergoing dialysis that she'd seen online. Maybe she'd read too much. Dialysis and then the next step—kidney transplants. How could a four-year-old be in danger of dying? As soon as the tears started, she couldn't stop them. She sat on the edge of the bed, praying through her silent tears. Carly's blood work would get better. It was only the infection that had made everything look as bad as it did...

Footsteps came down the hall and then by the sounds she guessed Reed had entered the room. She didn't look over at her. Reed didn't need her crying. She was supposed to be here cheering Carly up, not adding any burden. Wiping her eyes, Julia stood up slowly, her back still to Reed. Once she'd mastered her face, she slipped past Reed and out into the hall. She took another minute in the hallway to compose herself and then looked up to find Reed staring at her.

"She'll be upset she missed you," Reed said quietly. She'd closed the bedroom door and was leaning against the wall.

"I could stay for a bit. Help with some laundry."

Reed shook her head. "It's a mess up here, but I'm not comfortable with you doing that. I'll get to the laundry tonight after Bryn's in bed."

"Do you ever let people help you?" Julia regretted the question when she saw the look on Reed's face. She pressed on, thinking she could salvage something by clarifying. "I'm not saying you need help. I'm saying I want to help. At least let me fold some clothes and put away a few toys. Bryn and I can make a game of it."

Seconds passed with Reed not meeting her eyes. Julia exhaled, knowing her help wasn't wanted and hating Reed in that moment while knowing she couldn't be blamed. Bryn's voice shattered the quiet. She was calling Julia's name.

"I promised her a game of Hungry Hippo before I go," Julia said. "Then I'll be out of your way."

"Wait." Reed closed her eyes and took a deep breath. "I'm not trying to kick you out. I'm just tired...And I can't deal with anything else right now. My plate's full."

"Well, maybe you should let a friend help."

"A friend?"

Julia regretted her word choice as soon as she heard Reed's tone. Yes, of course they were more than friends. But what was she supposed to say? "I'm sorry. I'm not trying to make this harder. I'm trying to help. Tell me what I can do."

"I can't handle your help right now." Reed hadn't raised her voice, but her tone was sharp. She seemed to instantly regret it, shaking her head as she glanced over her shoulder at Carly's bedroom door. "Look, I'm sorry. But I'm tapped out. What's going on between you and me—I can't fix any problems we have. I get that it's not enough for you and I'm sorry I never responded to that voice mail you left, but I told you from the beginning I couldn't do more."

"When I left that message I didn't know what was going on with Carly," Julia said, straining to keep her voice calm. "Now that I know what you're going through, I don't expect you to be thinking about us at all. If there ever was an 'us.'"

Reed exhaled, her head dropping back against the doorframe. "I can't deal with this. With us."

"I'm not asking you to." Julia squeezed her hands into fists. She wanted to yell, but they were both still only whispering. "Jesus, Reed. Will you listen? I'm not asking you for anything. I'm here because I love your kids. I'm attached. I'm sorry I got attached. I didn't plan on it—but it happened."

Reed didn't respond, so Julia continued, "And yeah. I'm attached to you too. And you've made it painfully clear that I'm an idiot for wanting you because you aren't available. Fine. Can we pretend for the next half hour that I don't like you and I'm here only because I like your kids? Can you deal with that?" She paused, shaking her head. "Dammit, Reed. What are you scared of? Getting close? Letting me down? What the hell is it?" She exhaled, knowing she shouldn't be saying any of this. Not now. "I'm here because I want to be—you don't owe me anything in return and it isn't your job to take care of me."

Reed eyed the laundry basket and then Carly's door again. "I think we need to break things off."

"We aren't dating. What are we going to break off?" Julia whispered the last bit through clenched teeth. God, she wanted to scream. Reed wasn't even looking at her. "Is it okay with you if I go downstairs to play a game of Hungry Hippos? If Carly is still asleep after the game, I'll leave."

Reed nodded.

"And I really am sorry I left that phone message. The last thing I want to do is fight. I hate how much you're hurting and that you don't even want me to give you a hug." Bryn called again and Julia turned for the stairs without another look at Reed.

As much as she wanted Reed to say something to her before she left, she wasn't surprised when that didn't happen. After twenty minutes of Hungry Hippo with Bryn, she went upstairs to check on Carly again. She was still sleeping, but tossing enough to have wrestled off her blankets. Julia pulled the blankets up to her chin and then slipped out of the room.

When she announced that she had to go, only Bryn, hopping from the couch to the loveseat to jump on Julia's back, whined for her to stay. Reed turned on the television finally to calm Bryn down with a show and then walked Julia to the door. Julia started to say good-bye and then on impulse stepped forward for a hug. Reed stiffened in her arms and she immediately let go.

By the time she'd buckled her seat belt, she was crying again. This time the tears didn't fall quietly. She pulled away from the curb, struggling to see the road, and resolute that she wasn't making the drive up to Davis again. Reed had made her point loud and clear.

She'd send Carly and Bryn texts, mail them packages, or talk to them if Reed answered when she called. Maybe someday Reed would let her back as a friend. But Julia would need time to be ready for that. At the moment, she wasn't strong enough to fight her way through Reed's defenses.

CHAPTER TWENTY

Julia's phone buzzed and she rubbed her eyes, squinting to see the time and then reading the text—a strange list of dates, abbreviations, and numbers. She hadn't expected to wake up to a text from Reed, that was for sure, and this one made no sense.

Two weeks had passed since Reed had broken off their non-relationship and the only contact she'd had was from Carly, who'd somehow twisted Reed's arm enough to let her Skype with Julia. Their conversation had been short. Carly wanted to show her the troll, now covered in bandages because Bryn had thrown it down the stairs. She'd asked when Julia was coming back, wanting to put a mark on her bedside calendar, and Julia thought her heart would break again as she told Carly that she wouldn't be able to drive up for a while. A while. "How long is a while?" Carly had wanted to know.

Julia wished she had an answer. How long would it take until she could look at Reed and not feel a hollow ache in the middle of her chest? She got out of bed and flipped open her laptop.

As the computer booted up, she scanned Reed's text again. The second time through made no more sense than the first. She typed the abbreviations into the search engine and finally realized Reed had sent her Carly's blood work. The blood work dated March 14th was from after the Hawaii trip. Then the next list of numbers was from three weeks ago when she was still in the hospital. The last blood work was from yesterday. Her cell phone rang and Reed's name popped on the screen. She answered the call, wishing she already knew if this was bad news or good.

"Mom said I could call you."

Julia smiled at the sound of Carly's voice. "Hi, sweetie."

"What are you doing?"

"Well, I'm trying to decide if I want to wear my pajamas all day or get dressed."

"You're still wearing pajamas? What color are they?"

"Blue. With pink bows. And dancing cats." And at nine o'clock on a Saturday it was entirely reasonable to still be in pajamas, Julia wanted to add. Carly was telling someone else in the room about the pajamas and judging from the giggling that followed, she guessed it was Bryn.

"Why do you have cats on your pajamas?"

"My mom thought they were cute. She sends me pajamas every Christmas."

"You have a mom?"

Julia instantly wished her mom could meet Carly. "I sure do. And I bet she'd love you. She'd probably send you cat pajamas too."

Carly giggled. "Guess what?"

"What?"

"Mom said I can ask you if we can come over," Carly said. "Are you still going to be wearing the cat pajamas then?"

"Well, that depends on when you come." Julia took a moment to decipher Carly's sentence. "Wait, you want to come to my apartment?" And Reed was in on this conversation?

"Yeah because you can't drive up here for a while."

A while…"Right. That." The way Carly repeated the same phrase she'd used in their last conversation made her heart sink further in her chest. She hated that Reed had put her in this spot and Reed probably hated that Carly was asking to see her. Of course, there was no doubt Reed would put her kids' needs before her own.

Maybe Reed was relenting to making a visit because Carly was about to start on dialysis. But Carly certainly sounded better on the phone…Julia realized the reasons behind this didn't matter. She wanted to hug Carly—and Bryn too.

"I'd love it if you guys came down to see me."

First Carly shouted that they could go to Julia's and then Bryn echoed the same sentence in a higher octave. Hopefully that meant Reed wasn't in the room for the conversation about pajamas. The call ended before Julia had a chance to ask when they were coming.

She set the phone down, eyed her pajamas and then the rest of the room. Her bedroom was reasonably clean, but the rest of the apartment wasn't. Mo had taken up residence on the sofa and several of her boxes and suitcases had moved in as well. With some finessing, she could probably convince Mo to do a grocery store run while she cleaned.

Julia went into the living room and found Mo already awake and reading the paper. She usually liked the sports section, but this morning the classifieds were spread out on the coffee table in front of her.

Mo looked up from the paper. "Do you know how much they're charging for one-bedroom apartments? It's highway robbery…I'm giving up on Craigslist. Before I can even call on an ad, someone's rented the place."

"I don't think the newspaper will be much better. Places are probably spoken for before that gets printed. You need to consider living somewhere besides the City."

"I know." Mo sighed. "Or I get another roommate and keep my place after Kate moves out."

"Those are the options." Julia sat down next to Mo. They'd been through this more than once. She knew Mo was reluctant to get a roommate. Even if she wasn't saying it, the problem was that it'd be hard living in the same place without Kate. For the past few months the coolness between Kate and Mo had felt distinctly like a breakup, but neither would admit anything was wrong.

"You know you're welcome here as long as you need it."

"Thanks." Mo glanced at her duffel bag of gym clothes and then at the suitcase against the wall. "I take up a lot of space. I know it's probably driving you crazy with all this mess."

"About that...I was thinking we could move a few things into my closet. There's plenty of room if I use the lower racks and squish a little."

Mo squinted at her. "What's going on?"

Julia couldn't keep anything from Mo and there would be no hiding this secret anyway once the kids arrived. "Reed and her kids are coming over. This place is tiny and—"

Mo straightened up. "Hold on a minute. I thought we were done with Reed. And now, out of the blue, she's driving all the way down here?"

"We are done." Julia shook her head. "It's her kids..."

"You're letting her waltz in here after everything she did? Did you forget what happened? First she asked you to drive all the way up there and then when you get there—with dinner that you spent half the day making—she dumps you. And now you're inviting her here?"

"Mo, I remember. Thanks. But you know there was a lot more going on. She's had a lot on her plate with Carly being sick and—"

"But you're not on that plate, Jules. And that's the problem. I don't want her hurting you again." Mo stood up. "Where's your phone?"

"What are you going to do? Call her and tell her not to come over?"

"No. I'm going to text her." Mo glanced at the kitchen table and then at Julia's hands. "I'm going to tell her exactly what you should have said all along. Where'd you leave your phone?"

"And what exactly should I have said all along?"

"That you're too good for this crap. She needs to stop stringing you along. And I'm going to tell her that your friend Mo is gonna beat her ass up for this shit if she doesn't leave you alone."

Julia caught Mo's hand as she started for the bedroom. "Wait, Mo. I love that you have my back and that you want to protect me. I really do. But I need you to stay out of this."

Mo's shoulders dropped. "You're going to keep seeing her—after all the crap she pulled?"

"No. I'm done." At Mo's skeptical look, Julia added: "I'm not sleeping with her again. I can't do it. And maybe one day I'll tell her all the reasons why she missed out."

Julia smiled sadly. She didn't want to see Reed today. It was too soon. But for Carly, she was going to put a game face on and pretend she was fine. Reed would doubtlessly be doing the same thing—except she wasn't hurting the way Julia was. She'd gotten exactly what she wanted out of the arrangement.

"I know her kid's been sick and she has all she can handle, but I'm still pissed at her. I hate that this never became more than sex for her. And I hate that the way she deals with problems is to cut ties and run." Julia paused. All of that was true and yet she was still aching over the breakup. "But whatever. We're done. I'm only letting her come here because I honestly love her kids."

"I'm sorry, Jules. I feel like I pushed you into this with all that learning curve stuff. Clearly I was wrong, but I thought she'd be good for you."

"Don't apologize. I don't regret sleeping with her…I needed that learning curve." Now the question was how long it would take to recover from her lesson. "Maybe my next girlfriend will send her a thank-you card."

Mo smiled. "You sure you're going to be okay with her coming here?"

"I'll get through it. And you'll be here."

"I'm not leaving you two alone for a second," Mo promised.

"Are you protecting me from Reed or from myself?"

"Both."

She probably needed some protection from herself. But not from Reed. She had no expectations that Reed would bring up what had happened or ask to start things again. She'd made it clear she was done.

All along Reed had told her she couldn't do a relationship. But it wasn't that she was too busy. For some reason, she couldn't open up and let anyone in. Julia had felt it all along. Her heart was sealed. Maybe it was her sister dying or maybe it was some lover had hurt her. Either way, she was damaged goods. Handsome and seemingly perfect but damaged all the same. And when the going got tough, she was gone.

* * *

Staying in the cat pajamas wasn't an option. She needed all the courage she could muster and she also planned on giving Reed a few reasons to regret what she'd let go of. At the same time, she had to make it look like she was enjoying a relaxing Saturday and the visit was no big deal. Finding an outfit to fill all those roles wasn't easy.

After a few false starts in front of the bedroom mirror, she decided on what Mo called her sexy jeans and a snug, scoop-neck, cream-colored sweater. She left her hair down and went for light makeup. Unfortunately, she was still nervous when the bell rang.

Mo hit the buzzer and then went to stand by the front door, looking every bit like the bodyguard she intended to be. Julia smiled. It was both sweet and completely Mo.

"You can relax for a minute. She's got two four-year-olds. It'll take a while for them to make it up the stairs," Julia went up to Mo and stood on her tiptoes to kiss her cheek. "And I love that you're here for me, but remember her kid's sick."

"She's still an asshole."

Julia stopped herself from arguing that Reed was also caring, thoughtful, and genuine. She wished she was only an asshole. Then her heart would have moved on months ago.

At their knock, Mo opened the door. Reed stood on the doormat for a moment, glancing from Mo to Julia, with Bryn hanging on her back and Carly standing on her toes. Carly hopped off Reed's shoes and dashed past Mo to wrap herself around Julia's leg. After the hug, she raised her arms to be picked up.

As soon as Julia scooped her up, she noticed that Carly had gotten much too thin. She was a shadow of what she'd been only a month ago and had nothing more to lose with every bone too prominent in her frail frame. But she was smiling. Julia spun around in a circle and Carly laughed, begging her to spin again when she stopped.

"Someone's feeling better," Julia said.

"Me!" Carly shouted.

Julia's cheeks ached from the smile she couldn't hold back. Meanwhile her heart was threatening a full mutiny. How could she have told this kid that she wasn't going to drive up to see her? So what if dating Reed hadn't worked out. Somehow, she had to be part of Carly's world.

"Did you get Mom's text?"

"I did. But it didn't make any sense," Julia admitted. "It was a bunch of numbers and letters that I think probably only make sense to a doctor."

"I told her to send you what Dr. Terri sent because it made her so happy she cried." Carly glanced over at Reed, as if asking for permission, and then leaned close to Julia's ear and whispered, "I don't have to go back to the hospital."

Julia choked up with a sudden rush of emotion. *Thank God.* "Your kidneys are all better?" Carly nodded and then turned to look at Reed again, still standing in the doorway with Mo partly blocking her from entering.

"Nearly. She's back down to stage three. Which means no dialysis and no transplant on the horizon." Reed's gaze was still on Carly.

"And I'm not throwing up all over the place," Carly added.

Bryn slid off Reed's back then and came forward to tap Mo's knee. "Do you remember me?"

Mo grinned. She squatted in front of Bryn and said, "I don't know. Hop up and down for a minute." When Bryn's shoes lit up, Mo's eyebrow arched. "Oh, yeah, I remember. Those shoes are trouble." Bryn giggled and hopped closer while Mo pretended to be scared and scooted back.

"Have you ever jumped up and down on a bed in those shoes? I bet it'd be super cool to jump on your mom's bed in the dark. While she was sleeping."

Bryn's mouth dropped in awe at Mo's suggestion. She looked up at Reed. "Can I?"

"That depends. How much trouble do you want to get in?" Reed asked.

Before Bryn could answer, Mo said, "Or you could try it first when she's not watching. You could see if she notices that her bed's all messed up."

"Oh, she'd notice. She makes her bed every morning so it looks perfect."

In a loud whisper, Mo said, "That's why you need to mess it up every day while she's brushing her teeth."

Bryn giggled again. "Want to see how fast I can run?"

As soon as Bryn took off, Mo was right on her heels. Carly wiggled out of Julia's arms and ran to follow. In no time, they'd skirted through the living room, past the kitchen to the bedroom, and then circled back.

"Is this the whole house?" Bryn asked, trying to dodge past Mo to find somewhere else to run. "Where are all the other rooms?"

"There aren't any other rooms. You're cornered," Mo said. She took a step closer and then scooped Bryn up. Between giggles, Bryn hollered for Carly to help. Mo dropped her a second later, and said, "Last one to Julia's bed is a rotten egg."

Bryn started to run, but Mo scooted in front of her and then slowed down to give Carly the lead. When the three of them tumbled onto the bed, with much laughing, Julia glanced over at Reed to find her staring at her.

"Hey."

Julia nodded.

"Thanks for letting us come over," Reed started. She jammed her hands in her pockets and squared her shoulders. Walking toward the breakfast nook with the bay windows facing the city skyline she said, "You have a nice place. The view is pretty amazing."

"I like it." Julia had the distinct urge to ask Reed to wait in the car. She wasn't ready to pretend with her—pretend that she was fine chatting, pretend that Reed hadn't broken her heart, and pretend that she still wasn't holding it hostage.

"And you have nice friends. Who hate me." Reed eyed the hallway and the open door to Julia's room. Mo was on her back on the floor, taking turns giving the girls airplane rides.

"Mo's always going to protect me. Kate, on the other hand, told me I got what I signed up for and that I can't blame you."

Reed met Julia's eyes. "I know you probably don't want to be in the same room with me. And I know you're doing this for Carly. It means a lot that you'd put her first." She paused. "Not that you should care what I think or how I feel or anything like that. I know how much I screwed up."

Julia nodded again.

"I'm sorry."

Whether or not she had more to say, Reed didn't get a chance. Bryn came tearing into the kitchen screaming. Mo and Carly—teetering on Mo's shoulders—were one step behind her.

"They're monsters!" Bryn said, hiding behind Julia's legs. "They tickle you if you're wearing shoes."

Both Mo and Carly were shoeless and Reed had slipped off her shoes at the front door. Julia, however, was wearing her house slippers, which looked deceptively like Mary Janes, and Bryn of course was still in her disco light-up shoes. Mo lumbered toward her making menacing growling sounds while Carly wiggled her fingers in the air threateningly.

"The shoe tickle monsters are coming," Mo said. "You better run."

Julia pointed to the kitchen and Bryn caught her hand as they dashed to safety on the far side of the table.

"We're in big trouble," Bryn warned.

"Maybe we should take off our shoes," Julia suggested.

"No way," Bryn said. "We're the shoes-on team." She eyed the food on the table and then reached for a grape.

"Do you think we could feed them and make them nice monsters?" Julia wondered.

"Good idea," Bryn said, reaching for a plate. "Do you think shoe monsters like pineapple or grapes?"

"Both," Mo roared. Carly tried to roar too but sounded more like a sick frog.

But she wasn't sick, Julia reminded herself. At least, not like she had been. The relief from all that had her almost forgetting about what had happened with Reed. Almost.

"Who wants a monster plate?" Julia asked. She'd looked up food options for kids with kidney disease, thinking of making a full lunch, but Mo talked her down to snacks only. Still, the table was overflowing.

Bryn ended up on her lap and Carly settled into Mo's, leaving two extra chairs for Reed to pick from. She sat down on Mo's side, likely so she wouldn't have to suffer through Mo's dagger glances, but she looked decidedly uncomfortable. *This isn't about making her happy*, Julia reminded herself.

In no time, they'd made a dent in the fruit and veggies, with the kids debating over whether the carrots tasted better in the "healthy" yogurt dill dip or the peanut honey spread. When Reed awkwardly asked for the recipes for both, Bryn said, "Julia knows how to cook. They won't taste as good if you make them, Mom."

Mo chuckled and winked at Bryn, while Reed shrugged and said, "Yeah, you're right."

When the kids were excused from the table to go explore, Mo pulled out her phone and said, "Kate wants to go back to that cake place this afternoon."

Julia studied her for a moment, temporarily thrown from her internal debate on if there was something wrong with her that she could still be sitting here wanting Reed. "I thought she decided on the strawberry with vanilla buttercream frosting."

"She did. And then she texted me saying she was worried she'd made the wrong choice."

"About the cake or Ethan?"

Mo cocked her head. "Maybe you can ask her that but if I do…"

"Right. Never mind. Well, I'm glad you two are talking again." Maybe they were moving past whatever had happened that neither Kate nor Mo would tell her about.

"We'll see. This is the first time she's texted me in a month. I think she was hoping we'd both meet her there."

"What time?"

"Three."

Julia glanced at her watch. It was half past two. They'd need to leave now if they were going to make it on time.

"You should go," Reed said, standing up and beginning to gather the water glasses. "This was great." She avoided eye contact as she reached for the utensils in front of Julia. "Thank you for letting us drop by and for feeding us. It was delicious."

"We're not leaving already, are we?" Bryn whined.

Carly looked up from the *Landscapes of California* table book she was leafing through. Her gaze tracked from Reed to Julia and then she bit her lip, as if she somehow sensed she couldn't get involved in this. This was a grown-up thing.

Julia knew she was crazy for wanting to stay in Carly's life. And yet she did want that—so much so that maybe it was worth getting over Reed in a crash course. She turned to Mo. "I think you and Kate need a chance to talk alone. Maybe cake will help."

"What about—" Mo pointedly turned toward Reed as her sentence trailed off.

"It's fine, Mo," Julia promised. She could hold her own. "They've only been here for a little while. I haven't even shown them my roof garden."

"You have a garden on your roof?" Carly asked.

"That's where I grow all my tomatoes."

"Why don't you grow them in your backyard?" Bryn asked.

"Because I don't have one. I have a roof instead." She'd told them both about her obsession with tomatoes one night while they were making spaghetti. Carly loved to help in the kitchen and Bryn never wanted to be left out. They'd passed many evenings together, each kid standing on a stepstool on either side of her, one peeling carrots or potatoes or snapping green beans, while Julia worked on a sauce. A fresh pang of loss tightened her chest. Those little moments in Reed's kitchen were a thing of the past. "But it's early for tomatoes. Right now I have lettuce and more kale than anyone wants to eat."

"Kale?" Bryn screwed up her face and then stuck out her tongue.

"Are you kidding? Kale's delicious," Mo argued. She eyed Reed as if her kid's palate was somehow her fault as well.

"Can we see the garden?" Carly's eyes pleaded with Reed.

Julia swallowed, hoping Reed would say yes and at the same time wishing she didn't want the extra time with them. She didn't look over at Reed.

"Maybe for a quick peek. But then we have to get out of Julia's hair."

"Out of her hair?" Bryn laughed.

"And we need to help clean up first. Can you guys take your plates to the sink?"

While Bryn and Carly came to get their plates, debating possible ways to get to the roof garden—Bryn thought there might be a secret passage through the hall closet and Carly thought a ladder could be hidden in the bathroom—Julia overheard Mo, who had cornered Reed, say in a low voice, "Your kids are cool. Just so we're clear, that's why you're here. Don't overstay your welcome."

The icy air between Mo and Reed could have put out a fire. Fortunately, neither Bryn nor Carly heard what Mo had said. Reed didn't say anything in response and instead started consolidating the remaining fruit in one bowl.

Julia eyed Mo. Mo had crossed a line, and from her guilty expression, she knew Julia wasn't happy about it. Mo spread her hands as if to say she couldn't be blamed and Julia shook her head.

"Go give Kate a hug from me," Julia said. "If a tiebreaker is needed my vote is for buttercream over fondant."

Mo motioned to her phone and mouthed, "Call me later." When she went to say good-bye to Bryn and Carly, she joked with them about the roof garden, half convincing them that the entire thing had been planted by fairies, and then both kids clambered to hug her good-bye.

Just as Mo was leaving, Reed said, "Mind if I walk out with you?"

Mo looked as surprised by the request as Julia was. She shrugged in response and then Reed turned to Julia. "I'll be right back. I just need to grab Carly's medicine from the car. She was supposed to take it with her lunch."

Reed was back a few minutes later. Her tense shoulders and balled-up jaw muscles had noticeably relaxed now that Mo was gone, but she still avoided looking at Julia. After convincing

Carly to swallow a spoonful of something pink, she sent the kids on a hunt for the entrance to the roof garden and then came to the kitchen. Without a word, she began filling the sink with dishes and started the water.

Julia pulled a clean dishtowel out of the drawer and tossed it to Reed. "I'll clean. You dry."

Reed stepped back from the sink and stood to the side waiting to dry what Julia handed her. She seemed to be paying extra attention to where she placed herself—not close enough to bump elbows but close enough for a hand off of a wet platter. In the narrow kitchen, she didn't have much choice where she stood, but having her close was agony for Julia. Why did she have to long for her still?

They worked in a heavy silence, Julia more aware than ever of Reed's body, of how straight she stood, and of the muscles and curves she knew well that were partly hidden under the T-shirt and jeans she was wearing. Her clothes had a freshly laundered scent Julia wanted to lean into, and her new haircut, buzzed short in the back and stylishly longer on top, was tempting to dishevel. Julia thought of all the head massages they'd shared in the past months and a tightness settled in her throat. That was only one thing she'd miss.

As she handed Reed the last bowl, Carly came into the kitchen, wanting to know how much longer it would be. Before Julia could answer her, Carly had stopped in front of the refrigerator and let out a squeal.

"It's all of us at the waterfall!" She tugged the photo off the fridge and held it close, studying the picture. "Bryn, come see— Julia has our picture! We look like a family!"

Reed's hand stalled on the dish she was drying and Julia watched her eyes track to the photo. In the bustle to clean the rest of the house, Julia had forgotten about taking the picture off the fridge.

"Why don't we have this picture, Mom?" Bryn said, tugging it out of Carly's hands to take a closer look. "I want a picture of all of us together. We don't have any pictures of Julia."

"Hey, I was holding it first," Carly complained, trying to tug it back from Bryn.

Before the fight could escalate, Reed reached between them and held her palm out. "That's Julia's picture."

Bryn stuck her tongue out at Carly as she dropped the photo into Reed's hand. "If you hadn't said anything we could have kept looking at it."

"You pulled it out of my hands!"

When Carly whined to have it back, Reed raised her voice enough to get their attention. "That's it, you two. Out of the kitchen. Both of your butts better be on Julia's sofa waiting for us to finish if you want to go up to her roof garden."

"Mom said 'butts,'" Bryn whispered to Carly. Carly laughed and then pushed past her sister to race to the sofa. When they reached the living room, they flopped onto the sofa and then rolled on top of each other, still joking about butts.

Reed carefully replaced the picture on the refrigerator and then looked over at Julia. "I know I probably shouldn't say this but...Carly's right. We do look like a family. That day was—"

"You're right. You shouldn't say that." Julia held Reed's gaze, determined not to break. "And I should have taken that picture down. The truth is, I forgot about it."

"Is there any chance we could talk about us?"

"Us?" Julia cut Reed off. "There is no us. You already made that clear." She took the dishtowel out of Reed's hands and tossed it on the counter.

Reed started again, her voice still soft, "I know you're mad at me and you have every right to be. I wish I could take back what I said that day. I wish we could go back to what we had—"

"You don't get it. Even if we could go back, I don't want what we had. That wasn't enough for me. I want more. And you can't give me that."

Reed opened her mouth to respond, but Julia raised her hand to stop her. "You missed your chance on having this conversation."

"Can we go see the garden now?" Carly asked.

Julia forced a smile. "Sure, sweetie."

She half hoped Reed would volunteer to wait in the car, but she didn't. Instead, she took up the rear position as all four of them climbed out the bedroom window onto her narrow balcony and then up the fire escape to the roof. Once they were on the roof, Julia realized the handrail around the edge wasn't as sturdy as it seemed when a kid pushed it and she was glad then to have Reed there for backup. Fortunately the four raised garden beds, while not hosting many live plants, held Bryn and Carly's interest. She explained what she planned for her summer crops and gave them both spades to dig for potatoes.

Reed sat down on an overturned bucket and watched them, noticeably quiet. Julia could tell she still wanted to talk, but they both focused on the kids. Every time she looked over at Reed, her stomach clenched up. This was not how she wanted it to be between them, but she couldn't give Reed another chance.

After a few minutes of digging, Carly crawled into Reed's lap, looking spent. "The sunshine is making me tired."

"We should head out soon anyway. Julia has to meet up with her friends." Reed continued, "You ran around today more than you've done in about a month. It made me happy to see you laughing and having so much fun."

Carly's eyes half closed and she snuggled closer to Reed's chest. "When can we come back to Julia's house?"

"I don't know, sweetie," Reed said. "But it was fun, wasn't it?"

Carly murmured her agreement.

Julia pretended to be interested in the tiny snail Bryn had found in the dirt. She had given up on looking for potatoes and begun digging a Dixie cup-sized hole for a mouse to sleep in, but she had stopped at the sight of the snail. Worried that she'd hurt it with the spade, she turned it upside down in her palm and searched for injuries.

"I think it'll be fine. Those little guys are sturdy." Julia held out her hand and Bryn deposited the snail. "I've got to get some marigolds planted. They keep the snails out."

"Why do you want to keep out the snails?"

"They eat holes in my plants." Julia pretended to scold the snail, wagging her finger at it before dropping it in an empty water jug. Usually she chucked them over the edge, but it seemed harsh with Bryn staring at her.

Bryn looked concerned about the snail's fate as it was. She peered into the water jug and then said, "Julia, can we give the snails their own garden?"

Before Julia could answer, Reed said, "I think we better say good-bye before Carly falls asleep. The snail will be fine, Bryn. Julia will take care of it."

Julia glanced at Carly. Her eyes were closed and her small frame was curled completely in Reed's lap. Reed jiggled her knee and Carly opened her eyes, giggled, and then pretended to fall asleep again.

"Come on, sleepyhead. I don't want to carry you down that fire escape. You know I'm scared of heights." Reed stood up and deposited Carly on her feet. She stretched her arms up to be carried, but Reed pointed to the fire escape.

It took some convincing for Bryn to leave the garden bed. She would have been happy digging in the dirt for hours and was still worrying about the snails.

"Why do we have to leave?"

"Julia has things to do," Reed said. "And Carly needs a nap."

"Carly can sleep on Julia's bed. She sleeps all the time," Bryn complained as they climbed back through the window.

"Her body needs to rest so she can keep getting better. She's getting stronger every day," Reed said.

"We never do anything fun anymore because of her," Bryn said. "It's her fault we have to leave."

Carly's tears started immediately. Reed kissed Carly's head, murmured something, and then turned to Bryn. She dropped down on one knee and tilted Bryn's chin up to hers. "You know what? We're leaving because of me. I messed up with Julia and said something I shouldn't have. This isn't Carly's fault. You're right—Carly could sleep on Julia's bed, but because of me, we have to go. And now I need your help. Do you think we can leave without making this into a big deal?"

Bryn looked from Reed to Julia. "You and Carly can leave. I don't want to."

Carly's sobbing worsened at that and Reed stood up. She took a deep breath and exhaled slowly. "Can you guys say thank you to Julia for letting us come down to see her?"

"No." Bryn climbed onto Julia's bed and then crossed her arms. "I'm moving in with Julia."

"Bryn, get off the bed and march your butt to the door." Reed's voice had lost the understanding tone. She hadn't yelled, but it was clear her orders weren't up for debate. When Bryn hesitated, Reed added, "Now."

The last bit got Bryn moving. There was no long good-bye. Julia gave one hug to each kid and that was it. She didn't make eye contact with Reed and only nodded when Reed thanked her again. *Maybe it's better this way*, Julia thought. If this was the last time she'd see them, she didn't want to make a big deal out of good-bye.

As she closed the door behind them, the finality of it all set in. She sank to the floor mat and leaned back against the door. The apartment, emptied of the chaos that was the past hour, was suddenly too quiet. She brought her knees up to her chin and stared at the living room, the kitchen, the hallway, and then her bedroom. Her assorted furniture—the sofa and loveseat set that she'd spent too much money on, the kitchen table with the sleek modern look she'd coveted when she'd seen it on Craigslist for an unbelievable steal, the bureau her mom had shipped all the way from home—all of it ought to have filled the small space and made the apartment feel like home. But the apartment had never felt like home. Not the way Reed's place did the first weekend she'd spent there and all the nights since. She fought the tears that threatened, determined not to cry. Maybe Reed truly was sorry. Well, so was she.

Julia stood up finally and went to the table where she'd left her phone. When Mo answered, she said, "Tell me you guys are saving me a slice of cake."

"They were closing early. But I'm two blocks from your place and I bought us a whole cake."

"I love you, Mo."

Mo chuckled. "You know my mom and you are the only ones who say that to me these days. So, I'm guessing Reed and the kids are gone."

"Yeah. God, that was hard. What kind of cake did you get? Please make it be chocolate."

"Dark chocolate with chocolate buttercream and a raspberry filling. You're gonna want to skip dinner." She paused. "And Jules, Kate's coming too. You won't believe what she did."

CHAPTER TWENTY-ONE

"You told your parents?"

Kate licked the chocolate off her fork. "It happened so fast that I surprised even myself. My dad was going on and on about how we should consider Florida for the actual ceremony and then my mom piped up with how she thought it was ridiculous we were making everyone fly all the way to St. John...And then right when I was about to say it didn't matter since the invitations had all been sent, I just said it." She stabbed her fork into her cake and a smile crossed her face. "I still can't believe I did it."

"What did Ethan say when you told him?"

The smile slipped off Kate's lips, but before she could answer, Mo said, "It's possible he doesn't know yet."

"You told your parents you were gay before you told Ethan?"

"I know I'm going to have to tell him. Honestly, I'm a little worried that my parents will call him first." Kate's brow furrowed. "I'll do it tonight. It's going to crush him, but I have to end things…"

"You'll let him down easy. You always manage to have ex-boyfriends who still love you after you've broken up with them," Julia said. "And it's a good idea telling him on a Sunday night. He'll have work tomorrow to distract him."

"All his friends are gonna make him feel better saying this is all the fault of the lesbians," Mo added.

"Except that's only partly true. It's not like I've had an affair with a woman." Kate set her fork down. "I'm not in love with Ethan and I should never have agreed to marry him. I don't know how I let it get this far."

"You don't like to disappoint people," Julia said. "But you have to make yourself happy too."

"And this is step one," Kate said. "Someday I'm getting married to someone I love and we're going to order this cake."

Kate left not long after they'd boxed up the rest of the cake. The resolute look on her face derailed any doubts that she'd go through with her plan. For the first time since she'd met him a year ago, Julia felt sorry for Ethan. It wasn't his fault Kate didn't love him. Of course, he could take some blame for being oblivious and self-centered. But despite what Mo thought, Julia maintained that he wasn't a bad guy. She honestly hoped he'd weather the breakup and maybe find someone who wanted that fancy wedding in St. John.

"Do you think they can get some of their money back?"

Mo shrugged. "It was all Kate's money they used for the deposit and you know she's got plenty to spare. At this point, I doubt she cares about losing ten thousand dollars."

"At least Ethan's not out any money…" Julia paused, eyeing Mo. "Okay, admit it—you feel a little sorry for him."

Mo held her thumb and her index finger an inch apart. "Maybe this much. He never liked me either."

"He was jealous of you."

"Which is ridiculous," Mo argued. "He had Kate. If he'd tried harder—or at all—she would have stayed. She wanted to love him. She's been trying for months." She paused. "What would Reed have to do to get you back?"

"You're seriously asking me that?" Julia didn't want to answer the question despite the fact that she'd been mulling over her answer ever since she'd closed the door on Reed.

Mo went to the kitchen and found the open bottle of wine. "Want more?"

Julia held up her empty glass. "I'll take half a glass. I still have work to do tonight. Tomorrow morning I have to meet with one of our new clients."

Mo poured and then settled back into her spot on the sofa. "The truth is I feel sorry for Ethan and Reed. For entirely different reasons."

"Okay, Ethan first."

"He never had a chance," Mo said. "But Reed had a chance. She let you slip through her hands. And I don't think she ever realized what she had...You two would have been perfect together."

"Now you tell me this? Two hours ago you hated Reed."

"She hurt you so I had to hate her," Mo defended. "But we all saw it coming—even you. What I didn't see coming is Reed asking if she could call me later to talk."

"She asked you that when she was here today?" Julia tried to remember a time when Reed and Mo would have been alone together long enough for a conversation. Then it hit her—when Reed had gone out to get Carly's medicine...

"So answer my question," Mo said. "What would Reed have to do?"

"We want different things. It's not happening."

"Then that's what I'll tell her," Mo said.

Julia felt her heart drop at the finality in Mo's voice. It really was over. Mo reached for her phone and started typing out a text to Reed. Julia didn't move, staring numbly at the words on the screen. *Sorry dude. She's done.* After Mo had sent the text, she started scrolling through her contact list. Her finger stopped at Andi's number.

"Guess who keeps asking about you? Want to give this one a second chance?"

"No." Julia felt nauseous. There was no way she was going to go out with Andi, or anyone else for that matter, anytime soon. "I want to spend the next year watching plants grow. I'm done thinking about women."

"That's what I always say after a breakup. It lasts about a month." Mo chuckled. Mo set her phone down and looked over at Julia. "I still can't believe Kate told her parents."

* * *

Julia climbed into bed that evening in no mood to face the morning. She had a week full of meetings and a host of new messages from Val that were waiting for responses. But she didn't want to think about work. Her mind was still spinning through the afternoon's events—Kate had finally come out, Mo was happier than she'd been in months, and she'd officially ended the relationship that never was.

No matter how she tried to focus on the book she'd picked to help her wind down, she kept seeing Reed's smile. When she'd first walked in and met Julia's eyes, a smile had popped on her face as if she couldn't hold it back. Julia's heart had bounced up to her throat in response. But then there was Reed standing in front of the refrigerator with the waterfall picture in her hand. The words of that conversation repeated in her mind and she wished she could forget the pained look she'd seen on Reed's face. It was over then—not two weeks ago in the hall outside of Carly's room. Even if it hurt Julia to hear it, Reed hadn't meant it then. But Julia had meant it today. And what she'd told Mo was the truth. There was no reason to try and patch things up when they wanted two different things.

She stared down at her cat pajamas and then reached for her phone. Waiting for the ring, she pictured her parents' living room with the pair of old sagging couches, the long dark walnut coffee table, and the Turkish rugs arranged about the room like pieces of a jigsaw puzzle waiting to be connected. She knew her mom would answer even though it was after ten in New York. She'd be sitting in one of the couches rereading one of her favorite torrid romance novels.

"Julia? What's wrong?"

"Hi, Mom. Nothing's wrong."

"What time is it? Are you in the hospital?"

She smiled, despite herself. "It's not that late in California. And I knew you'd still be awake reading. How's the book?"

"You know me too well." Her mom laughed. "I love this book—I've read it three times. But the cover is terrible. Thank God your father doesn't have a hairy chest like this man."

"Maybe he secretly waxes." Julia felt the tension in her neck easing already.

"All these years? I'd know. He's terrible at keeping secrets."

Julia smiled at the love in her mom's voice. All these years… Despite how her mom teased her dad, they were perfect for each other. Still.

"How are you? It's been a while…" How long had it been since their last phone call? She couldn't remember. Too long. "And how's Dad?"

"My knee's aching and I've got a hemorrhoid flare-up. Aren't you glad you asked?" She laughed. "Your father's fine. He's here with me on the sofa snoring away. Can you hear it? Ever since his hair fell out he sounds like an elephant when he sleeps."

"I don't think it's because of the hair," Julia said, smiling again.

Her mom sighed. "Maybe not. I told him it might be that we're getting old…Now tell me what's wrong."

"I think I'm homesick." Tears sprang to her eyes when she said the words. "And I need a Mom hug."

"You broke up with the woman you were seeing? The one with the kids?"

Julia exhaled, not wanting to say the words that would confirm her mom's guess. She hadn't explained the nature of her relationship with Reed, but she'd let a few details slip. After Hawaii, her mom had asked if she was seeing someone, partly because their phone calls were further apart and partly because she heard the excitement in Julia's voice when she did call.

"Oh, Julia." Mom clicked her tongue three times the way she used to when Julia had a scraped knee or had a cold and then said something in Mandarin. Julia recognized the phrase, but she didn't know the exact meaning. It was something her mother used to say to soothe her, and for not the first time, she wished she'd learned more from her mom. "I'm going to wake up your father and get him to buy you a plane ticket. You need a slice of my cheesecake."

"Your cheesecake is the best." Julia sniffed, trying to keep the tears in check. She couldn't swing time off, but maybe she could squeeze the trip in over Memorial Day weekend. "I could go for a slice right now."

"Did I ever tell you the time Charlotte tried to steal my recipe? We were playing cards one night and I'd left that old church recipe box out. I got up to check on your father and when I got back to the kitchen, I found her rifling through those cards." Mom laughed. "She didn't know I keep the cheesecake recipe in my head!"

Charlotte was the neighbor her mom always complained about. They had a love-hate relationship that had started when Charlotte's now deceased poodle decided he liked Julia's mom better than his owner.

"Good thing you got your father's stomach instead of mine." Her mom laughed again. "If I eat more than a bite of my cheesecake, I'm in the bathroom for the rest of the night." She grumbled something about lactose intolerance and then there was a pause before she shouted, "Paul, wake up!"

Julia heard a clatter and then her father's sleep-slurred voice asking, "What is it?"

"Julia's coming home for cheesecake. You need to buy her a ticket." Back on the line, Mom said, "When can you come? I can't wait long. I'm old you know."

"I can buy my own ticket, Mom."

"I know. My successful daughter can do everything herself. But I still want to take care of you."

Julia couldn't argue then. After promising to check her work calendar and exchanging a few sentences with her father, who was only half awake, she hung up the phone. The fact that she was too old to need her mom didn't matter. For the first time all month, she felt loved. She switched off her bedside light and pulled the covers up to her chin.

CHAPTER TWENTY-TWO

The windows were open and a warm June breeze carried in the smell of the bay. Kate was scrolling through pictures on Instagram and Mo was hunting for the beer she'd left in Julia's refrigerator. She found it finally behind a bottle of hot sauce and then started to close the refrigerator.

"What's this?" She'd spotted the platter on the top shelf. "Is this one of your mom's cheesecakes? Tell me she sent you home with a whole cheesecake." Mo's eyes widened as she pushed back the aluminum foil to get a glimpse.

"She made two—one for us to eat last weekend and one for me to bring home. She made me promise to share some with you and Kate. You know how much she loves you two."

"Why didn't you tell me before we made dinner reservations? We could stay home and eat this entire thing."

Julia pushed the refrigerator door closed. "That's for dessert. But it'd make my mom's day if you took some of it home with you."

"Can I have your mom?" Kate asked. "I need a temporary replacement."

"Is yours still not talking to you?"

"Oh, I wish." Kate sighed. "The not-talking thing lasted one week. Now every night I listen to her daily voice mail about how I've turned my back on God, my family, my country—sometimes she even throws in how Peeves needs a man in his life for a stable family. And the shitty thing is, I think Peeves does miss Ethan."

"Eileen's a piece of work," Mo said. "But at least your dad's coming around."

Kate nodded. "He called me up the other day to tell me that he loved me. It was sweet. He said I could date whoever I wanted, but he still thinks the wedding in St. John was impractical. That's my dad for you."

After spending the past weekend with her parents, Julia was reminded of how lucky she was, particularly in the Mom department. Her mom's only concern was that she thought she looked thin. In addition to pushing multiple slices of cheesecake, she'd convinced Julia to go out to Dim Sum two nights in a row. "My mom would adopt you in an instant."

"Great. I'll get the documents in order." Kate set down her phone. "I keep hoping my mom will eventually realize that I only want to be happy."

Mo's phone buzzed. She eyed the text and then went over to the papers crowding the kitchen table. "We're up to five players for fantasy football. Guess who just decided to add?"

"Who?" Kate asked.

By Mo's look, Julia knew the answer. Reed and Mo had formed a friendship, and the two had been texting way too often.

"Reed. But she doesn't think she can come to any of the games. Apparently she's got the whole summer planned out and the kids start kindergarten in the fall...I think she's more of a planner than I am—which is impressive." Mo flipped through the pages of her calendar. "Jules, could you make it to an August

17th game? It'll be pre-season and I think I can get us better seats."

"My schedule's wide open." She hated to admit it, but she doubted that would change anytime soon.

Mo nodded, making marks on her chart under her name. She had two lists going—one for game dates and another for fantasy football. "What about you, Kate?"

"You know how I feel about football. It's absurd how many concussions those players suffer in one season and the long-term brain damage—"

"I'll ask your girlfriend," Mo said, scrolling through the contact list on her phone. "Didn't you say she was a Niners fan?"

"She's a Forty-Niners fan, yes, but she's not my girlfriend," Kate argued.

"You've been seeing her for two weeks and you haven't dated anyone else in that time, right?" Mo waited for Kate to respond. She only folded her arms however. "In the world of dating women that means Chris is your girlfriend."

"We've gone on two dates. And she's nice but I'm not going on a third date."

"Why not?" Julia asked at the same time as Mo.

Kate shrugged. "She's not the one. Anyway I think I'm still getting over Ethan."

"That's why you have rebound relationships," Mo said.

Kate shook her head. "I don't want to put Chris through that."

Mo gave up the argument surprisingly quick. There was no doubting the fact that both Mo and Kate were happy that the other was single. Julia's stomach growled and she eyed the clock. "When do you guys want to head out?"

"Soonish…Reservations are at seven," Kate said. "But it's so close we could probably walk and not bother with parking."

Dinner had been Mo's idea—she'd wanted to set up a monthly dinner at a fancy restaurant for the three of them before anyone got engaged again. The way Mo said "engaged" made it sound like a death sentence—yet another reason Julia was glad Mo was part of her life. The first restaurant they were trying was a new place that had opened up a few blocks from Julia's apartment. Kate insisted they all get dressed up for the occasion, but Mo was still in shorts and a T-shirt.

"Can you guys give me five more minutes? I've almost got this schedule set up, and I'm texting back and forth with three other people. Reed's schedule is tricky."

"How exactly did she become friends with Reed?" Kate asked Julia.

"Reed texted me first," Mo said. "But you both know I'm an amazing person who everyone wants to be friends with."

"Obviously." Kate rolled her eyes, but a smile edged her lips. She looked over at Julia. "I hear Reed's been texting you too."

Julia nodded. She hadn't mentioned it to Kate, but she had known Mo would say something sooner or later.

"And?" Kate pressed.

"And nothing. Part of me knows I should block her number. But I can't bring myself to do it." Reed had been texting Julia daily for the past few weeks. Often it was a funny or sweet thing the kids had done, but sometimes it was only one line— "thinking of you."

Julia knew better than to respond, but one night she broke down and sent a smiling emoji back when Reed relayed a conversation she'd had over dinner with the kids. Then the phone calls came—Carly wanted to wish her "sweet dreams," and then Bryn wanted to check in on the snails in the garden.

Once Reed had called. She started with: "If you want me to stop texting, I will. And if phone calls are crossing the line, tell me. But Mo says there might be a slim chance you don't hate me."

Mo and Reed had patched things up and become fast friends. They'd met up to take the kids to matinees more than once and even all gone fishing—something Julia had trouble not being jealous about when she learned of it after the fact. Despite this and the phone calls, every time Mo asked if Julia was interested in meeting up with Reed, her answer was always the same. She wasn't ready to be Reed's friend.

Unfortunately, she didn't hate her. The problem was she still wanted her too much. She'd even let her heart wonder if there was a chance of getting back together again. But for that to happen, she'd need to know it wasn't a game this time. How Reed could prove that, she wasn't sure, but texts and phone calls weren't enough. As it stood, she couldn't think of dating anyone else, but she was in a limbo land with her feelings on Reed.

The doorbell rang and Julia guessed someone had pressed the wrong apartment number. Mo, however, jumped up and went to hit the buzzer without even asking who was there.

"Expecting someone?"

"Yeah. Pizza delivery guy."

"Wait, you ordered pizza?" Julia glanced down at the dress she was wearing and then looked over at Kate, also dressed as if she were ready for a black-tie dinner. She'd been expecting Mo to change clothes but maybe she wasn't planning on it.

"You know Mo," Kate said. "She doesn't think you get enough food at the trendy expensive places."

"But we are still going, right?"

"Sure. I just like to have a backup plan," Mo said, reaching for her wallet. She went to the door and was ready to hand over cash when the pizza guy knocked.

Julia shook her head when she carried not one, but two pizza boxes to the kitchen. "Mo, I know you lift weights, but how many calories can you eat? It's not fair that you never gain any weight."

"They had a buy one-get one free offer," Mo explained. "I figure I'll be set for lunches this week."

When a second knock came at the door only a moment after the pizza guy had left, Julia assumed Mo hadn't paid the right amount, but Mo, who was on her phone, only shrugged, and Kate waved her hand toward the bathroom, indicating she needed to visit it. Julia tried not to be miffed as she went to open the door.

Her breath caught in her chest when she saw Reed on the landing. What the hell was she doing here?

"Hi." Reed gave her a sheepish smile. She was wearing a suit and holding a pallet of marigolds. Over a dozen plants were squeezed onto the huge tray.

Julia looked up from the flowers to find Reed's eyes waiting for hers. She shook her head but before she could think of what to say, Bryn shot past Reed to hug her leg. After a quick squeeze, she made a mad dash for Mo, shrilly calling, "Aunt Mo!"

Julia glanced from Mo, who was swinging Bryn in a circle, to Reed. Finally her throat seemed to loosen. "Why are you here?" The words sounded harsher than she'd intended and Reed's brow furrowed in response.

Carly peeked out from behind Reed's legs. "Mom's surprising you with flowers."

Julia opened and closed her mouth. She didn't know what to say. Her heart was thumping in her chest, and God, Reed was handsome in a suit. But this was not supposed to be happening.

"We also brought chocolates," Carly added, coming forward to hand Julia a box of chocolate-covered macadamia nuts. "Aunt Mo said we might need an emergency plan."

"Contingency plan," Mo said. She leaned around Julia. "But that was before I knew about the cheesecake. Carly, come help us pick out our movie."

Carly stepped out from behind Reed and, then exactly as Bryn had done, hugged Julia's leg. She held on for a long time, and when she looked up at Julia she said softly, "I missed you."

Julia choked up instantly, but Carly let go and ran to join Mo and Bryn on the sofa. Kate came out to the living room then and started chatting with the kids about movie options. She held up the DVDs she'd bought. Three cartoon movies.

"They were both in on this and I had no idea," Julia said, realizing it only in that moment.

"I needed some help. And a babysitter." Reed's smile was tentative. For the first time, she looked truly nervous.

Julia could tell Reed was putting everything on the line. How could she send her away now? She didn't want to but…

Reed continued, "I was wondering if you'd like to go out to dinner with me. I heard there was this great new restaurant a few blocks from here. Interested?"

Julia held her breath. She wanted to throw her arms around Reed and not have to bother with talking. But she had to keep the lines clear in her head and not take a step closer.

"And if that answer is yes, would you like to go on a hot air balloon ride tomorrow morning at six a.m?" Reed paused. "I know it's early, but I have a hotel room reserved in Napa near the launch spot. They'll wake us up and give us a ride right to the balloon." She shifted the tray of marigolds, balancing them on one arm, and then pulled out a brochure with a picture of a hot air balloon soaring over a vineyard.

Julia took the brochure. "You're scared of heights."

"I'm scared of a lot of things," Reed said.

Stalling, Julia pointed to the plastic container squished in amongst the flowers. "What's that?"

"A snail transporter." Reed set the tray of flowers down and pulled out the plastic container. A single leaf of kale sat at the bottom of a Tupperware container with holes punched in the top lid. "Bryn made me build a garden bed in the backyard for your snails. She wanted me to make them a little car so they could drive up to Davis, but I told her this might work."

Julia cracked a smile. "I love that you'll do anything for them."

"I'd do anything for you too." Reed caught her gaze.

If only she could trust that Reed meant what she said… Part of her desperately longed to go to Napa, regardless of what happened afterward. And part of her knew it was a mistake.

Tears pushed at the corner of her eyes, and she quickly looked up to keep them from falling. She stared at the cracks in the wood along the top of the doorjamb, determined Reed wouldn't see her cry. *Dammit*. She couldn't do this again. "I'm not sure Napa's a good idea."

Reed was quiet for a long moment. Finally she said, "Will you have dinner with me anyway?"

CHAPTER TWENTY-THREE

Their conversation over dinner covered everything from Bryn kissing a kid in daycare to Julia's new client who'd sent her a troll as a thank-you. Every time Reed laughed Julia felt a warmth spread through her. She knew Reed was nervous and the laughter was her defense, but it was something she'd so missed hearing that she couldn't help joining in.

Sitting across from Reed and not having touched her yet was painful. She longed at least to clasp her hand. But any touching was a bad idea until she figured out the mess of feelings fighting a battle in her head. There was a certain distance that hadn't been crossed and things that were waiting to be said. Until that happened, she couldn't touch Reed. Still she watched her lips as she talked and the unsettling desire to kiss her was impossible to ignore.

With Reed finally in the same room with her and, for once, no distractions, some things were clear. She wasn't mad at her. That emotion, which had been so strong before, had completely evaporated. But she wasn't ready to open up and trust her with her heart either. Cautious—that was a good description.

Except she didn't feel cautious when Reed's eyes met hers, when her hand brushed Reed's as she was setting her empty wineglass down at the same moment Reed was reaching for the check and then again as they were leaving when she cut a corner too close skirting the crowd in the waiting lounge and ended up bumping into Reed's chest. Reed was a magnet then and all she wanted to do was lean in. She could think later.

They stepped out of the restaurant and the cool evening air cleared Julia's head. She needed to figure out what to do next. Saying yes to dinner was one thing, but Napa…

Reed caught her hand. Her grip was warm and sure, and Julia couldn't ignore the tingling sensation that shot from their clasped hands up to her chest. Everything about Reed felt too right. A passing car honked at them and Reed only looked over at Julia and shrugged. She didn't let go.

They held hands all the way to the parking garage. Reed opened Julia's door and then went around to her side. When she'd settled into the driver's seat, she turned on the ignition and then switched it off again.

"I wasn't sure what you were going to say when I showed up tonight," Reed started. "I thought maybe you would tell me to leave as soon as I got there. The last time we were at your apartment…I could tell you didn't want me there."

"Actually I wanted to pretend I'd never met you."

"Ouch." Reed's jaw clenched.

"By the way, you broke my heart. Did you miss that text?" Julia laughed, trying to prove at least to herself that she could joke about it, but the tone was flat and Reed had never looked more somber. She exhaled, knowing the next part was going to be hard. "I was pissed but only part of that was your fault. Mostly I was upset that I'd let you get close when you could toss me aside that easily."

When Reed tried to speak up, Julia cut her off: "And unfortunately, I couldn't just be mad at you because I was in love with you. So, yeah. It sucked."

She hadn't planned on admitting the part about loving Reed, but once it was out there, she didn't want to take it back. At least she'd used the past tense.

Reed seemed to wait for Julia to say more, and when she didn't, she said, "I could explain all the things that were going on in my head, but it wouldn't make what I did any less shitty. I'm sorry." She looked over at Julia. "I probably don't deserve a second chance, do I?"

"Probably not." Julia held onto her gaze. No one had ever been able to look straight into her heart like Reed could do and being close to Reed again made her realize how alive she felt with her, how her whole body seemed to buzz. She didn't want to move even a few inches away. Despite everything she'd said, she knew that meant something. She wanted to give Reed another chance.

"Do you want me to drive you home?"

"No. I want you to take me to Napa."

"So you're open to dating again?" Reed sounded surprised but happy.

"I didn't say that. And we weren't dating, remember?"

"I don't know if it's a good idea for us to go to Napa," Reed said.

"Why not? Worried we won't be able to be in the same room without having sex?"

Reed shrugged. "Well, yeah."

"It wouldn't have to mean anything." Julia tried to keep her voice balanced. "We've had sex before without it meaning anything."

"I don't think that's—"

"Relax," Julia interrupted. "I'm not even sure I want to kiss you. But the more I think about it, the more I realize I don't want to let you off the hook on that hot air balloon ride."

"Okay. That's fair."

Reed's smile was perfect, and Julia felt something shift between them when she smiled back. "You know you told me once that you'd never show up on my doorstep with flowers."

"Mo said I was crazy, but I had to try."

"You were nervous."

"Yeah...well..." Reed paused. "I still am. It's been a long time since I've tried to date someone—really date. I don't want a hookup with you. I want something serious."

"So you decide to take me out to dinner and then to a hotel as a first real date? You might need a brush up on dating rules."

"I didn't think it all the way through, I guess." Reed paused. "It was more the hot air balloon ride that I was planning...We don't have to have sex. Obviously."

"You think we're going to go to a hotel room and keep our pajamas on?" Julia shook her head. She couldn't imagine keeping her clothes on with Reed lying next to her, and she knew the limits of Reed's self-control.

"We could try and be friends first. Then if more happens down the line..."

"Friends first? We blew past that months ago."

"But we could start over fresh."

Julia eyed the parked car next to them. Being in close quarters with Reed was hard enough in a car. The hotel room wasn't going to work. "I can't be just friends with you."

"Why not? I think we're doing okay so far," Reed said.

Julia turned halfway in her seat and set her hand on Reed's knee. As she slid it up Reed's thigh, she held her gaze, knowing exactly what she was doing to her. Reed groaned when she inched close to her center.

"Still think we can be friends?" Julia asked softly.

When Julia reached for her zipper, Reed caught her hand. Their eyes locked and Julia felt suddenly exposed. She was certain Reed was about to call her bluff. Before Reed could say anything, she pulled her hand away and sank back in her seat. She'd intended to make Reed uncomfortable, but she hadn't expected the effect she'd have on her own body. Her hands were shaking and she hid them against her legs, hoping Reed wouldn't notice.

"I want you in my life," Reed said. "If there's a chance that you want that too…I'm willing to do whatever it takes. But this needs to be about more than sex."

"What if I only want sex?" Julia argued. "Maybe I don't want a relationship anymore."

"I can't have sex with you and pretend it isn't more," Reed said. "Not now."

"You could. It doesn't feel great, but you could do it."

Reed's jaw clenched again and Julia thought of all the times she'd whispered "I love you" after Reed had fallen asleep. Or the times she'd silently breathed the words after they'd shared a climax. Reed hadn't heard her but the truth was there. For her, they'd been making love every time.

Reed exhaled. "I know I screwed up from the beginning. I wish we could go back and—"

"I don't want to sit in a parking garage talking," Julia said, cutting her off. What she really didn't want was to start crying. Not now. "Can you get us out of here?"

Julia could feel Reed's gaze on her, but she stared out the window and a silence stretched between them. Finally Reed started the car. The truth was, she wanted to talk. She wanted to figure everything out. But she needed Reed's arms around her, needed to feel what she wasn't saying. She didn't trust her words yet.

When they'd merged onto the highway and shifted into the fast lane, Julia took Reed's hand off the gear stick and brought it to rest on her thigh. The warmth of Reed's palm pressed through the thin material of her dress.

"You're going to make it hard to concentrate on the drive," Reed said quietly.

"I have no intentions of making tonight easy for you."

Reed chuckled. "Well, that's deserved."

But Reed wasn't the only one who had trouble concentrating on the road. After a while, Julia hardly noticed anything outside their car. The cars they passed, the gathering darkness, the changing scenery, all was a blur. She ran through all the reasons she should keep her clothes on, but then there was Reed's hand, reminding her of all the reasons she wanted to give in. By the time they finally got to the hotel, she was wet with anticipation and more uncertain than she'd been at the start of the drive that she should be in Napa at all.

The check-in process with a talkative innkeeper only made things worse. Standing close to Reed without touching her was torture. She wanted Reed to kiss her, but there'd been no move that direction and only an uncomfortable silence that she was responsible for.

They took the stairs up the one flight and then walked down the hall to their room. It was a boutique hotel with only a few dozen rooms and the innkeeper walked them right to their door. After he'd gone, Reed carried in their overnight bags and then called Mo to check in on the girls—both had fallen asleep watching the second movie.

Julia sorted through the overnight bag that Kate had managed to pack without her noticing. She still couldn't believe they'd planned all this…She spotted a new lingerie set and wondered if that had been Mo's idea or Kate's. When Reed looked her direction, she buried the black silk under a pair of jeans.

"Want to check out the balcony?" Reed said. "According to the website, every room has a view of the stars."

Julia followed her, missing her coat as soon as the night air met her skin. Reed noticed and stepped close. When Reed wrapped her arms around her, Julia leaned back against her. She breathed in Reed's scent. God, she loved that smell. Reed's arms held her tight—as if she didn't want to let go. It wasn't fair how good it felt being close to her.

"Well, they're right," Julia said. "No shortage of stars."

"I've missed this."

"No stars in Davis?" Julia knew that wasn't what Reed meant, but she needed to keep things light.

"I meant I missed holding you," Reed clarified.

"You have no idea how many times I had to stop myself from driving up to see you," Julia admitted. "One time I made it all the way to your freeway exit before I turned around. Then I decided that I was going to get over you. Somehow."

"Do you want me to back off?"

Julia didn't answer and Reed's grip on her loosened. When Reed moved back a step, Julia stepped back with her, settling in against Reed's chest again.

She needed to ask something, but the words caught in her throat every time she tried. Finally she closed her eyes, blocking out the night sky, and said, "I get why you wanted a fling when we were in Hawaii. But after that...how was it not more for you?"

"I didn't want a fling," Reed said. "Remember that drive we went on—when we went to the waterfall?"

Julia nodded. She'd never forget that day.

"I wanted that to be our first date..." Reed paused. "My therapist says I can't let anyone in because I won't risk another loss."

"You see a therapist?"

"I started a few months ago."

Julia pulled Reed's arms tighter around her body. She wasn't cold anymore, but she didn't want her letting go now. The fact that Reed was seeing a therapist gave her some hope, but it was no guarantee things would be different this time.

"I don't know if your therapist is right. You did let me in. Then you pulled away as soon as things got hard. That's why it hurt so much. When Carly was sick, I wanted to be there for you but..." Julia didn't want to go on.

"That night when you came to the hospital, I realized how much I wanted you there. How much I needed you," Reed said. "But I didn't want to need you. And I was so worried about Carly...What I wanted was the last thing I could think of. By the way, I never smoked that cigarette. I went outside to cry."

"Do you know when I started to fall in love with you?" Julia wanted to see Reed's face, but she didn't dare turn around. She wouldn't be able to go on. "When you told me how much you wanted your sister to see that waterfall. I thought you were so brave when you let yourself cry. You weren't scared of what I'd think."

"It's easy to be brave if you don't have anything to lose."

Julia turned then and the tears at the corner of Reed's eyes broke down the last bit of her wall. Who was she kidding? She'd already bet her heart on this woman. "How brave are you feeling now?"

"I'm terrified." Reed leaned forward and met Julia's lips. The tingling shot down to her toes, and once again she was glad Reed's arms were around her. As the kiss deepened, there was no turning back.

When their lips parted, Reed looked as shaken as Julia felt. She stepped back, eyeing the stars for a moment, and then met Julia's gaze again. A shy smile turned up her lips. "The thing is I love you, so I figure being scared is pretty normal, right?"

"I love you too," Julia said. Saying the words out loud gave her a rush and the look on Reed's face gave her more courage. "But I still want to have hot unbridled sex with you tonight so don't get too mushy on me."

Reed laughed as she caught Julia's hand and pulled her into another kiss. She tugged her inside the room, closing the sliding glass door and then stepping backwards to the bed with one kiss for every step. She let go only to pull back the covers.

"You know it's a nice place when they leave chocolate on the pillows."

Julia took the chocolate that Reed held out for her and unwrapped it. She kicked off her heels and let the chocolate melt on her tongue. Reed was pouring the wine that had been left for them. Wine on the bedside table seemed quintessential Napa. Maybe a drive through the vineyards would be nice. They could sleep in…

"We could skip the hot air balloon ride and do a little wine tasting instead. I know how you feel about heights."

Reed handed her one of the wineglasses. "Do you remember how nervous you were the first night we had sex?"

Julia felt the blush hit her cheeks instantly. "I wasn't *that* nervous."

"You were," Reed said. "But you went for it anyway. And it was amazing."

"It was amazing." Julia took a sip of the wine and then set down the glass. The red wine paired perfectly with the dark chocolate, but she wanted something else. She stepped closer to Reed and started undoing the buttons on her shirt. "So you're hoping our first hot air balloon ride is going to be as good as the first time we had sex?"

"I'm hoping I get over being scared as fast as you did. I figure it's possible I'll even enjoy it as long as I don't look down." Reed took a sip of her wine, watching Julia's hands work. "What do you think?"

"I think you should stop talking and start taking off my clothes. Who knows when we'll have an all-night babysitter again? We should make the most of this."

Reed grinned. "Is it too early to ask if you'll move in with me?"

"Way too early. We need a six-month trial period." But the fact Reed was even making that suggestion sent a warmth through her that had nothing to do with how much she wanted her at the moment.

"Can I at least call you my girlfriend?"

Julia considered it. She reached for Reed's tie. Tonight was different—she saw it in Reed's eyes and felt it in the slow way her hands were moving up her body. Reed was taking her time. Tonight they were making love. "Yeah, I'll give you that."

"Then how long should I wait before I ask you to marry me?" Reed smiled. "I'm a planner."

"Two years at least."

"Two years is a long time. I might not be able to wait that long. By the way, I like this dress," Reed said, her hand moving up Julia's back and sending a shiver down her spine. "But it's been distracting me all night. I keep thinking about how easy it'd be to take it off you..."

"You're sure that means you like it?" Julia teased with her eyes, stepping back when Reed caught the side zipper.

"Well, you're gorgeous wearing it. But I like you even better naked."

Reed tugged and the zipper gave way. Her hand slipped under the fabric and her fingertips touched Julia's skin. Julia opened her mouth, unable to hold in the gasp, as Reed's hand moved lightly up her back.

"Is this okay?"

"As long as you don't stop there."

Reed smiled. "Good thing we're not trying to be friends." She caressed Julia's neck and then pulled her closer. When their lips met, Julia closed her eyes. She wanted Reed more than ever.

EPILOGUE

One year later...

"Shoes off, Bryn."

"But Mo said she didn't mind if I accidentally kicked her seat."

"Trust me, she'll mind after an hour of that." Julia held out her hand, waiting. With a huff, Bryn pulled off the first shoe and handed it over. She took her time with the second.

Carly waved the airplane safety guide in front of Julia's face. "Mama, can you read this to me again?"

"Mom could read it this time," Julia suggested. They'd only been in the air for twenty minutes and she'd already read it four times. For some reason Carly was intrigued at the idea of a crash landing and wanted to know all the details.

"No, I want you to read it. You do all the funny voices and Mom's too serious."

Reed looked over at Julia and smiled. "You do have good voices, babe. I especially like the one you use for the people hopping on the raft. Everyone sounds so happy even though they're probably about to die."

"See what I mean?" Carly's eyes begged Julia. "You're better at being funny than Mom is."

"All right. Give me a second with Bryn. She's still working on her shoe."

"I'm not working on it, Mama. I'm giving up. It won't come off my foot."

Mama. After she'd moved in, Reed had asked how she'd feel about the kids calling her "Mama." She'd quickly realized that living together meant it was impossible not to share at least some of the parenting responsibilities and Reed thought it would help Bryn accept Julia's rules as well as give Carly the comfort of knowing that she wasn't going anywhere. At first Julia wasn't convinced it was a good idea, but she'd agreed to a trial and the kids latched on. Six months later and it was who she was.

"Let me know when you want to switch seats," Reed said.

"I'll be fine until Dallas. You're on for the flight to Cozumel."

At the girls' insistence, she was in the middle seat between Carly and Bryn while Reed was across the aisle. Kate and Mo were in the row ahead of them along with an older woman who seemed slightly confused at the fact that they were all together.

"How long before we can get our swimming suits on?"

"Seven hours," Reed said.

"That's forever," Bryn moaned.

"But then we'll be here." Julia pulled out the book she'd bought and pointed to the cover. A kid with a snorkeling mask stood on a sandy beach with an aquamarine ocean behind him. "We're going to have so much fun we won't want to leave. According to this, they have iguanas all over the place. But I want to see a coati."

"What's a coati?"

"They look like little raccoons," Julia said, flipping pages to find a picture.

She found a picture of an iguana instead and Bryn leaned over her lap to get a better look. "They're so cute."

Carly scrunched up her face and said, "So not cute. Do they bite?"

"Only a little bit," Mo said, suddenly leaning over her seat to stare down at them. She opened her mouth wide and made chomping sounds. Carly and Bryn both giggled when she tried to tickle them. "Want to see a magic trick?"

At the girls' nods, Mo momentarily dropped back to her seat and then reappeared with a wide grin on her face. "I got something for my favorite nieces." She opened her hand showing that it was empty and then reached for Bryn's ear and pulled out a peso. When Bryn squealed, Mo laughed and handed her the coin. She repeated the trick on Carly and then both kids were clambering for an encore.

"We're switching seats if you get them anymore riled up," Julia said.

"I can't help it," Mo said. "I love your little family."

"I love them too…" Before Julia could go on, Carly and Bryn were jumping out of their seats as Mo tried to tickle them again. Predictably, Aunt Mo tired of the game before the twins did. She dropped back into her seat, leaving Julia to quiet them down and wrangle seat belts.

When she looked over at Reed, the smile lines were at the corner of her eyes. They were something Julia had noticed more lately. She loved that Reed smiled more these days. And she loved the lines.

"I love you, babe," Reed said. "Hey, I got a question for you."

Bryn groaned. "Mom, you already know what she's going to say. You've asked her about a thousand times and she always says the same thing."

"But you don't know what I was going to ask," Reed said.

Carly shook her head and gave Julia a knowing look while Bryn said, "You were gonna ask her the same thing you ask her every day, 'When are you gonna marry me?'"

"How'd you know?" Reed feigned a look of surprise.

Carly cocked her head. "Because you always sound like you want to kiss her when you say it."

Julia laughed when Bryn agreed, making "ew" sounds about the kissing. She met Reed's eyes and smiled. "These two know you pretty well."

"Apparently." Reed sighed.

"We know you pretty well, too," Bryn said to Julia. "Every time she asks, you think she's kidding. So you kiss her and then say, "Keep asking," and then you start talking about something else."

Julia avoided looking at Reed then. Bryn never seemed as perceptive as Carly, but she'd laid the truth out plainly. "Who knew five-year-olds were so smart?"

"Mom, I think you've been doing it wrong," Carly said, half leaning into the aisle to whisper to Reed. "Next time when you want to ask her, pick a really good spot. Then go down on your knee. And you should probably have a ring."

"That's good advice," Reed whispered back. She unbuckled her seat belt and stood up. When she pulled a black velvet box out of her pocket, Julia's breath caught in her chest. What was she doing?

Reed moved to the aisle and kneeled on one knee. Then she looked over at Carly. "Like this?"

"Is there a real ring in there?" Carly asked, wide-eyed.

Reed opened the box and the diamond sparkled. Julia could hear her pulse thumping in her ears. Reed wasn't joking this time. Bryn and Carly ooh'ed at the same time and then Mo leaned over her seat. "What are you up to back there?"

"Mom got Mama a ring," Bryn said. "She's gonna ask her to marry her."

"Kate, you gotta see this," Mo said, her voice just as excited as Bryn's. Kate's head popped up and then she was leaning over the seat, grinning down at them.

Julia turned to look at Reed again. Blue eyes held her gaze. She could hardly breathe when Reed looked at her that way.

"I want to marry you," Reed started. "If you're not ready yet, that's okay. I'll keep asking another thousand times. But I really hope this is my lucky day." She paused, taking a deep breath. "Will you marry me?"

Carly turned to look at Julia, her fingers crossed, and then Bryn whispered, "Please say yes."

Julia felt her throat tighten. She never would have guessed that she could love three people so much. "Yes. A thousand times yes."

"It's okay with me if you kiss her," Bryn told Julia, and Carly nodded her agreement. "This one time."

Julia met Reed's lips. She'd never get tired of kissing her. And now she'd never have to worry about when this all would end. This—all of it—was what happily ever after felt like.

Bella Books, Inc.

Women. Books. Even Better Together.

P.O. Box 10543
Tallahassee, FL 32302

Phone: 800-729-4992
www.bellabooks.com